Murder in the Moonlight

Penrose & Pyke Mysteries, Book 4

Rose Pascoe

Published by Flax Bay Books, 2023

Copyright

MURDER IN THE MOONLIGHT

ISBN: 978-1991181336 (Softcover POD)
978-1991181329 (Epub)
Publisher: Flax Bay Books, New Zealand

Cover design: Rose Pascoe
Cover images from Adobe Stock Images by fotomaximum, dervish15 and Irina Korsakova

Table of Contents

Table of Contents 3

Trouble At The Hospital 5

Glittering Soirée 13

Moonlit Stroll 28

Unexpected Arrival 38

Reunion 43

Prime Suspect 51

First Client 65

Apologies 75

Toxic Shock 87

Moonlight Revisited 99

Natural Remedies 104

Unnatural Remedies 113

Under The Bed 124

Where There's A Will 131

The Housekeeper 139

Ladies Of The House 145

The New Surgeon 156

The Butler And The Valet 162

Mischievous Maids 173

Missing Heir 183

A World Away 194

Voice From The Past..205

At The Hospital 213

A Hive Of Suspects 227

The Lady's Maid 233

Memory Box 243

The Stables 248

Joy 261

Read On..266

Historical Notes...267

Acknowledgements 269

About the author..270

Trouble At The Hospital

"Nurse, nurse!" The patient in bed twelve waved a stick-insect arm. "Och, sorry, Miss Penrose, I couldn't see who it was in the gloom."

Grace Penrose, the first female medical student in the country, was often mistaken for a nurse, regardless of the ambient light. At the end of a dull May day, with clouds as grey as the row of metal bedframes stretching down the women's ward, the patient would be hard pressed to distinguish her from the ghosts of patients past.

She glanced at her notes: *Mrs Mackle, paracentesis to remove fluid from the abdomen.* "Anything the matter, Mrs Mackle, aside from the dismal lighting in here?"

"I've no mind to that. After all, money's that tight, ye can have the gaslights on, or ye can have yer treatment, but ye cannae have the both."

Mrs Mackle's pitch-perfect impersonation of Matron would have made Grace laugh out loud, if it hadn't been for Matron's disturbing habit of appearing at inconvenient moments. Grace glanced around before risking a smile. "At least our fine hospital spares no expense on the quality of the cuisine."

Her patient let out a derisive snort as she flicked a glance at the congealing sludge on the enamel plate beside her. "Oh, aye, straight from the kitchens of the Grand Hotel, that is. Smells even worse than the air in here, and that's saying something."

"The rain has certainly made the swampy ground outside smell worse than usual," Grace agreed.

The medical staff had been told not to mention any other source of odour, including the mould in the cracks in the walls, the rot slowly eating away the floorboards, the stench of carbolic, and the vile smell emanating from the hospital kitchens and laundries. All blown in courtesy of the draughts that plagued this decrepit ward. In

5

short, the hospital would have disgraced even a provincial town. For Dunedin, the most distinguished city in New Zealand, it was intolerable. Their city might be a dot on a distant corner of the globe compared to the great cities of the world, but its citizens had their pride.

Grace palpated the patient's abdomen. "Swelling's all but gone, I'm pleased to see. How are you feeling, Mrs Mackle?"

"A stone lighter and keen as mustard to get back to my own home."

"I'll get Doctor Beechworth to discharge you as soon as possible." Grace moved on to the next patient. As a third-year medical student, she ought to have been working under close supervision, but the hospital was short-staffed because of an influenza outbreak. Grace had volunteered to stay on to cover the ward while the overworked nurse had a dinner break. Grace's own stomach had passed the rumbling stage several hours ago, leaving her innards shrunken into a tight mass inside her thin frame.

Mrs Mackle nodded towards the woman in the next bed and lowered her voice. "Mrs Jamieson ain't right, Miss Penrose. Groaning and tossing all day she was, but now she ain't moving."

Grace leaned over the patient in bed thirteen. Mrs Jamieson might have been made of wax for all the signs of life she showed. Sightless eyes, sallow skin, and the sickly odour of infection dreaded by doctors the world over. Only the drops of sweat on her brow and the erratic pulse in her neck declared her to be alive. Grace lifted the bedclothes, revealing a stained bandage that ought to be white.

Two days ago, Grace had sat in the gallery of the operating theatre and watched Doctor Beechworth perform an exemplary abdominal surgery on Mrs Jamieson. Such a rapid post-operative deterioration did not bode well. She covered the patient and hurried off to find the attending doctor.

Doctor Beechworth, the hospital's specialist in gynaecology, was leaving the consulting room at his customary pace, carrying a pile of documents. He moved with such dignity and grace, his speed was deceptive. Many an unwary medical student had been left floundering in his wake as he swooped around the ward on rounds.

The doctor glanced around at the sound of Grace's hurried footsteps. His raised eyebrow pulled up the bristles of his moustache on one side, under a prominent nose. "Problem, Miss Penrose? I'm due in an important meeting." Beechworth glanced down the corridor, before adding. "Last chance to overturn Ormsby's duplicity. I really don't want to miss the meeting."

Grace didn't want him to miss the meeting either. Doctor Ormsby had convinced the Dunedin Hospital Trustees to change the plans for the proposed new hospital extension at the last minute. The hospital desperately needed a women's ward up to the medical standards of 1892, to replace the disgraceful current facilities. Ormsby, a surgeon, had fed the trustees with promises of the financial benefits of another new operating theatre and surgical consulting rooms.

With the hospital finances in tatters after a prolonged economic depression, the trustees had been swayed by his honeyed words. After all, they argued, would anyone of importance really care if the women's ward was left to moulder for a few more years? All respectable women had their medical needs seen to at home, anyway. The embarrassing problem of the maternity ward – a dilapidated wooden structure accessed down a flight of dangerous steps – had already been neatly solved by transferring maternity patients to the Benevolent Institution across the other side of town.

Grace, of course, cared a great deal, as did Beechworth. So did all the women who had raised a vast sum of money to fund the new women's ward. But right now, a woman's life was at risk and everything else was of secondary importance.

"Should I get someone else, Doctor Beechworth? It's Mrs Jamieson, bed thirteen. Signs of post-operative infection. Waxy countenance, erratic pulse, semi-conscious."

Doctor Beechworth was off before Grace had finished her sentence. She trotted after him. Aside from her desire to save the patient, she took every opportunity to learn from the experts, especially those who were willing to overlook the inescapable handicap of her gender.

By the time they had drained and cleaned the infected wound, and waited for the patient's vital signs to stabilise, every muscle in Grace's body was sagging.

Beechworth looked equally weary. He drew out his pocket watch. "No chance of me making the meeting now. I hope my wife, Ivy, and the rest of the women's group have been given the opportunity to make their views known in my absence."

"My great-aunt is at the meeting too, Doctor Beechworth," Grace replied. "I can assure you that she will not be silenced. I only hope she hasn't had to resort to desperate measures to get her way. I've seen enough bloodshed for one day."

Grace was living with her great-aunt while she trained to be a doctor. To her friends and allies, Anne Macmillan was a woman of modern ideas and robust character. Her detractors used rather less complimentary adjectives. If Anne's fury at Ormsby and the trustees was anything to go by (and it usually was), the meeting would have been fiery. Especially so in combination with Mrs Ivy Beechworth, another formidable force on the side of women's rights.

From the apprehension writ large on the doctor's face, he was well aware of it. "May I offer to take you home, Miss Penrose? Once the meeting has finished, we can all go together." Beechworth set off down the corridor to the meeting room without waiting for her reply.

Grace brushed back wayward strands of her dark hair as she hurried after him, thankful for the lack of mirrors on the ward. Working long hours was to be expected as a medical student. Returning home in the dead of night was the worst of it, especially for a young woman. More often than not, Grace curled up in a chair in the consulting room or collapsed on a vacant bed, rather than risking the short journey home, even in a hansom cab.

Doctor Beechworth pushed the door to the meeting room open a crack. The Chairman of the Hospital Trustees, Mr Horncastle, was speaking in an officious drone. With his top hat beside him, his

8

monocle framing iron grey eyes above a neatly trimmed beard, and his cravat so perfectly tied it could only be the work of a superior valet, Alfred Horncastle was clearly a man of substance.

Grace failed to understand how his success at selling imported furniture and homeware (*"Turn your home into a castle with Horncastle's quality goods!"*) qualified him to make crucial decisions about Dunedin hospital. But Horncastle was no worse than any of the other merchants and attorneys who made up the trustees. At present, not a single medical man sat with them, a situation she found both incomprehensible and dangerous.

Horncastle droned to a close. "… therefore, it is agreed that Doctor Ormsby will commission the architect to prepare a variation to the original plan, with the final decision to be made after Doctor Beechworth has had his chance to speak on the matter. Ah, there you are Beechworth. Late again."

"My sincere apologies," Doctor Beechworth said with a distinct lack of sincerity. "A woman almost died tonight from an entirely unnecessary post-operative infection, caused by the abominably insanitary conditions in the women's ward. If the next death is a woman of means, the hospital might well be sued for gross negligence."

Horncastle blanched but continued as if he hadn't heard. "I therefore declare this meeting adjourned until next Thursday."

Even as Horncastle banged the gavel, the meeting attendees were pushing back their chairs and jostling to escape. The women were allowed out first, as dictated by good manners. Strange that these men could be so gracious about polite trivialities, thought Grace, when their decisions consigned women to early graves. She hurried to catch up with her great-aunt and Ivy Beechworth, who had surged past in a wave of grim-faced ladies.

Doctor Ormsby caught up with their group in the foyer, a smirk hovering above his swaying jowls. "Sorry to hear you've had another post-operative infection, Beechworth. Operating by bicycle lamp again, eh? You ought to get into private practice like me. Never a single infection under my watch."

9

Doctor Beechworth ignored the jibe. He was rightly proud of his successful treatment of a haemorrhage by the light of the wardsman's acetylene bicycle lamp, after the gaslights failed. "The patient suffered a secondary infection as a result of the appalling conditions in the women's ward, Ormsby, not because of my surgical skills. If the Hospital Trustees proceed with your proposal for an additional operating theatre instead of the planned women's ward, I will hold you personally responsible for the unnecessary deaths of women for years to come."

Ormsby wiped his brow with a monogrammed handkerchief. His rotund figure was not made for any pace beyond sauntering. "Come now, Beechworth. No need to be a sore loser." He turned to Grace and took her hand in his gloved fingers. "You must be Miss Beechworth. I am enchanted to meet you at last. I insist you join your parents in attending my soirée on Saturday evening. No elegant gathering is complete without a pretty girl. My eldest son, Richard, is particularly desirous of making your acquaintance."

His last sentence was spoken with exaggerated emphasis, leaving Grace in no doubt that Richard Ormsby was an eligible young man in want of a suitable wife. Grace hadn't the energy to respond without appearing rude, so she said nothing. Her great-aunt and Ivy Beechworth were too busy stifling unseemly laughter to come to her aid.

Doctor Beechworth was left to respond. "How kind of you to invite this charming young lady, Doctor Ormsby. I'm sure she will be delighted to attend with us."

Grace glared at Beechworth, silently beseeching him to rescue her from the perils of the Ormsby soirée.

Beechworth ignored her unspoken plea. "However, I must inform you that the young lady is not our daughter. Indeed, I am surprised you failed to recognise her, as she is acquainted with your younger son, Henry, a fellow medical student. May I present Miss Grace Penrose."

Ormsby's eyes widened for an instant before narrowing to fleshy slits. He hoisted a thin smile over sour lips. "Miss Penrose.

You will be welcome, of course. Indeed, Mr Horncastle is eager to extend a welcome to the ladies, to acknowledge the 'changing face of medicine'." The words, emphatically in quotes, assured his listeners that his arm had been twisted. "I have already invited the new Matron and the head nurse. A lady medical student will round out the party nicely." Ormsby bowed his head briefly and hurried away to his carriage.

Mrs Beechworth took her husband's arm, exchanging an intimate smile with him that spoke of mutual devotion. "That was very wicked of you, Frederick darling. You must know Ormsby was a fierce opponent of admitting a woman to medical school. And his vile son, Henry, has abused Grace abominably from the first day she stepped foot inside the lecture theatre."

"A woman having the gall to answer the questions that stumped the male students," Anne added, with a cackle. "Shockingly unladylike behaviour, Grace dear, showing up the men like that. But, Frederick, I have to agree with Ivy. What on earth were you thinking? Edgar Ormsby would sooner welcome a leper to his soirée than an aspiring female doctor."

Doctor Beechworth waved away their admonitions. "All the more reason for Ormsby to meet Miss Penrose properly, so that he realises the error of his ways. Besides, I have a feeling that Ormsby's determination to derail the women's ward might waver under the persuasive powers of Miss Penrose's intellect and charm."

"If Grace doesn't strangle him first," Anne retorted. "One minute in Ormsby's company would be enough for me to contemplate skewering him with a hatpin. I give thanks I am too old and too outspoken to warrant an invitation to his tiresome soirée."

Mrs Beechworth had to retrieve a handkerchief from her reticule to cover her mirth. "Rat poison might be the more appropriate method to silence a scheming rat, don't you think, Anne? Or throw him into a vat of boiling whale blubber. Ormsby might actually be of some use to the world if his blubber was turned into oil to keep the hospital lights running."

An unexpected voice from close behind them cut through the merriment. "Good evening, Doctor Beechworth, ladies," Mr Horncastle said. "I look forward to seeing you again at the soirée."

Doctor Beechworth watched Horncastle's progress down the street until he was out of earshot. "Ivy, dearest, your rapier wit will get you into trouble one of these days. Might I beg of you to be on your best behaviour at the soirée? Charm and logic are needed to sway the Hospital Trustees to our viewpoint. Ormsby and Horncastle wield a great deal of influence."

"Do come, Grace," Mrs Beechworth pleaded. "After all our exertions to raise funds for the new women's ward, I couldn't bear to have it denied to us at the whim of a pair of pompous idiots."

The last thing Grace wanted to do was to attend a social gathering of superior people who disapproved of her, especially as the soirée was a thin excuse for Ormsby to entice the trustees with fine wine and talk of wealth. On the other hand, Doctor and Mrs Beechworth deserved her support. She found herself agreeing to attend, even as her intuition flashed a warning that it was a very, very bad idea.

Glittering Soirée

On the Saturday evening of the soirée, Doctor Beechworth threaded his arm through Grace's, with his wife on his other side. "Come, ladies, let us face the enemy with all the bravery of the Light Brigade at Balaclava."

"Hardly an apt metaphor, my dear," his wife grumbled, "given the disastrous results of that battle." Ivy Beechworth stiffened her spine, rendering her imposing presence even more formidable.

The Ormsby residence was more of a mansion than a house, spread across a double-width section of Royal Terrace, looking down upon the lesser folk of Dunedin. The city lay within a natural amphitheatre of hills around a harbour. A town belt of trees ran around the upper slopes, forming a cloak of greenery above the most prestigious houses. Washed clean of the persistent coalsmoke by recent rain, the glorious view was rendered dramatic by the light of a full moon.

Grace would have happily stayed outside all evening, but Doctor Beechworth tugged her through the gate. They walked up a path lit by lanterns, through a manicured garden, to the wide two-storey villa beyond. Light from the upper storey poured through stained glass, throwing a colourful pattern between the spaces in the fretted timber balustrade of the balcony.

A black-suited butler with snow-white gloves removed the fine woollen cloak Grace had borrowed from Anne for the soirée. Her chaperones led her down the entrance gallery, flanked by portraits of stout men, whose narrow eyes gazing down upon them over snub noses and receding chins. A reception line greeted them, guarding the entrance to a large salon. Beyond, the crystal-cut light from chandeliers sparkled over the impeccable evening attire of the gathered crowd.

Edgar Ormsby was effusive in his welcome to Doctor Beechworth but sparing in his acknowledgement of Grace. Their host's gaze moved on to the next arrival of significance. Grace caught a momentary flaring of Ormsby's nostrils, followed swiftly by a pursing of lips. Mr Horncastle pushed past, not doing Ormsby the courtesy of even the merest nod of greeting.

The woman beside Ormsby, presumably his wife, recovered her composure quickly. She offered their group a sweet smile. "Mrs Beechworth, how delightful to see you again." Mrs Ormsby leaned forward, as if to kiss her guest's cheek, but instead she whispered, "Good luck, Ivy. I have had a word with my husband to smooth your way. I believe Edgar might yet be swayed."

Interesting. So Ormsby's wife was on their side. Mrs Ormsby was as graceful and delicate as a sprite in a beautiful gown and jewels, but her sun-touched face and the way she tugged at her lace sleeves left Grace with the feeling that she would have been happier in a garden than at a formal soirée. Perhaps the evening would not be too awful after all.

Mrs Ormsby's eyes lit up with a genuine smile. "And this, I presume, is the famous Miss Grace Penrose, of whom we have heard a great deal. You are most welcome. I very much look forward to claiming you later for an intimate chat."

Famous? More like infamous in this house. "I would be honoured, Mrs Ormsby."

The line was building behind them, so they moved along to a man in his mid-twenties, who was a less rotund version of his father and the men in the portraits. The man bent over her hand with such formality that Grace found herself bobbing in response.

"Mr Richard Ormsby, at your service, Miss Penrose. I too wish to make your acquaintance. Any young lady who can put my younger brother in his place is a woman I am eager to get to know better. And Mrs Beechworth, delightful to see you again."

The younger brother in question, Henry, stood in stony silence beside Richard. He, too, favoured his father's unfortunate physique over his mother's delicate good looks. When Grace moved along the

14

line to greet him, Henry stretched his lips in a half-hearted attempt at a smile, succeeding only in appearing surly. "Miss Penrose. Welcome."

Grace smiled angelically. "Mr Ormsby. What a splendid evening."

She was not about to give him the satisfaction of intimidating her. Henry Ormsby was one of Grace's fiercest adversaries, outdoing even his father in opposing a woman's right to study at the Otago Medical School. Unlike most of the other students, he had not come to accept her over time, after she had shrugged off their insults and proved herself up to the intellectual challenge. If Grace had to play the part of a refined lady for the evening to prove she was worthy, so be it.

The final Ormsby in the receiving line was a pale woman, who was glaring at her father with narrowed eyes and a belligerent pout. Older than her brothers, but cast from the same mould, with a round face and receding chin. Richard reached around his brother to nudge her shoulder. Her gaze shifted back to Grace.

"Miss Cecilia Ormsby," she murmured. Her lips stretched into a forced smile reminiscent of Henry's.

"Miss Grace Penrose," Grace responded. "Delighted to make your acquaintance, Miss Ormsby."

The Ormsby sister fiddled nervously with the small, plain brooch pinned to her gown. "I must say, Miss Penrose, you do not look at all terrifying." Cecilia clapped a hand over her mouth. "Oh, my goodness, that didn't come out as I had intended. I hope I haven't offended you?"

"Not at all, Miss Ormsby." Grace presumed Cecilia's nervousness was because of Henry's tall tales about his unwanted classmate. She struggled to think of a reply that wouldn't add to her low reputation in this household, settling on the age-old ploy of flattery. "What a lovely brooch."

Cecilia Ormsby's pale cheeks flamed. Her attention darted to a handsome young man standing nearby, conversing with Mr

15

Horncastle. "Doctor Alexander gave it to me. He has recently arrived from London and has taken up a position on the hospital staff."

The young man had agile fingers, which moved expressively as he talked. Grace concluded Doctor Alexander must be the new surgeon in town, fresh from training under the best in the world. She glanced back at Cecilia, who was twisting a blonde curl around a finger and frowning at the attention Grace was paying to her man.

Grace had no desire to spark jealousy. "How charming of Doctor Alexander. He must think exceedingly well of you, Miss Ormsby, to give you such a treasure." She bobbed her head and passed into the grand salon, carefully circling in a wide arc around the dashing young surgeon.

The reassuring chaperonage of Doctor Beechworth lasted only seconds. He melted into a homogeneous group of fellow doctors, who appeared to be discussing the weighty matter of whether Carbine was the greatest racehorse of all time.

Although the men were all known to Grace, as her lecturers or hospital staff, this was not a circle she cared to force herself into without an explicit invitation. Especially on this occasion, as she had nothing to contribute on the subject of horse racing, beyond the general knowledge – forced unwillingly upon her by the newspapers at the time – that the horse being discussed had won the most prestigious race in the Southern Hemisphere two years ago.

Yet she was loath to join Mrs Beechworth amongst the cluster of wives sipping sherry by the long stretch of windows looking out onto a wide terrace. This was why Grace disliked social occasions outside her own circle of unconventional friends. She was a dodecahedron-shaped peg in a world of round and square holes.

She glanced around to see if either Mr Edgar Ormsby or Mr Horncastle was free, so that she might press the case for the women's ward before they imbibed too much. Horncastle was nowhere to be seen. Ormsby was still standing at the door, although it appeared all his guests had arrived. As Grace drifted his way, she noted a scowl on Ormsby's face and a hunch to his shoulders that

16

was far from welcoming. Still, no battle was won without engaging the enemy. Had David not beaten Goliath against all odds?

Suddenly, Ormsby bent almost double and dashed down the hallway. As Grace was sure he hadn't noticed her approach, she concluded he was feeling unwell. Unfortunate for him, after going to so much trouble to put on a lavish party. She contemplated going after him, to see if she might assist, but dismissed the thought. He would not welcome her interference, especially when he had access to a roomful of male doctors.

Now what? Grace was left stranded, alone in the middle of a crowded room, looking and feeling like an outcast. She caught herself wishing that Charlie Pyke was by her side. What would he make of this glittering gathering? She stomped on the thought as soon as it crossed her mind. Much as she could have used Charlie's uncanny ability to fit into any social setting with ease, he was not here. He had left Dunedin, by his own choice. She would not think about him. End of story.

She wondered what Charlie was doing right now, picturing him in front of a roaring fire, sharing amusing stories with his parents. So far away.

Mrs Beechworth appeared at her side. "Grace, dear, you look so beautiful in that divine gown. People will think you are a lifelike statue if you stand so still and solitary in the middle of the room. Come and meet the council of war, better known as the fundraising committee for the women's ward at the hospital."

Richard Ormsby appeared at her other elbow. "Not so fast, Mrs Beechworth. I claim host's privilege to steal Miss Penrose away from you. If you consent to my request, I promise to have a word in Father's ear about the hospital plan."

"If Grace agrees, I am willing to try any stratagem that delivers us a dedicated ward for women's diseases." As Richard took Grace's arm, Mrs Beechworth added, "A decent children's ward would be a godsend too. The current one would do a Dickensian workhouse proud."

Richard bowed. "I shall do my best, Mrs Beechworth, but I doubt my influence would extend so far. Indeed, my father and I are so at odds at present, I suspect I might have a better chance of achieving the desired outcome if I declared myself in favour of his proposed operating theatre."

Richard steered Grace towards a waiter, who was balancing a tray of champagne. He liberated two glasses from the tray with a flourish. "Sherry is so overrated. Don't you agree, Miss Penrose?"

"As a matter of fact, I do, Mr Ormsby, when the alternative is champagne." Grace accepted the long-stemmed coupe, taking care to hold it firmly in her slippery evening gloves.

"I knew it. A spirited young woman in a shimmering midnight-blue gown ought not to be sipping on anything without bubbles." Richard raised his glass. "To spirited young women who take on the establishment."

"And the courageous men who support them." Grace touched her glass to his with an exuberance she never expected to feel tonight.

Doctor Ormsby had returned. He rested a moment against the doorframe, wiping his flushed face with a handkerchief. Grace almost felt sorry for the man, so unwell did he look. But then he looked their way, not disguising his surprise at seeing her with Richard. Grace turned away, determined to enjoy his son's more pleasant company while she could. Too late, she recalled Ormsby was in search of a wife for Richard. At least she might rest easy on that score, for female medical students would surely be low on Ormsby's list of desirable matches, right below factory girls and mudlarks.

Richard Ormsby tucked Grace's arm through his and guided her into an unpopulated corner, near enough to the black-jacketed musician playing the piano to cloak their conversation. With a twinge of disquiet, she wondered if Henry had shared his low opinion of her character with his brother. Henry might consider himself a gentleman, but he had no qualms about calling her virtue

18

into question. If Richard had been misinformed, she must nip it in the bud.

"You are most unlike your younger brother, if I may say so," Grace said, keeping her tone light, as if in jest. "He believes my desire to be a doctor is a sign of unnatural tendencies. I hope he has not left you under the impression that my liberal views on women's rights mean I am without morals."

Richard looked shocked for an instant before laughing. "And I hope you will not take me for a man of such arrogant opinions. I am trying to be charming to make up for the appalling behaviour of the other male members of my family. You have every right to despise us, Miss Penrose."

"By no means," Grace replied, although she was uncomfortably aware of his father's eyes on them from across the room. "Your father and brother have been honest and forthright in making their feelings about my place at medical school clear. And yet, I have prevailed. I hold no resentment, no matter their opinion of me."

"You might be surprised, Miss Penrose. Far from despising you, Henry admires your resolve. However, he also fears your success. Our father sets high standards, which my brother interprets as a need to eclipse all other students at medical school. Even Father, I believe, has come to have a grudging respect for you. His initial argument was based on the 'fact' that no woman would have the intellectual or emotional competence to handle the rigours of medicine. Father concedes the notion has long since been dispelled, as you carve a path to glory."

Grace acknowledged the exaggerated compliment with a smile, as it was kindly meant. "I confess, I have never understood the argument. Since the dawn of time, women have tended to the injuries of their children, the ailments of their husbands, and the agonies of childbirth. How could anyone believe that we would have a fit of the vapours at the sight of blood?"

Richard chuckled. "I doubt the average male has considered the matter with that level of rationality, Miss Penrose. We men have so

19

long presumed ourselves to be intellectually superior, we have come to believe it."

Now it was her turn to laugh. "You have a refreshing honesty, Mr Ormsby. Are you a doctor too?"

A mask dropped over Richard's face. "I am not. My stepmother is an herbalist, as well as a nurse. I became fascinated with her natural remedies and knowledge of medicines. To the horror of my father, I was inspired to pursue a career as a pharmacist."

"Ah, that's it. I knew I had seen you before, but I couldn't think where. You are the dispenser at the hospital, are you not?" Grace noted his use of "stepmother", which explained the oddity of the Ormsby children's lack of similarity to Mrs Ormsby.

"I'm amazed you noticed me, Miss Penrose. Most doctors believe us an inferior species, although they are happy to take credit for the miraculous outcomes of our medicines. Father practically disowned me when I informed him of my choice of profession. He dismisses my stepmother's work as 'my wife's little hobby'. Rather ironic, I feel, as she is responsible for his success. Not that he would ever admit it."

Grace found her admiration for Richard Ormsby increasing by the minute. A man who made his own choices and championed his stepmother was a man worth knowing. "You intrigue me. How is Mrs Ormsby responsible for her husband's success?"

"My stepmother acts as his surgical assistant. It is thanks to her meticulous attention to hygiene that Father claims so high a success rate. His own practices tend to the lax, but she insists he wash his hands with carbolic soap and ensure every instrument and surface is spotless. Mother is a devotee of Florence Nightingale and germ theory."

No wonder Mrs Ormsby was on their side over the new women's ward, if she had such high standards. Grace was very much looking forward to making her acquaintance. But first she took the opportunity to enjoy the champagne, which was perfectly chilled and decidedly delicious.

"I must say, this soirée is not at all what I expected, Mr Ormsby. It just goes to show that one ought not to prejudge based on incomplete information. I know my invitation was a mistake, but I am surprised to see so many of the ladies who fundraised for the women's ward."

"The majority of Hospital Trustees want to move ahead with the new hospital building without a fight, so Father agreed to extend an olive branch to the women's lobby." Richard Ormsby smiled at her over his glass. "My stepmother has been applying gentle persuasion too. I believe my father might agree to a slightly smaller women's ward, as long as he gets an extra consulting room for surgeons, along with a promise of an additional operating theatre after the new building is completed."

Grace raised her glass to his. "My Ormsby, I do declare that is the most sensible suggestion I have heard on the matter. I take it you wish this compromise to be put to the women's lobby discreetly, without your own name being mentioned? Or that of Mrs Ormsby, I expect."

"Your reputation for quick wits has not been exaggerated, Miss Penrose. I do hope this will not be the last time we have the pleasure of your company."

Cecilia Ormsby approached from behind her brother, clinging to the arm of the new surgeon. "Richard, you cannot keep Miss Penrose to yourself all evening. People will start to gossip."

Red spots flared on Richard's pudgy cheeks. "I'll leave the gossip to you, sister dear."

His sister ignored him. "Miss Penrose, Doctor Alexander insists on making your acquaintance. He has never met an aspiring lady doctor before."

The man at her side bowed. "Please excuse my intrusion into your conversation, Miss Penrose. I am Gideon Alexander, recently arrived to take up a surgical position in Dunedin."

Grace allowed him to take the tips of her fingers. "Doctor Alexander, a pleasure to meet you. I look forward to seeing you at work in the operating theatre."

"The pleasure is all mine, Miss Penrose. I understand you take a particular interest in medical jurisprudence. Your lecturer in that subject, Doctor Ogston, tells me you are his star pupil."

Two compliments on Grace's medical prowess in the space of minutes – a record. And not a single mention of her lovely gown. Grace tried not to let it go to her head. "I have been privileged to work for the police surgeon during term breaks, which has given me an advantage in medical jurisprudence. Do you have a specialty, Doctor Alexander?"

Alexander waved his expressive hands dismissively, which made a pleasant change from the smug arrogance Grace had observed in many of his ilk. "As a recently qualified surgeon, I do what is needed. However, I do have a special interest in orthopaedics and bone-setting. There have been some marvellous advances in the use of splints to reduce the need for amputation."

"You'll find plenty of patients in New Zealand," Grace said. "The colonies, I fear, are a dangerous place, abounding with broken limbs."

"So I've observed," Alexander replied. "I was fortunate to study in London alongside a man with contacts in this country. He kindly recommended me for a probationary position at Dunedin Hospital, subject to their approval naturally."

Grace didn't have Charlie's ear for accents, but Alexander's rounded vowels suggested a London not too far from the illustrious environs of Buckingham Palace. "I hope Dunedin is to your taste, after travelling halfway around the world to a foreign land. I fear we are rather lacking in splendid palaces and cultural attractions."

"I like it very much so far, Miss Penrose." Alexander's smile had that disarming quality of making the receiver feel special. "What Dunedin lacks in ancient buildings and equally ancient traditions, it makes up for in delightful people with a fresh outlook upon the future. I take it as a sign of advancement that a woman was allowed into the Otago Medical School. That must have caused a few of the old traditionalists to choke on their port."

"I'm delighted to report that none of the old codgers have died of asphyxiation yet. Nor have the hallowed halls collapsed with the shame of it."

Cecilia was watching the exchange with a blossoming pout. Grace redirected her attention to Cecilia, not wanting her to be left out of the conversation with all this talk of medicine. "May I ask what pursuits you enjoy, Miss Ormsby?"

"I like music." Cecilia glanced up at Gideon Alexander, fluttering her eyelashes prettily. "We both do."

"You play the piano beautifully, Cecilia," Richard said. "I'm sure we would all like to hear you play a piece or two later. We may not have the great opera houses of London, Doctor Alexander, but there are several musical societies in Dunedin, if you are interested. My sister can tell you all about them."

"I should like to hear of them, Miss Ormsby. Shall we refresh our glasses?"

When Cecilia Ormsby and Gideon Alexander had drifted away, arm-in-arm, Grace turned back to Richard Ormsby. "That was kind of you to praise your sister."

"My sister is twenty-seven years old and lacks your accomplishments, Miss Penrose," Richard replied. "Father has already turned down two suitors for their lack of wealth and position, fearing they are only after Cecilia's substantial dowry. She would never forgive him if he refuses Doctor Alexander as well. They appear to have fallen in love and he has excellent prospects. What more could Father want? I hope I have not upset you by turning Doctor Alexander away from the more intriguing prospect you might present."

"Not in the least," Grace assured him. "I'd sooner dip my toes in prussic acid than the marriage market at present. I am determined not to marry until I have qualified as a doctor. I do wish people didn't feel the need to meddle in the love life of every unattached

23

young woman, as if she was desperate for rescue from her shameful plight."

"Hear, hear, Miss Penrose. I applaud you on behalf of all unattached men who find themselves shoved at the nearest lace-fluttering, mindless debutante." Richard Ormsby took her empty glass and placed it on the lid of the piano, to the horror of the pianist. "Come. Mother has been waving at me these last five minutes. I expect she wishes to be rescued from the tedious company she has been landed with."

As they crossed the room, Grace could hear Mrs Beechworth attempting to put the women's case to a group of hospital trustees. Indeed, it would have been hard not to hear, as her voice had risen above the polite level of the conversation around the rest of the room. Horncastle, the chairman of the trustees, said not a word, but looked ready to explode.

Edgar Ormsby shushed Mrs Beechworth with his hands. "I must insist you leave these gentlemen in peace, Mrs Beechworth. Such matters should be addressed at a meeting, not at a social event." He moved closer, a polite smile fixed on his face. "Do come and speak to my wife and her ladies. I'm sure you would have a great deal in common."

Richard Ormsby leaned over to whisper in Grace's ear. "My father hates to be harangued. He's a man better lured with honey than vinegar. Let me distract him, so you can woo the trustees with your charms."

He stepped to his father's side. "Apologies for interrupting, Father, but there is an issue regarding the wine." Richard cut his father out of the herd with the skill of a sheepdog, prattling away about the best choice of claret, while winking at Grace over his shoulder.

Grace moved into the newly created space in the group of trustees. By great good fortune, she recognised the man beside her as an attorney friend of her Great-Aunt Anne's beau, Mr Drummond. The man had attended a dinner at Anne's house recently. Grace favoured him with her sweetest smile, which she had practiced in the mirror before attending tonight's soirée. "Mr McKinley, isn't it?"

He pushed his eyeglasses up his nose and squinted down at her between rampant sideburns. "Er, Miss Macmillan?"

"Miss Penrose, Mrs Anne Macmillan's great-niece. As I recall, you were about to become a great-grandfather, sir."

"Your memory does you proud, Miss Penrose. My great-grandson was born two weeks ago. An enormous relief, after a rather traumatic few weeks for my granddaughter. For a while we thought … well, no matter now, she survived, and the babe is a bonny wee lad."

Grace felt a surge of inappropriate glee. "You can be rightly proud of your own role in her survival, Mr McKinley. I applaud the decision of the Hospital Trustees to improve sanitation at the hospital and employ trained nursing staff. Even with their dedication, I expect you were shocked by the conditions in the current women's ward."

Mr McKinley had the grace to blush. "Oh, well, er, actually, we had my granddaughter admitted to a private clinic, on Doctor Beechworth's recommendation."

Of course you did, Grace thought. "A wise decision, Mr McKinley, giving the appalling state of the public facilities. It must give you great pleasure to know that the prospects of women like your granddaughter will be far better served with the new building, complete with a specialist ward for women's issues. We ought to toast the forward thinking of the Hospital Trustees, who are making women's lives safer, and by extension, securing the best prospects for the next generation of strapping young baby boys. For what man amongst you would wish to be without a bevy of healthy heirs?"

It was a grandiose speech, which wouldn't have fooled a medical person for an instant, but the trustees lapped it up.

McKinley gaped at her for a moment, before a wave of delight spread across his craggy features. "How very true, Miss Penrose. When you put it like that, I do feel proud to serve as a Hospital

25

Trustee. One really oughtn't to think of a hospital as merely bricks and mortar and endless expenses, after all. Yes, yes, saving people's lives, that's what it's about."

"Indeed, Mr McKinley." Grace raised her glass.

Mrs Beechworth, who was standing on her other side, put her hand over Grace's to halt the toast, giving it the tiniest of squeezes. "Miss Penrose, I am sorry to say that the proposed women's ward is no longer the preferred option for the hospital extension."

Grace raised a hand to cover her mouth. "Oh? Is it not? Goodness, you shock me. But surely the women's fundraising committee has already raised the funds for the new building? What crisis has arisen to forestall this essential work?"

Several of the trustees shuffled their feet. Horncastle was brave enough to fill the silence. "An alternative suggestion has been put forward. A new operating theatre, which will enhance the status of the hospital and provide much-needed income." Horncastle gave Grace a hard look, no doubt recalling her from somewhere he couldn't quite put his finger on.

Grace returned his gaze with puzzled incomprehension. "Was there not a new operating theatre opened relatively recently, Mr Horncastle? It is not for me to say, of course, but I cannot imagine anything that would enhance the status of our fine hospital more than a ward cherishing the weaker sex. Women do, after all, make up half of the population and the entire population capable of giving birth to the next generation of male leaders."

Gideon Alexander appeared at her shoulder. "Quite so, Miss Penrose. I have little knowledge of the local situation, but I can tell you that in England there are entire hospitals devoted to women and children, under the patronage of the royal family and other illustrious members of society."

"Is that so?" McKinley said. "Well, our decision has not yet been made, has it, gentlemen? I shouldn't care to deprive the good women of Dunedin of the best facilities, especially after the ladies have raised so much money for the building. It'll still have to be discussed at the next meeting, of course."

"I wish you well, Mr McKinley," Grace said. "The women of this fair city look forward to hearing your final decision."

With perfect timing, the butler rang a bell and announced that supper was served. Grace favoured the trustees with a demure smile and slipped away from their group, gliding elegantly, without a hint of the smug grin bubbling inside. By a stroke of luck, Richard Ormsby's suggested compromise might not be needed after all.

Moonlit Stroll

Having done her duty to her fellow women by raising the issue of the women's ward, Grace could enjoy the rest of the soirée. To her surprise, the evening was turning out to be decidedly pleasant, thanks to the unexpected support of Richard Ormsby and Gideon Alexander.

Because of the large number of guests and the informality of the occasion, there were a dozen small supper tables, which meant she could feast with a group of like-minded souls. Grace certainly couldn't fault the food. Ormsby had spared no expense. The lavish spread could have fed the poor of Dunedin for a week, if their stomachs could cope with the richness of the offering.

Mrs Ormsby flitted between tables, dropping a smile here and a compliment there, ensuring that all her husband's guests were enjoying themselves. Edgar Ormsby sat with a coterie of senior physicians and surgeons, although he ate little and spoke even less. Every now and then, Ormsby glared across the room at the table of women fundraisers and their husbands, where Grace sat.

"Doctor Ormsby has been glaring at me throughout supper," Mrs Beechworth said, as the men rose to take their port and cigars. "I must apologise for accosting him earlier this evening."

"He should apologise to you, my dear," her husband replied. "There was no call for him to have snapped at you so rudely."

"No, the fault was mine," Mrs Beechworth said. "I should not have criticized Ormsby at his own party, especially as I could see he wasn't feeling well. I need to learn the art of being subtle, like Grace, who achieved the objective without causing a hint of offense. In fact, I heard that several of the Hospital Trustees are now counting themselves proud supporters of the women's ward, as if it was their idea all along."

"Subtlety is hardly my forte," Grace admitted. "Fate intervened on my behalf, with the gift of Mr McKinley's granddaughter and great-grandson. If you wish to apologise, I've just seen Doctor Ormsby go out alone onto the terrace. It looks freezing out there. Shall I get our cloaks, Mrs Beechworth, so you can make your apology without your teeth chattering?"

"Thank you, Grace." Mrs Beechworth turned to her husband. "No need for you to come, my dear. I know you want to talk to your medical colleagues over a decent port. Doctor Ormsby is hardly likely to take advantage of me on the terrace." She swept towards the French doors without waiting for a reply from her husband.

When Grace returned with their cloaks, the tension on the terrace already hung like an icy fog around Mrs Beechworth and Doctor Ormsby.

Mrs Beechworth was not letting her rival get a word in. "No, sir, I will not listen to your justifications. I assure you, Doctor Ormsby, that I will not allow anyone to stand in the way of our new women's ward."

Ormsby responded to Mrs Beechworth's tenuous grasp on civility with raised hackles and spurious politeness. "In that case, I will accept your apology for your earlier discourtesy, Mrs Beechworth, and ask you to return to your husband, for I am in no mood to respond to threats."

Mrs Beechworth swept past, grabbing her cloak and gesturing for Grace to follow. The French doors slammed shut on Grace's indecision, leaving her standing out in the freezing chill of a late autumn night with a man who loathed her.

Grace would not have hesitated to return to the warmth of the salon, had it not been for the hunch of Ormsby's back and the pallor of his face. "Doctor Ormsby, if you will forgive my impertinence, you do not look at all well. May I send for assistance?"

"I do not wish to be prodded by a physician, only to be told what I know myself. I have merely eaten something that disagreed with me." Ormsby waved a hand towards a garden path. "Walk with me,

29

Miss Penrose. Fresh air and activity will benefit my ailing digestive system."

Grace glanced around, seeking rescue at best or chaperonage at least. The only other person outside was Henry Ormsby, who was skulking in the shadows at the opposite end of the terrace, smoking a cigar. Henry turned his back on her, leaving Grace with no choice but to refuse to accompany his father. "Doctor Ormsby, I do not think it is appropriate–"

"Really, Miss Penrose, your reputation for charging resolutely where other ladies fear to tread is well known. You do not need to be missish about a simple stroll with a gentleman old enough to be your father." Ormsby hooked his arm through hers. "Come, you need not fear either my disapprobation or my morals. I wish to talk to you."

Concern for the women's ward won out over deep-seated reluctance. Grace allowed Doctor Ormsby to guide her along the path, which wound through an immaculate garden to the wide stretch of trees rising up the hillside beyond. Truly, it was a lovely night – sharp with the promise of frost and fresh with the scent of autumn leaves, their gold turned to silver by the pale wash of the full moon.

Her eyes adjusted quickly until the path through the trees became as clear as a grainy photograph. Beside her, Ormsby gripped her arm tightly for support, as his feet struggled to maintain a straight line. He was either more unwell than he had admitted or more inebriated than he sounded. Rasps of laboured breath punctuated the silence, leaving white puffs in the night.

Before Grace could muster the courage to insist Ormsby return to the house, he stopped of his own accord, turning to face the otherworldly panorama. The path had taken them to a clearing, where the ground dropped away steeply, leaving them above the treeline and the rows of houses. In the distance, beyond the city, the harbour glittered in the moonlight, ringed by the dark hills of Otago Peninsula.

Ormsby scarcely noticed the stunning view. Although his body hunched in discomfit, his voice was tight but determined. "I truly believed the new operating theatre was the best option, Miss Penrose. Horncastle convinced me that the funds for running the hospital have all but dried up because of the collapse of wool prices. Government revenues are down, income from land holdings is evaporating. New Zealand is on her knees. The hospital must fund services by taking patients able to pay, if we cannot find enough wealthy donors."

"And what of those who cannot pay?" Grace inquired.

"Horncastle has worked it all out. The paying patients will subsidise the impoverished. Without them, the hospital cannot continue to pay for the staff and equipment we have, much less the necessary improvements we all desire."

Grace drew cool, fresh air into her lungs. Ormsby was not the pompous fool she had taken him for. Had the women's lobby driven him into a corner with their demands, not seeing the deeper funding concerns wrought by a decade of depression? "You make a fair point, Doctor Ormsby. And yet, women are dying unnecessarily in substandard, draughty wards."

"So my wife has informed me in no uncertain terms. And Mrs Beechworth has added her own rather strident form of protest. I do not like to be lectured, especially when I find myself between a rock and a ravine. To own the truth, I have already told Horncastle I plan to withdraw my support for the new operating theatre."

Which no doubt explained Horncastle's rudeness to Ormsby when he arrived at the soirée. "May I ask why Mr Horncastle is so set on the operating theatre? Is it only the money it will bring in?"

Ormsby's face contorted, leaving Grace uncertain whether he was annoyed at her question or suffering a spasm of stomach pain. He recovered quickly but reached out to a nearby tree for support. "I hope I can rely on your discretion, Miss Penrose, if I suggest that Horncastle may be looking to his legacy. His term as the Chairman of the Hospital Trustees ends soon and I suspect he would rather

31

have his tenure commemorated on a plaque above a surgical facility rather than on a ward for ladies' ailments."

Grace wasn't sure whether to laugh or cry. Could the failure to proceed with a desperately needed facility for the women of Dunedin really come down to one man's vanity? Perhaps this was why Richard Ormsby had dropped the hint earlier about the need for negotiation.

She considered her words carefully. "Doctor Ormsby, I appreciate your candour. I wonder if a compromise would be possible. A slightly smaller women's ward would free up space for a new surgical consulting room. The latter might be designated the Horncastle Surgical Suite perhaps, with a new operating theatre next on the agenda. If the suggested compromise was made by the women of the fundraising committee, it might be seen as a win by the Hospital Trustees."

Doctor Ormsby surprised her by letting loose a throaty chuckle. "You remind me of my wife, Miss Penrose. A strong, competent woman, who uses her strength in the service of compassion. Best decision I ever made, marrying her, despite the naysayers. I ought to have supported your entry to medical school too, and for that I apologise. You have proved yourself worthy of the honour, perhaps because you have had to fight so hard for it. I wish my son Henry had half your spirit."

Ormsby paused to wipe beads of sweat from his brow, despite the cold. "My son, Richard, also troubles me. He shows no inclination for the wealthy young society ladies I have encouraged him to meet, yet it is past time for him to settle down and produce a worthy heir. I have belatedly come to realise Richard is much more like myself that I had realised. If he married a strong woman, it would be the making of him." Ormsby cleared his throat. "If I may be so bold, I could not fail to notice his animation when speaking with you earlier, Miss Penrose."

Grace breathed out a long stream of white mist. "Your elder son impressed me greatly as an intelligent and charming young man,

Doctor Ormsby, but you should know that I am not in a position to consider any attachment at present."

Ormsby was silent, leaving Grace to wonder if she was expected to justify herself. His groan cut through her thoughts. He doubled over, clutching his chest and stomach. This man was seriously ill. What had he been thinking, dragging her into the woods for a walk? She had to get him home now, before his condition deteriorated further.

Suddenly, his arm jerked upwards, connecting painfully with her breast. Instinctively, Grace's arm shot out to protect herself, as his arms flailed around her. Ormsby lurched forward at the same moment, her hand catching him across the cheek.

In the still, silent night air, the unintended slap echoed along the path like the retort from a small pistol. Ormsby lurched towards the steep drop, leaving Grace with no choice but to yank him back towards the safety of the path. They both stumbled backwards.

Ormsby fell to the ground, writhing and jerking amidst the mush of autumn leaves, catching his thrashing limbs on tree roots. Grace fell to her knees beside him, trying to protect him from hurting himself.

When the fit stopped – it must have been mere seconds, although it felt like minutes – Ormsby went rigidly still. Grace slid her hand under his cravat, loosening his tight collar. His pulse was fast and irregular.

A voice cracked through the night. "Oy!"

Henry Ormsby rushed forward until he was standing over Grace with his fists bunched. "Leave my father alone!"

"For heaven's sake, Henry, don't just stand there. Your father was having a fit. Get medical assistance, as fast as you can." Grace felt his father's forehead for signs of fever and slipped a hand around the back of his head, checking for any injury. She stripped off her cloak and placed it under Ormsby's head. Henry still hadn't moved. "Give me your coat to keep him warm. Go! Send a stretcher party."

Henry stared at her for another precious second, as if he was about to protest. Then he yanked his coat off, draped it over his father's body, and ran back down the path.

Abruptly, Doctor Ormsby's limbs lost their rigidity. Although the fit had passed, the lack of focus in his gaze told her he was too befuddled to recognise her. He shook his head and mumbled something but was too confused to make any sense. Before she could utter reassuring words, his body spasmed. His hands flew to the left side of his chest, while his lungs gasped for breath. When the dreadful spasm finally ended, Ormsby lay deathly still.

Grace felt for a pulse with trembling fingers, praying that help would arrive soon, but knowing in her heart that it was too late. Nevertheless, she began chest compressions. There was always hope. She pumped his chest, ignoring the frosty chill that seeped through her gown, numbing her knees, not stopping even when she heard a flurry of footsteps running up the path at long last.

"Penrose, what the devil are you doing to my father?"

"Out of the way, Henry, she is trying to save his life." Doctor Beechworth dropped to his knees beside Grace, taking over the compressions. "Doctor Alexander, please take Miss Penrose, Henry, and my wife back to the house. Get them warm. Tell the stretcher bearers to make haste."

Alexander didn't waste time arguing. As Grace was dragged away, she heard the terrible wheezing thump of ribs compressing – the only sound that penetrated the still air, apart from the crunch of gravel under their feet and the quiet sobs of Mrs Beechworth.

Henry, who had looked upon his father's lifeless body, showed no apparent emotion. Shock, Grace assumed. When he caught her looking at him, Henry glared at her and dashed ahead, towards the house. Four men raced past in the opposite direction with a stretcher.

As Grace reached the steps up to the house, she heard Henry shouting, "My father's dead. She killed him."

Doctor Alexander used his body to shield Grace, as he bustled her and Mrs Beechworth past the rows of horrified faces lining the windows. Inside, Mrs Ormsby screamed and collapsed into Richard's arms. Cecilia took one look at her younger brother's expression and fainted.

The solitude of the library was a blessed relief, especially as a roaring fire burned amidst the fug of cigar smoke. As feeling returned to her chilled limbs, Grace realised she was shivering. Somebody tucked a blanket around her shoulders, another person put a tumbler of brandy into her trembling hand, a third comforted Mrs Beechworth, who was huddled on a sofa.

Grateful as she was for their care, all Grace wanted was for her beloved Charlie Pyke to appear miraculously in the doorway and tell her he had everything under control. But Charlie was hundreds of miles away. The thought of him reminded her of her duty. Doctor Alexander had left, leaving Horncastle guarding the door of the library, a task he clearly didn't relish. If he was expecting denials, tears or fainting, he was going to be disappointed.

Grace stood up and threw off the blanket. "Mr Horncastle, has somebody sent for the police?"

"The police? Why?"

"The police surgeon is required to attend any unexpected death to establish the cause."

"But surely the poor chap had a heart attack?" Horncastle said. "Dashed young to die, but Ormsby did have a weak heart. Young Henry was overwrought to make such an accusation against you, Miss Penrose. There is no need for you to be hysterical."

Grace bit back her frustration. "It was by no means a typical heart failure, sir. The police must be summoned."

"Well, I suppose so, but I will have to get Mrs Ormsby's permission for such an unwarranted intrusion at this tragic time." Horncastle wavered for a moment, then left, closing the door behind him.

Grace would have liked nothing better than to curl up in an armchair in front of the fire, but she had a duty to do. As occasional assistant to the police surgeon, she must ensure that correct procedure was followed. She went after Horncastle, who had halted at the sight of Mrs Ormsby's anguish. The stretcher-bearers kept their eyes lowered as they carried Ormsby's lifeless body through to another room. Doctor Beechworth looked up and caught Grace's eye, giving his head a slight shake.

Horncastle moved to Richard Ormsby's side. "Richard, old chap. My deepest condolences."

"The condolences can wait, Horncastle," Richard snapped. "Do me a favour and alert the police. Pugh, our butler, will show you where the telephone is. And get that Penrose woman out of our house. Henry told me she hit Father and knocked him to the ground. How could she be so stupid as to strike a sick man with a weak heart?"

Grace shrank back, out of their line of sight. Her eyes drilled into the back of Beechworth's skull, willing him to turn. When he did, she jerked her head toward the library.

Doctor Beechworth joined Grace by the fire. "Ignore them, Miss Penrose."

"Henry Ormsby is blaming me, but it is not my fault. I think it is best we leave at once, Doctor Beechworth. The police will need to question me, but Richard wants me out of the house right away."

"Ivy will take you home, Miss Penrose. I will stay to give an account to the police." Beechworth turned to leave, then thought better of it. "What happened out there?"

Grace edged closer to the warmth of the fire. "Ormsby had a grand mal seizure. His jerking arm caught me by surprise. When I put my hand up to fend him off, it connected with his face. That was the slap Henry must have overheard. I suppose Henry followed us, not trusting my motives."

"Or his father's. Henry seemed rather incoherent, but I heard him accuse you of strangling his father. I'm sure it's all a misunderstanding, but it is better the truth is known from the start."

"Doctor Ormsby collapsed during his fit, Doctor Beechworth," Grace said. "He was thrashing about on the ground, so I leaned over him to protect him from injury. As soon as the fit stopped, I checked his pulse. I had to loosen his collar to help him breathe, which might have appeared as if I was strangling him. It all happened so fast. He went rigid. I couldn't find a pulse. I tried–"

Beechworth put a gentle hand on her arm. "You did everything you could, Miss Penrose. I know Ormsby had a weak heart. A terrible tragedy, but nobody is to blame. Especially not you, who did everything you could to save him. If there is fault, it is mine. Ivy and I should have walked with you. I'm so very sorry. I know you didn't want to accept the invitation to the party in the first place."

"Do not blame yourself, sir. Ormsby insisted I join him for a walk. I thought the opportunity to talk about the women's ward at the hospital was worth the risk to my reputation."

"I understand," Beechworth said. "Henry Ormsby is a spiteful brat. Don't you worry about his bluster. I will stand by you."

Grace didn't bother pointing out that an accusation of murder could destroy a reputation in an instant, whether ill-founded or not. Even the impropriety of walking with a gentleman alone could destroy her career. Instead, she allowed herself to be escorted out a side entrance and bundled into the Beechworth carriage. Mrs Beechworth was already huddled in the corner of the carriage, pale and round-eyed in a shaft of moonlight.

After a tearful apology from Mrs Beechworth for abandoning her to Ormsby, brushed off by Grace, they travelled home in silence, each lost in her own thoughts. Grace's mind swung between rational analysis of what more she might have done to save Doctor Ormsby's life and irrational fear of what lay ahead. Expulsion from medical school? Arrest, if Henry stuck to his version of events? At best, a black mark that would be hard to erase, no matter what happened.

Unexpected Arrival

Anne Macmillan's house was still lit up when Grace arrived home from the disastrous soirée. Grace had expected her great-aunt to be in bed at this late hour. Their friend and lodger, Lily Wu, was not one for late nights either. Not wanting to face questions from Anne and Lily tonight, Grace turned the key gently and eased the door closed behind her. She needn't have bothered. The noise emanating from the drawing room was as merry as Hogmanay.

Grace hung up her cloak and stripped off her long gloves, which were soiled with leaf litter and mud. As she walked up the hallway, intending to sneak up the stairs, the changing angle of view revealed the silhouette of a tall, muscular man in the light of the drawing room. He stood with his feet apart, redolent with natural authority. Grace took a step back into the shadows of the hallway to calm her racing pulse.

Not an hour ago, she had been on her knees amongst the autumn leaves beside a dying man, praying for the miracle of Charlie Pyke's presence. And now here he was, and she was not sure she could face him. When last she saw him, she had laid her heart bare and Charlie had left anyway, intending to visit his parents in Central Otago, to decide his future. Part of her ached to hear his decision, part of her dreaded it. And the part of her trying to keep sanity afloat after Ormsby's shocking death screamed "not tonight".

Before Grace could retreat, Lily appeared in the doorway, arm-in-arm with a woman who could have been her twin. Not quite as petite as Lily, but with the same jet-black hair, litheness of movement and almond eyes inherited from their Chinese father. Even before the woman came close enough for Grace to note her emerald eyes, flecked with gold, she was in no doubt this woman was Mrs Jasmine Pyke, Charlie's mother.

38

Grace shuttered her mixed emotions behind a smile. "Mrs Pyke. How lovely to meet you. Had I known you were coming, I would not have accepted an invitation to Ormsby's soirée." How she wished she hadn't.

Jasmine Pyke closed the gap between them with the same disconcerting speed and dancer's grace as her son, flinging her arms around Grace and embracing her as if she was a long-lost daughter. "Miss Penrose, I have heard so much about you. I feel as if I have known you for years. I hope you will forgive my excitement at meeting you at last."

"I only received Jasmine's telegram two days ago, advising of their early arrival," Lily explained. "Being unsure of their exact arrival time and with Anne wanting you to attend the soirée, we decided to let it be a surprise. Did you achieve your objective tonight, Grace?"

"Er … in a way. Doctor Ormsby will no longer interfere with the original plan for the hospital." The last thing Grace wanted was to greet Charlie's mother with the news of a death. Grace's growing reputation for corpse-gathering was already far worse than any sensible mother would accept for her son. Grace was desperate to go upstairs and change her gown, which still showed traces of mud about the lower portions.

Jasmine linked her arm with Grace's. "Do come and meet my husband. May I call you Grace? Lily has assured me Anne prefers informality." Charlie's mother led her up the hall to the drawing room, giving her no option but to comply. "Thomas, darling, come and meet Grace."

The familiar silhouette turned, but it was not Charlie. Instead, Grace found herself staring at a grey-haired, brown-eyed version of what Charlie might look like in another quarter of a century. She tried to imagine life in 1917, but it was an inconceivably distant future for a woman of twenty-two to contemplate.

Sergeant Thomas Pyke stepped towards her with the vigour of a man half his age. Charlie's father took her hand and raising it to his lips with an elegance more akin to an aristocrat than a back-country policeman. "Miss Penrose, delighted to meet you at last."

"Likewise, Sergeant Pyke. Forgive my distraction. You are so like your son, it is quite disconcerting."

"Charlie will be sorry to have missed your arrival. When he heard you were out at a soirée, he and Alistair went off to deal with a matter of business at Mr Drummond's house. I expect they will all return shortly."

Grace nodded dumbly. It seemed she was not only going to have to face Charlie without time to prepare herself, after a harrowing evening, but also in the presence of his nearest and dearest. She had expected Charlie's parents to arrive next week for the wedding of Lily and Alistair Stewart. Alistair was already like family to them, being Charlie's former Detective Inspector, as well as an old friend of his father. Charlie had been delighted when his Aunt Lily and Alistair had fallen in love.

Grace felt a tug on her arm as Jasmine Pyke diverted her to a quiet spot in the corner of the room. Let the interrogation begin.

"Forgive our unexpected arrival, Grace. We didn't wish to risk missing my sister's wedding. Some years, autumn snow closes the road for days. Fortunately, Thomas now has a constable with sufficient gumption to take sole charge of the district for an extended period."

"Lily will be thrilled to have you here, Mrs Pyke. I know your sister misses you a great deal."

"And I her. Your great-aunt has been kind enough to offer us a place to stay for as long as we wish. Charlie and Alistair are staying with Mr Drummond." Jasmine contemplated her silently for a moment. "Grace, I'm not sure how much Charlie would wish me to say. Or rather, if I am honest, I know my son would prefer my silence."

Jasmine's eyes and expression were so close a match to Charlie's that Grace's mind played tricks on her, as if this woman was speaking his words. "I am a forthright woman, Mrs Pyke. I

40

would prefer to hear the truth, no matter the consequences. If your son does not wish to tell me himself, then I should be glad to hear it from you. I take it Charlie does not intend to stay in Dunedin after the wedding."

Jasmine cut in. "No, no, that's not it at all! Oh dear, I fear I am making a muddle of this. Charlie is not reluctant to see you, Grace. Indeed, he is eager to talk to you himself. He has been like a bee in a field of flowers since he arrived in Clyde, flitting from one thing to another, unable to settle. What he may not tell you is that he insisted on leaving early, because he had a strong premonition that you needed him. The rational-minded policeman in him puts it down to missing your company, which he undoubtedly does. He will be very relieved to see you in such an excellent state of health. Looking very beautiful, if I might say so, in that exquisite gown. May I ask – is there any cause for his troubling intuition?"

"I'm afraid there is, Mrs Pyke. It seems I am about to become embroiled in another police investigation. I hope my part in the matter is quickly over, so we can concentrate on the joy of Lily and Alistair's wedding. They are a fine match."

Jasmine glanced at her sister, who was chatting and laughing with Thomas Pyke. "To see Lily happy again was one of my fondest hopes. My husband tells me there is no better man than Alistair Stewart. The day you and Anne took Lily into your home was the turning point in her life. We will be forever grateful."

As that day was also the first time Grace met Charlie, she felt the same emotion. "Lily has been a blessing to us, Mrs Pyke. Anne would have struggled to cope alone with all the patients who flock to Lavender House, especially with me busy studying to be a doctor. Although, it is also true that I may not have gained entry to medical school if it had not been for the fortuitous meeting with your son."

Jasmine's eyes crinkled above an enigmatic smile. "Happenstance? Or destiny? Either way, a joyous day for both my family and yours. In more ways than one, I hope."

Out of the corner of her eye, Grace noticed Charlie Pyke enter the room, flanked by Alistair Stewart and Kenneth Drummond. As physically mismatched a group of men as one could imagine, although united in their intellect and compassion.

Former Detective Inspector Alistair Stewart was slight, dapper and middle-aged. He exuded the languid air of a gentleman of leisure, neatly disguising his stiletto-sharp brain and legendary detective skills. His elegant countenance softened into a smile at the sight of his betrothed enjoying her family's company. Mr Drummond's gaze swept the room for Anne Macmillan, before turning to Grace, with a nod. Drummond was tall, stooped, and elderly, looking exactly like the astute retired attorney he was.

And Charlie Pyke, whose presence dominated a room despite his youth, with his father's stature and natural authority, and his mother's feline grace, black hair and gold-flecked green eyes.

Charlie had been Alistair's detective constable until recent events curtailed his career in the police force. Now, his future was uncertain. Grace felt sure Charlie had the intelligence and character to make a success of any career that took his fancy, especially given his uncanny ability to pass for anything from a dim-witted, barrel-lugging labourer to a gentleman born to power and privilege. The question was, what did he want and would it be found in Dunedin?

Charlie stood observing her, not moving to greet her. He watched her from the corner of his eye, as if she was a suspect in one of his investigations. Grace wished she had had time to change out of her evening gown, which was far too formal for the occasion, but she was unable to move for fear that he would vanish again in a puff of smoke.

The conflicting events of the day rose in a concerted tangle of emotion and squeezed the breath out of her lungs.

Reunion

Charlie Pyke paused in the doorway, frozen by the sight of Grace in a sleek evening gown of shimmering midnight blue. He glanced around the room in case there was an elegant young man lurking in an evening suit, although he couldn't imagine any partner in his right mind abandoning her side.

Grace was talking to his mother as if they had known each other for years. She looked so in command of herself, it reminded him of the first time he had seen her, when she had subdued a corrupt police officer with the sheer force of her personality.

Charlie skipped a breath as he noted that Grace's elegantly coiffed hair was askew and her gown showed traces of mud from the knee down. A small matter compared to what his imagination had feared – seeing Grace with blood on her again, whether her own or somebody else's – but still cause for concern. Nothing short of a catastrophe would have caused her to kneel in the mud in that beautiful gown.

Grace noticed him watching and turned her piercingly intelligent eyes on him. The flint in her gaze made his welcome as uncertain as he had expected it would be. He had a great deal of apologising to do, if she would allow it. As he stood there, she sagged at the knees. He was across the room in seconds, catching her elbow and guiding her onto the nearby sofa.

"Grace, are you well? Should I get you water or brandy?"

"I'm fine, Charlie. I didn't know you were arriving tonight." A pause. "I wasn't sure if you were ever coming back."

"I promised I would return, Grace, after I had time away to see my parents." Charlie glanced back to see if his mother was hovering, but she had moved into the huddle around the new arrivals, listening intently to Alistair's words, as were all the other guests.

43

Grace followed his line of sight. "Your mother said you wanted to return because you sensed I was in trouble."

"I hope I was wrong." Charlie couldn't deny the strong presentiment he'd felt, although he wished his mother had been more discreet about sharing his concerns with Grace. The momentary tightening of tension around her mouth told him more than her silence. "Grace, what has happened?"

She sank back into the sofa, her gaze focussed on the clasped hands in her lap. "I had to attend a supper party tonight in order to persuade one of the local surgeons to withdraw his proposed plan for the new hospital building. He collapsed. I tried to save him, but he died. Or, as the police will see it, I was the last person to touch him before he died."

"The police? Was it not a straightforward death?" The words came out more sharply than Charlie intended. The cluster around Alistair broke apart with a collective intake of breath.

Anne's head snapped around. "Grace, did Charlie just say there was a death at the party tonight?"

"I'm sorry to report that Edgar Ormsby suffered a seizure and died."

"What an awful tragedy for his family," Anne said. "I cannot pretend that I cared for the man, but he was far too young to die. I hope it was a quick and natural passing."

"The police will be obliged to investigate." Grace had no intention of ruining the evening by elaborating. She turned to Lily. "I do hope I won't be dragged into it, when I need to be helping you with your wedding preparations."

"Of course you must assist the police inquiry, Grace," Lily assured her. "Our wedding plan is simple and well in hand, especially now Jasmine is here early. As long as Alistair shows up, all will be well."

"You may be assured I will be there, my darling," Alistair replied. "I'm relieved it's not me doing the investigating. And, naturally, relieved Grace came home unharmed." His unspoken words, "this time", hung in the air.

"Don't worry about me," Grace said, with a lightness she did not feel inside. "The police will want to talk to me tomorrow, but I promise not to let it interfere with my duties to you, Lily."

"Duties?" Charlie queried.

"I've asked Grace to be my bridesmaid," Lily said. "Dear Grace, I cannot believe you are worried about my wedding, when a man has died. You must be in shock."

"Only a little. Edgar Ormsby was no friend of mine and no friend of the women of Dunedin. I'm sorry that his passing will cause his family pain, but, to me, your wedding is infinitely more important."

Alistair, with his usual sensitivity, adroitly changed the subject. "Thank you, Grace. Now is not the time to dwell upon the grim side of life. In fact, now that we are all together at last, I propose we have a toast, to families reunited." He turned to Lily. "What would you like, my dearest? Champagne? Whisky? Nectar of the Gods?"

Lily touched her hand to his. "Would it be too disrespectful to the deceased to opt for champagne?"

Mrs Brown appeared with a trolley, laden with champagne, the best glasses, and a platter of tiny, fragrant savouries. Their housekeeper never missed her cue. Anne stepped up to her role as hostess, assisted by Kenneth Drummond, who was courting Anne with old-fashioned gallantry and ruthless determination. Even Mrs Brown was pressed to take a glass, to toast the uniting families.

While the celebration swelled with the tinkle of crystal and a renewed babble of voices, Charlie remained on the sofa with Grace. He had angled his broad back to the room to give them a degree of privacy. Despite her protestations, he could see that Grace was shaken by Ormsby's death. "Would you let me accompany you to the police interview, Grace? I know I have no right to ask, but if you wish me to, I would like to be with you."

"I can manage on my own," Grace replied. Her all-seeing blue eyes considered him for so long that he started to rise from the sofa. She put a hand out to stop him. "But I would prefer to have your company, if the prospect of revisiting the Dunedin Central Police Station is not too painful."

"I am looking to the future, Grace, not the past."

Grace's hand dropped from his forearm, landing softly on his fingers. "And what do you see in your future, Charlie, if I might be allowed to ask?"

Charlie contemplated linking his fingers with hers, but that was too presumptuous until they had addressed the wedge between them. "Of one thing I am sure. I do not wish to leave Dunedin unless I have exhausted all options for acceptable employment here." He tried to read her emotions. Grace's absolute stillness suggested … what? Full attention? Certainly. Hope? Possibly. Outright rejection? Definitely not. A promising start.

Grace made no response, so Charlie ploughed on. "Detective Inspector Wallace has offered to apply himself on my behalf to change the decision about my placement, with legal assistance from Mr Drummond. Alternatively, Mr Drummond has suggested a career in law. He has offered me the benefit of his experience, as well as a home for the foreseeable future, rent-free in exchange for work on the property, which became neglected while his wife was ill."

Grace raised an eyebrow a fraction of an inch. "And?"

"I am not hopeful that a lowly Detective Inspector like Wallace will be able to alter a decision made by the Deputy Commissioner of Police, although I am grateful that he still wants to recruit me to the Dunedin detective team. Law could be interesting, but rather sedentary for my taste. To be honest, I would value your opinion, Grace."

"Wallace and Drummond are both fine men, who have their own views on your best interests. But what is it that you want to do, Charlie? Not what is expected or well remunerated or has the best prospects. Rather, which of all possible options would give you the

46

most satisfaction?" She caught the flicker of his smile and blushed prettily. "In terms of your employment, I mean."

"Alistair and I have been discussing a more intriguing option," Charlie confided. "Risky, in terms of stability of employment. But I confess the idea has taken root inside me and I cannot shake it. In truth, if it worked, I think it would suit my character far better than policing. Alistair feels the same. For him, it would be a diversion to keep him occupied, as much or as little as he wishes. As you know, Alistair does not need the money. But for me, the decision is not so straightforward. I cannot build the future I yearn for with empty pockets."

"Yet your eyes are sparkling at the very thought of this idea," Grace observed. "Tell me more."

"Have you heard of Charles Field? Or Allan Pinkerton?"

"Should I have?"

"They have each set up private investigation agencies," Charlie explained. "Field in England and Pinkerton in the United States of America. They solve cases for private clients, who chose not to involve the police or who have not found satisfaction with a police investigation. Not only criminal investigations, but tracking down missing persons, recovering lost valuables, discreet inquiries about the background of men offering investments, even providing personal security. President Lincoln himself was saved from assassination in 1861 by the Pinkerton Agency. You will be fascinated to learn that a woman agent, Kate Warne, was instrumental in that success, amongst others."

Grace was leaning forward now, quivering with interest, just as Charlie had been when Alistair Stewart raised the idea of setting up a private investigation agency.

"Charlie, it seems the perfect solution. You and Alistair would make a brilliant team. The only issue is, would there be sufficient demand for such a service here?"

"That is the risk, Grace. Because it is new and untested in this country, it is impossible to know. The first few years would likely

47

be lean, until we could establish a reputation. However, Kenneth Drummond has excellent contacts amongst the legal fraternity. He believes there may be work investigating on behalf of people who have been wrongly accused of crimes, as well as more regular mundane work, such as tracking down lost relatives and beneficiaries of wills. With so many young men leaving Britain for our shores, Drummond says it is not uncommon for attorneys here to receive such inquiries."

Grace grazed the tips of her fingers across her lips, giving the idea due consideration. "I imagine there might be wealthy families who value discretion enough to prefer a private service instead of bringing their troubles to the attention of the police. And you and Alistair have your police contacts, for cases that the police have not the manpower or ability to solve."

"Precisely," Charlie replied, forcing himself to focus on her words, rather than the distraction of her lips. "Drummond believes we could charge a percentage fee for the recovery of stolen valuables. Pinkerton's Agency has been involved with embezzlements and robberies worth tens of thousands of dollars. Naturally, such large sums would be rare in New Zealand, but one would only need the occasional lucrative case to fund the bulk of lower paying cases."

"As well as to cover the inevitable cases you solve without charging a fee, because of your hopelessly soft heart," Grace suggested.

He raised an eyebrow. "You believe me to be too soft to run a profitable venture, Grace?"

"Charlie, you make it sound as if I think compassion is a bad trait. I would not have it any other way. Perhaps I am biased towards any scheme that keeps you domiciled in Dunedin, but I truly feel this might be your calling."

He threw caution to the wind, grasping her hands between his and leaning in close. "When I walked out, you said you would wait for me. I need to know if your feelings have changed. I could not bear to live here if we cannot remain friends, at the very least."

Grace smiled. "I might be persuaded – in time – to ignore your lapse of judgement in leaving me. On one condition."

"Anything you wish."

"You must tell me every detail of your cases, so that I might enjoy your detective work vicariously."

Charlie sat back on the sofa, sinking into its plump padding with a sigh, as if weighing a difficult decision. "I'm afraid that would not be possible, Grace. Client confidentiality, you understand. I could not disclose any details of a case to a person outside the agency."

She gaped at him, uncertain what her ears had just taken in, after being promised anything she wished.

Charlie help up a hand to forestall her indignation. "Of course, we will require the services of a medical expert on occasion. Alistair has already suggested we offer you a retainer for your services, making you part of the team. If you accept, the issue of confidentiality would not arise."

Her hovering rebuke transformed into a burst of laughter. Her hands spread wide, as if she was about to embrace him, before dropping. With the devilish grin he knew so well, she thrust out her hand and sealed the deal with a gentleman's handshake. He settled for the gesture of reconciliation, even if his preference would have been for the embrace.

Charlie could feel the weight of a dozen eyes upon them. "Alistair, perhaps we might have a toast to the establishment of your new business."

"*Our* new business, Charlie. I shall put up the initial funding and enjoy sitting back in my chair handing out advice, while you wear out your boot leather doing the real work of solving cases." Alistair raised his glass. "To New Zealand's first private detective agency … Hmm, we haven't discussed a name yet. What about Pyke and Stewart Investigations?"

Charlie raised his glass to Grace. "Grace has agreed to join us as a medical expert and skilled investigator."

Alistair bowed to Grace, before turning to Kenneth Drummond. "And we are most fortunate that Mr Drummond has agreed to be our legal advisor. However, Penrose, Pyke, Stewart, and Drummond Investigations does seem rather a mouthful."

"Our services are available too," Charlie's father said, "should any inquiry require a Central Otago branch office."

"I suppose you will need somebody to run the Dunedin office and screen the thousands of potential clients," Lily added. "When I can spare the time from my duties at Lavender House."

Anne tapped her walking cane on the floor. "I trust I will not be the only one left out of this crazy enterprise."

"Mrs Macmillan," Charlie said. "You are the most critical cog in the whole machine, for no detective can get by without an informant who knows everyone and everything that makes this city tick."

A wicked grin spread across Anne's face. "A spy? I might rather enjoy that. But Stewart, Wu, Pyke, Pyke, Pyke, Penrose, Drummond and Macmillan is not merely a mouthful, but an entire meal. Perhaps something more descriptive. Dunedin's Dashing Detectives has a nice ring to it."

"Southern Sleuths?" Grace suggested.

Lily chuckled. "How about Southern Investigations Agency?"

Alistair raised his glass. "To the successful launch of the Southern Investigations Agency, and all who sail in and around her, seen and unseen."

Prime Suspect

Grace awoke the next morning with a parched mouth and a delicate head. Too much rich food and champagne, especially alongside the large dose of medicinal brandy and the even larger dose of shock. Ormsby's sudden death had knocked her more than she cared to admit.

Anne greeted her with welcome silence, a warm embrace, and a full pot of spirit-bracing tea. A wave of affection for her great-aunt surged from Grace's heart into her carotid arteries and on upwards to soothe her pounding brain. "Formidable" was a word often used to describe her great-aunt, but Anne Macmillan was only truly daunting when fighting to make the lives of others better.

Grace waved away the eggs and bacon offered by their housekeeper, Mrs Brown. Dry toast was all she could face this morning. Anne waited until Grace had gulped her first cup of tea, before handing her a note.

Although it had all the appearance of an ordinary note, Grace opened it with marked reluctance. "It seems our police force does not wish to observe a day of rest on Sunday, like normal folk."

Anne glanced up from her scrambled eggs. "No doubt they would, if a lowly resident of the Devil's Half Acre had died. A prominent and wealthy surgeon is another matter. Do the constabulary wish to interview you?"

"Interrogate, more like," Grace replied. "How is it that the police can take a perfectly civil expression like 'We request your presence at your earliest convenience' and make it sound as if they are preparing instruments of torture?"

"Aren't you being a trifle melodramatic, my dear? All they need is a simple witness statement." Anne's suspicion sharpened at

Grace's silence. "Unless there is more to Ormsby's death than you admitted to us last night."

Grace dropped her head into her hands, propped up with her elbows on the table. Manners were not at the forefront of her thoughts today – even less so than usual. "Henry Ormsby made certain unpleasant accusations against me. False, naturally, but muck sticks to a clean boot as well as a dirty one."

Anne studied her with an air of resignation. "I will ask Kenneth Drummond to accompany you. How fortunate that my gentleman friend has the legal skills you seem to need so regularly."

This was why Grace loved her great-aunt. No hysterics at an implied accusation of murder, merely a practical offer of help from Mr Drummond, who was one of Dunedin's most renowned former barristers. "No need for your gentleman friend to forgo the pleasure of accompanying you to church. Charlie offered to come with me. If I am arrested, I will send him back to get Mr Drummond."

Anne was about to argue, when Charlie bounded into the kitchen on an annoying wave of youthful exuberance. Grace forced down a third cup of tea, as he allowed Mrs Brown to pile his plate with eggs and bacon. Mrs Brown adored Charlie. Whether it was his charm or his open admiration for her culinary skills, Grace had yet to decide.

"There now, Mr Pyke, get that down you," Mrs Brown crooned. "It does me the world of good to see a young man with such a healthy appetite. There's another rasher if you want it."

"I ought not to, Mrs Brown, having taken a perfectly sufficient meal at Mr Drummond's house already. Oh, go on then – you know I cannot resist your cooking. I suspect that is the real reason my parents agreed to come ahead of schedule, having heard so much of your talents."

"Charlie," Grace groaned, "must you talk of food this morning?"

"What would you like to talk about, Grace?" Charlie mumbled, through an indecently large mouthful of egg.

She slid the note across the table. "I need a moment to get ready."

Grace escaped to her room, where she swallowed a dose of Lily's special revitalising tonic, splashed her face with icy water, and opened the window to the chill of a southerly breeze. She wasn't sure if the cold helped, but at least it numbed her peripheral nervous system. With a last regretful glance at her cosy bed, Grace donned her hat, gloves and coat, before returning downstairs to face the day.

Charlie took her arm as they walked down High Street towards the police station. He stopped for a moment in front of the neighbour's house.

Grace hauled him onward, not caring to linger. "The house has been sold. I hope our new neighbours are more congenial than the previous occupants. They have certainly made enough noise over the past few weeks with all their hammering. The new owner has engaged workmen to remodel the house."

"I can assure you that you will be delighted with your new neighbours," Charlie said. "It was supposed to be a secret, but my Aunt Lily can sense subterfuge at a hundred paces. Alistair has bought the house for them to live in once they are married. He thought Lily would like to be near Mrs Macmillan and Lavender House."

"That's marvellous news." Grace's dark mood lifted a little at the thought of Lily and Alistair living next door. All the more reason for Charlie to visit. "No wonder Lily and Jasmine were discussing furniture and fabrics last night, while Alistair watched them with such a blissful look on his face, I wondered if he had overindulged in the whisky."

Charlie held her arm tight, as they passed over a shady patch, where the frost still clung to the pavement. "Just as well Alistair has deep pockets. My mother and her sister have a passion for silk and brocade."

"I admit, I took little notice of their conversation, other than to envy their happiness. Why is it, do you think, that some of us act as a magnet for trouble? Not a month has passed since we had a revolver pointed at us, and here I am accused of murder, whilst other people get on with their lives with apparent ease." Grace's sigh curled from her mouth as trails of white in the morning chill. "I do hope Detective Inspector Wallace is assigned the Ormsby case. At least then I might get a sympathetic hearing."

"I'm afraid not, Grace. I've already stopped by the station to see Declan Kelly. He told me Wallace is out of town, visiting his first grandson. The baby arrived early, which is just as well, as Declan says Wallace didn't want to miss his old friend Alistair's wedding. Detective Sergeant Elliot is in charge of the Ormsby investigation."

Grace recalled Elliot, an older man with a face worn low by gravity, who had been about to retire. Detective Inspector Wallace had wanted Charlie to replace Elliot, but circumstances had intervened. Detective Constable Declan Kelly had been involved with their last two investigations too, becoming a friend as well as a colleague.

Grace hoped that Charlie's new career wouldn't put too much of a strain on his relationships with his former colleagues in the police force. "Do Kelly and Wallace know about your new business venture, Charlie?"

"They do. Alistair took Wallace into his confidence, probably to make sure he was doing the right thing by me. I've encouraged Declan to apply for the detective sergeant position when Elliot retires."

At the police station, they were shown to the interview room by Constable Weston, whom they had never met.

Weston blocked Charlie's path. "You may wait outside, sir, while we talk to Miss Penrose."

"I would prefer Detect– ... Mr Pyke ... to stay," Grace replied.

Weston wavered, but didn't move. Charlie smirked at her over Weston's shoulder, waiting for her next move. One of the things Grace cherished most about their friendship was Charlie's willingness to allow her to act for herself.

This morning, she couldn't be bothered with arguments, so she brought out a rarely used weapon – her "surely you wouldn't deny a lady?" voice, learned from her great-aunt. Anne was a master at knowing exactly what levers to pull to get her way. Lavender House, a women's refuge and medical clinic, would never have survived without it.

"Constable Weston, surely you would not deny a young lady much-needed support, when she has had the misfortune to witness a sudden death?" Grace slipped past the hesitant constable, taking a seat at the far side of the table and patting the chair next to her. "Come along, Mr Pyke."

"Woof," Charlie breathed into her ear as he took the indicated seat.

The defeated constable took the seat opposite, opening his folder with a crisp flourish to regain his tenuous hold on authority. "Detective Sergeant Elliot will be along in a moment. I am to take your details. Name and situation?"

"Miss Grace Penrose, age twenty-two years, resident of the Macmillan household on High Street. I am a student at Otago Medical School."

The pen nib carried on scratching for a second before it abruptly halted in mid-sentence. "I beg your pardon, Miss, I must have misheard. Did you say your father works at the medical school?"

"No, DC Weston. I said I am a medical student, in my third year of study. In answer to your unspoken question, yes, they do allow women to study medicine. In the interests of full disclosure, I ought to advise you that I also assist the police surgeon."

Based on his creased brow, Weston failed to comprehend her words. "Assist the police surgeon? What, writing up records, making tea, and suchlike?"

Grace resisted the urge to lecture him on the place of women in society. She proceeded in a calm, if rather assertive, tone. "I assist at autopsies to earn money to fund my medical studies. Should I

55

describe the post-mortem process to convince you? The first incision is usually–"

Weston gulped. "I'm sure that won't be necessary." He glanced towards the door, before leaning forward, lowering his voice. "You wouldn't be pulling my leg, Miss Penrose, owing to me being new in the job?"

"I would not be so cruel. Ah, here is DS Elliot. He will vouch for me."

Elliot stopped in the doorway, looking from one to the other. "DC Charlie Pyke and Miss Grace Penrose. I might have known if there was trouble afoot, you two would be close at hand."

"It is not of our choosing, I assure you." Charlie picked up Weston's pen, which had fallen from his grip and rolled across the table, spreading a trail of ink. "It's Mr Pyke now, for the record. And no, you should not believe everything you hear about me, DC Weston. The worst half of the rumours are entirely untrue, while the better half are exaggerated."

Weston snapped his jaw shut, took the offered pen, and recorded the details, as given.

"I suspect we are not here to reminisce," Grace said. "Shall we proceed with your interview regarding the tragic death of Edgar Ormsby?"

Elliot glared at her. "First, tell us how you happen to have been invited to a party given by a notable surgeon to entertain the elite of the hospital fraternity."

Grace wondered if she should admit it was a mistake, but that would involve too much explanation. "Doctor Ormsby invited me himself, after a meeting of the Hospital Trustees on Thursday evening. I was in the company of Doctor and Mrs Beechworth at the meeting, as I was at the soirée."

"Are you on friendly terms with the Ormsby family then, Miss Penrose?" Elliot asked, emphasising *friendly* in a way that might have caused Grace to consider slapping another man, despite her natural aversion to violence.

"Not in the least. Doctor Ormsby opposed the construction of the new women's ward, which did not endear him to me. He also opposed my entry to medical school. His son, Henry Ormsby, my fellow medical student, most definitely shared his opinion. I had never met Richard Ormsby before last night."

"In which case, I wonder why Ormsby invited you," Elliot said.

"Doctor Ormsby had been urged to invite a few token women from the hospital, who do not fit within the established medical *fraternity*. Namely, the new Matron, the head nurse, and myself, the first female medical student. Several of the wives of the invited doctors are also on a committee raising funds for the hospital, so perhaps they might be counted as more than mere pretty decoration as well."

"Including Mrs Ivy Beechworth, the woman who was seen arguing with Ormsby prior to his death?"

"Hardly an argument," Grace replied. "In fact, Mrs Beechworth was apologising for raising the matter of the women's ward earlier in the evening. I believe Ormsby's irritated response reflected his being unwell."

"That's not what I hear, Miss Penrose," Elliot retorted. "In fact, I am reliably informed that Mrs Ivy Beechworth was overheard uttering a death threat against the victim just days ago, after the meeting of Hospital Trustees. I understand that the meeting was called to discuss a rather contentious dispute over Ormsby's plans to improve the hospital." Elliot flipped through his notebook with the slow deliberation of a man who believes he has the upper hand. "According to the Chairman of the Hospital Trustees, Mrs Beechworth was overheard saying: 'Rat poison might be the most appropriate method for killing a scheming rat like Ormsby.' What do you say to that, Miss Penrose?"

The constable choked back a gasp. Grace bit her lip to stop herself from reacting. Charlie squeezed her hand gently. "It's not what you think, Detective Sergeant Elliot. Mrs Beechworth spoke those words in jest. I assure you, she would not hurt a hair on

57

Ormsby's head. Nor indeed anyone else's head. She is a woman worthy of our highest regard."

Elliot gave Grace his best policeman's glare. "Furthermore, I believe that was right after Mr Horncastle overheard the other woman present say: 'if Grace doesn't strangle him first'. Two nights later, several guests at the party overheard Henry Ormsby accusing you of strangling his father, Miss Penrose. Quite a coincidence, isn't it?"

"I wasn't–"

Elliot cut her off. "Indeed, the woman who was overheard admitting your desire to strangle Doctor Ormsby then went on to describe her own yearning to skewer him with a hatpin. I'd call that a coven of conspirators, Miss Penrose. That was all our witness heard, but you can be sure we will interview the woman."

Horncastle must have overheard their unfortunate conversation after all. Grace knew better than to conceal any connection, however it might look. "The lady in question, Mrs Anne Macmillan, is my great-aunt. I live with her. She shares Mrs Beechworth's lively language, but nothing was meant by it. Mrs Macmillan is a frail lady in her seventies, so I trust you will treat her gently."

Elliot snapped his notebook shut. "Miss Penrose, from what I hear of your group of women agitators, I wouldn't care to approach any of you with less than a contingent of constables, armed to the teeth."

Grace felt Charlie's hand on hers again, a gentle reminder to hold her temper in check. She breathed in and out twice before replying. "The women's ward had already been approved in the plan for the new hospital building. It was Doctor Ormsby who sought the last-minute change, not the other way around. If Mrs Beechworth was cross at his duplicity, she had every right to be. However, she certainly had no intention of inflicting any physical harm on him. The same goes for me and Mrs Macmillan."

Grace and her inquisitor glared at each other across the table until Charlie intervened. "Perhaps if Miss Penrose gave her account of the evening in her own words, Detective Sergeant Elliot."

Grace was grateful to Charlie for breaking the tension, even if Elliot narrowed his eyes and thrust out his jaw out at being told how to do his job. She decided the best course of action was to proceed as if Elliot had made the suggestion.

"Thank you, Detective Sergeant Elliot. My account will clear up any misunderstanding about what Henry Ormsby thought he saw."

Elliot waved at Grace to proceed.

"I arrived with Doctor and Mrs Beechworth at the appointed hour of seven o'clock. I did not talk with Mr Edgar Ormsby at all during the first part of the evening. However, I did notice that he appeared to be in discomfort on several occasions and left the room in a hurry at least twice. When I mentioned this to his daughter, Miss Cecilia Ormsby replied that her father had been feeling unwell even before the party began but he was determined to proceed."

"Not very ill in that case?" Elliot said.

"Sick enough to return pale and shaking, holding his belly as if he was in pain. From the way Doctor Ormsby was hunched over, I would not be surprised if he had left the room to expel his stomach contents."

Elliot didn't disagree, indicating that her supposition was correct. "Yet the dinner proceeded to plan?"

"Indeed. It was a social gathering with a late supper, rather than a formal dinner, but a lavish affair, nevertheless. Doctor Ormsby tried to be a good host, but not without a certain difficulty, I observed."

"You appear to have taken quite an interest in this man you profess to dislike, Miss Penrose."

"Detective Sergeant Elliot, can I make one thing clear. I did not dislike Doctor Ormsby. He opposed my entry to medical school, but so did several others. By majority vote, I was allowed entry. There was no ill-feeling on my side."

"Then why were you watching him so closely?"

"I am training to be a doctor and the man seemed to be seriously unwell. I was concerned. Did none of the doctors you interviewed last night remark upon it?"

"They made discreet mention of it," Elliot conceded, "but did not consider it gentlemanly to comment on another doctor's indisposition at his own supper party. Ormsby had a minor health condition that might account for it."

Grace knew better than to ask, much as she would have liked to know the details of his ailments. She hoped the police surgeon had been given the information, because she still thought the circumstances of Ormsby's death were extremely odd.

She took up her account again. "After supper, the gentlemen retreated to the library. The next time I saw him, Doctor Ormsby was on the terrace with Mrs Beechworth. As I said, I know she was planning to apologise to him."

"Apologise for what?"

"Mrs Beechworth raised the issue of the women's ward and Doctor Ormsby took exception, it being a social event. Nothing serious, although I believe he was a little terse with her. Hence her desire to mend fences. There was certainly no indication of serious animosity between them. I went to retrieve a cloak for Mrs Beechworth, as the night air was chilly, but when I got back, she was making her way inside. Before I could join her, Doctor Ormsby asked me to walk with him."

Elliot eyed her up in drawn-out silence, not hiding his incredulity. "You agreed to go for a stroll – alone – with a man you didn't like, late on a freezing cold evening? Unchaperoned? You will forgive me, Miss Penrose, if I suggest that seems highly irregular."

"I agree with you, Detective Sergeant Elliot. I initially refused to go. However, Doctor Ormsby insisted he wanted to talk to me. I assumed he wished to discuss the women's ward, an opportunity I could not afford to let pass. However, my primary concern was for how unwell he looked. Ormsby insisted a walk would aid his condition. It was cold, but not unpleasant, after the overheated interior of the house."

"And did you discuss the women's ward?" Elliot asked.

"We did. Indeed, I found Doctor Ormsby remarkably obliging about everything we discussed. He apologised for his treatment of me and was amenable to a compromise on the new hospital design."

"I fail to see why Ormsby would wish to discuss confidential hospital matters with you alone, Miss Penrose. Were there other, more personal, matters perhaps?" Elliot stopped short of a leer, but his line of inquiry was clear.

Grace felt Charlie clenching his muscles beside her. A curse on Elliot and his snide insinuations. Did he really think a man of Ormsby's reputation would make unseemly moves on a woman less than half his age, under the gaze of his colleagues and acquaintances? There was nothing for it but to confess the truth.

"Doctor Ormsby was seeking a match for his son, Richard. As he noticed us talking earlier in the evening, he wanted to … suggest that I might be considered a potential candidate." The admission was met with a sudden rigidity in her companion. Grace glanced sideways at Charlie as she added, "I was quick to assure Doctor Ormsby that I was not available."

"Ormsby must have been highly affronted when you rejected his eldest son," Elliot said.

Grace ignored the implied barb. "He had no cause to be. I commended his son's character before declaring myself unavailable. By then, Doctor Ormsby's condition appeared to be deteriorating, so I urged him to consider returning to his house. Too late, unfortunately. He suffered a grand mal seizure–"

"A what?" Constable Weston asked, as his writing hand struggled to keep place with the revelations.

"A fit. Like an epileptic seizure," Grace explained.

"We have been told by more than one witness that Mr Henry Ormsby thought you were attacking his father, Miss Penrose," Elliot said.

"Witnesses?" Charlie interjected. "Have you not interviewed Henry Ormsby himself to hear his version of events?"

Weston leaned across the table, his eyes alight. "Henry Ormsby has disappeared. Vanished into the night."

"That's quite enough from you, Weston," Elliot barked. "The fact is, Pyke, that Miss Penrose slapped the victim very hard, leaving a mark on his face and causing him to collapse to the ground. Do you deny it, Miss Penrose?"

"Quite the opposite, I assure you. Ormsby's arms were flailing wildly during the fit. One hand caught me a painful blow. I was forced to put my arm up to fend him off, which was when his face connected with my hand, unintentionally. On such a still night, the slap probably sounded sharper than it was. Ormsby did collapse after that, but from the seizure, not my actions."

Elliot studied at her in silence, only speaking again when Grace refused to be intimidated into confessing. "And then?"

Memories of that dreadful night flooded back. Grace forced herself to remain calm. "Doctor Ormsby went into convulsions. I crouched beside him to prevent him hurting himself."

"Why would he hurt himself?"

"During a grand mal seizure, the patient alternates between the muscles being rigid and periods of uncontrolled jerky movement. It is safest to have the patient on the ground in a clear space to avoid injury. I cleared away a couple of fallen branches and sharp stones. After a minute or so of intense fitting, his seizure stopped abruptly. For a few seconds, Doctor Ormsby became rigid, then almost normal, although confused. I don't think even recognised me."

"Blimey," Weston said. His pen had stopped moving. The two policemen sat wide-eyed and slack-jawed.

Grace realised this was the first detailed account they had heard of Doctor Ormsby's death. Doctor Beechworth had arrived too late to witness it, while Henry Ormsby had obviously either misunderstood or deliberately lied about what he had seen.

Grace needed to ensure the police had the full facts. "Henry Ormsby must have secretly followed us. When he finally made his presence known, I was attempting to loosen Ormsby's collar and take his pulse. I presume Henry's false accusation of strangling must stem from him seeing my hands at his father's neck as I loosened the cravat and collar. I sent Henry back to the house—"

"Miss Penrose," Elliot interrupted, "do you expect me to believe that you undertook to care for Doctor Ormsby, while Henry Ormsby stood watching, despite him being at least as qualified as yourself?"

Anger swelled inside Grace. She had asked herself the same question over and over during the night. The best answer she could come up with was that Henry had either frozen in a crisis or he believed he had stumbled upon a secret tryst, not a medical emergency.

She swallowed her anger and pressed ahead, using her doctor's voice. "For unknown reasons, Henry did not offer to assist, so I sent him to get urgent medical assistance from one of the many qualified doctors at the party. While he was gone, Doctor Ormsby went into cardiac arrest. He clutched his chest and stopped breathing. I initiated resuscitation procedures. And before you say anything, I was not assaulting Ormsby, as his son may claim. I was attempting to restart his heart and save his life."

Grace took a deep breath and finished her account. "Doctor Beechworth arrived and took over. Doctor Alexander took me back to the house. Somebody gave me brandy. Mr Horncastle, I think. I don't recall much else. Everyone was shaken and distraught, not knowing what to say or do. I urged Horncastle to call the police, as is the protocol for a sudden death. As both Mrs Beechworth and I were cold and distressed, Doctor Beechworth sent us home."

Several seconds of silence followed her account, aside from the frantic scratching of the nib as Weston attempted to get it all down.

Elliot's sardonic expression had shifted into something more closely resembling sympathy for her ordeal. "In your opinion, Miss

63

Penrose, was Doctor Edgar Ormsby's death the result of natural causes?"

"I really couldn't say. If Doctor Ormsby had a history of epileptic seizures or a recent traumatic injury to the head, then it is possible. However, death would not be a common outcome of such cases. Also, the diversity of symptoms is atypical – the nausea, the weaving, the convulsions, the confusion, the elevated pulse and ultimately the heart failure. I am no expert, but the symptoms suggest a generalised debilitating effect on the nervous system, leading to a massive seizure. I wouldn't care to rule out some type of toxin or poison. A full post-mortem is indicated, without a doubt."

"It is already underway," Elliot admitted.

DC Weston looked up from his frantic scribbling. "Could I get you to repeat some of the medical details, Doctor Penrose? I'm not sure I got it all down right."

Grace passed over several sheets of paper. "I wrote a full account of what I witnessed last night, while it was fresh in my mind."

"Thank you," Elliot replied. "That will be all for now. Don't leave town."

First Client

Charlie took Grace's arm as soon as they left the police station. She had presented her evidence as a poised and confident professional in the interview room, but he couldn't help noticing the way she had gripped her hands in her lap to stop them trembling. Her account had been traumatic even in the retelling.

Charlie could scarcely envisage what it must have been like for Grace, trying to save a man's life in the dead of night, full moon notwithstanding. "A harrowing evening's entertainment, Grace, even by your standards. Let's get you home straight away."

Grace simply nodded and pulled her coat tighter around her shivering body.

Anne's house was silent. Everyone else had gone to church, as normal people do on a Sunday. Charlie guided Grace into the drawing room. While he stoked the fire, Grace cast off her outerwear with careless abandon. Her coat slithered off an armchair and pooled on the Turkish rug, while her scarf caught on a vase, sending it teetering to the edge of a side-table. The gloves and hat landed on a pile of books, knocking her toxicology textbook to the floor.

Grace went over to the window, leaning her head on the frame. "I'm glad you trusted your instinct to come back, Charlie," she whispered.

The desire to comfort her almost overwhelmed Charlie, but the defensive hunch of her shoulders held him back. After hurting her by insisting on time away to consider his future, he wanted to avoid any missteps as he fought his way back into her favour. Instead, he stood at arm's length, staring out the window without seeing. "Does that mean you might forgive me?"

"There is nothing to forgive. After a great deal of consideration, I've come to see you were right. It is better for each of us to

65

concentrate on our careers. Right at this moment, I need your detective skills more than anything else."

"Whatever skills I possess are entirely at your disposal, Grace. That goes without saying." Charlie felt his way carefully around the ambiguity of the rest of her words. "Aside from that, I trust we can still be friends. Close friends, I mean, not passing acquaintances."

"Yes, of course. I feel … stronger with you here."

Charlie watched the tension play across the muscles of her neck. "Grace, you are the strongest person I know, but even you cannot bear the entire weight of the world on your shoulders. Can I recommend sharing the load with a close friend?"

She closed the gap between them with a sudden lurch, falling into his arms. He held her in silence, stroking her hair, until her trembling ceased.

When Grace spoke, it was a whisper against his waistcoat. "What if I didn't do enough, Charlie? I've never had a patient die before, not without a qualified doctor present."

"Dearest Grace, I think it is a miracle that you kept your wits about you in such circumstances. I'm not a doctor, but I have seen many people reacting to an emergency – screaming, fainting, freezing, running away, crouching in a ball pretending they are elsewhere. Not one in twenty reacts with calm good sense, as you did. You only have to look at that damnable idiot, Henry Ormsby, who failed to act to save his own father."

The tension across Grace's slim shoulders eased at his words. "Can we sit and talk about something else for a while?"

Charlie led her to the sofa, where she sat down beside him, so close her hair tickled his chin. He struggled to think of a safe subject. "Have you been a bridesmaid before?"

"At my brother's wedding, but that doesn't count, because I only had to walk down the aisle at the end of a line of the brides' sisters and friends. I confess I am a little nervous, as this time I am the only bridesmaid. Your mother will be matron of honour, of course, so she will do most of whatever needs to be done. Lily says

66

all I need to do is attend a gown fitting and show up on the day, but I feel I should do more to help her organise it." The tension flooded back. "If Detective Sergeant Elliot and Henry Ormsby have anything to do with it, I might end up spending their wedding day in prison. Lily might never forgive me."

"That will not happen, Grace. I will not let you go to prison. And I'm sure Aunt Lily and my mother will have every detail of the wedding under control. However, you should know there is one other challenging duty you will be required to perform."

Grace sat up in alarm, bumping his chin. "I knew Lily wasn't telling me the full extent of it." She groaned. "I hope it isn't anything to do with decorating, dressmaking or cooking. Not my strongest talents. Or flower arranging … or etiquette or … Oh fiddlesticks, I'm going to the worst bridesmaid in history. Go on then, you'd better put me out of my misery – what is it I have to do?"

Charlie leaned closer. "You will be required to dance with the best man, after the bride and groom have taken a first turn around the dance floor. All eyes will be upon you and your fortunate partner. Your performance will have to be dazzling."

Grace sank back against his chest. "Oh Charlie, you had me worried for a moment. I expect I can manage a dance. Not the dazzling part, as I have had little dancing practice lately. Remind me who the best man is?"

"That would be me."

Graced exhaled rather forcibly, but her lips twitched into a smile. Charlie knew she was recalling the few times they had danced together – each time so memorable that she would have no choice but to accept they were meant to be together.

"Perhaps a little dance practice would take my mind off being a police suspect," Grace murmured.

Charlie had little doubt it would take his own mind to places he shouldn't go. Close friends he could manage, at a pinch, but not if he was circling the room slowly with Grace in his arms.

The bell at the front door came to his rescue, unfortunately. Charlie hoped it wasn't DS Elliot, back with more questions. Grace ignored the bell, but he knew they could not escape the visitor, as Mrs Brown was home, preparing the Sunday lunch. Charlie heard her welcoming the visitor in, followed by footsteps down the hall.

"Doctor Beechworth," Mrs Brown announced.

Dark smudges under Beechworth's eyes, combined with mismatched cufflinks and a skewed tie, suggested the doctor was short on sleep and long on anxiety. "Miss Penrose, please forgive me for arriving without notice. I see you have company, so I shall detain you no further."

"Not at all, Doctor Beechworth. Please take a seat. Allow me to introduce Mr Charles Pyke, a private investigation agent and close friend. Charlie was kind enough to accompany me to the police interview this morning. There is no one I trust more to find answers to mysteries that appear baffling."

Charlie extended his hand. "I wish we had met under more pleasant circumstances, Doctor Beechworth. If you wish to speak to Miss Penrose privately, I would be happy to oblige."

"Not at all, Mr Pyke. The more intelligent minds deployed upon the matter, the better, as far as I am concerned."

Charlie led the conversation, in the interests of sparing Grace. "How is Mrs Beechworth this morning? I assume she was also called to the police station to see Detective Sergeant Elliot?"

"Less a talk than an interrogation," Beechworth growled. "I came close to flooring the oaf on several occasions. Unfortunately, everyone at the soirée saw the heated exchange between my wife and Ormsby. It seems her later apology ended badly too. Worse still, Ivy had brought Ormsby a glass of port in an attempt to mollify him after confronting him earlier in the evening. Now, rumours are swirling that she poisoned him."

"Outrageous." Grace set aside her indignation with conspicuous effort. "I'm truly sorry, Doctor Beechworth. I know your wife did nothing untoward, as I told the police. However, I have to warn you that Mr Horncastle overheard your wife after the Hospital Trustees' meeting, joking about being cross enough to murder Ormsby. Elliot may not view this as the harmless venting of frustration that her friends understand it to be."

Doctor Beechworth sunk his head into his hands. "Don't I know it. Sergeant Elliot pressed her about it until Ivy was in tears. Not Horncastle's fault, of course, but I do wish he had kept it to himself. Especially the bit about using rat poison."

Grace grimaced at the memory. "I am not acquainted with Mr Horncastle, or his normal relationship to Ormsby, but he appeared to be actively avoiding his host at the soirée."

"That dratted new hospital building has everyone's hackles up." Beechworth stopped his fist from thumping down on the arm of the chair and gave her an apologetic smile. "We need the new facilities desperately, of course. If only I could get the Trustees out of their leather seats and into the women's ward, they'd change their minds in an instant. I must say, your manipulation of the Trustees to our point of view last night was masterful. With Ormsby gone, there is hope."

Beechworth's hand flew to his mouth. "I … I didn't mean that as it sounded. Ormsby's death is a great loss, naturally."

"I know exactly what you mean, Doctor Beechworth," Grace assured him. "Doctor Ormsby was a difficult character, at times. I must say, I saw a different side of him last night on our walk. In fact, he agreed to a compromise that would allow the building of the women's ward to proceed, so there was no ill will on his side. His death was untimely for our cause, as well as tragic. The only consolation I can offer to your wife is that the police's prime suspect appears to be me, not her."

"Hardly a consolation. Ivy would prefer to bear the brunt of accusations herself, rather than have your reputation impugned. Miss Penrose, I know it is a lot to ask in the circumstances, but I would be very grateful to hear exactly what happened, directly from you, as the only reliable witness. Young Henry Ormsby seems to have quite lost his head last night, when he accused you of causing his father's death. Foolish idiot, he mistook your brave attempt at resuscitation as further evidence of a concerted attack. Henry was suitably shamefaced about that mistake after I blasted him, but I doubt he bothered to retract his statement to the police."

"Henry Ormsby vanished before the police arrived," Charlie said. "His conduct in this matter has been deplorable."

Mrs Brown knocked and entered with a tray of tea. Grace poured and passed around cups as she spoke of the previous night, concentrating on the critical events, in the calm, coherent manner of an ideal witness. "I fear I did not do enough to save Doctor Ormsby," she finished, "but I cannot undo what is done."

Beechworth sat in silence for several seconds, crushing one of Mrs Brown's delicious shortbread biscuits into crumbs. "On the contrary, Miss Penrose, I must commend you on your quick thinking. You did exactly what I would have done in the circumstances, which is more than many qualified practitioners would have managed. From what you say, there is little doubt that Ormsby suffered something akin to a grand mal seizure. The question is, why?"

"Doctor Ormsby was clearly very unwell during the soirée," Grace replied, "but it seemed no more than a bad stomach upset until he had the seizure. He did not appear to have a fever indicative of some type of infection that affected his nervous system. A prior head injury is possible, but I checked his head and found no sign of anything abnormal. The most likely cause is epilepsy, unless the nausea and disorientation he had been suffering over the course of the evening was because of a toxin. Hopefully, his doctor will be able to explain it."

"I fear not," Beechworth said. "I spoke to Ormsby's personal physician last night. I am breaching no confidences in telling you that Ormsby had a weak heart and a tendency to stomach upsets, as that fact is widely known. He has never suffered from epilepsy or any other cause of seizures."

"Perhaps the police surgeon will find the cause of death at the post-mortem," Charlie said.

Beechworth shook his head. "I visited Doctor Cranston-Hartfield on my way here. He confirmed heart failure as the proximate cause of death and noted the presence of a slightly malformed heart valve, which explains his weak heart. The seizure Ormsby suffered likely led to the heart failure, but the cause of the seizure is as yet unknown. I hardly need to add that the police surgeon found no evidence of strangulation, although he did find a minor bruise on Ormsby's cheek. Aside from that, the police surgeon would only say that the stomach and colon were completely void, confirming that the malaise we all noted in him during the evening had been accompanied by retching and bowel evacuation. But if it was accidental food poisoning, why did nobody else suffer ill effects? And why the seizure?"

"Did the police surgeon view his death as potentially suspicious?" Charlie asked.

"All I can say is that Cranston-Hartfield is running further tests. Not that he suspects anything specific, but as a precaution. As you will be aware from the symptoms, Miss Penrose, there is considerable room for doubt. It is possible Ormsby took an accidental overdose of medication or ingested some toxin by mistake."

"As a detective," Charlie said, "I cannot help but wonder whether anyone held a sufficiently severe grievance against Edgar Ormsby to wish him harm."

"Good heavens, Mr Pyke, you cannot be suggesting a deliberate attack? Ormsby could be a little fixed in his ways, but who amongst us doesn't have minor disputes from time to time? I do wish Ivy had been a little more circumspect in her dealings with him. My dear wife has a heart of gold, but a loose way with words, which often causes unnecessary trouble."

"I fear that being in my great-aunt's company only encourages that type of sharp banter," Grace said. "We women are all guilty of it, whether spoken or unspoken, having little other outlet for our frustration. But your wife must take heart from the facts, Doctor Beechworth. Ormsby was seriously ill even before the party began

71

and therefore none of the invited guests was at fault. Whatever caused his illness was the most likely trigger for the seizure, and ultimately his heart failure."

Beechworth turned to Charlie. "Am I to understand that you are a private detective, Mr Pyke? Might I engage your services to clear my wife's name?"

"There is no need, as I am already looking into the truth of the matter for Miss Penrose."

"I beg you, Mr Pyke. My wife's reputation is worth a great deal to me."

Charlie looked to Grace for her assent before agreeing. "I can make no promises about the outcome, Doctor Beechworth. Like the police, a private detective must ask questions that people may prefer to remain unasked. I would advise waiting until the direction of the police investigation is clear. If the police accept that Ormsby's death was because of natural causes, such as epilepsy or accidental food poisoning, then it may be better to leave it at that."

Beechworth considered the advice for a moment, before shaking his head. "I don't believe that will be the case. I cannot allow my wife's reputation to be left open to slander while the police poke around making accusations for weeks or months. That Elliot fellow appears to have his mind made up already. If you don't act on our behalf, Mr Pyke, I fear the coroner will leave the verdict open. You know what that would mean. A lifetime of whispers."

"If you are determined to go ahead, Doctor Beechworth, I accept," Charlie said. "I would ask that you consider, as a medical doctor, what could cause the symptoms. Also, as an intimate of the medical community, who do you think might have wished harm to Doctor Ormsby? Did he have any fierce rivalries or bitter disagreements, or perhaps deceased patients whose families held a grudge?"

Beechworth gave the matter due consideration. "Offhand, I would say that Ormsby had no enemies who might wish him physical harm. He was not a man who was well liked, but nor was he a man to make bitter enemies. His private practice was well

72

regarded. He specialised in hernias and other types of abdominal surgery, largely for wealthy male clients. He's had a few patient deaths over the years, but that is normal for a surgeon. Still, it is possible that a bereaved family held a grudge against him. I will investigate further and compile a list of potential suspects for you."

Charlie shook Beechworth's extended hand. "Thank you, sir. That would be helpful."

"Meanwhile, please forward your contract terms to my residence. Miss Penrose has the address." Beechworth rose and bowed his head to Grace. "I have taken far too much of your time on the Lord's Day. I wish you success, Mr Pyke. And Miss Penrose, whatever I can do to assist, please do not hesitate to ask. I feel I have let you down most dreadfully by neglecting my chaperoning duties at the soirée."

Grace watched Beechworth stride from the room with far more energy than he had shown on his arrival. "It seems your Southern Investigations Agency has its first client, Detective Pyke. Beechworth didn't even ask what fees you charge."

"Just as well, considering Alistair and I haven't yet discussed the matter of fees, let alone contracts, premises and whatever else needs doing to set the business on an official footing."

Grace waved away his doubts. "I expect Mr Drummond will have a standard legal contract and a fair idea on the matter of fees. Don't undervalue your services, for heaven's sake. Recall that you have to cover many ancillary expenses, such as travel and office premises, before you make a healthy profit. Doctor Beechworth will expect to pay well for your professional services, as he is paid for his."

"So much to consider, Grace. Perhaps life as a simple copper would be preferable after all."

"Nonsense, you were born for this. And Charlie?"

"Yes, Grace?"

"Be sure to add in a hefty percentage to cover the consultation fee for your medical expert. That is, if one can be a consultant on a case where one is also the accused."

Apologies

Grace's gloom had evaporated, now that Doctor Beechworth had reassured her that Ormsby's death was not because of a misdiagnosis or medical omission on her part. If she was honest, the return of her spirits was also aided by clearing the air with Charlie. The concept of being close friends would take a little getting used to, but it was far preferable to not seeing him at all.

Everyone had gathered at Anne's house for Sunday lunch. Charlie's parents, the burly Sergeant Thomas Pyke and diminutive Jasmine Pyke, already felt like part of the inner circle of family and friends. Jasmine and Lily were relishing the chance to have a long-overdue sisterly catch-up. Thomas Pyke and Alistair Stewart were picking over the bones of infamous police cases, aided by Kenneth Drummond, who had an extraordinary memory for old court cases and legal precedents. As Anne's suitor, Drummond also made sure he assisted Anne with her hostess role.

Anne leaned in towards Grace. "You're very quiet, my dear. How was your interview with the police?"

"Detective Sergeant Elliot believes I am responsible for Ormsby's death," Grace replied. "However, he was less convinced of my guilt by the end of the interview, which I suppose is progress of sorts."

The noise level at the table dropped away at Grace's words. Spoons hovered in mid-air, glasses remained half-filled, amusing stories were left unfinished. Grace shot a pleading look in Charlie's direction.

Charlie reached down the table for the butter dish, causing a minor distraction as he knocked a salt cellar over. "Nothing to worry about. Elliot always approaches witness interviews as if he is interrogating a hardened criminal." He plopped the butter down and carved a chunk off. "If Grace isn't being lauded as a heroine before the week is out, I'll … I'll–"

"Give up eating for a week?" Charlie's mother suggested.

"A month," Charlie retorted. He waited for the gasps of disbelief to die down. "The good news is that Doctor Beechworth has engaged us to investigate Ormsby's death. Southern Investigations has its first case."

After a few moments of excited chatter, Charlie diverted the discussion by asking about his Aunt Lily's plans for her new home. Talk turned to a simply divine red silk, threaded with a gold motif, which Jasmine had spotted in the importer's catalogue.

"Only a little, here and there," Lily reassured her fiancé. "I promise not to turn our home into an Oriental palace. I thought perhaps tartan drapes for your study, Alistair?"

"Whatever you like, my dear," Alistair agreed, "as long as it is the Stewart tartan."

"But dearest, the MacDonald tartan goes so much better with the fabric for the chairs," Lily replied, with a straight face and twinkling eyes.

Grace devoured her soup, making up for a missed breakfast with an extra slice of fresh-baked bread, while Alistair launched into an imaginative description of the dire consequences that would rain down upon Lily if she allowed even a fragment of MacDonald tartan in the house. When Grace's brain jerked awake again after a pleasant little open-eyed reverie, Lily was listing the equipment she would need to extract the essential oils she used in her medicinal herb preparations. Everyone at the table watched on with amused delight at Lily's enthusiasm. Everyone except Charlie, who seemed to be off in another world, presumably plotting his first independent investigation.

Grace was determined not to let the Ormsby tragedy sour the joyful mood, despite the niggling disquiet that danced around the edges of her brain at Lily's words. What was it about essential oils and herbs that triggered a memory?

"By the time you have finished, Lily, you'll have more laboratory equipment than the hospital," Jasmine Pyke teased. "Poor Alistair won't have space to move, nor fresh air to breathe. All those flasks and chemicals and goodness knows what else. It almost puts me off this delicious food."

"One has to be able to guarantee precision and quality, for safety's sake," Lily said. "I must admit, I do love a nice conical flask. Such an exquisite merger of form and function."

Alistair put his spoon back into a scraped-clean soup bowl. "I am beginning to worry that I shall never see my wife again once she gets into her workroom with all her new apparatus."

"I can assure you that I will include you in my busy schedule, Alistair," Lily replied. "That is, if I can lure you out of the Southern Investigations' office."

Thomas Pyke dabbed his lips with a napkin. "You two have set yourselves up very nicely indeed. I do wonder, though, Lily, why you need to be so meticulous about safety. Aren't all your remedies made from natural extracts of herbs?"

"Just ask Grace how many common plants are toxic, Thomas," Lily replied. "She wrote an essay on the topic that would curl your toes to read. Even herbs and essential oils can cause serious illness when taken in excess. Eucalyptus, sage, fennel, hyssop, pennyroyal, tansy, rosemary, and that's leaving out the truly poisonous plants, like hemlock and monkshood."

"Poor Alistair will be rethinking his offer of marriage," Thomas joked. "Perhaps we all ought to read your essay, Grace, for our safety ... Grace?"

"What? Oh, yes, absolutely, Sergeant Pyke," Grace replied, although her mind was stuck on Lily's words, not those of Charlie's father. Lily was right. Medicinal herbs could be poisons, if the correct dose was exceeded. Could Mrs Ormsby have unwittingly made a mistake in one of her herbal preparations and poisoned her husband?

77

Alistair laughed. "I consider myself fortunate to be marrying a healer, especially given my advancing years. A lifetime of chasing down criminals can play havoc with the knees. What about you, Thomas? Ever considered stepping down from police work and taking time to smell the roses?"

"As a matter of fact, it has crossed my mind of late, especially now I have a replacement in training, who is showing promise. Local lad. Always best in a country district. Can't deny it would be strange, after decades of being called Sergeant Pyke. Not sure I'd know what to do with myself." Thomas held up his hand to forestall his wife's words. "Jasmine, on the other hand, would know exactly what to do with me. Most of it involving an axe, hammer, spade, broom or other implement, I don't doubt."

Sadie, their maid, came in and made eye contact with Grace. She slipped away from the table, leaving the rest of the company to their conversation.

"A Mr Richard Ormsby is requesting an interview with you, Miss Penrose, if you are available," Sadie said.

"Is he here?" Grace queried.

"No, Miss. Mr Ormsby sent a man with a carriage. You may return with him if you are free now, or Mr Ormsby will visit you here at a time of your choosing, whichever is most acceptable to you."

"We will come now," Charlie said over Grace's shoulder. He bent down to whisper in her ear. "A chance to visit the scene, while it is fresh in the minds of the witnesses. And to escape from this discussion. My father had hoped that I would replace him as Clyde's policeman. It pains me to disappoint him."

Richard Ormsby must have been waiting for Grace's arrival, because he was already on the terrace when the carriage pulled into the entrance to the stables. Grace was shocked by the change in him. Richard's mourning clothes hung on his stooped body like a sack, the black emphasising the pallor of his face. It seemed as if all the energy had drained out of the lively gentleman of the previous evening.

Richard hurried down the steps to greet her. "Miss Penrose. Thank you for coming. I wasn't sure you would."

"I wanted to express my most sincere condolences, Mr Ormsby, and give you the opportunity to ask any questions that have been troubling you."

"How kind of you to perceive the reason I wished to see you, Miss Penrose."

Grace motioned Charlie forward. "Mr Ormsby, may I introduce Mr Charles Pyke, a close acquaintance of mine."

The two men shook hands. On the journey over, Charlie had confessed he found it difficult to know how to act on the rare occasion he had dealings with wealthy households. As a policeman, society's elite had treated him as an unwanted but necessary tradesman. Akin to a rubbish collector, cleaning up the messy, unseemly aftermath of crime. How should he act now that he was a private detective, employed to sift through his clients' most intimate secrets? Grace had advised him to trust his instincts. If in doubt, assert his position as a gentleman of business, on an equal footing.

Charlie's instinct must have been telling him to melt into the background, because he shrank into what Grace thought of as his "submissive pose" as he greeted their host. A drooping of his muscular shoulders, a slight bend in the knee to diminish his height, a certain polite meekness of expression. Richard Ormsby showed no signs of noticing, which was the aim. He would certainly have taken notice if Charlie had used his "threatening pose", which he used when he wished to intimidate. The first time Grace had seen it, it had taken all her willpower not to cower behind the nearest solid object.

Richard ushered them across the terrace to the large salon in which the soirée had been held, showing them into a small drawing room beyond. A tea tray was being set out by a plain young woman with darting eyes – a Mona Lisa in a matronly dress. Her eyes slid

79

sideways towards Grace, but did not linger. Otherwise, her expression conveyed nothing.

"Thank you, Lawson," Richard said. "Please fetch Mrs Ormsby to see Miss Penrose."

Lawson sidled out without either looking at or acknowledging Richard.

Richard Ormsby's eyes followed Lawson to the door. Only when she had shut it behind her did he speak again. "Please, take a seat, Miss Penrose." Their host glanced at Charlie. "I confess, I had hoped to have this conversation in private."

Grace took a seat on the sofa, indicating that Charlie should do the same. He opted for an occasional chair nearer the wall. Grace turned her attention to Richard. "Mr Pyke knows about your father's tragic death, Mr Ormsby. He is a private detective, working on behalf of myself and Mrs Beechworth. There is no need to be alarmed, sir. Mr Pyke is simply ensuring that our interests are protected, in light of the accusations made by your brother last night."

The pallor of her host's face flushed scarlet as he took the armchair beside her. "Miss Penrose, I beseech you to forgive the appalling behaviour of my brother and myself last night. What was I thinking, to believe Henry's reckless accusations and have you thrown out of the house? I cannot apologise enough. When Doctor Beechworth told me that Henry was talking nonsense, that Father had died of heart failure, not strangulation, I wished I had never spoken so rashly. I can only pray that we have not damaged your reputation."

"That is very gracious of you, Mr Ormsby," Grace replied. In truth, it was probably far too late to protect her reputation. Gossip and rumour would already be spreading across town faster than measles through a schoolyard.

"I ought to have realised," Richard continued. "Father has had a weak heart for many years, but we thought Mother's tonic kept any serious problems under control. He often had digestive issues too, but again, her tonics kept the symptoms at bay. I can only plead for your understanding. The shock of seeing my father's corpse–"

The entrance of Mrs Ormsby to the room cut off the rest of his plea. Richard jumped from his chair and took her arm, shooing Lawson away. He guided his stepmother towards the most comfortable armchair, but she took the seat beside Grace instead. Mrs Ormsby, who had seemed delicate but bubbling with life on Saturday night, now looked no more than a sickly child on the overstuffed sofa.

Mrs Ormsby raised her head with obvious effort, as if weighing down by the flimsy black veil pinned in her hair. "Miss Penrose. I apologise for summoning you at this difficult time. I wish to hear what happened, as you were the sole witness."

Grace wasted little time on platitudes, for she saw the yearning in the other woman's eyes behind the thin veil. For the third time that day, Grace recounted the evening from her point of view, not leaving anything out, but downplaying the terrifying ending. She hesitated at the discussion of Richard's marriage prospects, wanting Mrs Ormsby to know that there was a legitimate reason for the walk, but not wishing to embarrass Richard. In the end, she softened Ormsby's remarks into a mild comment about his earnest desire to see his son happily married and his observation that Richard appeared to be enjoying Grace's company at the party.

By the time Grace finished, Mrs Ormsby was gripping her hands so hard that Grace could feel nail marks denting her skin, while Richard was surreptitiously wiping tears from his eyes.

Grace struggled to find words to ease their anguish. "The seizure came on very quickly, Mrs Ormsby, followed by heart failure. I believe your husband didn't suffer, because he was too confused to know what was happening."

The widow's grip on Grace's hand softened and fell away, until her hands had withdrawn into her lap. Her fingers interlaced, as if in prayer.

Grace risked a question, hoping it wouldn't give offence. "May I ask if your husband has ever suffered from epileptic fits or seizures, Mrs Ormsby?"

"No, never. Edgar could not have practised as a surgeon if he had any such condition." Mrs Ormsby fell silent for a time. Eventually, she lifted her veil, so Grace could see the full depth of her feeling. "I thank you, most sincerely, for your honesty and for attempting to save my husband's life, Miss Penrose. Doctor Beechworth assured me you did everything a qualified doctor would have done. I am very grateful Edgar did not die alone."

The raw emotion of Mrs Ormsby's gratitude brought Grace closer to tears than accusations or anger would have done. "I gained a new appreciation of your husband's fine character in his final moments, Mrs Ormsby. He obviously loved you very deeply and wished only that he could see his son as happy as he had been with you."

Mrs Ormsby gave way to the sobs she had been holding at bay. Nevertheless, Grace sensed her words had brought comfort. Richard rang a bell, which Lawson answered so quickly, Grace suspected she must have been waiting by the door. Judging by the redness of one ear, Lawson might well have been actively pressed against the door, listening to their conversation. Lawson rushed to take Mrs Ormsby's arm and guide her from the room.

Grace and Charlie rose too, but Richard waved them back into their seats.

"You must stay for tea. I would not wish to be inhospitable after all you have done. To be honest, I am struggling to believe my father is no longer with us. I want to talk about him, but Mother and Cecilia are too distressed, Henry isn't here, and poor wee Agnes has taken to her bed, claiming a stomach ache. Sympathy pains, I expect. It must be difficult for a seven-year-old girl to comprehend her father's passing."

Grace took over the teapot when Richard's shaking fingers threatened to spill tea into the saucer. "How is your brother coping, Mr Ormsby? I understand it must have been a terrible shock for

Henry to have witnessed his father suffering a medical emergency, but I do wonder why he was so quick to blame me."

Richard set his cup down, untasted. "I haven't seen the little bounder since last night, but his behaviour is typical. Henry always blames someone else in a crisis. If I may be frank – as I have no doubt you are already well aware of it – Henry has been aggrieved ever since you were admitted to medical school, Miss Penrose. What did he call it? An assault on the bastion of a noble institution? A travesty of decency? A monstrous insult to the medical profession? Take your pick of his imbecilic rants."

Grace sipped her tea. Those might well have been the words Henry Ormsby used in polite company, but she had heard far worse from Henry when he thought no one else could overhear. Grace had been left in no doubt that Henry Ormsby thought her depraved, unnatural and unscrupulous. A century or two ago, he might have demanded she be burned at the stake.

"Of course," Richard continued, with a wry grin, "the real trouble started when you proved yourself more than capable of keeping up with the gentlemen, both intellectually and practically. Henry grumbled about your unfair advantage when you came top of the class in medical jurisprudence, even though he would have scorned the role of assistant to the police surgeon himself. I confess I enjoyed seeing his arrogance brought to heel."

"I did detect a certain animosity from him," Grace conceded, recalling the vitriolic scene Henry had made when the examination results were announced. "He also made rather a fuss when I was included on surgical rounds."

"A 'fuss' is a polite way of describing it. Henry wants to be a surgeon, of course, like his father. Oddly enough, I believe it was your toxicology essay that upset him the most."

"Toxicology essay? I cannot imagine what you mean, Mr Ormsby."

"Your essay on poisonous plants, Miss Penrose. I gather it was read out as an exemplar to the class, as you had the wit to include toxic native plants. Henry was furious, because of course his

83

stepmother could have told him all about that topic, if he'd had the sense to ask. But no, she's been our devoted mother for the best part of a decade, yet he still refuses to acknowledge her. If you ask me, our stepmother is the best thing that ever happened to this family."

"I'm sure Mrs Ormsby must be grateful for your support, especially now." Grace could see that talking was helping to take Richard's mind off his father's death, if only for a while. After Richard welcoming her to the party last night and his apology now, she was glad to do what she could to ease his grief. "As an expert on medicines yourself, you must find your stepmother's work fascinating."

Richard took up his cup again, relaxing back into the armchair for the first time since they entered the room. "I do, Miss Penrose. I often help her in her workroom. My stepmother has an exceptional talent for developing herbal remedies."

"Including native plants?" Grace asked.

"Her view is that the native peoples of a country can be relied upon to know the applications and dangers of the local flora. The Māori people use plants like manuka and kawakawa for healing. My stepmother has experimented with them in her own formulations. With great success, I might add. Her creams and balms to soothe skin conditions and relieve infections are so good, I advocate their use at the hospital. Not that advocacy is required. Mother doesn't have the time to keep up with all the orders. Her workroom, which is a room off the stables, isn't large enough to cope with demand."

"How fascinating. I should like to see her at work, at some point in the future."

"I'm sure she would be happy to accommodate you, Miss Penrose," Richard said. "After reading your essay, my stepmother even sought out one of the poisonous plants you mentioned, thinking its toxin might work on the plagues of rats we suffer from time to time. Unfortunately, its effect on the test rats was unbearable to watch, so she discontinued the experiment."

Grace's eyes flicked to Richard, but he showed no sign of emotion other than subdued grief. "How interesting. Don't tell

Henry, but I expended very little effort on that essay. Our gardener is an expert on plants of all types, including natives. His grandmother was a Māori healer. I dashed the essay off in an evening after picking his brains."

Richard smiled for the first time. "Perhaps one day we can meet this fascinating gardener of yours." The smile faded quickly. Richard slumped in the chair, his eyes half closed.

Grace took the hint. "We must take our leave, Mr Ormsby. You have much to do, I am sure."

"Thank you for coming, Miss Penrose. I feel better for the company. I am more grateful than I can express that you have set my mind at rest over Henry's reckless accusations." Richard looked at Charlie for the first time since they had entered the house, appearing startled that this silent man was still here. "And you, Mr … Pyke? I trust your detective skills will no longer be required?"

Charlie stood up and took the proffered hand. "I must be honest with you, Mr Ormsby. The police will still be obliged to investigate, given the suddenness of your father's death and the lack of clarity around the precise cause. However, I do hope you will soon be left to grieve in peace."

Richard accompanied them out to the terrace, reiterating his apology for the appalling way he had treated Grace last night. The coachman had disappeared about other duties, which gave Grace and Charlie a moment alone as Richard went in search of him.

"Is this the terrace on which Ormsby and Mrs Beechworth argued, before your walk?" Charlie asked.

Grace indicated a spot at the far end. "Ormsby was standing there. You can see the garden path we took, which leads to the back of the property and on up into the trees of the town belt."

"May I leave you to go home alone, Grace? I feel the sudden urge to take a stroll. There's no need for you to come. I can see you need to rest and recover your spirits."

Richard Ormsby appeared again at the far end of the garden path, with the man who evidently doubled as a coachman and gardener. Grace had mere moments to make her suspicions known. "Charlie, that toxic native plant Richard Ormsby mentioned – the one Mrs Ormsby was testing as a rat poison. Its symptoms fit Doctor Ormsby's death exactly."

Toxic Shock

Grace entered the cold, cheerless domain of the police surgeon twenty minutes later, half hoping he would not still be there late on a Sunday afternoon. The possibility that her essay on a toxic native plant had precipitated Edgar Ormsby's death was beyond unsettling. Her gut churned with an unholy mix of guilt and fear. Nevertheless, she was obliged to report her suspicions.

Doctor Cranston-Hartfield was bending over a test tube, muttering to himself. He looked up at the sound of her tentative footsteps. "Grace. Good to see you. You've thrown me a tricky one this time. I know Ormsby died of a seizure and heart failure, but I'm darned if I can trace the underlying cause. Stomach cramps and vomiting over several hours, followed by sudden convulsions and heart arrythmia. Odd, to say the least."

Grace indicated the row of test tubes and open textbooks. "I take it you have been testing for poisons?"

"If it is a poison, I have been unable to detect it. Digitalis poisoning is the closest match to the symptoms, but the presentation is atypical. Perhaps it is simply one of those tragic coincidences. A stomach upset from food poisoning, vomited out, combined with undiagnosed epilepsy and a weak heart. I'll probably have to rule it as natural causes, unless the police team can find evidence of a crime. Nobody would thank me for recommending that the coroner should leave the cause of death open, especially for such a prominent citizen."

The police surgeon straightened his back with an audible click. "You really must stop getting entangled in suspicious deaths, Grace, especially so soon after the last one. But have no fear, I have ruled out strangulation. That so-called eyewitness must need his eyes testing."

Grace fiddled with her gloves, putting off the inevitable. "I'm grateful, Jamie. You must have been here all day, if not half the night, as well."

Doctor Cranston-Hartfield shrugged. They both knew that a police surgeon's hours were far from regular. "Doctor Beechworth came by earlier. Wanted to ensure I had all the facts. It seems you have another admirer." The police surgeon looked as ill at ease as she was. In the past few seconds, he had smoothed his sleek moustache, adjusted his cuffs, shuffled his feet, and developed a fascination with the spotless white wall behind her. "The thing is, Grace, you should know … that is, I'd like you to know … well, the fact is, I have been stepping out with Beechworth's eldest daughter of late."

Grace felt a small brick of guilt lift from her conscience. "Marvellous news, Jamie. I'm thrilled for you both. I hear she is an exceptional young lady." Grace's professional relationship with the police surgeon had been strained recently because of his personal interest in her. She had been dreading matters coming to a head between them, which would certainly have meant the end of their working relationship. The police surgeon might be young, but he excelled at his work. Thank heavens for the delightful Miss Beechworth.

The lines of exhaustion fell away from his face as he smiled the dreamy smile of a man in the first grip of a new love. "I do hope we can continue working together, Grace. There are few medical students who view the dark art of the post-mortem with the interest and aptitude you show."

"You may depend upon it," Grace said, with heartfelt enthusiasm. "I have learnt a great deal working with you, Jamie. In fact, I have come here to ask your professional advice on a possible, but highly unusual, cause for Ormsby's death. Have you heard of a toxic native plant known as tutu to Māori, or *Coriaria* to science?"

"Tutu?" Jamie Cranston-Hartfield's fatigue evaporated as he churned through his formidable knowledge of toxicology. "Haven't had a death in a while, but I recall a group of children who became severely ill from eating a large quantity of tutu berries. Happened while I was a medical student. By Jove, the little blighters had us worried. An extended period of nausea and vomiting, followed by bouts of convulsions and stupor, respiratory distress, heart palpitations..."

His jaw fell slack at his own description of the symptoms. The police surgeon rushed out of the room, returning several minutes later with a faded folder. "I did a little follow-up research on tutu. Hated that feeling of helplessness that none of us knew what to do."

Jamie flipped through the pages with flying fingers. His words came equally fast. "The Māori people knew all about tutu, of course. There's an account of them saving the life of one of the early settlers by stopping him from eating the berries. Livestock perished in devastating numbers in the early years after they gorged on the leaves and shoots. Did you know that Captain Cook put the first sheep ashore in New Zealand, only to have them die after eating tutu? Not many human deaths now that we know about it, although children must still be warned and educated about its toxicity. Toot, the settlers called it."

The police surgeon's monologue stopped abruptly when he found the page he was looking for. "Ah, here it is." He scanned the page quickly, the colour draining from his face. "You're right, Grace, the symptoms are a close match. If tutu caused Ormsby's death, it wasn't because he was feasting on berries. In fact, the berries are no longer in season. Besides, he would have had to ingest a massive quantity to die, although his weak heart would have made him more susceptible than most."

"I agree, Jamie. The thing is, Mrs Ormsby had experimented with tutu in an attempt to develop a rat poison. Richard Ormsby told us, which was why I hurried to see you."

"Richard Ormsby admitted it?"

Grace shook her head. "It wasn't an admission. The topic came up in another context, and Richard mentioned his stepmother's interest. He gave no indication of knowing that the effects were the same as the symptoms his father showed. In fact, he doesn't know

89

the exact symptoms associated with his father's death, as I only gave them an abridged account. Richard believes his father's death was because of his weak heart, following a seizure."

The police surgeon snapped the file shut. "I will have to advise the police officer in charge of the investigation immediately. Thank goodness Detective Inspector Wallace is arriving back tomorrow. This case will have to be upgraded to a homicide inquiry."

Grace arrived home to find Charlie sitting on the front step.

"Thought you'd be home before me, Grace. I was about to send out a search party."

"I felt obliged to inform the police surgeon about my concerns without delay. As luck would have it, he witnessed a tutu poisoning as a medical student and recalled the symptoms. He's recommending the case be upgraded to a homicide inquiry. Fortunately, DI Wallace is back tomorrow."

"That's good news." Charlie leaned back against the step and observed her. "How is my dear friend, Cranston-Hartfield?"

Dear friend? Charlie and Jamie circled around each other like pit bulls every time they met. "The police surgeon is besotted with Doctor Beechworth's eldest daughter, a lovely young woman. As you can imagine, I am delighted to see him so happy." Grace paused to gauge Charlie's reaction. "No pithy riposte, Charlie? You disappoint me. If nothing else, I thought the prospect of a murder inquiry would have you as lively as a bloodhound on the scent."

Charlie regarded her with a quizzical eye and the beginnings of a grin. "No wonder Ormsby fancied you as his daughter-in-law, with the police surgeon retiring from the field. I must say, I struggle to picture you married to Richard Ormsby. I am trying to visualise you a decade or two from now, surrounded by lively little girls with stethoscopes around their necks and pudgy little boys terrified by their sisters' intelligence and daring."

90

Grace swatted his arm. "Don't be ridiculous, Charlie. My little Ormsby sons will be treated no differently to their sisters. Women only want the same opportunities, not complete subjugation of men. Most men, anyway."

"Present company excepted, I hope." Charlie rose from the step. "We'd better go inside, I suppose."

Grace took his arm. "I'm looking forward to an hour's peace and quiet before dinner."

"I'm afraid you would have more chance of peace at a brass band concert, Grace. The entire extended Southern Investigations team has gathered in Anne's drawing room."

"Discussing the murder?"

"How I wish it were so," Charlie lamented. "Wedding matters prevail over crime. There's only so much discussion of tulle versus silk that a man can take before he breaks. I must say, I'm amazed at Alistair's capacity to cope. He smiles and nods at every suggestion Aunt Lily and my mother make, no matter how ridiculous."

"Alistair is a smart man." Grace sighed. "Let's set our smiles in place and sally forth. All I ask is that you rescue me if I show signs of a tulle-induced brain seizure."

"I promise, if I am here," Charlie said, as he opened the door for her. "I was planning to return to the scene of Ormsby's collapse this evening, to test a little theory."

"I beg of you, take me with you."

Grace was, as forewarned, dragged straight into a huddle with Jasmine, Lily and Anne, while Charlie made a coward's dash to the other corner to update Alistair and Thomas on the case. Kenneth Drummond, ever the gentleman, brought Grace a glass of sherry and topped up the other ladies' glasses, before hurrying away from talk of buttonholes and bouquets to pour more whisky for the men.

After Grace successfully deflected questions about her day ("are you still under suspicion for murder?" hardly seemed a polite topic of conversation, in the circumstances), she found herself enjoying the novelty of planning a joyous event. Perhaps, she conceded, the constant grimness of her life as a trainee doctor and occasional detective could do with a little more balance.

Grace sat back, sipped sherry, and chipped in with her opinions as required. "Yes, satin would be perfect ... definitely gold trim, not silver ... perhaps camellias given the season ... Alistair will be happy with whatever you decide, Lily ... yes, Jasmine, Charlie will make a handsome best man ... three courses at dinner will be more than enough ... champagne, naturally."

After what felt like several hours of discussions (less than thirty minutes, according to the clock on the mantelpiece), Jasmine Pyke made a final tick on her list, which extended to several pages. "Excellent. I believe we have a complete and comprehensive plan. Have we got time before dinner for me to take Grace's measurements, Anne?"

"Grab her while you can, Jasmine," Anne replied. "Without your intervention, she'll end up coming to the wedding dressed in her usual white shirtwaist and grey skirt, probably with a surgical apron on top. I know that look on Grace's face. She'll be off chasing suspects before pudding is settled in her stomach."

When his mother left the room, Charlie sidled up to Grace and whispered, "I don't wish to alarm you, but Ma has interrogation skills that would be the envy of any detective inspector. Good luck."

Jasmine Pyke came back to the drawing room, carrying a wooden box, which either contained sewing accessories or instruments of inquisition (or possibly both, Jasmine being an efficient sort of woman). She took Grace up to her room and directed her to take off her outer clothes and stand still, with her arms out. Thankfully, the thumbscrews were set aside in favour of a measuring tape. Grace took a leaf out of Alistair's book – keep smiling and follow orders – as the tape flashed this way and that, measuring every part of her anatomy with surgical precision.

"This won't take long," Jasmine assured her with a charming smile, as the tape slid around Grace's neck and tightened. "Anne is a lovely lady." The tape whizzed down the length of Grace's arm.

"So welcoming and wonderfully accepting of your choices." Whizz, underarm to waist.

"I am extremely grateful for my great-aunt's support and trust." Grace squirmed as the measuring tape tickled her torso. "I know medicine is not the usual path for a young woman to take, but it is what I have always dreamed of doing."

"That can't be right. Let me just measure your chest again." Jasmine slipped the tape around Grace's bust. "No, that's right. I'll have to make some major adjustments to the pattern, which was designed for Lily."

Jasmine mumbled her thoughts to herself, which was just as well, as Grace had no reply. The tape circled her waist. Grace had spent her life being told to eat more and stop rushing around, if she wished to have an attractive feminine figure. Now, she felt like an Amazon. She consoled herself with the thought that Lily was five inches shorter and practically invisible if she was standing side on. Jasmine was the same. How she had ever given birth to Charlie, Grace didn't care to imagine.

The tape moved on down to her hips. "Hmm, I hope we have enough material," Jasmine murmured. "You don't long for a husband and children?"

The sudden switch back to a personal question caught Grace by surprise. There was something ludicrous about being asked that question by Charlie's mother, when Jasmine was on her knees, measuring Grace's hips. Would Jasmine look at the tape and declare them child-bearing hips or would she tut in disappointment and stop this increasingly embarrassing interrogation?

"I want a family eventually," Grace assured her, "but only after I have qualified as a doctor. I mean to work, as well as raising my children."

Jasmine's face was hidden as she measured the hip to floor distance. Grace didn't want Jasmine to be getting the wrong idea, but she didn't wish to offend either. "Really, it is not so very different from what most women do. After all, Anne was both married and dispensing medical care, while you must have taken on a great deal of work to support Sergeant Pyke. Charlie told me you run the Clyde police station, while your husband is out patrolling the extensive area under his command. I'd love to hear more about it, Mrs Pyke. It cannot be easy, in so remote a place, with so many gold miners desperate to make a fortune."

"I suppose that's true enough." Jasmine stood up and recorded the measurements in quick, neat script. "At least you will be paid for your toil. The wives of country policemen are expected to help with no recompense. My Thomas is out all hours of the day and night. Perhaps our Charlie has made a wise decision after all, leaving the police. Let's double-check that waist."

"I am sure he has. Charlie has all the characteristics of an ideal detective."

"There, all done. You can put your arms down now." Jasmine rolled the tape up and deposited it in her sewing kit, alongside a rainbow of cotton, a score of wickedly sharp needles of various sizes and shapes, and no less than three types of scissors. She turned and favoured Grace with another charming smile. "Charlie failed to mention what a lovely figure you have, because he was too busy telling us about your intellectual accomplishments. I can see now that the pattern for the bridesmaid's gown is all wrong. Lily and I will look for one that suits you better tomorrow. I promise you, Grace, you will look perfect on the day."

Grace wondered what Jasmine's view of perfect might be. Time to make her feelings known, so there was no misunderstanding. "I don't wish to stand out, Mrs Pyke. Something simple and modest would be ideal, in a neutral colour, so the focus remains on Lily."

"Nonsense, Grace. You must look dazzling. Lily has chosen a gorgeous silk, which will be lovely with your dark hair." Jasmine snapped the sewing box closed. "Charlie certainly seems to be happy now that he is back in Dunedin. I'm glad he has been able to secure his first case so quickly, thanks to you. And, if I might be so forward, I am relieved to see the two of you on good terms again. He was worried you might not forgive him."

"There was nothing to forgive." Grace pulled her outer clothes back on with relief. "I have made it clear our friendship is in no way diminished. In fact, I understand perfectly that he needed time away to consider his career, which is as important to him as my medical career is to me."

"I'm eager to hear all about your medical studies, Grace. It's about time we had doctors who understand how a woman's body works. And you work with the police surgeon too, which must be absolutely fascinating. My husband is eager to discuss the subject with you. Thomas loves nothing better than to stay up late at night, reading about the latest techniques. He subscribes to many journals, which arrive by the box load once a year from the other side of the world. Charlie used to say that day was better than Christmas. Now, let's go back downstairs. I've been wanting to ask you more about the post-mortem process."

Round one of the inquisition completed satisfactorily, Grace made light conversation about the gentle art of autopsy to a surprisingly knowledgeable and interested audience. It appeared there wasn't much that could shock the wife of a long-standing country policeman.

Over dinner, talk turned to their first case. Grace explained about the rat poison Mrs Ormsby had developed from the tutu plant.

"Murder, do you think?" Alistair asked. "That old classic, a wife killing her husband with poison, with a new twist? Would you please pass the mint sauce, Lily, my darling?"

Charlie passed it, his arms being longer. "Could be, although Mrs Ormsby didn't strike me as the usual type of poisoner. We only met her briefly, but her grief seemed genuine. I must say, Mrs Brown has outdone herself with this lamb. An unpleasant way to die by the sound of it. The tutu poison, I mean, not the lamb."

"Charlie, is this really an appropriate conversation for the dinner table?" Jasmine asked.

"Would you rather Grace continued her fascinating description of autopsy methods?" Charlie replied. "Or should we talk about the

95

weather? Who's in favour of hearing more about The Case of the Poisoned Surgeon?"

After a chorus of ayes, Jasmine included, Thomas Pyke asked about the victim.

"I'd say Doctor Ormsby was genuinely devoted to his wife, and vice versa," Grace answered, "although they are very different in temperament. A hard man to fathom. Fickle, definitely. Ormsby seemed so set on the new operating theatre on Thursday but professed a different opinion to me on Saturday. Likewise, he was against me attending medical school, yet he wanted me to marry his son, Richard."

This declaration put a stop to the conversation. Fortunately, Anne filled the awkward silence. "Perhaps Edgar Ormsby was more cunning than I gave him credit for. Marrying you off to his son might be his way of getting you out of medical school. The theory being, you'd be too busy raising a nursery full of Ormsby heirs to practice medicine."

"Really, Auntie, you are putting me off my dinner," Grace said, as she helped herself to another slice of roast lamb. "I'd sooner remain a spinster forever than become Henry Ormsby's sister-in-law. Please don't tell DS Elliot, or he'll see it as another motive for me to do away with Ormsby."

"If not the widow, then who?" Alistair asked. "I suppose it will come down to who had access to the poison and how it was administered."

Charlie scooped up more of the deliciously crisp roast potatoes, which Mrs Brown had left conveniently near his plate, as she always did. "I suspect it is going to be a difficult case to prove, even if we can narrow down the suspects. Mrs Ormsby's workroom is near the house. I imagine it would be easy enough to find the key, take the poison, and slip some into food or drink, depending on how bad it tastes. Anyone might have done it. We must hope the culprit has left a monogrammed handkerchief or calling card."

"What about fingerprints?" Thomas Pyke suggested. At the general bafflement around the table, he explained. "Francis Galton has published several articles on the unique nature of marks made by the tip of the fingers and their potential for identifying individuals. His latest work proves the concept."

"I know Scotland Yard dismissed the idea," Alistair said, "partly because there is no method to match a fingerprint to a perpetrator, when there are thousands of criminals it might have come from."

Charlie's fork halted in mid-air as he considered the idea. "That problem is irrelevant in this case, as we have a limited number of likely suspects from within the same household. If we could get their fingerprints and match them to marks on the poison bottle, we might identify the murderer."

"Only if the murderer did not have legitimate reason to touch the bottle," Anne said. "Mrs Ormsby, for example, would have left her marks on the poison bottle during the production process."

Grace lifted her palm in front of her face. "I'm not sure I understand what you mean by fingerprints, Sergeant Pyke."

Thomas Pyke polished a wineglass with his napkin, then pressed his thumb and forefinger to it. "Do the same in a different spot, Grace, and you too, Charlie. Can you see the marks?"

Grace squinted at the glass. "I see three pairs of smudges."

Thomas Pyke excused himself from the table. He returned with a small dish of cocoa powder, which he sprinkled on the glass, before dusting it off gently with a pastry brush. By the light of a gas lamp, turned to full, he angled the glass until the audience crowding around him could see the marks.

Grace took the glass by the stem to observe more closely, with the help of a magnifying glass Charlie passed to her. "How extraordinary! I see them now. Lots of little curving lines, different for each of us."

Charlie's father leaned over her shoulder, pointing out the patterns of arches, loops and whorls. "Francis Galton showed fingerprints are unique to an individual, even within families and between twins. Aside from being a polymath, Galton has an interest in heredity, being a cousin of Charles Darwin. Unfortunately, he also believes in the so-called betterment of humanity through proper breeding. Eugenics, he calls it."

"Survival of the elitists," Anne grumbled.

"I wonder the police haven't thought to use fingerprints before now," Kenneth Drummond chimed in. "Since the dawn of civilisation, people have dipped their finger or thumb in ink and pressed it onto legal and business documents, in lieu of a signature. Still happens, amongst the illiterate."

"If fingerprints are unique, while signatures may be forged, it would seem the illiterate are the wiser," Anne suggested.

"How right you are, my dear," Drummond replied. "I must say, the next time I commit a crime, I shall be more careful about what I touch."

Anne favoured her beau with a smile. "With your legal skills, Kenneth, you'd talk the judge into believing you were innocent, no matter how many smudges were found in the cocoa."

Lily clutched her fiancé's arm. "Alistair, this may be a way for us to assist in the investigation. Now that we have set up the workroom in our new house, we have a place to experiment. How exciting it would be to try our hand at solving a case using fingerprints."

Moonlight Revisited

Later that night, Charlie pulled his heavy overcoat tighter against the freezing cold. Beside him, Grace exhaled regular puffs of white mist. She seemed remarkably calm as they waited for DC Declan Kelly to accompany them to the site of Ormsby's demise, to test a theory about Henry's evidence.

Charlie hadn't wanted Grace to come with them. Grace, true to form, had stuck her chin out, crossed her arms over her chest, and insisted that she should come. Charlie had wavered, knowing he would need her help to recreate the exact sequence of events. In the end, he left it to Grace's great-aunt to refuse to let Grace go out with him so late at night.

To his shock, Anne had agreed. The accepted rules of society, which banned unchaperoned contact with a young lady, meant little to Anne Macmillan. She backed her own judgement on character, telling Charlie more than once she was grateful to have somebody to protect her strong-willed ward from trouble. Thus, here they were, alone at the start of the path through the town belt.

Grace stiffened at the sound of approaching footsteps in the shadow of the trees. "Good evening, Declan."

"A lovely night to recreate a murder, Grace," Declan agreed.

Together, they went through the events of the previous night, with Declan playing the role of Henry and Charlie as Doctor Ormsby. Grace dredged her memory to make the re-enactment as exact as possible. First, she recalled how she and Ormsby had walked without talking until they turned to see the view. Grace's facial muscles tightened as she mimicked the tone and volume of Ormsby's last words, before his seizure.

The hardest part was the last desperate scene. Grace was now so immersed in the drama that Charlie experienced first-hand the rising tension in her voice as she urged Ormsby to return to the house, her terror at the seizure, her panic as she began chest compressions. Even knowing she was only acting, Charlie's heart was pumping like a piston.

Finally, Grace allowed the act to drop away, giving in to a bout of shivering that would not stop, even as he pulled her into the warmth of his embrace.

Declan emerged from behind a tree and hurried towards them. "By all the saints, Grace, you almost gave me heart failure just watching."

"Impressions, Declan?" Charlie prompted, letting Grace go, but wrapping his overcoat around her shaking shoulders.

"Henry Ormsby must have followed as soon as his father and Grace left the terrace," Declan said. "If he followed later, he would not have known which of the paths you had taken into the woods, as you were not talking. I had to stay back, so you didn't hear me, but I heard every word you said when you stopped. The tree on the bend is a perfect vantage point, especially with sound carrying in the still night air."

Grace gasped. "Henry was there, watching us, all the time? I assumed he had arrived right at the end. But that makes no sense. If Henry saw and heard us, why would he accuse me of killing his father?"

"Exactly the point I was puzzling over," Charlie agreed. "Henry gave the guests at the soirée the impression that he ran to the rescue after he heard arguing and fighting. Instead, what Henry heard was his father and Grace reaching a sensible compromise over the women's ward and calmly discussing Richard's love life. Given Henry's contempt for you, Grace, he must have been furious to hear his father praise you and offer you the coveted position of daughter-in-law and producer of an heir."

"Not only pushing Henry further down the chain of inheritance but forcing him into the role of brother-in-law to his nemesis. If I had agreed, I would not have put it past Henry to attack us in a moment of unbridled fury." Grace considered the fresh evidence. "If

100

Ormsby's death was because of tutu poisoning, then he must have ingested it much earlier in the day, before Henry knew what his father had in mind for me."

"We will have to question young master Henry," Charlie agreed. "Ormsby may have already informed the family of his intention to recruit you to their ranks. Henry seems like the type of arrogant elitist who would assume your eager acceptance of such an eligible match, especially if he knew of your … situation."

Grace was seething mad by now. "Oh, you may be assured Henry kept himself informed of all the scandalous rumours about me. He held me in low esteem even before the events of last month. You can imagine how he gloated at rumours that I had been deserted by a man he viewed as a lowlife murder suspect. He still clings to the falsehood that I was somehow implicated in a criminal plot, but wormed my way out of it by sharing favours with the entire Dunedin police force."

Her gush of bitterness subsided into remorse when Grace saw the pain scything across Charlie's face. "It's no worse than I hear every day at medical school, Charlie. I try to ignore petty name-calling, but it eats away at the soul, being called unnatural and a freak for wanting to be something more than a wife and broodmare. I survive by keeping rigid control of what I can."

"I'm so very sorry, Grace," Charlie said. "I left Dunedin to allow you to live a better life. Now I see how naïve I was. I admit I am shocked by what you have said – that such filth could come from the mouth of a well-bred young gentleman."

Grace couldn't hold back a derisive snort. "Medical students are as much gentlemen as that pack of well-bred louts whose lies and high connections caused you to lose your position in the police force. I don't want to be forced out of medicine the same way."

Declan Kelly interrupted, to everyone's relief. "I believe you are missing a critical point. Standing behind that tree, watching the scene unfold, it took every ounce of my self-control not to rush out and help, even knowing it was playacting. What on earth was Henry Ormsby thinking, standing back and watching his father dying,

101

while Grace threw herself into saving his life? He ought to be charged with failure to render assistance and booted out of medical school."

"I'd happily save them the bother by stringing him up by the–", Charlie growled.

"No need, Charlie," Grace interrupted. "Honestly, if I hadn't believed I was alone out here, I would have left it to somebody else too. Although, I do agree that Henry should have come forward to assist, rather than shouting accusations at me."

"That's another thing," Declan said. "There is no way Henry Ormsby could have been sure you were strangling his father. The moonlight is bright enough to make out the path, but nowhere near bright enough to discern what was happening between two dark bodies at ground level, in the shadow of the bushes. If Henry had come upon you at the last minute, he would have been more likely to have accused you of impropriety than murder, unless he had some other agenda."

Charlie stepped forward and shook Declan's hand. "Thank you for coming out so late on a Sunday night, my friend. Without you, we might have missed a crucial piece of evidence."

"DI Wallace is back at work tomorrow," Declan replied. "I'll see what I can do about bringing you into the police interviews, Charlie."

When Declan had gone, Grace and Charlie stood silently, surveying the eerie beauty of the moonlit view.

"I wish I hadn't been fool enough to walk with Doctor Ormsby," Grace said.

"Would you have agreed if he hadn't been unwell?" Charlie asked.

"No," she replied with instinctive certainty. "I would have insisted we talk on the terrace. Ormsby was adamant the walk would make him feel better. He would have gone without me."

"And died alone, without hope of aid."

"I miss your crystal-clear logic, Charlie." Grace watched a cloud flit across the face of the moon, throwing darkness on land and sea. "How strange it feels to be standing in the same spot, under the same beautiful moon, yet feeling entirely opposite emotions."

"Not so strange. I would be offended if you felt that being alone with me was in any way similar to being alone with a seriously ill adversary who wanted you to marry his rich son."

"Idiot," Grace said, jabbing an elbow into his side. "With hindsight, it was a most peculiar encounter with a perplexing man. Of one thing I am sure – there is no spark of attraction at all between me and Richard, although he was much more amiable than I expected of an Ormsby."

"And what about us, Grace?" Charlie whispered in her ear. "Is there still a spark, or has it been extinguished by me being a lowlife murder suspect and a deserter to boot?"

Grace stared, unblinking, into the silver-spun void for so long, he wished he had kept his mouth shut. Finally, she replied. "Whatever there is between us, Charlie, I would not call it a spark."

The shock of her dismissal passed through his brain and out of his heart, leaving Charlie wondering if this was what being electrocuted felt like.

Then Grace slipped one arm around his waist. "For me, it has always been less a spark than a roaring fire. I cannot seem to stop myself from being drawn ever closer to the warmth until I fear I will either be burned or I will smother the flames."

The heat of her arm around him threatened Charlie's own tenuous grip on control. How to answer when he felt the same fear? His arm slid around her waist, which felt slim and fragile next to his bulk. "One fire will smother another only if it dominates. If two fires of equal intensity join, together they burn all the brighter."

The cloud passed, revealing a full moon bright enough to illuminate Grace's smile. She swivelled to face him, drawing closer as his arms encircled her. "On a night like tonight, who am I to deny such logic?"

Natural Remedies

Grace arrived early for the first lecture on Monday morning, intending to catch up on the assigned reading. She settled into a seat in the back corner of the lecture theatre and pulled a battered pathology textbook out of her satchel. The words blurred in front of heavy eyelids. Ormsby's death, two sleepless nights, and the memory of lips crushed against hers, as if their lives depended on it. So much for her firm intention to put her career before her heart.

A trio of Henry's friends arrived before Grace had ingested a single paragraph. Fortunately, they were too busy talking to see her. Not simply talking, she realised, but gossiping with childish glee about the fatal soirée. Her first instinct was to blast them for disrespecting a friend's deceased father. But what good would that do, other than to provoke their taunts?

"My father was at Ormsby's soirée," the group's dominant male crowed. His favourite pastime was leaving body parts where Grace would come across them. Last week, he had slipped two eyeballs into her lunch tin. Rat, not human, but still… "Saw the whole sordid affair unfold. Pater swore the old man's face was contorted in terror when they carried him back through the house."

"Did Henry finally break and beat the old man to a pulp? Or did the evil stepmother get him with her poisons?" This from the cruellest of the three students – a sneaky, arrogant weasel.

"I heard Beechworth's wife had a slanging match with Ormsby right before he died." Student number three hovered on the edge of the group. Away from their influence, he verged on likable, but was far too easily led for Grace's taste.

"No, you imbeciles," Eyeballs replied. "The truth is far juicier than that. Penrose was there. The police suspect her of doing away with Henry's old man."

After a brief interlude of gasps and titters, during which Grace sank below the desk and started crawling towards the rear exit, the third student spoke again, his voice tinged with a glimmer of scepticism. "Grace Penrose killed a man? Are you sure? Why would Ormsby invite her in the first place? Gads, why would Penrose accept, when Henry has made her life a misery?"

Eyeballs sniggered. "Reckon old Ormsby had heard of her loose reputation and fancied a chance to lift her petticoats. Penrose joined Ormsby Senior on a cosy little stroll. Alone, late at night. Henry actually saw them going at it, before she strangled the old man."

"Gorblimey, might have a go myself if the Ice Queen has expanded her repertoire from scum to gentlemen," Weasel said. "On second thoughts, maybe not, if she is a lunatic murderess."

"Why didn't Henry stop her?"

Eyeballs lowered his voice, forcing Grace to stop crawling so she could hear. "Perhaps it suited Henry to get his inheritance early, before the wicked stepmother takes it all. If Penrose doesn't swing for this, I might even employ her myself to do away with Pater. My old man's even tighter with money than Ormsby, except when it comes to throwing it away on mistresses and horseflesh."

"Penrose will be kicked out of medical school, but I doubt she'll swing for it," Weasel sneered. "Everyone knows she likes a bit of rough with the coppers. She's probably desperate for it, after the lowlife she was consorting with was accused of murder and ran for the hills."

Grace was grateful for the dim light to cover the fire in her cheeks. She crouched on the floor under a desk, torn between defending herself and Charlie, and an aching desire to run for the hills herself. Before she could decide, she noticed that two pairs of legs were now visible at the entrance to the lecture theatre. She shrunk further into the shadows under the desk.

"If I hear any more of that foul language and scandalmongering, I'll have the lot of you sent down and banned for life. Good God, you're supposed to be gentlemen, not a bunch of back-alley guttersnipes."

Thank heavens, Grace thought. Her pathology lecturer to the rescue. Not that she liked being rescued, but she had yet to find an effective verbal method of countering her tormentors' so-called "harmless banter". How easy it was for them to turn a drop of truth into an ocean of malicious lies, not caring whom they hurt. Replying in kind was not only petty but harmed her reputation – a lady being held to higher standards than a gentleman. Ignoring their insults was the only option, hence the Ice Queen taunt. (Naturally, Grace had denied all knowledge of the debilitating diarrhoea Eyeballs suffered each time he taunted her. It was entirely coincidental that she had supplied laxatives to a grateful patient of Lavender House, who just happened to be married to the barman who poured her tormentor's midday ale at the local tavern.)

Grace was still frozen in place under the desk when the second man strode down the aisle towards the three students. His heavy boots drummed ominously on the floorboards. She heard an intake of breath and a porcine squeal as Eyeballs was hauled from his seat.

"What's your name, boy? I'll need it for the arrest warrant."

The voice of Detective Constable Kelly, growling with suppressed fury. Grace almost felt sorry for Eyeballs. Declan Kelly was a tender-hearted Irishman who doted on his wife and children. But that was not the side he showed to villains and scoundrels. Kelly had the battered face and physique of a rugby player and wasn't afraid to use it to his advantage.

"Arrest warrant?" Eyeballs squealed. "What for? Unhand me, you cur. I have done nothing wrong."

"I'll have you for assaulting a policeman if you don't stop kicking me," Kelly retorted. "I am minded to arrest you for slander and obscene language, not to mention spreading false information about the circumstances of a man's untimely death. Perverting the course of justice is a very serious offence."

Grace heard a thump and a whimper as Kelly dropped Eyeballs back into his seat.

"On the other hand," Kelly continued, "I could let you go with a warning and wait for my best friend to find you and teach you a lesson you'll never forget. My friend would not be pleased to hear you slandering himself and Miss Penrose. I should warn you, he once killed a man for threatening her."

Grace knew a cue when she heard one. She scrambled to the rear door and stood up, pretending she had just entered the room. "Detective Constable Kelly, what are you doing here?"

Kelly swung around and grinned at her. "Come to get you, Miss Penrose. Your expert medical evidence is required as a matter of urgency. Your lecturer has given you leave." He turned a final contemptuous glare on Eyeballs. "You owe Miss Penrose an apology, boy. Far from being a suspect, she ought to be commended as the one person in a roomful of medical experts who recognised the seriousness of Ormsby's condition and acted on it."

Only when they were safely away from the medical school, heading up the hill to the Ormsby house, did Kelly speak again. "You overheard that bucket of slime, didn't you, Grace?"

"I'm used to it, Declan, but I am very grateful for your support. Would you mind not telling Charlie what the students said?" Declan nodded his understanding, which allowed Grace to change the subject. "I take it the police surgeon has passed on my concern over the possible cause of death."

"Doctor Cranston-Hartfield thought it brave of you to come forward with the information, given its potential to implicate you. Wallace wants you present when we inspect the workroom where Mrs Ormsby made the poison, given your knowledge of the plant used."

Grace took that as a welcome sign that Wallace did not view her as a serious suspect. "I'm willing to do whatever I can to assist, whether or not it implicates me. Besides, the whole of my class heard my toxic plant essay, which means many others within the medical fraternity will know of it too. Henry Ormsby apparently shared it with his whole family."

"We'll have to find out if Ormsby had any enemies," Declan said.

Grace rummaged in her satchel. "Doctor Beechworth dropped off a list of people who disliked Edgar Ormsby, as well as a list of his surgical deaths. The families of deceased patients occasionally hold a grudge, although I admit it is unlikely that any of them would have expressed it in such an unusual and lethal manner."

"You're a step ahead of us, Grace." Declan took the list and tucked it into his pocket. "If it was murder, I suspect we will find the culprit rather closer to home. Interesting that Henry Ormsby's so-called friends thought he wished his father dead for financial gain, especially as he stood back and watched his father die."

If there was a murderer, Grace would much rather it was Henry Ormsby than anyone else. She was still furious at him for accusing her, but couldn't decide whether Henry had been genuinely confused by what had happened in the pale moonlight or actively attempting to put the blame on her. If Grace let her imagination run wild, she might even be tempted to think he had given his father the poison mentioned in her essay to further implicate her.

However, there was no point in mentioning it. In her view, compelling evidence must be gathered before accusations were hurled. In truth, Richard Ormsby probably had the most to gain financially. And Mrs Ormsby would likely be the first suspect, as she was the one to extract the poison from the tutu.

At the Ormsby's house, the butler showed them through to the drawing room, next to the grand salon where the fateful party had taken place. Richard Ormsby sat in an armchair, his hands clenched white on the armrest.

Grace was not surprised at Richard's ill-disguised trepidation. The sight of Detective Inspector Robbie Wallace sitting a yard away, looking like a grizzly bear in a doll's chair, would be enough to unnerve the most innocent of men. Wallace's woolly grey eyebrows formed a double thundercloud over seen-it-all grey eyes.

Grace had the advantage of knowing that Wallace was a kind man and a fine policeman, who followed the rules without fear or favour. "Good morning, Detective Inspector Wallace. I hope your newborn grandson and his mother are well?"

Wallace's lips twisted up into a sentimental grin. "The bairn is the bonniest wee lad in the land, Miss Penrose. Shall we proceed straight to the workroom?"

Richard jumped to his feet and showed the way, keeping close to Grace, while glancing nervously over his shoulder. The workroom, where Mrs Ormsby produced her natural remedies, was on the far side of the garden from the house.

Charlie Pyke was lounging outside on a wooden bench. His eyes snapped open as they approached, settling on Grace for a long moment, before he rose with the lithe grace of a cat stretching after a nap.

As Richard appeared disinclined to talk, Charlie took the lead. "As you can see, the workroom Mrs Ormsby uses to prepare her tonics has been converted from the rear half of the stables. The workroom is accessible from the side road leading up to the stable entrance, as well as the garden path from the terrace, off the main house." Charlie pointed at the two paths, before entering the building. "The workroom itself has only one entrance, off this small lobby, to the left. The door straight ahead of us goes through to the stables. The door on the right leads into a dangerous goods store."

"Dangerous goods?" Wallace queried.

Richard stepped forward. "The active ingredients of my stepmother's preparations are often extracted with flammable substances such as alcohol and ether, which are also used in my father's surgery. They are stored separately, for safety."

Charlie inserted a chunky key into the lock of the left-hand door, which was solid enough to deter anything short of an axe-wielding intruder. "As I understand it, this is the main workroom. Is that correct, Mr Ormsby?"

Richard waved his hand around vaguely. "It is. The usual thing. Work benches, with sinks and gas connections for the burners. Under-bench cupboards for utensils such as mortars and pots. Overhead cupboards for general stores, such as glass vials and harmless chemicals. The door at the rear leads to the storage

109

cupboard, which is used for raw ingredients, finished preparations and chemicals requiring secure storage."

Charlie opened the rear door. "The storage cupboard is much bigger than it looks, as it has been pushed out into the stable at the rear."

"An old horse stall," Richard confirmed. "The workroom was the former coach house. Look, I don't wish to be obstructive to your inquiry, gentlemen, but why are you interested in my stepmother's workroom when my father died of a heart attack?"

"We are keeping an open mind. Can you–" Wallace's head jerked up. "What the blazes was that at the window?"

All eyes turned to a barred window, high on the exterior wall. There was nothing to see. A moment later, a pair of pigtails with ruby-red ribbons appeared, followed by an upside-down face. In a flash, the imp was gone again. Richard stormed out of the workroom. They heard a body scrambling down through tree branches, a few terse words, and a manic giggle.

Richard reappeared, red-faced. "I do apologise. My sister Agnes can be a little terror. Hence the security precautions. Mother had bars fitted to the window recently, after Agnes learned how to climb the tree and open the window. The little devil made a dreadful mess in here before she was discovered." He sighed. "I'm sure I wasn't half so naughty when I was seven."

"And the keys?" Wallace prompted.

"My stepmother and I both have a key to the workroom door. Mother keeps a spare key on the top shelf of her wardrobe. I think Lawson uses that key, if she is here without Mother. Lawson is her lady's maid, but she has proven herself a capable laboratory assistant. Nobody else should be in here, unless one of us is present."

"You assist too, Mr Ormsby?" Wallace asked.

Richard's expression showed the first sign of animation since their arrival. "I am a pharmacist by training, but I find natural remedies to be a fascinating area of study and a useful adjunct to modern drugs. My stepmother trained as a nurse. She's a great proponent of the Florence Nightingale approach to germ theory and hygiene. She is also an exceptionally able chemist, when it comes to herbal preparations. Her kawakawa products show great promise. Indeed, we were working on a proposal to sell them more widely, only Father … Well, suffice to say, my father was not in favour of investing in the business. 'Mother's little hobby', he called it."

"Do you keep poisons here, Mr Ormsby, as well as remedies?" Wallace asked casually.

Richard did not so much as flinch. "Most chemicals are toxic if ingested or used at the wrong dose, Inspector, which is why they are under lock and key. I expect there is some arsenic or strychnine in the storage cupboard to get rid of rats too. Quite a plague of them last summer, as I'm sure you'll recall."

"You mentioned your stepmother had experimented with a native plant as a rat poison," Charlie said, looking at Grace with a raised eyebrow.

"Tutu," she supplied.

Richard planted his knuckles on his hips. His bottom lip thrust out over his receding chin, which only made him seem petulant. "I want to know, right now, the reason for all these questions."

Wallace nodded at Grace, who reluctantly took up the baton. "Mr Ormsby, you will appreciate that I know the effects of tutu on the human body, having written of it in my essay. I have to tell you that nothing else so closely matches the odd array of symptoms your father showed before his death."

Wide eyes and open mouth formed a trio of circles within the circle of Richard's face. Outside, a rustle of leaves segued into the rending sound of ripped fabric and a childish shriek. Grace and Richard reached the door simultaneously, to see Agnes racing across the garden, bawling at the top of her lungs.

Her half-brother started after her, but Wallace's meaty hand gripped his shoulder. "Pyke, go to the house and get someone to see to the little girl. Mr Ormsby, I need you to show me the poison."

Richard stumbled across the workroom to the storage cupboard. At the far end, he pointed to a jar of arsenic on the top shelf and a glass bottle beside it. Kelly found a stool and stood on it to reach the shelf. As Charlie had already mentioned the idea of fingerprinting the poison bottle, Kelly used a clean handkerchief to remove the glass bottle, touching only the narrow neck.

Grace stepped closer. Less than half an inch of dark oily slurry sat at the bottom of the bottle.

Richard stared at it too, his face a mask of shock. "The bottle was more than half full the last time I saw it."

"And when was that?" Wallace asked.

But Richard had slid down the wall onto the floor. He curled his arms around his head and sobbed.

Unnatural Remedies

Charlie walked through the garden without much hope of finding the vanished imp. He and the nanny had failed to find Agnes indoors, which the nanny took with a stoic resolution, suggestive of this being the usual state of affairs.

He had used the opportunity to question the nanny. On the day of the soirée, the nanny said she had taken Agnes out for a long walk in the park to keep her away from the party preparations. Both of them had fallen asleep early in the evening in their rooms off the nursery. Or so the nanny had thought. In fact, Agnes had escaped, of course, and eaten too many cream cakes, naturally. The nanny had not woken until Agnes had complained of a stomach ache, after which neither left the nursery. The woman was a saint.

Charlie didn't bother to search the depths of the shrubbery or the dingier corners of the stables. A small child could hide away in the tightest of spaces and he did not wish to dirty his clothes. He was wearing his second-best suit to show the household he was a man of standing. Or, rather, to give the appearance of such on his first full day as a private detective.

He even had a new necktie for the occasion. His mother had presented it to him, right before she burst into tears. It was weirdly reminiscent of a long-ago memory of his mother seeing him off to his first day at school. In contrast, his father had seen Charlie off this morning with a simple handshake. Thomas Pyke had slipped a leather-bound notebook into his pocket, complete with a hidden slot for a slim magnifying lens. His father was a recent devotee of a new author of detective stories, Arthur Conan Doyle, who was also a physician. Charlie dreaded the inevitable day when his father introduced Grace to Sherlock Holmes. Her disappointment would be unbearable, when Charlie failed to provide a complete description of the suspect from a single footprint or the ash from a specific type of pipe tobacco.

A commotion from the direction of the stables took an axe to his musings. Charlie dashed back to the workroom. Declan Kelly emerged, propping up Richard Ormsby, whose bones appeared to have dissolved within his body. Richard's low moaning resonated with anguish.

Wallace followed close behind, his expression grim. He waited until the others were out of earshot, before coming over to Charlie. "The tutu poison is down to the dregs. Richard Ormsby was sure the bottle was half full the last time he saw it."

Charlie watched Richard being dragged into the house. "From his reaction, Richard must know what a dreadful death his father suffered. Murder, then?"

"Can't entirely rule out accidental poisoning at this stage," Wallace said. "Would you ask Mrs Ormsby to come to the drawing room? Make sure you keep her lady's maid, Lawson, away. I want to ask each of them separately about how Doctor Ormsby was poisoned." Wallace paused. "That is, if you don't mind, Pyke. I know you're not mine to command any longer, more's the pity, but I would be grateful for your cooperation."

"Working together does strike me as the most efficient approach, sir," Charlie agreed. "I promise to inform you of any evidence I uncover. If it would help, I could talk to Miss Lawson while you interview Mrs Ormsby."

Charlie found Mrs Ormsby in her bedroom, showing as much sign of animation as the drawn curtains and the mirror draped in black cloth. While her mistress sat silently picking at her black lace shawl, Lawson sat equally silently, stitching a black border onto a handkerchief.

"The police request your presence in the drawing room, Mrs Ormsby." He held the door open to let her know it was a command, not a choice.

114

When they reached the drawing room, Charlie ushered Mrs Ormsby through but held Lawson back. "Please follow me to the salon, Miss Lawson. Miss Penrose will stay here with Mrs Ormsby."

The lady's maid looked as if she would resist but decided better of it when he placed his bulk between her and the door. "What's all this about, Mr Pyke? Poor Mrs Ormsby wishes to mourn in peace."

Charlie gestured her to a chair in the salon. "I am required to ask a few questions, Miss Lawson. First, can you tell me your full name and the nature of your employment?"

"Miss Nelly Lawson. Lady's maid." She took the offered chair, sitting upright, with her hands resting in her lap. A posture direct from the *Guide to Etiquette for the Discerning Lady's Maid*. Her voice was calm and precise, its origins obscured behind a standard English accent.

Charlie entered the details in his new notebook. "You also assist in the workroom, preparing herbal extracts and so forth. Is that correct, Miss Lawson?"

"Yes."

Charlie remained polite, despite her defiantly uninformative answers. "An unusual role for a lady's maid. Would you care to elaborate, Miss Lawson?"

"I do as I am asked. Mrs Ormsby and I met on the voyage out to New Zealand, during which I assisted with her work as a nurse. She's a qualified nurse, you know. I'm not, but she said I had an aptitude. When we landed, Mrs Ormsby was kind enough to employ me. I'm very grateful."

Charlie leaned towards her and smiled kindly. "I can see that, Miss Lawson, by the care you take of Mrs Ormsby. A trusted lady's maid is never more important than during a time of crisis, I imagine."

Miss Lawson did not so much as blink her doe eyes in reaction to the compliment. "Thank you, sir. I'm sure I do my best by her, as she does by me. Now, how may I help you, Mr Pyke?"

"Mr Richard Ormsby showed us through the workroom." Charlie noted that Lawson flinched at the sound of Richard's name, just as she had when she saw him yesterday. "He is most impressed by his stepmother's skills. I wonder if you might have a look at this bottle and tell me whether you have any like this in the workroom?"

Charlie dug into his Gladstone bag, which had been the doctor's bag used by Mrs Macmillan's husband when he was alive. Anne had always been very generous about passing on such items to him, including Doctor Macmillan's clothes, which allowed Charlie to supplement his own meagre wardrobe with a variety of useful disguises and formal wear. Grace had assured Charlie that no one else had been allowed to touch his possessions, which Charlie took that as a welcome sign of Anne's favour.

Touching only the top, Charlie drew out one of the small reagent bottles, which Lily had packed for him this morning, brand new from her workroom.

Miss Lawson took the glass bottle between her fingers and thumb. "A standard bottle. Smaller than we use." She held the bottle out to him, depositing it on a side table when he showed no signs of taking it.

"Mr Richard Ormsby told us Mrs Ormsby had experimented with a native plant called tutu," Charlie said.

"Oh yes, always trying new ideas is Mrs Ormsby. I helped her extract the active ingredient. Marvellous to think it might be the first time anyone has done it in a laboratory."

Charlie nodded encouragingly. "Fascinating. Did the poison work on the rats?"

Lawson grimaced. "Horrible to watch, it was. At first, it looked as if they were going to die quietly, but then the rats had the most awful spasms. It took hours for some of them to die."

"Did Mrs Ormsby throw the poison away afterwards?" Charlie tossed the question out causally. "Or had she used it all up on the rats?"

"There was more than half of it left." Dawning suspicion seeped into Lawson's voice, giving it a sharper tone. "Mrs Ormsby was going to throw it away, but other rat poisons were in short supply, so she thought she might keep it. I suggested doubling the dose, so the vermin died quicker, but we were busy with other preparations, so did not try it."

"When was the last time anyone touched it?"

Lawson's hands remained still in her lap, but with a definite tightening of the fingers. "To what do these questions tend, Mr Pyke?"

"If you would be so kind as to answer the question, Miss Lawson."

Lawson took a moment to think. "As far as I recall, it must be close to two weeks since the tutu extract was last used."

Her growing dismay appeared genuine as she asked the obvious question. "You're not thinking it had anything to do with Doctor Ormsby's death, I hope." Dismay turned to distress as she saw the answer in Charlie's silence. "Lord have mercy on him. What a way to go. Please, I beg of you, I must go to Mrs Ormsby now. She will need me."

Lawson darted away before Charlie could stop her. He let her go. She was right – Mrs Ormsby would need comforting. He tucked the reagent bottle carefully into a rack in his bag, labelled with Lawson's name. If their plan had worked, he had just taken his first fingerprints from a suspect.

After discussion with the Southern Investigations team, Charlie had come prepared with the small bottles of highly polished glass, lightly oiled to preserve fingerprints. His aim was to secure prints from every member of the household, by the simple method of getting each suspect to examine one of bottles. Not as effective as gathering prints using an ink pad and shiny white index cards, but less likely to alert the murderer to their attempts to identify him or her.

Charlie returned to the drawing room, where Lawson was already cradling her mistress. Richard Ormsby watched the pair with narrowed eyes. Charlie slipped across the room to whisper in Wallace's ear. "Sorry, sir, couldn't hold the maid back. Should we keep them apart?"

Wallace drew him into the corner to ensure their discussion remained private. "We will have to question them separately, but a few minutes of comfort will be needed after the shock they've had. Besides, if any of them caused Ormsby's death, I doubt they would have mentioned the tutu potion or kept the bottle. Mind you, poisoners tend to be more devious than the average criminal, in my limited experience. What did Lawson say?"

Charlie ran through the main points in a low voice. The evidence of Richard, his stepmother, and the lady's maid all indicated that the tutu poison had not been touched within the last two weeks.

Wallace nodded. "I've sent Kelly to telephone for Elliot and Weston, to assist at the formal interviews of the household. You may be present, Pyke, if the interviewee agrees, but I will reserve the right to eject you if circumstances dictate. No offence intended. Must stick by the rules, especially if the evidence is to be used in court—"

On the other side of the drawing room, Grace cleared her throat loudly. When they turned, she waved her hand at the empty chairs. Their suspects had absconded.

Wallace grunted. "Always the same with wealthy folks. Think they can leave whenever it suits them. I will search for them upstairs. Would you and Miss Penrose check the reception rooms?"

Charlie and Grace circled in opposite directions, meeting in a small room at the far side of the salon. The intimate arrangement of chairs and scatter of sheet music on a large chest in the corner indicated the room was used as both a private retreat and a music room. He took Grace's hand and led her to a beautifully upholstered, but ridiculously narrow sofa. The seat was stuffed to a rock-like consistency, while the backrest curled ornately up to the midpoint, giving no rest to the back of anyone not sitting right in the middle. A piece of furniture less suited to the name "loveseat" was hard to imagine.

Charlie lowered himself gently onto it, in case the spindly legs gave way. "What do you think of the relationships between Richard, Lawson, and Mrs Ormsby?"

Grace settled close beside him, the size of the loveseat giving her no other option. "Interesting. Mrs Ormsby and her lady's maid seem to be unusually close."

"They met on the voyage out to New Zealand and found they shared an interest in nursing and natural remedies."

"That might explain it. Those long voyages across the ocean can be the making or breaking of a friendship, according to my great-aunt. Richard seems very fond of his stepmother. He's proud of her skills, I would say."

Charlie lowered his voice to a whisper. "*Too* fond, do you think?"

"Charlie! Mrs Ormsby is almost twice Richard's age and his stepmother. I really don't see their attachment as improper."

"It wouldn't be the first time such a thing happened, Grace. Richard certainly doesn't seem to like Lawson. Both of them flinch when they see each other and go out of their way to avoid contact. Could be jealousy, given the strong bond between the women."

"Perhaps," Grace said. "But it struck me that the tension between Richard Ormsby and Nelly Lawson could be an act. It's only little signs, I admit. His eyes follow her when he thinks nobody is watching. Even when he is deliberately looking away, his body turns towards her. There's something in the way they both become alert, as a dog does when its master enters the room. You'll laugh at me, but I've often wondered if there is a scent or aura that can be sensed by two people who are attracted to each other. If so, those two are oozing it. Or rather, Richard is. I'm not so sure about Nelly Lawson."

Charlie's initial reaction was disbelief, but he could not deny that his own body reacted in exactly this way when Grace was near. He always knew when she had entered a room, even with his back turned. Without meaning to, he closed his eyes and sniffed the air.

"I see you know what I mean." Grace's smile verged on the mischievous as she leaned closer to him. "I'm not sure how I shall get any work done if you stay in Dunedin, unless the effect diminishes over time."

Whatever this scent or aura was, Charlie hoped it would linger for a very long time indeed. As he leaned over to close the distance between them – for who can resist the lure of an intoxicating scent? – a rustling noise emerged from behind the chest.

"You're not going to start kissing, are you? Bengali doesn't like kissing." A stuffed toy showed its tiger face around the side of the chest, growling not very ferociously.

"No kissing, I promise," Charlie replied. Not right now, at least. "Does Bengali have to put up with a lot of kissing in the music room?"

"Only Richard and Nelly." A small, pale face appeared from behind the chest. The pigtailed imp, last seen upside down in the workroom window. "I told Mummy, but she didn't mind. I'm not allowed to tell Daddy, because he would be cross."

Seen the right way up, Charlie noted little Agnes was very like her mother, with bright, curious eyes and delicate features. Grace slipped away, presumably to share the news that Agnes had been found. He hoped Mrs Ormsby wouldn't return too quickly. A bright, curious child invariably sees things that others overlook.

Agnes walked across the room and stood in front of Charlie, studying him intently. "My daddy died. That means he's gone to heaven to help in God's surgery. That's what Mummy said, but I'm not so sure angels need appendectomies and hernia operations."

Charlie stifled a smile. This must have been exactly what Grace had been like as a seven-year-old, questioning everything and using words like appendectomy with a confidence beyond her years. He tore a piece of paper from his notebook, folding it into a paper angel. "Maybe your daddy will fix the angels' wings if they hurt them."

Agnes gave serious consideration to his suggestion before shaking her head. "I don't think God would let anyone get hurt in heaven, especially not angels. My name is Agnes Siobhan Ormsby and I am seven and a quarter years old today. Who are you?"

"You have a nice name, Agnes Siobhan Ormsby. My name is Charlie Thomas Lee Pyke. Thomas for my father and Lee for my grandfather."

"My mother's name is Siobhan. She said as soon as I was born she knew I would be like her, so I ought to share her name."

"I'm very like my father. How did Bengali get his name?"

Agnes gave Charlie a withering look. "*She* is a Bengal tiger cub. Mummy made her for me."

"I'll bet she is a clever little cub who likes to explore secret places." Charlie waited for her nod. "Why is Bengali hiding today?"

Agnes planted her hands on her hips and rolled her eyes in a perfect parody of a disapproving parent. "She was naughty. *Again*."

"Curiosity and naughtiness tend to go together, don't you think?"

"She is *very* curious," Agnes agreed. "Bengali is going to be a scientist, testing things for herself instead of being a good cub and believing what she is told. She ruined mummy's best slippers by testing if they would float in the bath. They didn't."

Charlie struggled to keep a straight face. "I'm surprised the water damaged the slippers so badly as to ruin them."

Two circles of pink flared on the little girl's cheeks. "I tried to dry the slippers by the fire, but I put them too close and forgot about them." Agnes hung her head, pigtails swinging in contrition. "Bengali and I aren't allowed near fires anymore. Especially after we got into really big trouble for putting a candle to the curtains in the nursery to see if they would burn."

"Even young cubs like Bengali must know it's dangerous to play with fire." Charlie wondered how much the Ormsbys had to pay to keep the nanny from deserting.

Agnes nodded with all the sincerity of a reformed arsonist. "I wasn't allowed to see Bengali for a week after that. I had to climb up to Mummy's top shelf to get her so she wouldn't be lonely when everyone else was at the party. I wasn't allowed to go to the party because I am too small." After a pause for honest reflection, she added, "And because I ate too many of the cream puffs."

A scuffling from the adjacent salon indicated Grace had found Mrs Ormsby and was holding her back from entering the room. Charlie knew it wasn't his place to be interviewing this mischievous little pyromaniac, but he had a strong feeling that Agnes was upset about something, despite her boldness. He ignored the eavesdroppers and continued with his gentle probing, hoping Agnes would find it easier to talk to a kindly stranger than to her family.

"I love cream puffs too," Charlie admitted, "but if I eat too many, my stomach hurts. Was that why you had a stomach ache after the party, Agnes?"

Her eyes went wide. "How did you know I was sick?"

"Your brother Richard and your nanny both mentioned it."

"It wasn't the cream puffs. I only had four or five. Six at most." Her mouth turned down and quivered – the expression every adult recognises as a precursor to tears. "Bengali knows she must never, ever touch the bottles in the bathroom cabinet. But Daddy drinks his tonic every day, and she wanted a little taste too. It was no more than a dab on the tongue, honest. I didn't mean to knock the bottle over, but the taste was so horrible, I couldn't help it. It made me sick, just like Daddy." Agnes burst into tears. "Mummy will be very cross."

Charlie held up his hand to stop anyone entering the room. "Agnes, I think your mother will be proud of you for finding out something important that nobody else knows. Do you remember what you did with the bottle of tonic that made you sick?"

Agnes tucked herself into a ball around her tiger. "I hid it under my bed and put another bottle back in the cabinet so no one would know I had been naughty. Mummy said if I was naughty one more time this week, she would give Bengali away to the orphans."

"Agnes, I promise you can keep Bengali. But I would very much like to have a look at the bottle, being a curious kind of person myself."

"I suppose so. May I have the paper angel, Mr Charlie Thomas Lee Pyke?"

Charlie handed it over. "Your mother was worried about you when you disappeared, Agnes. Do you think if you closed your eyes and counted to ten, she would appear by magic and give you an enormous hug?"

Mrs Ormsby only had eyes for her daughter as she rushed into the room, passing Charlie as he left.

Under The Bed

Grace had been standing by the open door to the music room for the last few minutes, holding back Mrs Ormsby, while marvelling at the natural way Charlie had with children. Detective Inspector Wallace was listening too, at first with impatience, then with quivering intensity. Detective Constable Kelly had departed as soon as the bottle was mentioned, with a whispered reminder from Grace to touch only the top of the bottle.

Mrs Ormsby's expression had run the gamut from relief, to annoyance, to horror, before settling on concern for her child as she rushed into the room. As far as Grace could tell, fear and guilt were absent. Richard had been amused until the final revelation. He was now hunched in an armchair with his face shielded by his hands.

When Charlie emerged, his face raw with emotion, Grace followed him and Wallace back to the drawing room. Kelly was already there, with four bottles lined up on the table. Wallace raised an eyebrow at her.

Grace knelt in front of the table. Not that her expertise in poisons was much better than anyone else in the room, but her curiosity was roused. The poison bottle from the workroom was quite distinct from the others – a laboratory bottle, round, with a glass stopper, and a label clearly marking it as poison. The other three bottles were typical medicine bottles – rectangular, tapering to a narrow neck with a cork stopper. Two were labelled "Heart Tonic", the other "Digestive Tonic".

One of the heart tonic bottles had been sitting on its side, presumably the one from under the bed. The shape meant that a significant amount of liquid remained, despite the bottle having been tipped over by Agnes. Grace pointed out the tiny particles on the bottom and the faint dark oily slurry resting on the top of the red

124

liquid, matching the colour, viscosity and seed remnants of the poisonous tutu extract. The other two tonic bottles, which had come from the bathroom cabinet, had no such contamination.

Wallace looked on with the falcon-eyed intensity he used when murder was afoot. "Kelly, tell DC Weston to take these to the police surgeon for analysis. Make sure he packs them carefully to ensure no breakage or spillage."

Charlie intervened. "Sir, may I suggest we take samples of the liquid for the police surgeon to analyse the poison, while we keep the bottles for fingerprint testing?"

Grace thought Wallace was about to refuse. He would be right to do so, as there was a standard procedure to follow and fingerprinting was not yet in the police manual. But Wallace nodded. He directed Kelly to make a formal note on the decision. Both policemen watched closely as Grace drew off liquid from each bottle into labelled vials, which Charlie packed to give to DC Weston. Lily's newly arrived glassware and laboratory equipment were getting a fine start to their working life.

Grace was packing the tonic bottles into the Gladstone bag when they heard a hesitant knock at the door.

"Come in," Wallace barked.

Richard Ormsby edged his head around the door. "May I speak to Mr Pyke and Miss Penrose?"

Wallace eyed him suspiciously, but evidently saw no downside. He nodded and turned back to his notebook. Grace wondered how far they could assert their presence at the police investigation, before Wallace put his foot down. For now, she and Charlie followed Richard to the library. Cigar smoke still tainted the air, reminding her of the gut-churning minutes she had spent there after Doctor Ormsby's death.

"You think my father's medicine contained poison," Richard stated, as soon as he had closed the door behind them.

"I'm afraid so, Mr Ormsby," Charlie replied. "Do you know what was in the tonics?"

"Both were my stepmother's formulations. I believe the heart tonic is based on hawthorn berries, steeped in alcohol, in a honey syrup. The digestive tonic is a mixture of ginger, garlic, kawakawa and honey, in apple cider vinegar. Father took the heart tonic every day, the digestive tonic only as needed."

Grace noted the flick of Charlie's eyes towards her. She took Richard's arm and sat him down, drawing up a chair beside him. "We realise this is dreadful for you, Richard, but is there any conceivable way the tutu poison could have been added to the heart tonic in error?"

"No. Absolutely not." Misery dragged Richard's face down, from eyelids to jowls. "I took Father his heart tonic myself once during the week. Wednesday, I think. He was always forgetting. The bottle had already been in use for several days, with no previous ill effects, so it cannot have been faulty preparation. Besides, there was no way poison could be added by mistake. The preparation procedures are meticulous."

"Do you have any idea what dosage of tutu poison would be needed to have a fatal effect?" Grace asked.

Richard shook his head. "If Agnes was ill after touching it to her tongue, then the poison must have been highly concentrated. Father is supposed to take a spoonful, but he tended to swig it from the bottle. You would think a doctor would know better."

In Grace's experience, doctors were far more casual about their own health than that of their patients. She was no better, having recently discharged herself from hospital far earlier than was good for her. From what the police surgeon had told her, the seeds of the tutu berry were highly toxic, and Mrs Ormsby had further concentrated the poison by extracting the active ingredient from ground seeds.

"I saw how the poisoned rats died." Richard clutched Grace's arm, the agony on his face revealing his understanding of what his father must have suffered. "I know how this looks. There are only three people who had access to the workroom. Me, my stepmother and Lawson."

"And anyone who had access to the spare key," Grace reminded him.

After a moment's pause, Richard pulled up his sagging shoulders and turned to Charlie. "Miss Penrose said you are a private detective, Mr Pyke. I beg you to investigate this on my behalf. The police will surely jump to the false conclusion that one of us is to blame. I saw the look on that detective inspector's face."

"Mr Ormsby," Charlie replied, "I can assure you from personal experience that Detective Inspector Wallace is an exemplary officer. I must also tell you that I am obliged to pass on any information you reveal to me, if it constitutes relevant evidence. The sole aim of my investigation is to uncover the truth, wherever it takes me."

"And I am telling you that I want the truth, Mr Pyke. Please, I must know who did this to my father."

Charlie glanced at Grace. "Unfortunately, I have already been engaged to investigate this case. It would not be ethical to work for two clients."

"I presume Miss Penrose is your other client," Richard said, "after my brother's appalling accusations against her. I understand your loyalties, Mr Pyke, and I don't wish to be ungallant, but Miss Penrose is no longer a suspect."

Charlie hesitated.

Richard rushed to fill the pause. "I can afford to pay whatever you ask, which will save Miss Penrose the expense. Please, I want this whole awful situation to go away. I should be arranging my father's funeral and supporting my family, not dealing with the police. There are so many decisions to be made. Mrs Simpson is asking for a list of people to inform. The vicar wants to know Father's favourite hymns. Finch wants to know which printer to use for the black-bordered stationery. As if I cared a damn about hymns and stationery at a time like this!"

Richard flushed. "Apologies, Miss Penrose, for my unseemly outburst. It's all too much. Please, I need your help."

Charlie drew Grace aside. "Working for Richard Ormsby would give us much better access to the family and the house, and he can afford our services. However, I do not wish to break my promise to Doctor Beechworth."

"I agree, Charlie," Grace said. "But Beechworth won't care for whom you work, as long as the truth is uncovered. Richard is right. Ivy and I will no longer be suspects, as the poison must have been administered before the soirée."

Charlie returned to Richard, who was waiting with ill-concealed desperation. "I agree to investigate on your behalf, Mr Ormsby, but with conditions. I must have free access to the house and grounds, and permission to question all persons in the household and guests at the soirée. I will seek the truth, wherever that leads me. Are you absolutely sure that is what you want, bearing in mind that the most likely suspects are your own family?"

Richard met his gaze squarely. "I accept, Mr Pyke, gratefully and unconditionally. I know it wasn't me who poisoned my father and I would swear on my life it wasn't my stepmother or Lawson."

"Objectively, I hardly need to point out that your father's wealth provides a motive to all the beneficiaries of his estate." Charlie met Richard's defiance with a hard stare of his own. "As for Miss Lawson, she might have the strongest motive of all. I suspect her chances of marrying well will be materially improved by your father's death."

Richard rose from his chair, fists curled. "And I tell you, Lawson is innocent. You have proven yourself an able detective, Mr Pyke, to sniff out our secret so fast. Please proceed without delay. Whatever it costs."

Grace could see that Charlie still hadn't decided on the financial aspects of his new business, so she stepped in. "I believe the standard fee is ten pounds, assuming the case can be resolved within a week."

"Ten pounds?" Richard queried.

"A special rate," Grace assured him, "as Mr Pyke's findings will benefit me as well. You will have the services not only of Mr Pyke, the Lead Detective, but also his business partner, a detective inspector with over thirty years of experience, as well as a team of legal and medical experts."

"My apologies if it sounded as if I was questioning the fee, Miss Penrose. I am simply having trouble taking in extraneous details. Father undoubtedly spent far more on the ill-fated soirée. To be honest, I wasn't even aware there were private detectives working in Dunedin."

"Discretion is a vital part of their service, as you will appreciate," Grace replied. "I ought not to mention it, but Mr Pyke was behind the successful resolution of the recent Choral Hall case. Naturally, he works with his contacts within the police force and allows them to take the credit, to avoid any unwanted attention from the press."

"Really? I admit I am impressed, Mr Pyke. A shocking state of affairs when citizens are not safe from anarchists on the streets of their own city."

Charlie did not wish to dwell on that case, nor did he wish to stand like an idiot while Grace negotiated a ridiculous fee on his behalf. Ten pounds indeed. On his detective constable's wage, he would have had to work for two months to earn that much. Still, he was not about to object, given his precarious financial situation. Time to take control and prove his worth.

"As Miss Penrose has indicated, Mr Ormsby, I will do my best to investigate discreetly. However, I will have to ask about every aspect of your father's life. I will need to see your father's current will and ask about any animosities within the circle of family and wider acquaintances, as well as the movements of all persons on the day of the soirée."

"Of course," Richard agreed. "Whatever you need."

"As the police will question you on those matters as well, may I suggest we save time by attending their interview together?"

Richard nodded. "I'll get Father's will from his study, Mr Pyke."

Charlie took the small glass bottle Grace had passed him from the Gladstone bag. "Before you do, Mr Ormsby, can I ask if you have any bottles like this in the workroom?"

Richard took the reagent bottle. "It's possible. I do little of the practical work in the workroom. Is it important?"

"Probably not." Charlie took the bottle back, touching only the top.

Richard departed through a hidden door in the back of the library.

Grace waited for the door to close behind him, before rising on her toes to kiss Charlie on the cheek. "Now that the poison is discovered, I should get back to my medical studies. Make sure Wallace knows Ormsby was already feeling unwell before the soirée began. From what is known of the onset of symptoms, it is likely he ingested the poisoned tonic around mid-afternoon to early evening."

"A shame you cannot stay, Grace," Charlie said. "Would you let the rest of the Southern Investigations team know I will update them on developments this evening?"

"You had better or I'll come looking for you."

Charlie trailed his fingertips down her cheek. "Is that a promise?"

"No, Detective Pyke, that is a threat." Grace slipped out of the room before he could think of a suitable reply.

Where There's A Will

Charlie settled into a chair in the drawing room, positioning himself at an angle to and behind DI Wallace and DC Kelly, to make it clear who was in charge of the interview. In the interests of future cooperation with the police, he didn't want to usurp too much of Wallace's role.

Richard Ormsby sat in front of them, rigidly calm, but failing to control a twitch in his right eyelid. Only to be expected for a man who had just found out his father has been murdered with rat poison. Charlie had seen far more extreme reactions in his time, from catatonic collapse to fist-flailing belligerence.

Richard passed over a sealed envelope. "The Last Will and Testament of Edgar Robert Ormsby, may he rest in peace."

Wallace slit the envelope with a silver paper knife and read through the document silently, before passing it back to Charlie. The provisions were much as Charlie had expected, except that the sums involved were startlingly large. How did a middle-aged surgeon accrue such wealth, as well as a grand house? He passed the document on to Declan.

Edgar Ormsby had bequeathed a generous sum to the hospital for new surgical instruments and left a few minor bequests to servants. Charlie did not discount these as a motive. A few pounds could mean as much to a poor man as thousands of pounds to a rich one. Not ten minutes ago, Charlie had been aghast when Grace had set his fee at ten pounds, an amount he now realised that Richard Ormsby would see as a trifle.

Not for the first time, Charlie wondered at Grace turning down the financial security of a wealthy husband like Richard, in favour of following her heart. Intoxicating vapours had a lot to answer for in creating an undeniable attraction, but would they be enough to stand the test of time, especially when times were tough?

Charlie forced his thoughts back to the will. The bulk of the estate went to family, which meant all of them would gain financially from Edgar Ormsby's death. Mrs Ormsby was to receive the interest from a very substantial lump sum, with the capital passing to Agnes on reaching her majority. They would also have the right of residence in the house for as long as they wished. Even so, Mrs Ormsby's future depended a great deal upon the goodwill of her oldest stepson. The widow was fortunate indeed to get along well with Richard.

Doctor Ormsby's daughter, Cecilia, received the same amount outright for her dowry. Charlie wondered if Gideon Alexander knew Cecilia would be a wealthy young woman and whether that influenced his attachment to her. Given the opulence of the Ormsby house, Alexander cannot have been unaware of it. Charlie hadn't met him yet, but Grace had given a good account of Cecilia's suitor.

Henry Ormsby also received a lump sum, and his father's surgical instruments, while his older brother inherited the house and the residual estate. Henry would be well-off, whereas Richard would be extremely rich.

Miss Nelly Lawson was not mentioned as a beneficiary of the will. Nevertheless, she would benefit from Edgar Ormsby's death, if she had hopes of marrying Richard Ormsby. From what Charlie had gleaned of Doctor Ormsby's character, he would have refused consent to any alliance between his heir and a servant. Lawson's character was harder to discern. Was her regard for Richard due to love, or ambition?

Charlie recalled his attention to the interview of Richard Ormsby, as Wallace moved from the standard personal details of the witness to substantive questions.

"If you will forgive the indelicate question, how does a surgeon come to be so wealthy?"

"My mother – my birth mother, that is – came from a very wealthy family. Tragically, she died of dysentery on the voyage to

132

New Zealand." Richard paused long enough to size up the detectives in front of him, evidently deciding that hiding the truth was a waste of time. "You might as well know my stepmother was a nurse on the ship. She cared for my mother night and day but could not save my mother's life. There was no hint of impropriety. My father grieved his lost wife throughout the mourning period, before asking my future stepmother to be his nurse. In due course, she became his second wife. They were very much in love, Inspector, as you can see from my stepmother's deep distress at his death."

"Miss Lawson travelled on the same ship and assisted your mother, I understand," Wallace said.

Richard struggled to keep his expression neutral. "She did, along with our old gardener and one of the housemaids. Long weeks at sea tend to build a strong community spirit, Inspector. It is quite common for shipmates to continue their associations after the voyage."

Long voyages might build strong community spirit, Charlie reflected, but he'd bet his last sixpence they also created strong enmities that persisted long after docking.

Wallace let the silence build until Richard could stand it no longer. "I am sure you are eager to know why my father left me nothing in his will. Let's not tiptoe around the issue, Inspector. My father and I have been at odds for some time over my choice of career and my failure to propose to any of the eligible young ladies he paraded before me. Not a one of them with anything but goose down between their ears. We argued last month. Father threatened to disinherit me. I refused to give in. I was determined not to be manipulated by his threats. At least you cannot suspect me of having a financial motive to kill my father."

Wallace tapped his fingers on the arm of his chair at this unexpected outburst. "Are you sure your father changed his will, rather than simply threatening to disinherit you?"

"The argument took place in Father's study. He took the old will out of his desk and ripped it into pieces in front of me, to make the point."

"Perhaps you might clarify who the beneficiaries of his will are, Mr Ormsby."

"I had previously been the main beneficiary, with provisions to ensure the lifelong support of all the family, including my stepmother and half-sister. The new will cut me out entirely." Richard spoke with the level of indifference one might show for a minor irritation, rather than a life-changing loss of a massive inheritance. "Father told me the new will left the house to Henry, while increasing the provisions for the other family members. He also made a very substantial bequest for the building of the new operating theatre at the hospital. But you know all this, as you have the document in front of you."

"Did others know of this rewriting of the will?" Wallace asked.

"Father made no secret of it, although I cannot tell you to whom he made the specific details known. All the family, I presume. Horncastle too, who did not bother to conceal his triumph. Giving the money to the hospital was Father's way of slapping me in the face, you see. To show me he put proper medicine ahead of his disappointing elder son. I took it to be a fleeting gesture, aimed at testing my resolve. But, as it happens, Father died before he could change the will back. It seems I must either live at the financial whim of my younger brother or make my own way in the world. I am content with the latter option."

Wallace leaned forward, nudging the document towards Richard. "I confess I am confused. The document in front of me names you, Mr Richard Ormsby, as the main beneficiary."

"What?" Richard seized the will, skimming the words in obvious disbelief. "This must be the old will. Perhaps Father left the revised version with his attorney."

"Note the date, Mr Ormsby. Signed and dated on Friday, the day before he died. I take it you were unaware that your father had changed his will back again?"

Richard stared at the document, shaking his head. "I had no idea at all. Neither Father nor any other family member said a word on the matter. This changes everything."

No doubt it did, in terms of who benefited from Ormsby's death. But Charlie was not so sure the new will affected the motive for his murder, depending on who knew of the change. If Ormsby had told the whole family that he had disinherited Richard, but failed to inform them he had reversed his decision, then Richard was still the only family member without an apparent financial motive. In fact, if Ormsby was prone to making rash decisions, then reversing them, whoever killed Ormsby might have felt the need to act quickly to secure a larger share of the estate.

After a final scan of the will, Richard folded it back into the envelope and placed it on the small table between him and the detectives. "I'll have to talk to our attorney. May I check again in my father's desk to ensure I have the current version? I cannot believe he wouldn't have spoken to me about the change."

Charlie caught Wallace's eye, nodding his head just enough to convey a subtle message. Wallace didn't so much as blink before sending DC Kelly off with Richard Ormsby.

"Have a look at the envelope," Charlie said. "The slight wrinkling of the paper suggests that the envelope has been steamed open and resealed."

Wallace turned the envelope in his hands. "Well spotted, Pyke. So, at least one person in this house knew that a new will had been signed. The question is, who?"

"I don't think it was Richard. His shock was too genuine."

"I must say, Richard Ormsby has risen in my estimation," Wallace said. "Standing up to his father, at the risk of losing his inheritance, shows admirable courage in his convictions. I wonder if he realises he may be the next target of the murderer, assuming this case is about money, rather than personal enmity."

Wallace broke off his whisper at the sound of footsteps. Kelly and Richard returned, their hands empty of further complications. Wallace waved Richard back to his chair. "Mr Ormsby, I must insist that you keep the existence of this new will from your family for the time being. Now, can we put the mystery of the will to one side and proceed with the interview?"

Wallace waited for Richard's nod. "When did your father normally take the heart tonic?"

"At afternoon tea, every day." Richard gritted his teeth and answered with his usual quiet dignity, although, on the inside, he must have been in a turmoil of grief, confusion, worry and many other emotions. "Father had no ill effects the previous day, so the tutu extract must have been added some time after three o'clock on Friday."

"What were your own movements between Friday and Saturday afternoon?"

"I was working at the hospital until about six o'clock on Friday evening, after which I went to my club to dine. I arrived home again at perhaps ten o'clock. I did another shift at the hospital early on Saturday morning, returning home in time for luncheon. The house was in chaos all afternoon, with cleaning, food deliveries, flower arranging, decorating, and so forth, so I made myself scarce until the soirée started. I had a light meal sent up to my room at around six o'clock, before dressing for the soirée."

Wallace paused for Kelly to get this down before proceeding. "What about the movements of your father and other family members?"

Richard thought for a moment. "I don't think I saw anyone except at luncheon. I left for the hospital before the rest of the family was out of bed on Saturday. Everyone ate together about one o'clock on Saturday afternoon. Aside from the delivery men and hired servers, I am not aware of any other visitors that day."

"We'll need a list of the delivery men and servers, Mr Ormsby."

"Mrs Simpson, the housekeeper, would know. I can't imagine any of them would have had the opportunity to poison the tonic."

"Always pays to be thorough," Wallace said. "How did your family seem at the meal?"

"My younger brother, Henry, was in a foul mood. Cecilia had had a furious row with Father and was refusing to speak to him. Agnes was being a little demoness. Father ignored everyone, while

136

my stepmother single-handedly tried to keep everyone civil." Richard paused for long enough to roll his eyes and expel a deep breath. "In other words, everything was exactly as normal."

"Mr Ormsby, how do you think the tutu poison came to be in your father's heart tonic?"

"I honestly cannot say, Inspector. The tonic is kept in Father's bathroom cabinet. Usually, his valet brings it down for Father to take with afternoon tea. The poison could have been decanted from the bottle in the workroom at any time over the last two weeks without anyone noticing, assuming the guilty party knew where the key was kept. The workroom and the front door of the house are kept locked, but the other doors of the house are generally unlocked during the day. Therefore, anyone in the house, or indeed an intruder, might have added the tutu poison to the tonic."

"Who knew the spare key was kept in your stepmother's wardrobe?"

"I really couldn't say, Inspector. Nothing is ever secret within a busy household, although none of the servants besides Lawson and the housemaids ought to be in Mother's room. The main reason the key was hidden was to keep Agnes out of the workroom. As you will have observed, she has a propensity for mischief. She's a sweet little thing, but too clever and curious for her own good."

Wallace leaned forward, his fingertips forming an arch under his chin. "Whom do you suspect, Mr Ormsby?"

Richard flinched, but he held Wallace's gaze. "I cannot believe that any of the family or anyone else in the household could have committed this atrocity, Inspector. Truly, if it wasn't a ghastly mistake, then I don't know. Perhaps a disgruntled patient or madman? Someone who bore Father a grudge, who had visited the workroom?"

Wallace raised one of his woolly eyebrows. He allowed a moment to pass, while his target squirmed. "Anything is possible, Mr Ormsby. However, I can see you do have somebody specific in mind. From your reaction, I can only conclude you wish your intuition is wrong."

Wallace waited for a reply, ignoring the misery on the face in front of him. "Better to raise the possibility now, rather than having a troupe of policeman stomping around in your house for the next month."

Richard folded his arms around his body, as if warding off a chill. "It's nothing really … Only a terrible thought that sprang to mind when I mentioned my half-sister's propensity for mischief." He hesitated, before plunging ahead, his words tumbling out in a tangle. "It's just …. Well, you heard how Agnes likes to test things. The workroom, which is forbidden to her, has become a source of fascination. What if she added the poison to the tonic, thinking it was a medicine rather than a poison? With no ill intent, just to see if it would help her father. I mean … I hope not … nothing more than a crazy thought, probably because I'm so damnably tired. I don't think she would have really …"

The Housekeeper

The three policemen exchanged glances at Richard's stuttering admission. None of them looked the least surprised that Richard was worried about the possible involvement of little Agnes in her father's death. A child who could set fire to curtains for the sake of curiosity would certainly be capable of experimenting with her father's heart tonic.

Nevertheless, Charlie wondered if putting the blame on a child wasn't a convenient diversion. Richard must surely have considered the possibility that his beloved Lawson had taken matters into her own hands. Lawson had every opportunity to take the poison and tamper with the tonic, as she had access to all areas of the house and workroom. If her willingness to listen at doors was an indication of her character, then Lawson might well be the person who steamed open the will. Thus, she might be the only person who knew the will had been changed back in Richard's favour.

Wallace dismissed Richard Ormsby from the interview, with orders to take a stiff brandy and get some rest. The twin burdens of grief and shock dragged down Richard's shoulders as he shuffled out of the drawing room.

Wallace waited until Richard had closed the door. "Pyke, you seem to have a rapport with the little girl. See if you can find out if she added the poison to the tonic."

Charlie tracked Agnes down in the nursery, with the nanny standing guard over her. The little girl denied putting anything in her father's tonic, even in the noble interests of scientific experimentation. Bengali hadn't either. Charlie returned to the drawing room.

"I'm almost certain Agnes didn't tamper with her father's tonic," Charlie told Wallace.

"Children will tell whopping fibs to save themselves from punishment," Kelly reminded him.

"True," Charlie conceded, "but they rarely have the skill to lie convincingly at that age."

"Ain't that the truth," Kelly said. "My nephew will swear he hasn't been in the larder, while licking a thick smear of sticky red jam off his lips. The very thought of it makes me hungry."

They were interrupted by a discreet knock on the door. The woman who opened the door could be none other than the housekeeper, with her air of quiet command, crisp white cuffs and chatelaine of keys. Charlie rushed to hold the door open, eager to facilitate the entry of the accompanying trolley, which held the promise of a full Devonshire tea.

"That's a most welcome sight. I'm parched." Wallace consulted his list. "Mrs Simpson, I presume? Might we have a word, since you are here?"

"Of course, Inspector." As Mrs Simpson gave her version of events on the day of the soirée, she handed out plates, napkins and scones with a combination of silver tongs and smooth efficiency, borne of years of service. Her evidence failed to advance their investigation, as the housekeeper's entire day had revolved around menus, decorations, flowers, arranging tables, ensuring the silver was spotless, and the thousand other details that make a successful supper party appear effortless.

Since Doctor Ormsby's death, Mrs Simpson had been equally busy, seeing to mourning rituals and assisting with funeral arrangements. The housekeeper never said it in so many words, but it was clear from the tasks she and the butler had attended to that Richard and Mrs Ormsby were not coping with the practicalities of their bereavement.

Mrs Simpson also declared she had no knowledge of Mrs Ormsby's workroom, while handing a reagent bottle back to Charlie. She promised a list of delivery men and hired servers, although she assured Wallace that the delivery men never made it past the scullery and the servers didn't arrive until just prior to the start of the soirée, too late to have poisoned the heart tonic.

When the tea was poured and set on lace doilies in front of each man, Mrs Simpson lingered. "Inspector Wallace, might I ask a question?"

"You may, Mrs Simpson."

"It is human nature to gossip. I would like to be able to dismiss the dreadful rumour circulating below stairs, suggesting that Doctor Ormsby died of poisoning, not a weak heart. Aside from being an abominable accusation, it has created friction in the kitchen. Cook has threatened to walk out if her food is called into question. She is very strict about Doctor Ormsby's food and far too good a cook to lose over unfounded gossip."

"You may inform the cook and all the staff that it was not food poisoning," Wallace replied.

"Thank you, Inspector. I'm glad to hear it."

"However, Doctor Ormsby's death was not from natural causes. Mrs Simpson, I trust I can rely upon your discretion, if I ask a sensitive question?"

"Yes, of course, Inspector," the housekeeper said quietly, keeping her expression neutral, but with just a hint of growing unease.

"Mrs Ormsby produced many remedies, using a variety of herbs and other plants. Were the staff aware of that?"

"Naturally. Anything remotely different from the usual routine is discussed endlessly below stairs, Inspector. But what have Mrs Ormsby's remedies to do with–" Only years of strict training stopped Mrs Simpson from uttering the "Oh" that formed on her lips.

"And was it generally known that Mrs Ormsby had experimented with the use of various substances as rat poison?" Wallace asked.

The housekeeper momentarily looked as if she had swallowed the poison herself, before she collected herself. "Mrs Ormsby talked about it over the dinner table, which means that everyone in the house would have heard of it. Was that ... was that how Doctor Ormsby died?"

"It is an avenue that is currently under investigation," Wallace acknowledged. "Please keep this to yourself for the time being, Mrs Simpson. It would be helpful for us to have a tour of the house to better understand how this tragedy occurred, with particular attention to who had access to Doctor Ormsby's bedroom and private bathroom."

Mrs Simpson gave them a quarter of an hour to finish the refreshments before returning to conduct the tour. Needlessly, as it took barely five minutes for the three burly coppers to squeeze the last drop out of the teapot and dispatch the pile of scones, including licking stray blobs of jam and cream from the plates.

The housekeeper had used the break to recover her poise. She nodded with satisfaction at their effusive thanks for the tea. "Follow me, officers. I take it you wish to see the entire house, including the private rooms?"

"Yes, please, Mrs Simpson." Wallace stepped aside as a pretty housemaid with cherubic curls entered the drawing room.

"See to the rest of the airing after you've cleared the tea, please, Betsy," the housekeeper instructed the maid, who bobbed at the knees and began gathering cups.

Charlie noted the dark bags under the housekeeper's eyes and the chafing on the housemaid's hands. A death in the family was always hard on the household staff, whose role it was to smooth the disruption, whilst preparing the house for the rituals and extra visitors brought by a funeral. He wondered if they mourned the loss of a respected master of the house, or not. If Charlie had to hazard a guess, it would be that Richard would be a welcome change from his father. Not that any of the staff would admit it outside their own tight circle.

The housekeeper guided them across the parquet floor of the large room that adjoined the drawing room, which she referred to as the grand salon. The room the soirée had been held in. French doors

142

led to the terrace, and the stables and workroom beyond, which were partially screened by a luxuriant garden.

"Music room, connecting corridor to the dining room, kitchen and butler's pantry," Mrs Simpson intoned, as she swept past each of these locations, giving them just enough time to glimpse the efficient layout of the house.

They circled past the main hall, stopping before they completed the full circuit back to the drawing room. Mrs Simpson opened another door. "As you see, the drawing room adjoins the library, which leads to Doctor Ormsby's study."

Mrs Simpson led them through the two rooms, emerging into another corridor. Every room seemed to have two entrances, providing multiple routes through the house from front to rear, besides the main hall, which ran from the main entrance to the grand salon.

"Doctor Ormsby's private operating theatre is across this side corridor, at the front corner of the house," Mrs Simpson said. "It has a separate side entrance. And here we are, back at the entrance lobby."

The main entrance was in the centre of the front façade, opening into a lobby and staircase to the upper floor. As the kitchen also had an exterior entrance, that made four entry points in all, only one of which was locked during the daytime.

On the second floor, the family bedrooms formed a line along the front half of the house – parents to the north, children to the south. On the garden side, the guest bedrooms were opposite the rooms of Richard, Cecilia, and Henry. At the other end, the nursery was opposite Mr and Mrs Ormsby's rooms, incorporating a room each for Agnes and her nanny. The rest of the second floor comprised a bathroom and three staff rooms, for Mrs Simpson, Miss Lawson and the valet. The maids slept in the attic space, while the butler had a room off the butler's pantry downstairs, and the cook had in a space off the kitchen.

Thus, anyone in the household, with the possible exception of the cook and downstairs maids, might have accessed Doctor

Ormsby's private bathroom and tampered with his tonic. The murderer must have been bold, to risk an encounter with other members of the large household. However, on a day when most of the household was busy in the grand salon preparing for the soirée, the risk was lessened. Moreover, an outsider might easily have come through the side door, or even the main door, and sneaked up the stairs without being seen. With delivery men coming back and forth, and the house in a state of organised chaos, anything was possible.

Charlie returned from his examination of the second floor to find Wallace and the housekeeper engaged in a whispered disagreement over the merits of leaving Mrs Ormsby to rest versus the urgency of the police viewing the scene of the crime. The impasse was broken by the appearance of the lady of the house from out of her room.

"Thank you, Mrs Simpson," Mrs Ormsby said. "I have indulged my grief long enough. Detective Inspector Wallace is right. The priority must be determining how my husband met his death. If there is a killer on the loose, it behoves us all to do whatever is in our power to catch him. Me most of all, as it appears I have been the unwitting source of the poison that killed my husband."

144

Ladies Of The House

Mrs Ormsby ushered them into her private room, which appeared to be more of a lady's dayroom than a boudoir. Evidently, the Ormsby's marriage was affectionate enough to share a bed. The furnishings were orderly and feminine, without crossing the line into frills and fancies.

Mrs Ormsby went straight to the connecting door, rightly perceived their interest lay in her husband's domain. "As you can see, our rooms connect through a dressing room and private bathroom." She waved her hand around the inner space, which was a sizable area lined with clothes, shoes, a pair of dressing tables and drawers for smaller items and jewellery. "We have a small safe for valuable items, which was not touched."

Wallace opened the door to the private bathroom, another substantial space, with a full-sized bath and a washstand. Mrs Ormsby shrank back against the wall as Wallace opened the cabinet that had contained the heart tonic. The cabinet was crammed with a range of medicines and the usual soaps, perfumes, and shaving items.

Charlie noted the cabinet was locked, but the key was in the lock. A curious child would have no problem standing on a chair and taking whatever took her fancy. He took advantage of her distraction to hand Mrs Ormsby a reagent bottle, which she said was not one of hers. She passed it back to him without a trace of curiosity. She agreed without question when Charlie asked if he might take Doctor Ormsby's silver-backed brush with him. He did not explain that he wanted it so he could eliminate her husband's fingerprints from the inquiry.

The policemen went through to the master bedroom, which showed signs of Mrs Ormsby's hasty retreat from a nap. Wallace pretended to ignore the scattering of intimate clothing and rumpled sheets. "Perhaps we might have a word with you in the drawing room, Mrs Ormsby?"

When they were seated in the drawing room, Mrs Ormsby smoothed her heavy black gown, lifted her veil and looked Wallace directly in the eye. "Please ask whatever you wish, Inspector."

"Shall we start with your full name and place of birth?"

"Mrs Siobhan Agnes Ormsby. Edinburgh, Scotland."

"You are Doctor Ormsby's second wife, I understand," Wallace said.

Mrs Ormsby replied in a subdued monotone, as one does with a tale oft told. "That is correct, Inspector. I came to New Zealand in 1883, after my first husband died and left me without support. This country desperately needed trained nurses, and I felt a fresh start was in order. I met Edgar Ormsby and his family on the ship, under tragic circumstances. Edgar's first wife became seriously ill and died during the voyage. I nursed her, with the assistance of Miss Lawson. Edgar and I met again at the hospital here in Dunedin. As fate would have it, he needed a nurse for the private surgical clinic he planned to establish. I accepted the position and eventually married him eighteen months later. Agnes was born less than a year afterwards, to our great delight."

Mrs Ormsby waited patiently for the next question. When Wallace hesitated, she did not falter under his imperturbable gaze. "In answer to your unasked question, Inspector, I can assure you it was a love match. I didn't marry Edgar for his money or position, although I admit I viewed a surgeon as an ideal match for my skills and interests. Indeed, until I first visited this house, I did not know he was truly wealthy, rather than merely a well-to-do professional man. I suppose you find that hard to believe, but it is true."

"I have no reason to doubt it, Mrs Ormsby," Wallace replied. "Did you know either Doctor Ormsby or Miss Lawson before the voyage?"

146

"No. Nelly and I were assigned bunks next to each other. We quickly became friends. She showed an aptitude for nursing and her assistance was much needed on that long voyage. Dysentery afflicted more passengers than the ship's surgeon and I could handle alone."

"Miss Lawson is now your lady's maid, I understand."

"Officially, that is her title, although Nelly is more of a companion. I have looked after myself for many decades, without the assistance of servants. She also assists me with preparing my natural remedies, as I'm sure you know." Mrs Ormsby shot a stern glare in their direction. "I have complete faith in her. She is not the author of this tragedy, no more than I am. Less so, in fact, as I suffer the guilt of preparing the rat poison. Oh, how I wish I had never heard of tutu."

"Mrs Ormsby," Wallace said, "you will appreciate that the critical issue is how the poison came to be in your husband's heart tonic."

"I have no idea, I assure you, Inspector. An intruder, I can only assume, as it cannot have been anyone within the household."

Wallace raised an eyebrow fractionally but let the comment pass. "Did you see anyone in the private bathroom used by your husband and yourself between afternoon tea on Friday and Saturday?"

"Only the usual people. Edgar's valet shaved him in the bathroom every morning and the housemaids cleaned our rooms while we were at breakfast. Nelly would have been in the bathroom and dressing room at various times, to see to my requirements. Nobody else would have cause to be there. However, I spent most of Saturday downstairs, attending to preparations for the soirée. Thus, I cannot say for sure if anyone else entered the bathroom."

"What about your husband's bedroom?"

"Only the valet and the housemaids. Edgar's valet was in and out during the day, attending to my husband's clothes for the evening. Other than that, only myself and members of the family."

"Family?"

For the first time in the interview, Mrs Ormsby's composure slipped. Nothing dramatic – no pacing or hand-wringing or cross words. No more than a tightening of her lips and a narrowing of her eyes. "Unfortunately, Edgar chose the day of the soirée to stir up a hornet's nest. I suppose you will have to know that Edgar had been at odds with all three of his older children in the preceding weeks."

"I will need to hear the details, Mrs Ormsby." Wallace's own composure was faultless, although his very stillness hinted at his eagerness to hear her answer.

"Must you hear it from me? I try to avoid coming between Edgar and his children."

Wallace did no more than raise an eyebrow.

"Oh, yes, of course. I suppose it will have to be me now Edgar is no longer with us. I keep expecting him to come through the door…" A tear squeezed from under her eyelid. Mrs Ormsby dashed it away. "Well, if you must know, Cecilia was angry with her father over his failure to accept her suitor. Doctor Alexander had made his intentions known, but Edgar insisted on making him and Cecilia wait a week before he gave them his decision."

"Why was that, Mrs Ormsby?" Wallace asked gently.

"Doctor Alexander has nothing but his skill and character to recommend him. He is a fine young man and an excellent surgeon, which was more than enough for my approval. However, Edgar wanted the best for his daughter, in terms of wealth and position. Despite Alexander's failure to be born into wealth, Edgar planned to consent to the match. To be honest, I think he was pleased with the idea of a surgeon as a son-in-law and he truly did wish to see his daughter happy."

"You're sure your husband agreed? We were under the impression Miss Cecilia believed her father had denied her suitor."

"I'm afraid Edgar had rather an unfortunate tendency to tease and spring surprises on us." Mrs Ormsby sighed. "Edgar told me he had made up his mind but he had not made that known to his daughter. He would have had to finalise the matter with Gideon Alexander first, of course. Perhaps Edgar intended to tell them the good news at the soirée."

Charlie was rapidly coming to the conclusion that Doctor Ormsby was a man who relished being in control. Raising hackles by professing to be of one view, then changing his mind, presumably to appear magnanimous. Ormsby didn't seem to realise that this approach was gaining him more enemies than friends. Horncastle and the women fundraisers, whom he had played against each other over the new operating theatre, and now his own daughter. Even his wife and son, after refusing to support the proposed expansion of his wife's "little hobby".

"I'm sure it was well meant," Mrs Ormsby hastened to add. "Edgar was right to take the time to investigate Doctor Alexander's situation before he agreed to the marriage. Henry was pushing his father to do so, as we knew so little of Alexander's background. He hadn't been in New Zealand long, but he came with excellent references."

"I understand Henry was also angry with his father that day." Wallace said.

Mrs Ormsby's face tensed, as it always did when Henry's name was mentioned. "Henry is frequently angry about something. He seems to find life very unfair, although I cannot say why. He is fed, housed and educated as well as any young man in the land."

"May I ask about your own relationship with Henry, Mrs Ormsby?"

"If you must. I do my best to be a fair and loving stepmother, but Henry sees me as an usurper. He has never accepted me, unlike dear Richard, and now I doubt he ever will. Unfortunately, I am now rather at Henry's mercy."

"How so?" Wallace softened his tone, knowing what was to come, but unable to put her out of her misery at this critical point.

Mrs Ormsby tried to lighten the situation with a little laugh, but it sounded a little too desperate to all present. "I'm sorry, it's rather

149

frustrating. Edgar was trying to push his older son, Richard, into an unwanted society marriage. Their relationship had long been strained, after Richard chose to become a pharmacist rather than a surgeon. A few weeks ago, the tension erupted into a furious argument. Edgar ripped up his will and made a new one, cutting Richard out entirely. It was a moment of foolishness, which Edgar intended to reverse as soon as Richard 'saw sense'. Nevertheless, the fact is, Edgar had not yet done so. Thus, Henry is the now primary beneficiary of his father's will. I cannot remain in this house under Henry's rule."

"Are you sure your husband didn't change his will back in favour of Richard, as he intended?"

"I know he went to see his attorney on Friday, but I presume the new will remains undrafted and unsigned."

Wallace leaned a little closer. "Your husband didn't discuss it with you?"

Mrs Ormsby fluttered her delicate hands helplessly. For all her outward semblance of calm, tears welled again at the corner of her eyes. "Edgar makes his own decisions on such matters. I make a point of not being involved, as I do not wish to be perceived as influencing him against the children of his first wife."

Wallace sank back into the armchair, but kept his eyes fixed on her. "As a matter of fact, it would seem that your husband did change his will. The new will was signed on Friday, the day before the soirée."

Astonishment and hope rose to replace the misery on Mrs Ormsby's face. Her lips moved, but no words escaped.

Wallace filled the silence. "Your husband's meeting with his attorney must have been to sign an already drafted document. Richard was as surprised as you are, when he retrieved the document from Doctor Ormsby's study."

"Oh, well, my goodness. I cannot pretend that I am not relieved. For Richard, as well as for myself and Agnes." Her moment of joy passed quickly. "Henry will be furious. I wonder if –"

150

Mrs Ormsby cut the sentence short. From the way she clamped her lips together, she was unlikely to say anything more. Charlie had little doubt that she was wondering if Henry knew of his father's plan to reinstate Richard as the main beneficiary. Henry would indeed be furious.

"Richard will be able to make his own choice of a bride now." Wallace leaned forward again as he said it, inviting her confidence.

"Yes, he will. And much the happier he will be for it." Mrs Ormsby met Wallace's gaze but declined to elaborate.

"Perhaps his choice will be similar to his father's? A match for love, not money?"

"You have put your detective skills to good use, I perceive, Inspector. Suffice to say, I will leave the decision entirely in Richard's capable hands. He is a far better man than anyone gives him credit for, his father included."

Wallace let the statement sit in silence, waiting for any further admissions. But Mrs Ormsby was not one to babble confidences into a gap in the conversation. Wallace tried a new tack. "I believe you and your stepson had plans to develop and expand your natural remedies business. Plans that were thwarted by your husband's refusal to fund the venture."

Mrs Ormsby's head perked to one side, a touch of vexation crossing her rosebud lips. "I hope you are not thinking that minor disagreement was a motive for murder, Inspector. I assure you, with time and persuasion, Edgar would have accepted our plans."

Charlie had little doubt of it. This woman had all the powers of persuasion at her fingertips. She was clever, determined, and far too sweet-natured to refuse. "Mrs Ormsby, forgive me if I am being too forward, but why would your husband not wish to support your venture? It cannot have been that he didn't want you to be employed, when he readily accepted your assistance as his nurse."

The rosebud lips quirked into amusement. "Edgar did not wish me to sully my reputation by engaging in business for profit, Mr

Pyke. Nor did he want me to lure Richard away from 'pure' medicine."

"Perhaps he thought his own wealth was sufficient, without need of supplement," Wallace ventured.

"If you must know, I intended to donate the profits to a charitable medical service, which has been set up to benefit the native peoples. I attended a lecture by the director of the venture, who is of Ngāi Tahu descent. Indeed, it is from him that I first learned about the use of native plants as remedies."

Mrs Ormsby paused, as if judging their characters before continuing her disclosure. "The British came to this far corner of the world to seize land and natural resources. We left the Māori people with little more than devastating new diseases and broken promises. Providing the means to cure the diseases we gave them is surely the very least we can do, don't you think?"

Mrs Ormsby watched her words land on chastened ears. She rose from her chair. "If that is all, officers, I suppose you would like to speak to Cecilia."

Wallace rose and saw her to the door. "Miss Cecilia and Miss Lawson, as well as the household staff."

Edgar Ormsby's widow paused at the threshold. "I will send Cecilia and Nelly to you first."

While Wallace and Kelly conferred, Charlie slipped out of the room. He found Richard in his father's study, sorting documents with glum resolve.

"If you will pardon the intrusion, Mr Ormsby, I wanted to ask about your knowledge of your stepmother's plans to expand her natural remedies business and your father's views on the matter."

Richard set aside a pile of papers and gestured Charlie to the ladder-back chair in front of the desk. He sat back in his father's larger, well-padded leather chair behind the desk. "Mother and I plan to be partners in the venture. All we needed from Father was the capital to move to larger premises, in order to increase the production of her skin creams. Father opposed the scheme, because

152

he did not want his wife or son to be involved in 'sordid commerce', as he put it."

"How did you feel about his refusal?" Charlie watched for signs of anger, but Richard merely seemed resigned.

"Annoyed, naturally. The profits were going to a charitable foundation, so it wasn't as if Mother was attempting to amass independent wealth. I responded to my father's refusal by preparing a detailed business plan, complete with test results, in order to convince my father of the prospects. The doctors and nurses at the hospital couldn't get enough of my stepmother's hand cream. Hygiene is essential for reducing infection, you know. Medical practitioners must constantly wash their hands using carbolic soap, to the point where painful rashes develop. The cream was a godsend. I have no doubt at all that the business would have been a great success."

"Did your business proposal change your father's mind?" Charlie asked.

Richard shrugged. "We'll never know." He got up and went to a cabinet, rummaging through it until he found the document. "Here, you can see for yourself what I gave him. He probably never read it."

Richard had been impressively thorough, Charlie realised, as he flipped through pages of projected costs and profits, test results and endorsements. Each new meeting with the elder son raised his opinion of the man.

Tucked inside the document was a loose sheet of paper, on which someone had scribbled notes in a different hand, presumably that of Edgar Ormsby. He had clearly been convinced of the merits of the hand cream, to the extent of projecting potential profits from export of the product into the much larger British and American markets. The final paragraph said much of Edgar Ormsby's character – a note to talk to his attorney about setting up the business in his own name and altering the flow of profits accordingly, with a small percentage to be donated to worthy medical charities of his choice. The scoundrel planned to pull the business venture from under his wife and son's feet. He hadn't even had the decency to tell them.

Charlie kept his expression blank. "May I keep this copy for a day or two?"

"If you wish. I have my own copy. If you have no more questions, Mr Pyke, I had better return to my task, unless you have any information to share on the villain who sent my father to his grave."

"Not yet." Charlie rose from the chair. Surely Richard would not have handed the document over so calmly, if he had been aware of his father's notes. Even Richard Ormsby's mild temperament would have been driven to rage at his father's treachery, if he knew of it.

Charlie could hear Miss Cecilia Ormsby coming down the stairs, complaining loudly about being disturbed from her rest for the tedious task of talking to the constabulary. Time to return to the drawing room.

Cecilia entered in a swirl of black crepe. Whereas Mrs Ormsby's heavy black mourning gown made her look smaller and more vulnerable, Cecilia's fashionably cut and perfectly pressed gown achieved the opposite effect.

Edgar Ormsby's daughter was unable to add any substantive evidence to the investigation. Cecilia did not so much as glance at Charlie, reserving her remarks solely for the senior officer. After castigating the police for disturbing a household in mourning, Cecilia declared she knew nothing, heard nothing, saw nothing. Furthermore, she refused to believe her father's death wasn't anything more than a tragic heart attack. She flatly refused to take the reagent bottle, declaring herself entirely without interest in her stepmother's silly little hobby.

Wallace persevered until Cecilia admitted she had been in her bedroom most of Saturday (not helping her stepmother with the soirée), after arguing with her father at breakfast over his delay in approving her engagement. The rest of her statement, delivered

154

amidst pouts and recriminations, was centred around Gideon Alexander and the absolute importance of their marriage.

When Wallace informed her that her father's will had been rewritten again, Cecilia didn't so much as blink. "I know nothing about it, Inspector. I trusted my father to look after my best interests, as is proper." She rose from the chair. "And now, you must excuse me, for I feel a headache coming on."

Cecilia walked out the door. Wallace let her go. They heard a flurry of footsteps and a door opening nearby.

"Off to see brother Richard," Kelly said, "to see if she has lost or gained in the new will. I'll wager a shilling on sweet Cecilia convincing Richard to agree to the engagement before the day is done."

Not a wager Charlie would bet against, even for a penny.

"We'll need to interview her suitor," Wallace said. "If Doctor Ormsby turned him down, that's two more people with a motive."

The New Surgeon

Grace dashed through the doors of the hospital just in time for ward rounds. She was ill-prepared, but fortunately she was assigned to Doctor Beechworth, who went easy on her. On the positive side of the ledger, she was pleased to see Mrs Jamieson had recovered from her brush with a post-operative infection.

After rounds, Beechworth sent the other students off on assigned tasks, leaving Grace until last. "You've done more than your share of hospital work lately, Miss Penrose. Why don't you have a bite to eat, then observe surgery until it's time to go back for your afternoon lectures. But first, may I ask if the police are making any progress in the Ormsby investigation?"

Ordinarily, Grace was reluctant to accept any favours that might be mistaken as signs of feminine weakness. But a moment to sit and watch somebody else at work would be blissful. "I'm delighted to say that your wife and I are no longer suspected of contributing to Doctor Ormsby's death. However, the case is now being treated as a murder. I know I can rely on your discretion not to share that information, Doctor Beechworth. I cannot say anything further at this point."

"A terrible turn of events. But Ivy will be relieved that her part in it is over. Go and have a well-deserved break, Miss Penrose. You have achieved a great deal over the past few days."

Grace wasted no time in accepting his suggestion. She gulped down a plate of a substance that might optimistically be classified as edible sludge, served lukewarm by the hospital refectory, and made it to the viewing gallery of the operating theatre in time to see the first incision.

To her surprise, the surgeon was Gideon Alexander. The agile fingers she had noted at the soirée seemed to dance across the patient's body, making precise cuts, staunching bleeding, and stitching with finesse and speed. Despite his show of skill, Alexander didn't have the single-minded bluntness of most surgeons. He thanked the assistant who handed his instruments, shared a joke with the anaesthetist, and failed to anger at a dropped tray.

Two other onlookers shared the gallery, close enough for Grace to overhear their conversation.

"Who's the new surgeon?" one of the pair asked.

"Alexander's his name. On probation. Had to take over from Ormsby today, but I dare say he will become permanent given his obvious skill. He's a natural."

"Ormsby won't be happy to have his position taken. Where is the old boy today?"

"Haven't you heard? Ormsby suffered a fatal heart attack on Saturday night. I heard the old rogue took a young lady for a moonlit stroll. Must have been a rousing encounter to cause a heart attack. Lucky old coot, what a way to die."

Grace slipped out the back, wondering just how long it would be before the incident faded in people's memories. Faded? What was she thinking? Titillating rumours only ever grew. Her error of judgement might well follow her to her grave. She slunk out of the hospital, taking a seat in the sun in a small park nearby, which she shared with a handful of patients sporting plaster casts, bandages, crutches and sallow complexions.

Putting aside the onlooker's gossip, he had made a fair point. Gideon Alexander stood to benefit from Ormsby's death, by creating a vacancy on the small surgical team at the hospital. Hardly a strong motive to kill one's presumptive father-in-law, especially as there was more need for surgeons than qualified practitioners to fill the role. A man of Alexander's skill would have no trouble finding a job anywhere he went.

Speak of the devil. The man himself strolled across the park, nodding at the patients and stopping to exchange a word with one or two. No wonder Cecilia Ormsby guarded her suitor, for he was that rare being – a man attractive on both the interior and exterior. The miserable-looking patient opposite her was now laughing, as the surgeon signed his cast. Alexander stood up and spotted Grace.

"Miss Penrose, what a delight to see you again." He gestured at the seat beside her. "May I?"

"By all means, Doctor Alexander." Despite Alexander's bonhomie. Grace thought he looked exhausted. As a young surgeon on probation, she had little doubt the hospital got their pound of flesh.

"Do call me Gideon. I am not one for needless formality, especially as we will be working together at the hospital for the foreseeable future, I hope."

"And you must call me Grace." Was it her memory playing tricks on her, or was his upper-class accent distinctly more provincial today than it had been at the soirée? Not that she would blame him for covering up humble roots. People with the cards stacked against them did far worse than that in pursuit of a career and an advantageous match. "May I say how impressed I am with your surgical skills, Gideon. You made it look easy."

"Nothing more than a steady hand and a little needlework. Most ladies show equal or greater skill in their embroidery, but with rather less bloodshed, I trust." Gideon Alexander leaned back on the bench seat, stretching his limbs and breathing deeply. "I find a spell in the fresh air restores me after the intense concentration required during an operation. I noticed you in the viewing gallery, Grace. Are you interested in a surgical career?"

"Not in the least. Embroidery was never my strong suit. I intend to go into general practice. It was decent of you to step into the breech and fill in for Doctor Ormsby, especially as you must be mourning his passing."

"Keeping his practice going until other arrangements can be made seemed like the best way to help his family at this difficult time," Gideon replied. "Although I do wish I could spend more time comforting Cecilia. She is overcome with grief, as you might imagine. Despite his weak heart, nobody expected her father to die so suddenly."

Grace realised Gideon did not know the death was now being treated as murder. She debated between polite commiseration and probing further, with her curiosity winning out over decorum. "What will happen to Doctor Ormsby's practice?"

"I don't know. It will be up to his two sons, Richard and Henry, I daresay." Alexander blew out a long breath. "I don't mind admitting that Doctor Ormsby's untimely death has dealt my own prospects an unfortunate blow."

He slumped into silence, leaving Grace unsure as to exactly what he meant. "I'm sorry to hear that. May I ask why?"

"Forgive me if it sounds like I am thinking only of myself," Gideon replied. "I am, of course, devastated at Ormsby's passing. It's just … Well, the truth is, I asked Doctor Ormsby for Cecilia's hand in marriage last week. He requested a week to consider and made an appointment to give me his answer on Saturday at noon. I have to say I was on tenterhooks all week. I doubted Ormsby would agree, as Cecilia had told me her father was determined to find her a wealthy match."

"How cruel of Doctor Ormsby to make you wait a week for a response."

Gideon rallied to Ormsby's defence. "On the contrary, Miss Penrose. I viewed his deliberation as the sign of a caring father. Although it was awful watching my poor darling worrying herself into a terrible state. For no reason, as it turned out. Ormsby said he was delighted to accept my proposal. He said he had intended to do so all along."

"Congratulations, Gideon," Grace said. "How wonderful for you and Cecilia. Did he give a reason for the delay?"

Gideon let out a hollow laugh. "Oh, I think it's fair to say Ormsby wanted to make me wait, to test my character. Although he said the delay was to give him time to discuss the development of a new surgical facility with Mr Horncastle, the Chairman of the

159

Hospital Trustees. Ormsby saw it as a way of providing more work opportunities for me, as his future son-in-law. Unfortunately, he found himself in conflict with his wife and the other women supporting the women's ward."

"A difficult position for Doctor Ormsby to be in," Grace conceded. "We ladies would not have been so hard on him if we had known his motivation was to help you succeed."

"Ormsby may not always have made his intentions clear, but he was a man of principle. The solution he arrived at was simple in the end. He offered me a position as a surgeon in his own private practice, to supplement my earnings at the hospital, and withdrew his support for the new operating theatre at the hospital. I gather Ormsby suffered the slings and arrows of two rather stormy meetings on Saturday morning. One with Horncastle, who was understandably angry at the withdrawal of support. The other with Henry, who was furious with his father for offering me a position in his private practice."

Having been on the receiving end of Henry's spite herself, Grace didn't envy Gideon Alexander's position, although she felt sure his good nature would carry him through. "I suppose Henry had expectations of being taken into his father's practice eventually, although he is years away from being a trained surgeon. And you would be his brother-in-law, not an outsider."

"Exactly. It wasn't as if Ormsby was offering me a partnership, although he hinted that was an option if he was satisfied with my work. I confess he indicated his doubts about Henry's capacity to follow in his footsteps. Please don't share this information with Henry, Miss Penrose, but Doctor Ormsby was kind enough to refer to me as the son he always wanted. Perhaps Ormsby was simply angry that his own son wouldn't accept his decision."

"I assure you, Gideon, the reaction is not unique to you," Grace said. "With Henry, self-interest is always paramount. He sees the world for what it can give him, not what he can give back. Take comfort in the delight Cecilia must have had at hearing her father's decision. Richard and Mrs Ormsby too, I am sure."

Gideon sighed so deeply that his body slipped further down the bench seat. "Therein lies my misfortune. Because of work commitments, I left my meeting with Doctor Ormsby and came straight to the hospital. I had no time to share the good news with Cecilia. Besides, Doctor Ormsby wanted to announce the engagement and surgical collaboration as the finale to the soirée. And now he never will. As far as I can gather, he didn't even inform his wife of his decision. As it stands, I have neither the position nor the engagement."

If Henry had been high on Grace's list of suspects before, he had certainly shot to the top now. The police would have to know immediately. However, it was not her role to drag Gideon Alexander up the hill to convey his information to the investigating team. "My commiserations, Gideon. What rotten timing. But surely the family will honour the commitment Doctor Ormsby made to you? Indeed, I suspect nothing will stop Cecilia from securing both your engagement and your position. I know Richard likes you and will see the sense in keeping the practice going."

"I hope so, Grace. Talk of an engagement must wait, of course, for the mourning period to pass." Gideon glanced at his pocket watch. "I must get back to the hospital. Thank you for your kindness in listening to my problems, Grace. I hope to see you again soon."

Grace watched Doctor Alexander walk away, wishing she could warn him that the Ormsby family problems were a great deal worse than he imagined.

The Butler And The Valet

After Cecilia left the drawing room, Charlie showed Wallace and Kelly the business proposal written by Richard Ormsby. Wallace scanned it quickly and groaned.

Kelly shook his head in disbelief as he read of Doctor Ormsby's intention to take control of his wife's natural remedies business. "More suspects and motives than sand on St Kilda beach," Kelly grumbled. "Edgar Ormsby certainly had a flair for sowing dissent amongst his family and colleagues."

A rap on the door interrupted their discussion. A rap so similar to Mrs Simpson's that Charlie's mouth watered at the prospect. His prayers were answered when the housekeeper entered. Unfortunately, her trolley was absent.

"Mrs Ormsby requests you see Mr Pugh and Finch now," Mrs Simpson said, "as they have other duties to attend to. Afterwards, I will serve your luncheon, if that is acceptable. Mrs Ormsby asked me to convey her regrets that Miss Lawson is unavailable."

"Unavailable?" Wallace growled.

"Absent from the house, whereabouts unknown. Mr Henry is also still missing."

In the absence of Henry Ormsby and Miss Lawson, Wallace agreed the next priority was to interview the household staff. He looked relieved. Perhaps, like Charlie, he'd had more than enough family drama for one day.

Mr Pugh, the butler, refused the offered chair, preferring to stand with his white-gloved hands clasped behind his back. His uniform was immaculate and his face devoid of expression, despite the stiffly starched white collar digging into his neck under his perfectly shaved chin. A black armband circled his left upper arm in

162

a precise hoop. Pugh was as far away geographically as any butler could be from the stately drawing rooms of England, but he set a standard that would be familiar to his peers in Kensington or Mayfair.

Wallace settled into the familiar routine. "May I have your full name, age and place of birth, Mr Pugh."

"William Logan Pugh, age thirty-two, born in Lambeth, England."

Charlie took a closer look at this South Londoner who had polished his accent to fit his role. He had thought the butler was much older than thirty-two, because of Pugh's pinched face and receding hair. Despite being relatively young for a butler, Pugh had that special ability of fading into the background until needed, that marked a professional. Charlie was going to have to come up with an excuse to get Pugh's pristine white gloves off, if he was to get a fingerprint sample.

Pugh answered Wallace's questions with dignity and careful consideration, not giving in to the temptation to gossip or speculate. The butler agreed that Doctor Ormsby had appeared unwell at times during the soirée, but soldiered on regardless, as a gentleman ought to. The only discordant note of the evening had been when Mrs Beechworth caused a minor contretemps with her intemperate manner of questioning her host.

The butler had not seen Doctor Ormsby go out onto the terrace, as he was busy serving the port to the gentlemen in the library. Pugh's first inkling of the disaster to come was when Mr Henry Ormsby ran into the house, yelling "she killed him" and begging for a doctor and stretcher team with the utmost urgency. Pugh had run into Doctor Ormsby's surgery to gather a blanket and stretcher, before commanding three other men to sprint up the hill to his master's rescue. Pugh's composure slipped only when he described returning with the corpse and telephoning the police.

Charlie was impressed with the butler's combination of stately control and swift action in a crisis. A former military man, perhaps? He must be in fair shape, to run up a hill with a stretcher.

Wallace moved on to the events leading up to the soirée. Pugh's answers corroborated what they already knew. The house was in a state of organised chaos, with deliveries arriving throughout Saturday and extra staff hired to serve at the party.

"Mr Richard Ormsby was out on the Saturday morning, I understand, working at the hospital."

"That is correct, Inspector," Pugh said. "I let Mr Richard out before seven o'clock that morning. He returned via the side entrance not long before luncheon was served at one o'clock, as he had mislaid his keys again."

Wallace arched one of his woolly eyebrows. "Was he in the habit of forgetting his keys?"

"Mr Richard is a busy gentleman, Inspector. When I took the liberty of reminding him before he left, he assured me he had his keys. Nevertheless, one of the housemaids, Betsy, found them the next day, on the mantlepiece."

Kelly scribbled a note, while Wallace proceeded with the questioning. "Aside from the delivery men, were there any other visitors on Saturday, prior to the soirée commencing?"

"Two gentlemen had appointments with Doctor Ormsby in the morning. Mr Horncastle arrived on time for a short meeting at eleven o'clock. A matter of hospital business, I expect. Doctor Alexander had a private meeting with Doctor Ormsby at noon."

Wallace's nostrils flared, as they did when he scented vital new evidence. "Do you know the purpose of Doctor Alexander's appointment?"

"A personal matter, Inspector," Pugh replied. "I should not care to speculate, other than to say the gentlemen appeared to be on the very best of terms."

"How long did Alexander stay?"

"Almost three-quarters of an hour. Doctor Ormsby saw Doctor Alexander to the door himself and shook his hand with marked enthusiasm."

Charlie watched Pugh's rigid expression soften into a hint of a smile. The butler presumably knew, or deduced, that Alexander was about to be welcomed into the family. "I'm surprised Doctor Alexander did not stay to luncheon, given his intimacy with the family."

"I believe his services were required at the hospital."

Charlie made a note to check Alexander's arrival time at the hospital. He could have slipped upstairs to tamper with the tonic while the family was dining. But why would he, if he and Doctor Ormsby had parted on such good terms?

Wallace drummed his fingers on the small table beside him, signalling a difficult question was being formulated. "Did Doctor Ormsby have any interactions with family members, beyond the normal civilities?"

Pugh's lips pressed so tightly together, he appeared to be physically holding back his words. "I am not certain I know what you are asking, Inspector."

"Did he have any arguments or minor disagreements? Or other unusual discussions? Please bear in mind that we are investigating a death, Mr Pugh. Your admirable discretion will only impede truth."

Pugh straightened his already stiff spine. "Mr Henry had a meeting with his father at about ten o'clock in the morning." He cleared his throat. "I overheard raised voices, but I do not know the nature of their disagreement. Suffice to say, Mr Henry slammed the door so hard on his departure that a vase was toppled and shattered. Royal Worcester. Irreplaceable, of course."

"That will be all for now, Mr Pugh. If any other information comes to your attention, I want to hear about it without delay. Could you send in Doctor Ormsby's valet, please?" Wallace consulted the staff list. "Finch."

Finch walked into the room a step behind Pugh, imitating the butler's posture and actions. The imitation fell short of perfection. Finch's black armband was slightly wrinkled, his collar askew, and his expression betrayed an unseemly curiosity – but that only made

165

him seem more human than the butler. He also had a fresh-faced youthfulness that made him seem much younger than Pugh. Finch hesitated at the offer of a seat, before choosing to stand to attention.

The valet gave his name as Ronald Ian Finch, aged twenty-five. A recent immigrant to New Zealand, born in Glasgow but raised in London, which explained the Scottish lilt Finch struggled to disguise under a layer of the Queen's English. Charlie wasn't one to judge. His own Chinese ancestry was rarely on display outside of his own family circle, because of the pervasive bigotry shown by British immigrants to anyone whose origins lay east of the English Channel.

Under Wallace's gentle probing, Finch confirmed he acted as both valet and footman, attending to the needs of Doctor Ormsby and his sons, serving at the dinner table, and other tasks as required. He professed to being upset at Doctor Ormsby's death, with a strong undercurrent of distress at the possibility of losing his position. He showed no reaction to being asked about his activities on the Saturday of the supper party. Finch reeled off a long list of duties, involving spots removed from lapels, the shining of shoes, selection of the correct evening attire, and his usual job of ensuring Doctor Ormsby was given his medicine at afternoon tea.

"Are you sure he took his heart medication?" Wallace asked. "On such a busy day, it would be easy to forget."

Finch's poise slipped at the question. His fingers twisted together as he rushed out his answer. "Mrs Ormsby was most insistent that Doctor Ormsby took it every day. As soon as I heard the bell ring for afternoon tea, I retrieved the tonic from the bathroom cabinet and brought it down to him, as I always do. I'll swear to it, Inspector. If Doctor Ormsby died of heart failure, it was not because I forgot his medicine. God's truth, sir."

"No need for alarm, Finch. We are merely establishing the facts. Did you notice anything different about the heart tonic that day?"

The genteel accent dropped away entirely under stress. "I was so busy, I just grabbed the bottle and ran downstairs. I handed him the spoon, but he took the tonic and gulped it, as he always did, then took a wee gulp of coffee and a bite of cake."

166

"Did you notice if the bottle was full, Finch?"

Finch shook his head, then reconsidered. "As I recall, I had opened a fresh bottle several days before, so it was probably more than half empty by Saturday."

"And when a new bottle is required, do you fetch it yourself from Mrs Ormsby's workroom?" Wallace asked.

"No, sir. Miss Lawson brings in the tonic as needed and puts it in the bathroom cabinet."

Charlie held out one of the reagent bottles and asked if Finch had seen one like it. Finch took at the bottle as if he'd been asked a trick question, then shook his head.

Wallace took over the questioning again. "You must have been in and out of Doctor Ormsby's bedroom and dressing room frequently during the day. Did you notice anyone else there?"

Finch paused to consider his answer. Unlike Pugh, the valet wore his emotions on the surface. In this case, it was a deepening frown. "Did Mr Ormsby not die of a weak heart after all, Inspector?"

"Just answer the question, please, Finch."

"Yes, sir, of course. Mrs Ormsby came through the connecting door twice during the morning, as I recall. Once to remind me to press her husband's suit and once to select his tie and cufflinks. When I came back from pressing the suit, Miss Cecilia was coming out of her father's room. She appeared cross and asked me if I had seen her father, which I had not. Miss Cecilia came close to colliding with Mr Richard on the way out. He stayed only long enough to pass on to his father a message from Mr Pugh about the selection of wine and port for the evening."

Wallace sensed a hesitation. "Anybody else?"

Finch appeared to be taking an inordinate interest in a picture over Wallace's shoulder. "Mr Henry visited his father not long before afternoon tea. I left the room, as words were exchanged that were not meant for my ears. Mr Henry pushed past me on the stairs a few minutes later, as I returned. Doctor Ormsby had gone into his wife's room, so I busied myself with preparing his clothes for the evening. More than that, I am unable to say."

"Unable or unwilling?" Wallace queried.

"Unable, sir. I did not wish to be accused of eavesdropping, so I went downstairs to fetch a fresh jug of water."

"Very commendable, Finch. Were you away from Doctor Ormsby's room for any period of the day?"

"Frequently, Inspector. While Doctor Ormsby was occupied with meetings and luncheon, I completed other tasks downstairs. And had my own midday meal, of course."

"Finally, I have to ask about Doctor Ormsby's illness. Were you aware he was feeling unwell on Saturday evening?"

"Yes, sir. He began to feel unwell when I was dressing him for the soirée, shortly after taking a light dinner. Doctor Ormsby blamed the meal, presuming it to have contained cheese, which upsets his stomach. Cook is normally very careful, but I suppose it is possible she made an error, with all the other food preparation to be done."

"Can you describe his symptoms?"

Finch's nose wrinkled at the mere memory of it. "I confess I did not know his reaction to cheese was so severe. He had to ring for me twice during my evening break, to remove spots of … stomach contents … off his clothes. I don't mean to be indiscreet, Inspector, but Betsy, the housemaid, told me she was called to, er, freshen the water closet, several times. A very nasty stomach upset, Inspector."

Wallace hastened to move on to the next question. "Indeed, Finch. One final question. You will be aware that Mr Henry Ormsby disappeared after his father's body was brought back to the house. An odd reaction to his father's death, I'm sure you would agree. Have you seen Henry? Do you know where he might be?"

"No, sir." Finch's hand flicked up to touch his lips. Charlie was sure he was lying.

Wallace evidently thought the same. "Might I remind you that this is a formal police inquiry? Any person withholding evidence may be charged with obstruction of justice. If you have any information about Henry Ormsby's disappearance, I strongly suggest you divulge it now."

Finch's hands dropped behind his back, the intensity of his grasp showing in the tension in his shoulders. He wavered for a moment, before coming down on the side of his own interests. "After Mr Pugh had telephoned the police, he sent me to the gate to flag them down and show them to the rear entrance. I saw Mr Henry leave the house with a travelling bag."

"Alone?"

"Yes, Inspector."

"Did Henry see you? Talk to you?"

"Not at first, as I was in the shadows. I called out to him to find out if he needed assistance. Mr Henry was startled by the sound of my voice but assured me he did not need my help." Again, a downward flick of the eyes.

"How did he seem?"

This time, Finch answered instantly and instinctively. "Frightened."

Wallace frowned at the unexpected answer. "Did Henry say anything else? Any hint as to why he would be frightened when his father had, as far as he knew, suffered heart failure?"

"Mr Henry said something like: 'I'll not stay in that house a minute longer, Finch. Tell them I'm devastated by my father's death and need time to come to terms with the tragedy.' He tossed a coin into my hands and hurried off down the road. That's all, I swear."

Wallace continued to look at Finch for several seconds, but the dangling silence did not draw forth any further admissions. "If you hear anything at all regarding the whereabouts of Henry Ormsby, you will inform the police directly."

"Yes, sir."

"Thank you. That will be all for now, Finch."

The valet departed with more speed than dignity. Wallace rose from the armchair and circled his neck until it clicked. "At least we know that Henry Ormsby left of his own free will. I can't say I like

169

the sound of him being too frightened to stay in his own home. He clearly believed right from the start that his father's death was not from natural causes. We need to know why."

"When he came back to the house after seeing his father die, Henry's first words were: 'She killed him'," Kelly reminded them. "Everyone assumed he meant Miss Penrose, but perhaps he had some inkling that another woman in the house wanted Ormsby dead. A woman who might not stop at killing Doctor Ormsby, if Henry was believed to be the main financial beneficiary of his father's will."

"The obvious suspect is his stepmother, whom he mistrusts," Charlie said. "Or Lawson, who is close to his stepmother."

"Cecilia was angry at her father too, over his apparent refusal to allow her engagement to Alexander," Kelly added. "If she believed her father had disinherited Richard, then her share of the estate might be larger, making her more of a catch to an eligible bachelor. It all comes down to who knew about the provisions of the will."

Wallace paced the room, looking grim. "We'll have to get the attorney to confirm what happened with the wills. I don't like the smell of this. Far too much drama going on in this household, if you ask me, all of it orchestrated by Edgar Ormsby. I would give my right arm to know what was said at those meetings Ormsby had the morning of the soirée, with Henry Ormsby, Gideon Alexander, and Mr Horncastle."

Kelly finished scribbling his notes and got up to stretch. "I hate these domestic murders. Everyone had a motive and everyone had access, especially as Richard had left his keys lying around. No doubt the whole family is hiding secrets and long-simmering tensions. Give me a simple stabbing any day, preferably committed by a ruffian I can run down and tackle to the ground. All this sitting around in a stuffy drawing room makes my brain hurt."

"Ah, Declan lad," Charlie said, rocking back in his chair with a grin, "after all the scones you ate, you'd be hard pressed to run down a wee lassie like that pretty housemaid, let alone tackle her to the ground."

Declan let out a derisive puff of air. "You're a fine one to talk, Charlie boy. I didn't see you holding back when food was on offer."

"There'd be no need for me to run, as she'd not be running away from me. Unlike your good self, I am blessed with a face that doesn't scare the ladies away."

"You're so full of blarney, Pyke. Any maid in her right mind would run a mile."

Wallace shook his head, as if in despair at the younger generation, but failed to hide a smile. "If you ask me, you'd both be laughed off for acting like a couple of foolish schoolboys. Now, lads, we'd best remember it's not only the family who had access to the poison. Any of the servants could have taken the bottle of tutu from the workroom and added it to Ormsby's tonic, despite their claims to the contrary."

Charlie knew Wallace was right. In fact, with all the comings and goings upstairs, the safest time to enter Ormsby's bathroom unseen was when the family was at luncheon. Who knew what went on behind the discreet façade of servitude? He certainly didn't envy Finch being at his master's beck and call all day. A man would have to crack under the pressure, eventually.

"If this was a ladies' novel," Kelly said, "Ormsby would have a secret love-child plotting revenge from below stairs. My pick is the housemaid, Betsy Dean. Pretty little lass, perfect for the love-child character. Or perhaps she was harbouring a burning passion for one of the Ormsby sons."

"Spare me your fevered imagination, Kelly," Wallace begged. "We are not living in a Brontë novel, thank the Lord. As if there are not enough complications in the real world."

"Did you say the housemaid's surname is Dean?" Charlie asked. "Beechworth's list of patients who have died under Ormsby's scalpel included a Euan Dean."

"There now, did I not tell you it was the housemaid?" Kelly crowed.

Wallace glared at his detective constable, although the reprimand was lost when the side of his lip ticked up at the same time. "What a day. I'll be happy to see the housekeeper with our promised lunch. And for goodness' sake, Kelly, don't accuse Mrs Simpson of being Ormsby's secret mistress or any other ridiculous fantasy."

"A Prussian spy come to overthrow the country and steal all our sheep?" Charlie suggested.

Declan stifled a snort of laughter. Even Wallace had to bend his head over his notes to conceal a grin.

Mischievous Maids

In the manner of all superior housekeepers, Mrs Simpson chose that precise moment to rap on the door. Charlie was on his feet in an instant, helping her to wheel in a trolly bearing a welcome pot of tea and platter laden with dainty savouries, cakes and triangular sandwiches (crusts removed).

Mrs Simpson confirmed that Betsy Dean's grandfather had died on Ormsby's operating table. "Nobody blamed Doctor Ormsby, Inspector. Dear old fellow didn't say a word about his inflamed appendix until it burst. Our Mr Dean never uttered a single complaint in his life and always went about his work with cheerful diligence."

"Had Mr Dean worked here long, Mrs Simpson?"

"Ever since the Ormsby's arrival, Inspector. The Dean family travelled to New Zealand on the same ship as the Ormsby family, nine years ago."

Mrs Simpson assured the detectives that Betsy Dean had no cause to enter the workroom. Betsy did clean the bedrooms, always working alongside the other housemaid. On Saturday, the maids had been ordered to spend as little time as necessary attending to the upstairs rooms, so they could help downstairs with the party preparations.

When Mrs Simpson left, the trio of ravenous detectives attacked the food like a flock of kea around a picnic, pronouncing the cook a marvel and the housekeeper a saviour. Charlie and Declan Kelly were eying up the remaining slice of seed cake, when there was another knock on the door.

Charlie's heart skipped a beat at the welcome sight of Grace Penrose, her face red with exertion. "I hope you haven't run up the hill to get the last piece of cake, Grace?" Charlie asked, as Declan extended a talon and whipped it from under his fingers.

"Forget the cake. I have news," Grace panted. "I've been talking with Gideon Alexander. He was here on Saturday."

"Your timing is impeccable, Miss Penrose," Wallace replied. "Alexander's meeting with Ormsby was top of my mind. Please enlighten us."

"Gideon came by invitation, expecting to be turned down as a suitor to Ormsby's daughter. To Gideon's surprise, Ormsby not only accepted his proposal of marriage to Cecilia but offered him a position as assistant surgeon in Ormsby's private practice. Ormsby told Gideon that he had supported the new operating theatre at the hospital to give his prospective son-in-law more work. However, with Mrs Ormsby being strongly in favour of the women's ward, Ormsby had to devise a solution that would keep both his daughter and his wife happy. Needless to say, Gideon was also delighted."

Charlie did not comment on Grace's informal use of the new surgeon's first name, but he couldn't help but wonder how well they knew each other. "Presumably this also explains the meetings earlier in the day with Henry Ormsby and Mr Horncastle."

"Exactly," Grace said. "Gideon confirmed that Doctor Ormsby had broken the news to Henry and Horncastle that morning. Horncastle was angry at Ormsby for withdrawing his support for the proposed new operation theatre."

"And Henry?" Charlie asked.

"Absolutely furious, according to Gideon, and I don't doubt it. Henry has ambitions as a surgeon himself, so he did not react well to the news that his father was taking on Gideon as an assistant surgeon. His father assured him it didn't alter his intention to keep a position open for Henry, once he was qualified, as long as his son proved himself able. Gideon indicated Ormsby had his doubts that Henry would be up to the role. Ormsby even called Gideon the son he always wanted."

Grace was certainly earning her consulting fee for the case, Charlie thought, although she didn't seem to consider talking to Gideon Alexander a chore. More to the point, Henry Ormsby's fury at his father gave him a compelling motive, especially if he was still under the impression he would inherit the bulk of the estate if he acted quickly. Henry's disappearance after the soirée looked more suspicious at every turn.

Wallace evidently agreed, as he was practically purring with satisfaction. "We need to make Henry Ormsby our top priority. What is this Alexander fellow like, Miss Penrose? Has he any cause to want his future father-in-law dead?"

Grace glanced sideways at Charlie, before fixing her gaze on Wallace. "Doctor Alexander is an exceptional surgeon who treats assistants and patients with respect and consideration, which is rare. I find him pleasant to talk to, and he's handsome without being vain. I don't wonder at Ormsby welcoming him as a son-in-law, despite Gideon's lack of wealth and position. He is a recent immigrant, having trained in London, so he can have no grudge against Ormsby. Indeed, Ormsby's death is a major blow to Gideon's prospects, as Doctor Ormsby had not yet made a formal announcement about either his engagement to Cecilia or the assistant surgeon position."

"Sounds like Henry Ormsby had far more reason to murder his father than Gideon Alexander did," Kelly said.

"Have you talked to Henry yet?" Grace asked.

"Nobody knows where Henry is," Charlie replied. "Perhaps you could ask your fellow medical students, Grace?"

"You might mention that we have half the Dunedin police force looking for him, so he'd better hand himself in," Kelly added. "Getting back to Doctor Alexander, I find it odd that Ormsby approved of the match, yet Cecilia was reported as being angry at her father on Saturday."

Grace had an answer for this too. "Ormsby asked Gideon to keep their agreement a secret, so he could announce the engagement and the assistant surgeon's job at the soirée. Cecilia was still under the impression that her father disapproved of the match. A cruel

175

tease, given the depth of Cecilia's feelings for Gideon Alexander. Frankly, I'd scarcely blame Cecilia for being angry with her father."

"Doctor Ormsby seemed to have a talent for infuriating everyone around him," Kelly agreed. "On the day of his murder, we know that Cecilia, Henry, Richard and Mr Horncastle all had cause to be angry with Ormsby. Agnes too, for that matter, and Lawson and Mrs Ormsby."

"Probably most of the rest of the household and half of Dunedin too," Grace agreed cheerfully. "If you have no further questions, I must depart. I have already missed half of my anatomy class. I'm sure you wouldn't want me to qualify as a doctor without understanding the form and function of the mitral valve." With a twirl of skirts and a jaunty wave, Grace headed for the door.

Charlie lurched from his seat in time to open it for her. "My mitral valve is in your hands, so go easy on it," he whispered. "I'll even throw in my atrium and ventricle, so you have the full set."

Her eyes sparkled, then she twitched her nose and sniffed, just enough for him to notice, and was gone.

Kelly burst into laughter. "Is it not enough that Grace has started to talk like a detective? Now you're spouting like a doctor."

Charlie was still standing by the door, inhaling the last traces of the intoxicating scent. He turned and sauntered back to his chair. "Better get used to it, Declan. I'm not going anywhere."

"What the blazes was that all that about?" Wallace said. "In my day, young lads used to court their sweethearts with flowers and the uplifting words of Robbie Burns."

"Anatomical parts of the heart are romantic too, to the right woman," Charlie assured him.

"If you say so," Wallace replied. "I'm off to telephone the station to find out if they've located Henry Ormsby yet."

Declan Kelly went back to scribbling notes, while scooping crumbs off his plate with a forefinger.

Charlie stood at the window, fidgeting. As he watched, two girls walked across the garden, carrying a heavy basket between them.

One was dark and sturdy, the other was all plump curves and coppery-brown curls escaping from under her starched white cap. When the curvy one turned, Charlie realised she was the maid who had cleared the morning tea, Betsy Dean.

The urge to move his limbs and breathe fresh air had him dashing for the door, before Wallace returned. As Charlie hurried to catch up with the girls, Betsy glanced back and stumbled. She extended her hand to him, which left him with no option but to help her up. He picked up the basket and carried it to the clothesline, where rows of blankets were already airing in the breeze on this unseasonably warm day. The basket was heavy, but he flexed his muscles and gave the girls his most beguiling smile. He was rewarded with a batting of eyelashes and giggles from Betsy and a rolling of the eyes from the sturdy lass.

"Name's Charlie," he said. "This basket is mighty heavy for two bonny lasses to be carrying on their own."

"Get away with ye," Betsy replied. "Cheeky copper."

"Cheeky maybe, but not a copper." Charlie picked up one end of a blanket and pegged it out, passing the other end to her. The other girl grabbed a rug and went to the far end of the line, beating the dust out with forceful strokes. "And what would your name be, seeing as I am offering to help?"

"I'm Betsy and her with the sulky face is Flo."

"You must be Betsy Dean, granddaughter of Euan Dean? I heard your grandfather passed away recently. My condolences for your loss." It was a clumsy start, but Betsy took the bait.

"Aye, my granddad was dear to my heart. Kept an eye on me all my life, what with me being an orphan. My uncle's family took me in, God bless them, but it was my granddad who cared the most. Got me this position, when I was old enough."

"Everybody needs somebody special on their side," Charlie agreed. "Must be hard to stay on here without him, especially if he died here."

177

Betsy stood back, planting her hands on her hips, taking the measure of him. "I've a good place here, Mr Charlie Whoever-you-are. Doctor Ormsby even paid for a headstone, though my granddad's death was not his fault. Or so they say, on account of my granddad being so poorly before he asked for help. I only wish Mrs Ormsby had been home, for nothing ever goes wrong when she is helping."

Betsy's big eyes sparkled with tears, but she held them back. Instead, she picked up a blanket and angled her face away from him. Charlie was left with the feeling she was not as forgiving of Ormsby as she suggested, but unlikely to admit it.

He took up the other end of her blanket. "Does Mrs Ormsby help with the surgical operations?"

"Oh, aye. She's a nurse. Keeps the operating room spotless, she does. She's training me to clean it properly with carbolic. Gotta scrub right into the corners on account of The Germs. Terrible on the hands, but she has a cream to fix that too. I know she hands the doctor his tools and whatnot during surgeries and even stitches the patients up, but I'm not supposed to tell anyone."

"An impressive lady, Mrs Ormsby. Does she get you to clean her own workroom like that too?"

"Not likely. Lawson insists on doing it. What business does a lady's maid have with a mop in her hand, is what I'd like to know, though she's no better than the rest of us. Poking about in there, making who knows what potions and poisons. It ain't right. Henry's been in to see what they're up to. Wouldn't surprise me if Nelly was brewing a love potion to lure the heir of the house into her bed, just like—"

"Betsy Dean, that's quite enough of that foolish gossip." The other housemaid glared at Betsy until her curly head bowed in contrition. "You are such a gabbleguts. You ought not to be talking to strange men, especially about the family what pays your wages."

Betsy's cheekiness bounced back in an instant. "Strange man indeed. If you can't trust a copper, who can you trust?" She ran her eyes down his body with a brazenness that shocked Charlie. "I'm

178

not going to turn down a bit of help, am I, with all the work we've got on. Polishing the silver, airing and pressing all the mourning clothes, covering the mirrors, cleaning the guest rooms before the funeral. Blimey, just put him in the ground and get on with life, I say. That's what us poor folks have to do."

"Betsy Dean, you have gone too far. If the mistress heard you spouting such disrespectful claptrap, you'd be out on your plump rear end. I'll tell her myself if you don't shut your trap and get on with your work." Flo yanked the last blanket out of the basket and stalked off, not seeing the rude gesture Betsy made behind her back.

"All very well for her to say, but it wasn't Flo who had to clean up the disgusting mess after Doctor Ormsby was sick. Both ends firing at once, if you know what I mean. I was ready to hand my notice in, I can tell you, especially with that little imp of a daughter hanging around, making fun of me." Betsy shot a glance at the other girl. "I'd better do as Flo says."

Charlie didn't want to get the feisty Betsy into any more trouble. "Well now, Betsy Dean, it would seem we are out of blankets and out of questions, so I'll be wishing you a good day."

"Cheeky blimmin' copper," she called after him, with a chuckle in her voice. "Don't be a stranger now, Charlie me lad."

Charlie was on his way back across the garden, when the gardener-stableman stepped out from behind a camellia bush. The young man tugged his cap politely, but his hand gripped a rake so that it blocked Charlie's path.

"Lovely afternoon," Charlie said.

"Aye, that it is, sir," the young man said. "I'm sure you're just doing your job, but you don't want to be taking no notice of our Betsy. Reads too many silly stories, does Betsy. Puts foolish ideas in her head. No good can come from reading, for the likes of us."

In Charlie's opinion, it was the gardener who was foolish. Telling a policeman not to listen to a witness was the best way to make the policeman want to know more. "I was just out for a breath of fresh air, Mr …"

"Grant."

"Were you working on Saturday, Mr Grant?"

"No. I worked until my back ached all week to get the garden looking perfect. Mrs Ormsby said I could have Saturday off."

Charlie stood his ground until Grant withdrew the rake and mumbled about getting on with his work. Charlie watched him disappear into the camellias, making a mental note to come back with reagent bottles to fingerprint Grant and Betsy. Not that he thought them likely suspects, but the gardener's defensiveness seemed excessive. Probably it was nothing more than Grant protecting Betsy, or perhaps fancying her himself.

"Chatting up the pretty housemaid, Pyke?" Wallace said, from his spot at the window, when Charlie came back into the drawing room.

"All in the name of duty, sir."

Wallace grunted. "Worth the hardship, was it?"

"I reckon so, sir," Charlie replied. "Betsy Dean was devoted to her grandfather, but she doesn't seem to harbour murderous feelings towards Ormsby for his death. She also confirmed that Ormsby was seriously ill, 'firing from both ends' as she poetically put it. More importantly, she has seen Henry snooping in the workroom. She called him Henry with such familiarity, I wonder if their relationship is entirely proper. Betsy has a flirtatious way about her, to say the least."

"I know the type," Wallace sighed. "Too many tawdry novels putting ideas in her head."

"That's just what the gardener said, when he warned me not to believe anything Betsy told me. The gardener certainly didn't like me talking to her. Bordering on aggressive, he was. He says he wasn't here on Saturday, but it might be worth checking."

Wallace made a note in his notebook. "Betsy's relationship with Henry Ormsby warrants a closer look too. If the maid was sweet on Henry, how far would she go to help him? Betsy had daily access to Doctor Ormsby's bathroom cabinet, after all."

"Henry would have had to make it worth her while to take such a risk." Charlie paced back and forth across the drawing room, trying to fit all the pieces of the puzzle together. "Betsy is no wilting violet. She saw how Mrs Ormsby elevated her position by marriage after the first Mrs Ormsby died."

"You think Betsy may have been persuaded that Henry would marry her?" Wallace asked. "I suppose they have known each other for a long time. In fact, they would have been thirteen or fourteen years old when they were on the voyage over from Britain. An age where social class is less of a barrier to friendship. It must be odd to be living in the same household now in such divergent roles."

"True enough," Charlie said. "Betsy called the lady's maid Nelly and Lawson in the same sentence, so she must find it confusing. Betsy knows Lawson has designs on Richard Ormsby. Her exact words were: 'Wouldn't surprise me if Nelly was brewing a love potion to lure the heir of the house into her bed, just like–'. She never finished the sentence, but I can only assume she thought Mrs Ormsby had lured her husband by such means too."

"Love potions? What a load of horse manure. Mrs Ormsby is not the type of woman to need any inducement beyond her own natural charms."

Charlie had to hide a smile at the thought of the crusty old detective noticing Mrs Ormsby's undoubted charms. "Getting back to Henry Ormsby, have Elliot and Weston had any luck tracking him down?" Charlie wished he hadn't asked when he saw the thundercloud gathering over Wallace's head.

"Not a peep. I've sent Kelly out to do what he can. The Chief had to reassign Elliot and Weston to a fatal stabbing on the wharves. Lucky sods. How in the name of all that's holy does the Chief expect me to solve a case when I've insufficient men to do a proper job? Sure you won't change your mind about joining the team, Pyke?"

"You've got my full attention on the case already, sir." To Charlie's surprise, he felt not a single pang of temptation to re-join the police force. If asked, he would have put it down to the lure of

181

receiving ten pounds to solve a single case. The truth was that he was relishing the greater freedom to make his own way in the world.

Wallace ran his finger down a list of people in the household. "I believe there is only the cook, the kitchen maid and the laundry maid left to interview, not that they'll have anything worth saying. After that, I'll rouse the Chief to give us more men to search for Henry Ormsby. Kelly is setting up meetings with the attorney, Doctor Alexander, and Mr Horncastle for tomorrow morning."

"What would you like me to do?" Charlie asked.

Wallace grunted. "After cavorting with the pretty housemaid, I dare not let you near the kitchen maid. Nor the cook, who will take one look at you and get side-tracked into feeding your insatiable appetite with dainties. You may as well go home, Pyke."

Charlie wasn't fooled for an instant by Wallace's gruff dismissal. "Or I could team up with Miss Penrose to interrogate Henry Ormsby's known associates."

Wallace met his smile with his own predatory grin. "I'm beginning to see the advantages of this arrangement. Two skilled investigators at no cost, whose methods I trust, but whose behaviour I am not responsible for. Track down Henry Ormsby and there's a pint of best bitter with your name on it."

Missing Heir

The last lecture for the day finished with a long-winded explanation of something or other, which Grace had been too distracted to catch. Several students dashed for the exit as soon as the tedious drawl of words sputtered to an end. Others had sneaked out early or dozed off.

Grace had spent most of the lecture watching Henry's group of friends passing notes and carving obscenities into the desktop. She dreaded the moment she would have to approach them to ask where Henry was hiding. With luck, they would leave before she had a chance to catch them.

Unfortunately, they lingered at the end of the lecture, almost as if they were waiting for her. Grace certainly didn't want to be caught alone with them, so she grabbed her satchel, intending to wait for them at the entrance to the medical school building. They followed close behind her, setting the hairs on the back of her neck on end.

Outside, the grounds seemed unusually quiet. Henry's friends quickly surrounded her.

She had no choice but to brazen it out. "Gentlemen, how fortuitous. I was hoping to ask if you knew where Henry Ormsby is staying."

"Well, isn't that convenient? As it happens, Ormsby wishes to speak to you, Penrose."

The speaker was a student called Clement, who wasn't one of Henry's inner circle of friends. Clement had a reputation for getting things done for money, such as supplying exam answers and drugs to facilitate late-night, last-minute cramming. Perhaps he had branched out into harbouring criminals. Ironically, Clement came from one of the wealthier families in Dunedin, suggesting his dubious dealings were more for pleasure than desperation for funds.

Grace held her ground, despite being unnerved by Clement standing so close. "If you give me Henry's address, I will arrange to see him."

"Do you take me for a fool, Penrose? You'll bring the rozzers." Clement seized her arm in an iron grip, while his accomplice grabbed her other arm. "You're coming with me. I'd advise you not to scream, like the pitiful woman you are, or I might be forced to hurt you."

Henry's friends had backed away at the first sign of aggression. Still, that left two against one. Grace considered the option of breaking Clement's grip and throwing him to the ground. After previous experiences with men like him, Grace had taken the precaution of learning the art of defence from a street-wise friend. However, she did want to speak to Henry and had no wish to make an enemy, despite the temptation of showing up her abductor as a braggart. Besides, there was a fair chance it wouldn't work and she would end up getting hurt for nothing.

On the other hand, Grace was not willing to go quietly and risk the other students claiming they did not realise anything was wrong. "Unhand me, Clement, you are hurting me." She struggled, ineffectually, before turning to the crowd cowering behind her. "You gentlemen bear witness. I am being abducted without my consent. Don't just stand there, get help."

Clement raised a hand to slap her but thought better of it as rumblings spread through the crowd. Instead, he yanked her towards an enclosed carriage, already waiting on the street. The two men hoisted Grace inside. Clement followed, keeping a painful grip on her arm, while the other directed the coachman.

As the carriage rolled up the street, she glimpsed a large mass bursting through the goggle-eyed onlookers, scattering them in all directions. Grace prayed it was Charlie, coming to her rescue. She had never quite fathomed how he knew when she was in trouble, but she was profoundly grateful for his sixth sense.

Fortunately, they didn't have far to go, and most of that was at a slow uphill plod. Grace had a moment of doubt when her captor pulled her from the carriage outside a grand house overlooking the city. The street was empty. Grace put up a struggle, to allow her rescuer time to catch up, but Clement was having none of it. He dragged her into the house, took her to a quiet parlour, and departed.

Henry Ormsby huddled close to the fire. "Penrose, you came."

"Your pet ape gave me little choice. Do you know how many years in gaol you would get for abduction?"

Henry lifted tired eyes to her. "Don't be annoying, Penrose. I simply asked Clement to tell you I wanted to speak to you."

"Clement abducted me in front of a crowd of witnesses, forcibly enough to leave marks on my forearms. However, I do wish to speak with you, Ormsby, so perhaps we can overlook the commission of a serious criminal offence for the moment. Especially if you can provide a cup of tea. Being accused of murder makes one thirsty."

Henry got up and rang a bell, then resumed his seat by the fire. "I wish to apologise for the misunderstanding on Saturday night, Penrose. When I yelled 'she killed my father', I naturally assumed everyone would know I meant my stepmother. I had no intention of implicating you. I knew if I didn't leave the house, I would be the next corpse."

Grace allowed that to pass, although she hoped Henry would be given a stern talking to by DI Wallace. "Why would anyone believe your stepmother a murderess?"

They were interrupted by tea, which arrived so quickly, Clement must have seen to it. Henry had to be paying him well to hide him, and act as his servant and henchman. Grace waited for Henry to play the host and pour but saw to it herself when he didn't move. He seemed a diminished version of the conceited rich boy she knew from medical school. Either he was worried about being charged with murder or he was frightened of whoever really did kill his father.

No sooner had Grace poured and taken her first sip, when there was a scuffle outside and the door burst open. The snug parlour assumed doll's house proportions in the presence of a six-foot male frame, bulging with muscle, sinew and fury. Grace almost dropped the cup in surprise. Her rescuer was not Charlie after all.

Henry's eyes bulged at the apparition. He shrank into a ball and whimpered. "Don't kill me, I beg you. I haven't hurt her."

"You'd better not have, lad. And don't bother calling your vile associate. He fell onto my fist and is taking a short nap on the floor, prior to being arrested for abduction and the attempted assault of a policeman."

Grace gaped at her heavy-breathing saviour.

"Are you hurt, Grace?" Charlie's father asked, mistaking her shocked silence for distress.

"A little scalded, as your dramatic entrance made me spill my tea, but otherwise fine. Charming of you to drop by. May I introduce Mr Henry Ormsby, who was about to tell me why he thinks his stepmother is a murderess. Ormsby, this is Sergeant Pyke."

Henry looked between her and Charlie's father, his alarm tinged with confusion. "*This* is your admirer, Penrose. The policeman who killed a man for you? Isn't he a little…"

"A little what, Mr Ormsby?" Sergeant Pyke asked, his eyes twinkling.

Henry was struck dumb. His confusion and alarm doubled a moment later, when a second six-foot male shoved his way into the parlour. "How many more of you are there?" he squeaked.

"I'd have thought two Pykes quite enough to deal with any situation," Grace said, as she went to the sideboard for more cups. "In fact, I usually find one Pyke to be more than sufficient."

"Thanks for leading the way, Pa," Charlie said. "I'd have left you to it, only I was too embarrassed to stay outside the medical school, watching Ma tear shreds off those young fellows who stood by while Grace was abducted. Now, how about you take a seat, while I squeeze the truth out of this little scumbag."

"Perhaps we could all take a seat," Grace suggested. "Ormsby, allow me to introduce Mr Charles Pyke, private detective and personal protection agent. Or rather, one of my team of personal protection agents, or so it would seem. Charlie, dearest, do stop terrifying the witness and have some of this excellent tea. Can I pour for you too, Sergeant Pyke?"

"That would be delightful, Grace. Just a drop of milk, please."

Charlie rolled his eyes and sat directly opposite Henry, pulling his chair close. He took the proffered cup, holding it by the delicate handle with his little finger extended, in a parody of a genteel tea party. The other hand sat on his knee, clenched in a fist. "Talk, Ormsby."

Henry's gaze flicked between the two Pykes and the door. Charlie glared back with glacial green eyes. Henry talked.

"I was just apologising to Penrose – Miss Penrose – for implicating her unintentionally. When I was running back to the house, I realised that what I had first understood to be an altercation between my father and Miss Penrose was the same type of fatal seizure I had seen in the rats that were poisoned by my stepmother. It was my stepmother I meant when I said 'she killed him'. I suspect the evil witch killed my mother too, to get her hands on our family's money."

"That's a bold accusation, Ormsby," Charlie said. "Your stepmother seems a perfectly amiable lady who loved your father deeply. What evidence do you have that she is a cold-blooded killer?"

"Don't let that 'loving wife' act fool you," Henry sneered. "She is out for what she can get. You must have seen what she does in that lair of hers, brewing poison and potions. My mother was the only one on the ship who died, you know, despite dozens falling ill with dysentery. My stepmother played the saviour, 'nursing' my mother day and night, not letting anyone else get close. My gullible father hung on her every word. Did you know my stepmother was already a widow before the voyage? I'd very much like to know why she fled her homeland after her first husband's death."

"Did the ship's surgeon voice any doubts as to your mother's cause of death?" Charlie asked.

"What do you think, Pyke? My stepmother is like a siren, luring men to do her bidding. I may not have enough evidence for a court of law, but I know how she acted. Furthermore, I have the evidence of a girl who was acquainted with her on board. The girl told me my future stepmother was fleeing her past and prepared to do whatever was necessary for a better future in New Zealand."

Grace was sure that Henry had convinced himself he had the classic wicked stepmother of fairy tales. Nevertheless, Henry's conviction and obvious fear for his own life opened a crack in her previous trust in Mrs Ormsby. Could there be a grain of truth in his story?

"Everyone who emigrated was fleeing their past for a better future," Charlie said. "The lure of a new country and fresh opportunities was only strong for those who were either struggling to make ends meet in Britain or those with a sense of adventure."

Grace couldn't rid herself of the feeling that Henry believed his version of events. "Henry, you said you left the house because you thought you would be next. Why would your stepmother want to kill you?"

"She hates me," Henry said. "And I am my father's heir. I stand in the way of her getting her hands on our wealth."

"Surely Richard is your older brother," Grace said, "and therefore, the heir?"

"Richard and Father had a falling out. Besides, the witch was already lining up her acolyte, Lawson, to marry my older brother. I don't like his chances of making old bones, do you? Father was standing in the way of that disgraceful union, as you can imagine, which is why he disinherited Richard. One more nail in Father's coffin. That Lawson is a wily one, always listening at doors and poking in drawers when she thinks nobody is watching."

Charlie leaned forward. "If you were the main beneficiary of your father's estate, surely you had the most to gain by killing him. By your own admission, you knew of the rat poison and had as much opportunity to kill your father as anyone else in the house. I have to say, Ormsby, your disappearance immediately after your father's

188

death has thrown suspicion on you. I would strongly advise you to present yourself to Detective Inspector Wallace without delay. I suspect he will be issuing a warrant for your arrest very soon, if you don't come forward."

Henry jerked upright. "The police suspect *me*? That's outrageous."

"You must have considered the possibility," Grace said. "Presumably you 'invited' me here so I could convey your side of the story."

"Finch warned me that the police suspected me. I didn't believe him, but I thought you would know. I didn't kill my father. Why would I? My father and I have an excellent relationship. He was proud of me, choosing to follow the same career he did, like a good son should. Unlike Richard."

"And yet you were overheard on Saturday morning having a loud and acrimonious argument with your father," Charlie said. "May I ask what that was about?"

"Hardly acrimonious, although I suppose I did lose my temper, as did he. Father was coming around to the notion of Cecilia marrying Gideon Alexander. I was merely reminding him that the fellow hadn't been in Dunedin long and lacked the qualities desired of an acceptable suitor."

"By which you mean?"

"He lacked the financial assets to provide my sister with the life she deserved. She is my only sister, after all." Henry waved away Grace's attempted interruption. "I know what you are going to say, Penrose. Yes, Cecilia had fallen in love with Alexander, but the rush of feelings that comes with so-called love at first sight is a fleeting passion, not the basis for a marriage contract. Especially when Alexander was after her money, not her love."

"In fact, I was about to query you calling Cecilia your only sister," Grace replied.

Henry looked down his nose at her. "Agnes is a half-sister and quite as unhinged as her mother, if not more so. I wouldn't put it

189

past the little devil to have stolen the poison and tried it out on my father. She was cross at him after he gave her a well-deserved thrashing for setting the curtains alight."

"I think we have heard quite enough, Mr Ormsby," Charlie said. "I will accompany you to the police station now, to state your case."

Henry rose from his armchair with visible effort. "I'll get my bag." He nipped out the door and up the hall with an unexpected turn of speed.

Charlie and his father both jumped up to go after him. The Pyke double-act lunged for the narrow door at the same time. Grace cringed at the sickening thud of bodies colliding. By the time Thomas stepped back to let Charlie through, Ormsby's footsteps were no longer audible. A groan from the corridor indicated Clement was waking up.

"Stay here, Grace, while I go after him. Pa, see to the prisoner." Charlie sprinted after Henry.

Grace heard a scrapping and banging, followed by a curse from Charlie. Meanwhile, Sergeant Pyke unclipped the handcuffs from around the radiator pipes and pulled the woozy prisoner to his feet.

Charlie came back wearing an expression that would freeze an ocean. "Curse it. Wallace will have me boiled in oil. Henry scrambled out a window and escaped. I didn't even get a fingerprint from him, as he didn't pick up his cup. I'd better take his accomplice to the police station straight away. Wallace will squeeze him until he tells us where Henry is."

"His name is Clement," Grace said. "Do ensure you treat him as gently as he treated me. And you might suggest that Wallace send a man to investigate this house for evidence of drugs and other crimes. Not a nice fellow, Mr Clement."

"I'll see Grace home," Thomas Pyke said. "Tell DI Wallace that Henry's escape was my fault, for getting in your way. Sorry, son. Not used to being second in command."

"I ought to go with Charlie," Grace said. "I'll need to make a statement at the police station."

"Declan can take it tomorrow, Grace," Charlie said. "Alistair will have taken witness statements, if Ma hasn't terrified those medical students into silence. You go home and recover from your ordeal." He clipped the open cuff to his wrist, took the key from his father, and departed, dragging a sullen Clement behind him.

As luck would have it, two ladies were alighting from a hansom cab further up the street. Thomas Pyke hailed it and helped Grace up into the cab. The cab lurched sideways as he climbed up after her.

Grace shuffled to the far side of the seat. "I must thank you, Sergeant Pyke, for coming to my rescue."

Thomas Pyke squashed his bulk into the other corner to give Grace space. It felt decidedly odd, sharing the narrow interior with a man who was almost exactly the same size as Charlie.

"It was pure luck that we were strolling around the university looking for the medical school, when we saw you being manhandled into the carriage. I don't know where Charlie appeared from, but he must have seen your abduction too. I must say, you seemed in fine fettle when I caught up to you, Grace, so perhaps you didn't need to be rescued after all."

"Henry Ormsby I could handle," Grace replied, "but I was very relieved to see the last of Clement, thanks to your intervention."

The horse plodded unsteadily down the steep hill, jostling them in the narrow confines of the cab. Thomas Pyke had to fold his broad shoulders like wings to avoid squashing her. "My apologies. Not used to sharing tight spaces with young ladies. I can't get over how many people live in Dunedin these days."

"I take it you don't travel to the city often, Sergeant Pyke?"

"Very rarely. With Lily and Charlie both settled here, that will have to change. Jasmine and I would like to get to know you better too, Grace. I had assumed my son was exaggerating your exploits, but it seems he was understating your role in solving cases. You two make an excellent team."

Grace felt her cheeks redden and cursed her pale skin. "Your son is a born detective. I hope you don't feel too disappointed Charlie is not following in your footsteps."

"Disappointed? Is that what Charlie thinks? I assure you, I couldn't be prouder of what he has achieved in so short a career."

"Henry Ormsby certainly feels he earned his status as heir by choosing the same vocation as his father. His older brother, Richard, resented his father's disdain for his choices."

Thomas Pyke's harrumph was forceful enough to vibrate down his arm and into Grace's shoulder. "This Ormsby fellow sounds like a fool to me. Changing his will to punish his eldest son like that is asking for trouble. Far better to let one's children choose their own paths in life and to treat each equally in terms of inheritance. Easy for me to say, of course, with only one child, no fortune, and nothing but unbounded delight in my son's choices in both career and love."

The sincerity of these last words triggered a rush of warmth through Grace. In the two days since she had met Thomas and Jasmine Pyke, they had had a ringside seat to her failure to save a man's life, followed by an accusation of murder, a police interview, a late-night sortie to the scene of the death with their son, and now an abduction. Not to mention leaving Lily without the help of her bridesmaid in preparing for one of the most important days of her life. Hardly the type of young lady most parents dreamed of for their only son.

Rather than drawing attention to her dubious accomplishments, Grace used the golden opportunity to pick the brain of an experienced policeman. "Sergeant Pyke, you heard what Henry said about his stepmother being driven by greed. The same might be said of every member of the Ormsby family, including Henry. And they all resented Doctor Ormsby for thwarting their ambitions. Do you think such resentments and greed could be a sufficient motive for a deliberately planned murder? It does not seem enough to me, when they suffered no financial or personal hardship in their present lives."

Sergeant Pyke considered the question, displaying the same thoughtful intensity as his son. "I had a case a few years back, when a miner killed another over a mining claim. The killer had spent years watching other miners find bigger nuggets of gold. He never showed the least reaction other than mild envy. However, when he moved to a new claim, and the next man found a big nugget in his old patch, he lost his mind completely. It wasn't about the wealth, so much as the sense of injustice, that it should have been his nugget. Resentment and entitlement can be powerful motivators, especially for people of weak character."

The horse was leaning hard into the traces now, as they went up the steep stretch of High Street to Anne's house.

"As to the Ormsby case," Sergeant Pyke continued, "I really couldn't say without meeting the suspects. In a family, resentments can build up over time, until the smallest incident can cause a person to commit a heinous act. For women, years of violent abuse can be a powerful motive too."

Doctor Ormsby had many faults, in Grace's opinion, but she didn't see him as an abuser. At least not in the physical sense. "Mrs Ormsby seems genuine in her love for her husband. Why kill a man who has given her love, security, career and family, even if he dismissed her work as a hobby? As for Richard, he may not see eye to eye with his father, but he had no cause to kill him, especially as he believed he had nothing to gain financially. Henry had the financial motive, but he put on a good show of being in genuine fear for his life. And I really cannot see Cecilia contemplating murder simply to get her chosen suitor. It's all quite baffling."

Sergeant Pyke helped her down from the cab and paid the fare. "Let's hope Charlie has a better idea after his interviews today. I expect you find it as frustrating as I do, Grace, not being present for every twist and turn of the case."

Grace smiled at their shared understanding, having enjoyed the chance to get to know Charlie's father better. More than anything, she felt grateful that he hadn't told her to keep her nose out of it and leave it to the men.

A World Away

After delivering the obnoxious Clement into custody, Charlie returned to his lodgings at Kenneth Drummond's house, only to find it deserted. A note on the table told him to come to Anne's house as soon as he could. Charlie took the time to freshen up first, after a gruelling day. As he splashed cold water on his face and dragged a razor through day-old stubble, he reflected on Wallace's reaction to his failure to secure Henry Ormsby.

Wallace had said little, but Charlie had read his thoughts in his bushy eyebrows. Astonishment at Grace's abduction (two raised brows). Amused disbelief at Grace's cool reaction to abduction (one raised brow). Incredulity at Henry's accusations (one up, one down). Annoyance at Henry's escape (brows joining in the middle). And, finally, straight brows and a clenched jaw, signifying an ocean of trouble for both Clement and Henry Ormsby.

Charlie was relieved to have escaped without the terrifying sight of conjoined brows above a charging-bull expression, which Wallace reserved for policemen who committed the cardinal sin of letting a criminal get the better of him without just cause. They had parted with an agreement to send DC Kelly to the medical school tomorrow morning, seeking information on Henry's whereabouts. Clement had refused to say where Henry was hiding.

Washed, shaved and clad in a freshly laundered shirt, Charlie was ready to change from detective to dinner companion. Disengaging from the whirlpool of evidence and suspects in a complex case was never easy, but Charlie was determined to share in the excitement of the approaching nuptials. He owed a great deal to Alistair Stewart, who had taken him on at a low point in his life and taught him to be a detective.

Charlie arrived at Anne's house to find it deserted, except for his father, who was snoring gently in an armchair. Although he did his best to sneak out quietly, his father woke and sprang from the chair. Decades of being the sole policeman in a small town had taught him the art of switching from deep sleep to fully alert in an instant.

"Ah, Charlie, at last. The others are inspecting the new headquarters of your Southern Investigations Agency. Come along, we don't want to miss the tour." Thomas flung a muscular arm around his son's shoulder and marched him next door. "Wonderfully convenient location, don't you think? Lily is delighted to be so close to Anne, and vice versa, I imagine."

The house brought back memories for Charlie, none of them pleasant. Anne's former neighbour had never liked him, from the first moment she clapped eyes on him, and the antipathy had only increased. Charlie hoped Alistair and Lily had wrought sufficient changes to make the house unrecognisable.

His father chattered on, unaware of Charlie's mixed emotions. "They have set aside a room for you. I imagine you won't mind being so close to Grace. What an extraordinary young lady she is. I can't tell you how delighted I am that you have found someone so perfect for you."

"Er, yes," Charlie agreed, as he struggled to absorb the rapid flow of words from his usually taciturn father. To his astonishment, his father paused at the gate and enveloped him in an embrace. Charlie had never once in his life doubted his father loved him, but physical contact, beyond a friendly slap on the back, was not his usual way of showing it.

"Sometimes I forget you are a grown man, Charlie, not the wide-eyed lad I remember when you left home. Alistair has told me many times what a fine detective you have become, but it wasn't until this visit that I realised the full truth of it. I have to admit, I envy you the excitement of becoming a private detective. You'd have wasted your talents doing anything else."

Thomas Pyke pushed through the gate, changing the subject before Charlie could respond. "Come and see. Alistair has installed an office and a workroom for Lily to prepare her remedies."

Charlie followed meekly, still taken aback at the unexpected outpouring of emotion and praise, and suspecting Grace Penrose's subtle hand behind it. But he had to admit it was a relief to know his father approved of his new venture.

Charlie wandered through the house, admiring its transformation from old English fussiness into a perfect home for Lily and Alistair. He left the fingerprint-covered reagent bottles in Aunt Lily's care in her new workroom, which already looked the part of a functioning laboratory. Lily and her team had spent most of the day experimenting with different methods of examining their own fingerprints. Fortunately, Charlie's father had an excellent memory for the detail provided in Galton's publications on fingerprints.

Charlie wasn't convinced it would work in practice, but he had to admit the test prints looked promising, once Lily pointed out the distinct patterns that distinguished her own prints from her sister Jasmine's. If they could use fingerprints to identity people, their investigation agency would be at the forefront of detection. The criminals would never know they had left incriminating evidence. For a while, at least. As soon as word spread, the smarter crooks would start wearing gloves, if they didn't already. All respectable citizens already wore gloves, except within their own homes or while eating.

The tour finished in the room nearest the front door. Their new office, complete with a shiny brass plaque engraved "Southern Investigations Agency". Whether it was the unexpected embrace from his father or sight of his own nameplate ("Detective C. Pyke") already sitting on the desk by the window, or both, Charlie had to turn away to blink moisture from his eyes.

Alistair walked into the room and looked around with satisfaction. "Hope you don't mind me taking the liberty of setting up the office, Charlie. With you hard at work on our first case, I had to do something worthwhile, even if it was only amassing stationery and legal documents."

Charlie took the seat behind his new desk, admiring the nameplate. "What if I hadn't agreed to your business proposal, Alistair?"

"Och, laddie, I had plenty of other options. Robbie Wallace is getting as fed up with the police hierarchy as I was, and young Declan Kelly would have jumped at the chance. Even Thomas here might have been persuaded to leave his beloved Central Otago."

Charlie put the nameplate down, aligning it perfectly with the front of his new desk. "Enough of that. You knew darn well I wouldn't be able to resist. You and Lily have done an amazing job, Alistair. It's perfect."

Lily appeared in the doorway. "It is wonderful, isn't it? I cannot wait to be married, so I can move in."

"I hope you're not just marrying me for the house, Lily," Alistair teased.

"Can you think of any other reason I should marry you?" Lily shared a smile of such intimacy with her fiancé, Charlie felt obliged to turn away to give them privacy.

Anne joined the growing crowd in the office. "Time for dinner next door, for those of us who prefer food to other distractions."

Charlie, being firmly in favour of both, made haste to return next door. He nabbed the seat beside Grace at the table. Over the clatter of serving dishes, he leaned close to her ear. "Had a pleasant chat with my father about me, did you?"

"We had a delightful discussion about what motivates a person to commit murder. Now, do stop hogging the potatoes and tell me everything you found out today, before we are dragged into a discussion about the most desirable number of cushions for a sofa."

"You'd rather discuss murder than interior decorating?" Charlie scooped another serving of potatoes onto his plate before passing the dish.

197

Grace took the dish with both hands, trapping his fingers under hers. "By all means, Detective C. Pyke, do tell me your opinion on cushions, if that is your preference."

"Miss Penrose, I believe you know my preferences all too well." Charlie's eyes held hers, before withdrawing his fingers slowly. "Murder over cushions, every time."

He launched into a summary of the day's evidence. The rest of the Southern Investigations team were soon weighing in with questions and comments.

"Interesting that so many of the suspects emigrated on the same ship," Thomas Pyke said. "The Ormsby family, his future second wife, the lady's maid and housemaid. I wonder if there is something in their joint past that led to murder? Poison seems to me a cold and deliberate method of killing someone, suggestive of a deep and burning hatred."

"We can't rule out a sudden flare of anger, Thomas," Jasmine countered. "The poison was conveniently near to hand and known to all the household. Even an outsider might have known about it, if he was familiar with Mrs Ormsby's work. A rival surgeon, perhaps? Or a spurned lover, since poison is often said to be favoured by women."

Charlie caught the amused look Grace was giving his parents at their enthusiasm for the investigation. He was used to it, having grown up with discussions of policing, just as she had been raised on talk of medicine. "I agree with Pa. We need to find out more about the voyage. I'll have another word with the Ormsby's housemaid."

"We might be able to find the ship's passenger list," Anne suggested. "The log book will note any untoward issues that occurred on board. The captain on my passage to New Zealand certainly had plenty to write about."

"Already done." Alistair dug into his pocket and pulled out several sheets of paper. "Mr Peters, the police records clerk, has a marvellous network of contacts throughout the country. I didn't want to wave it around at the dinner table, but perhaps expediency overrides good manners."

Charlie had the documents out of Alistair's hand in an instant. "The ship sailed in 1883, nine years ago. A steamship, so it only took about seven weeks to get here."

"The Ormsby family travelled first class, naturally," Alistair said. "Mrs Ormsby died of dysentery two weeks out from Dunedin, according to the records. Many others were sick as well. Mr Peters found the report on her death and there was no evidence of foul play. Indeed, Mrs Ormsby's dedicated nursing was specifically mentioned as being exemplary. Or rather, Mrs Conway, as she was known then."

Charlie ran a finger down the passenger list, stopping at the familiar names. "Very useful, Alistair. I didn't know they recorded not only names, but ages, family relationships and occupations."

"Immigration to New Zealand was carefully planned from the start," Anne said. "Only certain age groups and occupations were given passage, so that the new colony would have the skills and people it needed to grow. Masons, farmhands, domestic servants and the like. All meticulously documented. None can rival British colonial administrators for rigorous attention to profit, efficiency and glory. Assisted immigration was almost at an end by 1883, but the records still had to be kept."

Grace leaned over Charlie's shoulder. "What information was recorded for Mrs Conway, the future Mrs Ormsby? Was she with her first husband?"

"Mrs Siobhan Conway is listed as a nurse, travelling in third class. Aged thirty-nine and a widow. A year younger than her future husband, Edgar Ormsby. Hardly a youthful siren, as portrayed by Henry, although still an attractive woman, nine years later." Charlie went on down the list. "Here's Miss Nelly Lawson, domestic servant, travelling alone, although she was only sixteen. I can't see Betsy Dean."

199

Grace leaned closer. "Is that her, amongst the long list of Grants? Must be two or three Grant families at least, with all those names."

"Oh, yes. Betsy Dean, aged twelve. Betsy emigrated with her sister, but no parents are listed. She told me she was an orphan. She was with her grandfather, Euan Dean, and the extended Grant family." Charlie recalled the hostility with which the gardener had accosted him after speaking with Betsy. If he was one of the Grant family related to Betsy, that would explain his protectiveness. It took Charlie a moment to untangle the family relationships, which were listed in relation to the head of the family, Duncan Grant. "Looks like Duncan Grant's wife, Elizabeth, is Betsy's aunt and Euan Dean's daughter."

"It was common for entire extended families to emigrate together," Anne said, "so they could start a new life amongst loved ones."

Charlie pulled the Ormsby's list of servants out of his pocket. "The Ormsby's current gardener is a Grant. He must have taken over his grandfather's job when Euan Dean died. His name is Duncan Grant too. Named after his father, I presume. That would make him Betsy's cousin. Odd that they all ended up in the same household."

"Not in the least, Charlie," Alistair said. "The Ormsby family would have been wise to recruit their household staff before the ship arrived, not knowing what they would find on arrival. Better the devil you know."

Anne smiled dreamily. "The shipboard experience is one that made friends or enemies for life. I can vouch for that. All our best friends for years afterwards came on the same ship. Our families intermarried, our fortunes rose and fell together, we all helped each other. The future Mrs Ormsby must have become friendly with these people and wanted to help them when her own fortunes took a turn for the better."

With a start, Charlie remembered Henry Ormsby's assertion that a 'girl on the ship' said his stepmother would do anything to secure her future, which Henry took to mean dispatching his mother with the aim of replacing her. Could that girl have been Betsy Dean? Surely it must be, as Henry would not have talked to anyone outside first class on the ship, except perhaps Lawson. If Betsy and Henry were on familiar terms now, perhaps together they had discovered evidence enough for Henry to suspect and fear his stepmother.

As far as Charlie was concerned, there were still too many suspects and motives and not enough evidence. The first couple of days of an investigation were often like this, in the rare cases where the murderer was not obvious from the beginning. Most murders had a dismally easy-to-spot culprit, arising from either domestic violence or drunken men fighting each other in front of equally inebriated witnesses.

Charlie was still ruminating on the various suspects when he realised his plate was being taken away. Grace and Lily were discussing the merits of various poisons, while his mother, Anne, and Alistair were sharing their most terrifying memories of their voyages to New Zealand. His father and Kenneth Drummond were helping to collect plates and debating the legal penalties for abduction. What a fine bunch of eccentrics they were. How lucky he was to have fallen into such company.

Mrs Brown had to clear her throat loudly to be heard over the din. "Doctor Beechworth is here, ma'am. I've put him in the drawing room."

Everyone followed Anne into the drawing room, resulting in a round of introductions to the entire Southern Investigations team.

"My apologies for interrupting at this unsociable hour," Beechworth said. "I've done a little more investigating around Edgar Ormsby's potential enemies and I thought you would prefer to know as soon as possible. Do you have that list I sent yesterday, Mr Pyke?"

Charlie took out the list, which comprised two short columns.

"The first three on the left are medical people who have disagreed with Ormsby. I've looked into the circumstances and none were significant enough to warrant murder. Minor rivalries or brief disputes at worst. I added Horncastle to that list, as he was disgruntled over Ormsby revoking his support for the operating theatre. Again, not even close to a motive for murder. The longer list on the right are patients who have died in Ormsby's care over the past decade. Again, none of the circumstances were untoward, although the patients' families may feel aggrieved at their loss."

"Would this be a normal fatality rate, Doctor Beechworth?" Charlie asked.

"More or less. Operating is always a hazardous business. Ormsby was a respected surgeon here in Dunedin, having built up a successful private practice as well as performing surgery at the hospital. The Dunedin Hospital Trustees were delighted to have attracted a man of his standing and they have not regretted it. Ormsby's rubbed a few people up the wrong way over the years, including me and a few other medical men, as well as the ladies fundraising committee, but that's about all."

"Did I detect a certain emphasis on 'here in Dunedin'?" Alistair asked. "Did Ormsby leave Edinburgh under a cloud?"

Beechworth hesitated. "The information I have is third hand, so I am reluctant to put any weight on it, Mr Stewart."

Charlie could understand his reluctance, especially with so many eager eyes upon him. "Every person here is associated with our Southern Investigations Agency, Doctor Beechworth. Your information will go no further."

"Very well, Mr Pyke. Apparently, when Ormsby applied for the position here, a check of references threw up a suggestion of his involvement in the negligent death of a prominent citizen in Edinburgh. The referee was critical of Ormsby, although another surgeon was holding the scalpel when the patient died. Ormsby was officially cleared of any wrongdoing, while the other surgeon was struck off and died tragically soon after. That's all I know."

An unpleasant situation for Ormsby to find himself in, Charlie thought, but hardly a motive if Ormsby was cleared of wrongdoing. "I'm afraid we had another unpleasant incident to deal with today, Doctor Beechworth. Miss Penrose was abducted by one of your

202

students. Mr Clement is now under arrest. Grace, as you can see, is not seriously harmed."

"Good heavens, how shocking." Beechworth glanced at Grace. "Unharmed maybe, but still a traumatic experience, I imagine, Miss Penrose."

"Detective Constable Kelly will be at the medical school tomorrow morning, seeking information from your students," Charlie added. "Several of Henry Ormsby's associates were present when the abduction took place."

"I will make sure they cooperate fully," Beechworth assured them. "I promise sharp words will be spoken and appropriate actions taken. Miss Penrose, I suggest you remain at home tomorrow. Please take as much time as you need to recover."

Grace, of course, insisted she would not be taking time off, with her usual defiance. Beechworth accepted her refusal as if he expected no less and departed.

Alistair duly changed the subject. "If Ormsby had an enemy in Edinburgh, somebody here is bound to know about it – Dunedin being a small city with a high proportion of Scots."

"Time for me to earn my keep as a spy," Anne said. "I'll soon find out which of our local doctors were in Edinburgh back then. It shouldn't be hard, as many of our medical people trained there."

Mrs Brown returned from seeing Beechworth out. "What about Doctor Harvey, ma'am? The late Doctor Macmillan's friend. With that accent of his, Doctor Harvey must surely be an Edinburgh man."

"An excellent idea, Mrs Brown," Anne said. "Andrew Harvey would be perfect. Indeed, I vaguely recall him and my husband discussing the arrival of Doctor Ormsby. Must have been nearly a decade ago. Andrew did not hold back his poor opinion of Ormsby, as I recall. Quite angry he was, that Ormsby was coming here. I'll make an appointment with Doctor Harvey tomorrow morning."

Mrs Brown looked pleased to have helped with the investigation. "I'll bake some gingerbread for you to take. Doctor Harvey was always partial to my gingerbread."

"One taste of your gingerbread and he will spill all his secrets," Charlie agreed. "I vote we add Mrs Brown to the Southern Investigations team as Head of Culinary Inducements."

"Seconded," Alistair said. "Welcome to the agency, Mrs Brown."

"I'm sure if I can be of any help, it would be my pleasure. I haven't had so much excitement since the last time you were here, Mr Pyke. And don't you worry, young man, I'll be sure to pop in a second batch of my gingerbread for you." Mrs Brown collected the last plates and disappeared into the kitchen, her cheeks flushed a becoming pink.

Charlie could already taste the spicy ginger on his tongue. He sat back with the satisfaction of an evening well spent. "That leaves Mrs Macmillan to see Doctor Harvey, Grace to give a statement to Declan Kelly, me helping Wallace with interviewing suspects and witnesses, and Aunt Lily and her team finding the killer's fingerprints."

"I feel like a spare wheel," Alistair complained.

"Not at all, dearest," Lily replied. "With your help, we can get the fingerprints done tonight, leaving us free to shop for linen tomorrow."

"I'm beginning to think I shouldn't have resigned from the police force," Alistair muttered.

Voice From The Past

On Tuesday morning, Grace arrived early and sat at the rear of the lecture theatre. The other students avoided eye contact with her and sat as far away as they could, leaving her as an island from which the sea had retreated. Common sense had urged her to stay home today, as Beechworth had advised, but giving in now would waste two years of fighting to establish her right to be at medical school.

Grace's spirits lifted a little as John Hargreaves and his friends entered at the front. After initial disbelief that a woman had been honoured with a place in their ranks, Hargreaves had been the first student to accept her and treat her with consideration. The day he had volunteered to be her laboratory partner had brought her as close to tears as she allowed herself to be in these hallowed halls. How would Hargreaves react to the blatant shunning of her today?

Hargreaves glanced around the lecture theatre and walked straight to the back, sitting beside Grace and filling the rest of the row with his friends. The next students through the door detected no unusual cross-currents and sat where they normally would. Soon, the silence ebbed as the tide of normal chatter rose. Grace eased the tension in her back and nodded her thanks to her saviour.

Hargreaves leaned closer, under the guise of getting his books out. "We ought to give you a medal, Penrose. That swine Clement made my life hell throughout school. A bully and a blackguard before he was out of short pants. If his family hadn't been so wealthy, he would have been expelled a dozen times over."

At two minutes to nine o'clock, Doctor Beechworth entered the lecture theatre beside their usual lecturer, with DC Declan Kelly a solid presence behind them. Kelly planted himself in the doorway, arms crossed over his broad chest, scanning the room with a policeman's distrustful scrutiny. Several students around the room suddenly found their shoes to be of overwhelming interest.

Beechworth strode to the very front of the class, neither hiding behind the lectern nor disguising the anger in his voice. "No doubt you have all heard Mr Clement has been arrested for abducting a fellow student. Appalled as I am by his offence, I am equally shocked that many of you stood by and allowed it to happen. Medical students are supposed to be the cream of our society. You will sign an oath to help your fellow citizens. We expect higher standards of you."

He inspected the hanging heads in the audience. "The police are here today to take official witness statements from those who were present. You will do so, fully and honestly, if you wish to retain your place at medical school. Detective Constable Weston is waiting for you in the anatomy room. Furthermore, if anyone here knows where Henry Ormsby is, or has been, or even where he might be, you will come forward immediately and share that information with Detective Constable Kelly here, who will see you in my office."

Beechworth waited for the students to make their way out of the room. When the room was silent again, he faced the remaining students. "The rest of you should take the time to contemplate how you have treated your fellow students. Not merely the overt cruelty, but the subtle disparagements, the refusal to engage, the arrogant and unwarranted assumptions about who is fit to be a doctor. Because becoming a doctor is not about being rich or setting yourself upon a pedestal but being a compassionate human who strives to make people's lives better."

Grace exited through the rear door as Beechworth stormed out via the front door. She had proved she would not be intimidated, but she had no intention of staying for a day of sidelong glances and half-hearted contrition. Besides, if she hurried, she could visit Doctor Harvey with her great-aunt.

Grace arrived at Doctor Harvey's surgery in time to help Anne down from the buggy.

Doctor Harvey welcomed Anne with old-fashioned gallantry. "Anne, my dear, do come in. We haven't seen nearly enough of you since Gordon passed."

Anne kissed the doctor's cheek. "How well you look, Andrew. May I introduce my great-niece, Miss Grace Penrose. George Penrose's granddaughter."

"Ah, yes, Miss Grace Penrose. Making your many medical relatives proud, so I hear."

Grace acknowledged the compliment with a smile. Harvey was a jolly old fellow. A shame to ruin his day. "It's kind of you to make time to see us, Doctor Harvey."

Harvey took the seat behind his desk and waved them to two chairs. "I don't take many patients these days. Ought to be retired at my age, but I only get under my wife's feet if I stay at home all day. My next patient isn't due for another ten minutes."

Anne retrieved a parcel from her bag and put it on the desk. "Mrs Brown sent some of her famous gingerbread."

The elderly doctor leaned forward to breathe in the aroma. "In that case, I can spare you twenty minutes at least. Your message indicated it was in relation to Ormsby's death."

"I'm not sure if you know Ormsby was deliberately poisoned, Andrew," Anne said.

Harvey's jolly smile slipped away behind bushy white whiskers. "News to me, my dear. Can't say I was heartbroken by his passing. But murder? How dreadful for his family. What can I do to help? I understand you are interested in Ormsby's life in Edinburgh."

"We are hunting for a person who harboured a murderous grudge against him. Our sources suggest Ormsby might have been implicated in a negligent death on the operating table. The other surgeon was found to be at fault, as far as we understand. It would have been a decade or more ago, so I won't be surprised if you cannot recall the incident."

Grace watched Harvey's face turn an ever-deeper shade of crimson as Anne spoke. She prayed she wouldn't be required to attempt a second resuscitation.

Harvey rallied, but his voice took on a harsher tone. "The old grey matter isn't what is used to be, Anne, but that case is etched into my memory. The surgeon who took the blame, Iain Thayne, was my son's best friend from the moment they met as children. Young Iain spent many hours in our home. We saw him grow up, get married, have children, become a fine man and a first-class surgeon. Because of Ormsby, Iain Thayne was struck off. His career was destroyed with the stroke of a pen. Iain died not long after that. Drowned. Accidentally, after imbibing too much whisky, so they said, but the suspicion was that he took his own life. The date of Iain's tragic death is fixed in my mind. The fifteenth of May 1882, my son's fortieth birthday."

Ten years ago on Saturday, Grace realised. The day Ormsby was murdered. Surely, that could not be a coincidence. The suspicion that Ormsby's death had its roots in a deep-seated antipathy had been growing steadily, like an itchy rash. For a planned murder is not undertaken lightly, except by a rare type of mentally unstable killer.

Doctor Harvey continued, oblivious to Grace's quickening pulse. "Surgery is often a life-threatening last resort, especially back then, but the death during this particular operation was inexcusable. The procedure was a straightforward one – a piece of small shot imbedded in the patient's thigh after a hunting accident. Ormsby nicked the femoral artery, then panicked and froze, leaving Iain to try to save the man's life. The patient was an influential man. His family demanded a sacrifice."

"Why was Ormsby not the one who was struck off, rather than Iain Thayne?" Grace asked.

"Ormsby lied to save himself." Harvey almost spat the words out, indicating the depth of emotion he still felt all these years later. "The scoundrel insisted Iain made the mistake, when Ormsby allowed him to close the wound after completing the difficult part

208

of the operation successfully. Ormsby implied he was doing Iain a favour by providing training, but everyone knew Iain was by far the better surgeon, even though they were the same age. In fact, Iain had been placed in the operating theatre by the Chief Surgeon, to ensure that Ormsby did an exemplary job on such an important man."

"Was there expected to be a problem with Ormsby's work?"

"Not really. Ormsby was an adequate surgeon, who had convinced the rich and illustrious he was the best. Ormsby was the type of man to blow his own bagpipe, and he had all the right contacts through his wealthy wife."

Grace had no trouble believing Harvey's assessment of Ormsby's character, but she was appalled that he could be so despicable as to leave another man to take the blame for a patient's death. "Thayne must have put up a fight, surely."

"Iain told his version of events, naturally, but was not believed. Or, rather, Iain was the easier of the two to sacrifice, not having the wealth or connections that Ormsby had. Iain had stepped up in the crisis and done his best to staunch the bleeding, but the damage was done. Ironically, it was the fact that Iain was covered in blood that was his downfall. The Medical Council believed Ormsby's sworn oath that it was Iain who made the fatal cut, not himself."

"What about the other people present?"

"The surgical assistant didn't see what happened, as he was tending the instrument tray. The anaesthetist was concentrating on his job too. If they had their suspicions, they didn't voice them. Possibly threatened or paid off, who knows? Iain Thayne was a broken man – struck off, vilified, cast out of society."

"How dreadful," Anne said. "It cannot have been long before you came to New Zealand, Andrew."

"It wasn't. My son had already been offered a position here. My wife and I had decided to travel with him and his family to see them settled. As you know, I found this country very much to my taste and set up a practice here. Your husband was one reason I stayed. I always valued Gordon's friendship and advice, you know."

209

Harvey's flicker of a smile at the memory faded quickly. "My son begged Iain to come to New Zealand with us to make a fresh start. I don't know why he refused, but I can tell you that his sudden death came as a terrible shock to us all. If only we had done more. I ought to have paid for his ticket and forced him to join us."

"You did what you could, Andrew," Anne said. "I hate to bring up these awful memories, but can you tell us what happened to Iain Thayne's family?"

"Iain had a lovely wife and three children. Two girls and a boy. His wife was a pretty, delicate thing, a nurse, who fought like a tiger for his reinstatement. After her husband died, the poor lass was found hammering on Ormsby's door, screaming that he was a liar and a killer and threatening revenge. Ormsby refused to come out and talk to her. A cowardly act, although perhaps it was a wise move, given Mrs Thayne's fury. She had to be dragged away."

Grace had no problem imagining how devastated Thayne's widow must have felt, to be robbed of her husband and her future by Ormsby's duplicity. Her blood was boiling merely hearing about it. "Do you know what happened to Mrs Thayne and the children, Doctor Harvey?"

Ten years had passed, but Harvey still had tears in his eyes when he replied. "I believe they went to stay with Mrs Thayne's relatives, although I heard her mental health was beyond repair by then. I will never forget seeing them standing at Iain's graveside. His wife was so grief stricken, she had to be held up by her uncle. Ormsby had the nerve to attend the funeral. If looks could kill, Thayne's entire family would have slayed Iain's killer that day. It drove a stake through my heart to see them so bereft. Our ship sailed only a couple of days later. My wife wrote to Mrs Thayne, but never heard back."

"Do you recall Mrs Thayne's name?" Grace struggled to keep her own words from choking with the appalling unfairness of the Thayne family's fate.

Harvey paused to think, presumably as he did not know Iain's wife as well as he knew the boy who had been his son's best friend.

"As I recall, it was something like Marie … No, it was Mairi, a lovely Scottish name for a lovely lass."

Grace let out the breath she had been holding. Her imagination had run away with her. For a moment, she had been sure that the doctor was going to say "Siobhan". She pictured little Agnes giving her name as Agnes Siobhan Ormsby, after her mother. Mrs Ormsby – a pretty, delicate widowed nurse from Edinburgh, who had never quite seemed like the right match for Edgar Ormsby, despite her protestations of love for her second husband.

But, in truth, it was never likely that a broken woman could be so set on revenge that she would travel halfway across the world, marry the scoundrel, and wait all these years before acting on her hatred. Unless something had triggered the long-awaited moment – the ten-year anniversary of Iain's death, perhaps?

Grace looked up to see Harvey watching at her, his head perked to the side.

"Miss Penrose, you look as if you were expecting a specific name."

"Not really, Doctor Harvey. It would have fit with one of my many wild theories if you had said her name was Siobhan, but I am not surprised to be wrong."

"Siobhan?" Harvey sat back and tapped his fingers on the desk. "Funnily enough, that does ring a bell. Many Scots families seem to call their children by their second names, don't they? Hmm, Siobhan Mairi Thayne. Could be, but honestly, I cannot say for sure. It was a long time ago."

Grace sucked in a breath. "Do you recall Mrs Thayne's maiden name?"

"That I wouldn't know, although I believe the family reverted to using her maiden name to avoid notoriety. I'll ask my wife. My dear Ava remembers every person she has ever met, while I struggle to recall the names of my own grandchildren. Unfortunately, my wife won't be home until this afternoon. I shall send her a note to expect you."

211

Grace and Anne thanked Doctor Harvey for his time and left him tucking into a large slice of gingerbread. Out on the street, Grace helped her great-aunt into the buggy. "Can we stop at the medical school? I'd like to tell DC Kelly what we found out as soon as possible."

It might well be a dead end, but Grace's senses were tingling. The Thayne family had lost everything – their husband and father, their respectability, their financial support, their peace of mind. A powerful motive for revenge, if ever she had heard one.

And Ormsby had left a good position in Edinburgh to travel to the other side of the world not long after Thayne's death. A coincidence? Unlikely. Perhaps it was the unbearable shame of enduring the accusatory glares of Thayne's friends? Or concern that Iain Thayne's vengeful widow would make good on her threats?

Grace was looking forward to seeing the sparkle in Charlie's eyes when she told him.

When Grace and Anne arrived at the medical school, they found DC Declan Kelly writing up his notes, having finished his interviews. Grace listened without surprise to Declan's certainty that he had enough evidence to convict Clement of abduction – as long as his wealthy father didn't hire a well-paid attorney to get him off on a technicality.

None of the medical students had admitted to knowing where Henry Ormsby was hiding, but several had suggested that they might try the hospital, which was used as an occasional overnight resting place after late nights in town.

At The Hospital

Charlie met with Wallace and Kelly early on Tuesday morning, eager to share news of the discoveries made by the Southern Investigations team.

The fingerprint team had worked into the night to examine the samples. After careful comparison of the patterns of arches, loops and whorls, the team had agreed that the original poison bottle – taken from the workroom – held prints that matched Mrs Ormsby, Miss Lawson and one unidentified person. A promising start to narrowing the suspect pool, assuming the murderer was not wearing gloves.

The poisoned tonic bottle, which Agnes had hidden in her room, was dotted with dozens of fingerprints. Unfortunately, many of the prints were layered on top of each other and impossibly smudged. Nevertheless, Lily had identified impressions left by Edgar Ormsby and Finch, his valet, along with smaller smudges that must have been Agnes. One partial impression appeared to match Richard, who had a distinctive scar on his thumb, while others appeared to match Mrs Ormsby and Miss Lawson. At least two other people had handled the bottle, if not more. The variety of prints was to be expected, as many people had contact with the bottle since it had been opened the previous week.

Alistair had the clever idea of examining the remaining bottle of heart tonic from the bathroom cabinet. Agnes had admitted to putting a replacement bottle back in the cabinet to disguise the fact that she had spilled the poisoned one. Alistair reasoned the killer would want to come back and remove the poisoned bottle, so no one would know how the poison had been administered. Charlie had no trouble imagining the killer's shock when he or she discovered that the bottle showed no trace of the poison. With luck, the killer had then replaced the untainted bottle in the cabinet, rather than drawing suspicion by throwing it away.

This bottle had fewer prints. Mrs Ormsby and Miss Lawson, presumably from contact in the workroom when filling the bottle, as well as Finch, Agnes, and an unknown fingerprint. The same unknown print as on the original poison bottle.

Thus, only Mrs Ormsby, Miss Lawson, and the unidentified person had touched both the poison bottle and the bottle of heart tonic. The fingerprints of Mrs Ormsby and Lawson proved nothing, since both had legitimate reasons to touch all the bottles. Either of them might still be the murderer.

Charlie needed to figure out the identity of the unknown person who had handled both the poison and the tonic bottle. He had yet to collect fingerprint samples from Henry and Cecilia Ormsby, Mr Pugh, Betsy Dean, Duncan Grant and all the outsiders who had been at the house on the day of the party. That included Mr Horncastle and Doctor Alexander, who were next on Wallace's interview schedule.

"Well, I never," Declan declared, after Charlie had finished explaining the findings. "Think of all the time we'd have saved over the years if we'd known about fingerprints before. You are sure they are unique to an individual, Charlie?"

"Apparently so," Charlie replied. He had presented the results impassively, but underneath, he was every bit as excited as Declan was.

"Might have trouble getting a judge and jury to place their faith in smudges," Wallace said, "but fascinating nevertheless. When this case is over, Pyke, perhaps you and your father could prepare a discussion paper for the police hierarchy to consider. Our superiors will be guided by what Scotland Yard is up to, no doubt, but they ought to be informed of the potential of this method. The fact that a private detective agency is ahead of the police force might rouse some action."

Wallace pushed his chair back and reached for his overcoat. "Right lads, enough mucking around with science. It's time to get some good old-fashioned policing done."

"I'd best be off to the medical school," Kelly agreed. "Charlie, you'll not have heard that I talked to Ormsby's attorney yesterday evening. Ormsby gave no explanation of his sudden change of mind or why he reverted to the original beneficiaries. Or perhaps the attorney was simply unwilling to share his client's motivation. Might as well have been talking to a stone."

"I'm interviewing Horncastle at the hospital at nine o'clock this morning, Pyke, if you wish to come." Wallace pulled his hat on, wrapped his scarf, and headed for the door, without waiting for a reply.

Quarter of an hour later, Charlie and Wallace were shown into a dim, wood-panelled room lined with the portraits of solemn, bewhiskered gentlemen. Horncastle stood up from the head of the oval table, which filled the room, gesturing them to the leather seats beside him.

Wallace stretched out a hand, which Horncastle shook, after a moment's hesitation. "Detective Inspector Wallace. I presume you are Mr Horncastle, Chairman of the Hospital Trustees."

"I am. Will this take long, Inspector, because I have important business to attend to?"

Horncastle spoke with an upper-class English accent that matched his appearance – top hat, silk cravat, bespoke tailoring, neatly trimmed beard. His accent seemed a little contrived. Charlie knew Horncastle had made his fortune importing quality furnishings. He diagnosed a self-made man, who had taken the opportunities available to him in a relatively young colony and made the most of them. He could be a Cockney barrow boy made good, as far as Charlie was concerned, but wealthy men often went to considerable effort to hide humble origins.

"I understand your role as Chairman is not a full-time occupation, Mr Horncastle," Wallace began.

215

"Indeed not, Inspector. All the Hospital Trustees are professionals and businessmen, who undertake the role for the benefit of the community. I confess, had I realised how much time it would take, I might have hesitated to accept. Nevertheless, one must do one's best for the betterment of society."

"I will come straight to the point, Mr Horncastle. You had a meeting with Doctor Ormsby at eleven o'clock on Saturday morning. Furthermore, you were observed to be angry with him during the soirée that evening."

Horncastle glared at Wallace, his monocle accentuating his irritation. "We met, yes, but I was not angry, merely frustrated at Ormsby's inconstancy."

"Perhaps you could tell me the reason for the meeting."

"Doctor Ormsby summoned me to his house on Saturday morning." Horncastle's pursed lips indicated he was not a man who appreciated being summoned by others. "Ormsby informed me he had altered his stated position on the new hospital wing. I had put my reputation on the line, supporting his suggestion of a new operating theatre. Ormsby himself had convinced me of the merits. I could see it would bring in fee-paying patients, which we desperately need, the financial situation of the hospital being precarious in these harsh economic times."

"Did Ormsby give a reason for his change of mind?" Wallace asked.

"He did not seem to feel I was owed an explanation." Horncastle tipped his head back slightly, causing the glass in the monocle to glint in the light. "I presumed Ormsby's wife pressured him to renege. Indeed, when I left, I saw Mrs Ormsby coming out of the stable across the other side of the garden, so I ventured across to ask her."

Wallace went absolutely still, a hound on a scent. "You stayed on, after the meeting with Ormsby?"

"I was merely returning to my carriage, which was standing by the entrance to the stables. Mrs Ormsby darted back into the building, snubbing me, which rather confirmed my suspicions. She is a leading member of the ladies' group agitating for a women's ward." Horncastle had dropped his voice for the last sentence, making it sound as if Mrs Ormsby was part of a dangerous gang of conspirators.

"You didn't follow Mrs Ormsby?"

"Absolutely not. I was quite put out by her rudeness, as you may imagine. I returned directly to my carriage. Frankly, Inspector, I blame the suffragists for giving women misguided ideas about their role in society. The women's group is incorrigible. One of them even harangued Ormsby during his soirée that evening. I don't know what their husbands are thinking, condoning such disgraceful conduct."

Charlie would have liked to shut this man in a room with Grace's suffragist friends for an hour or two, not that he expected a man like Horncastle would change his ways. He wanted to ask if Horncastle had ever walked the wards of the hospital he had such power over, to see with his own eyes the conditions patients endured. Fortunately, Wallace was of like mind.

"No doubt you and the other Trustees conducted a thorough investigation before coming to your decision to switch from a new women's ward to an operating theatre," Wallace said, in a sympathetic tone. "I expect these women were exaggerating the dire state of the current women's ward, eh? Perhaps you would have time to take us on a quick tour?"

Horncastle sniffed. "I do not have time to waste visiting the wards, Inspector, and neither do the other Trustees. We operate at a higher level, dealing with proposals and budgets and the wider overall vision for a modern hospital facility. We aim to build a legacy that will be the envy of the southern hemisphere."

Wallace stared at him for a long moment, unblinking, before continuing. "Of course, my mistake. Were you aware that Doctor Ormsby had made provision in his will for a substantial donation to the hospital?"

"He intimated as much to me. The generosity of wealthy men is vital to keeping this hospital from falling into disrepair."

"Ormsby's death, tragic as it was, would thus be of benefit to the hospital, Mr Horncastle, would it not? Perhaps to the benefit of your own legacy as well? I understand retiring chairmen are often remembered in the naming of new wards."

Horncastle removed his monocle, so he could glare all the harder. "I find that offensive, Inspector. Donations are always welcome, but it is hardly appropriate to talk of such things so soon after Ormsby's heart attack."

"It wasn't a heart attack. Edgar Ormsby was murdered." Wallace must have seen the shock on Horncastle's face, but he ignored it and ploughed on. "Did you know Ormsby changed his will again, the day before he died? Unfortunately for the hospital, the revised donation is a fraction of the previous bequest."

Shock turned to a mix of horror and disbelief. Whatever Ormsby had said to Horncastle at their Saturday morning meeting, it was abundantly clear that he had not mentioned his altered will.

Wallace waited until Horncastle had recovered his composure. "Mr Horncastle, do you know who murdered Edgar Ormsby?"

"No, of course not. Absolutely not. Why would I?"

"Do you recognise this type of bottle, sir?" Charlie asked, holding a reagent bottle out to him.

"No." Horncastle touched it briefly, when Charlie thrust it into his hand, before handing it back. "I trust that will be all, Inspector. I am a very busy man. If you require a character reference, you need look no further than your own Chief Inspector, who is an acquaintance of mine."

Wallace didn't so much as blink. He rose from his chair and gave Horncastle a brief nod. "Please notify me at the police station if you recall any further information, Mr Horncastle." Wallace left his suspect staring at the vast, empty table. Horncastle did not seem to notice their departure.

Charlie followed Wallace back down the corridor to the hospital lobby. Horncastle seemed like the type of man to take offence at every slight. Charlie had no problem imagining him slapping an

218

opponent with a glove and demanding a duel, had this been a tale of old. However, he couldn't imagine Horncastle killing Ormsby over a simple, if frustrating, withdrawal of support for the new operating theatre. Horncastle's motive was simply not compelling, unless …

Charlie hurried to catch up to Wallace. "Horncastle seemed excessively put out by the change of will. Perhaps it might be worth investigating the hospital accounts, to see if our honourable Chairman of Trustees is benefitting personally from donations and bequests."

Wallace grunted his agreement. Horncastle had made the mistake of annoying DI Wallace with his superior attitude – never a wise move. If there was wrongdoing, Wallace would sniff it out.

Fascinating as the interview had been, the most useful insight had been Horncastle witnessing Mrs Ormsby coming out of the workroom, late on Saturday morning. She had not mentioned this in her interview. Charlie was sure Wallace would head back up to Royal Terrace to have further discussions with Mrs Ormsby, her lady's maid, and Richard.

Cecilia too. The daughter's character seemed as insubstantial as mist, unless she really was as shallow as she appeared to be. Her one concern seemed to be marrying Gideon Alexander, a man who hadn't shown his face at the Ormsby house since Saturday night, as far as Charlie could tell. He was looking forward to meeting Cecilia's suitor, especially as Grace had given such a fine account of the young surgeon. That is, if he and Wallace could find their way through the maze of corridors to the duty surgeon's room, where Doctor Alexander had agreed to meet them.

A nurse took pity on them and took them to the right place. She halted in the doorway, her face full of sympathy as she held a finger to her lips and pointed to the man fast asleep on the narrow bunk. All that was visible of Doctor Alexander was a hand dangling from under a blanket and a tangle of light brown hair. He was so still, he might have been heavily sedated, or dead.

"Do you have to wake the poor man?" the nurse whispered. "He's been on call for days, we're that short staffed. After a nasty accident down on the wharves late yesterday, Doctor Alexander worked through the night, attending to an amputation, several broken bones and a crushed skull. Three ships in at once and the dockworkers labouring all hours, just like us. Shouldn't be allowed. An accident waiting to happen if you ask me. The House Surgeon told Doctor Alexander to go home, but he insisted on waiting for the police."

Wallace hesitated. Charlie knew he was eager to return to the Ormsby house, but they still only had Alexander's evidence second hand, through Grace. Alexander had no apparent motive and limited opportunity, but a policeman had to be thorough. Besides, he might have witnessed something suspicious.

The nurse's expression softened. "I heard what happened to his sweetheart's father. Terrible tragedy, right before they were to be engaged. I know Doctor Alexander was beside himself having so much work to do here, taking over Ormsby's operations as well as his own, when all he wanted was to be by his sweetheart's side. I hope Miss Ormsby understands he is wearing himself to the bone for her and her family."

No wonder Grace admired the man, Charlie thought. He felt a stab of guilt for thinking ill of Alexander for his absence from Cecilia's side. However, they still needed to question him. Charlie turned back to the nurse. "Do you know his future brother-in-law, Henry Ormsby?"

Compassion fell away to wariness. "The medical student. I know him all right."

"Have you seen him recently?" Charlie asked.

"Yes, I have. I found the little blighter sleeping in the duty surgeon's bed. Poor Doctor Alexander was asleep in a chair in between patients, because he was too soft-hearted to kick the Ormsby boy out. I don't care who Henry Ormsby's father is. That's not acceptable. Showed young Mr Ormsby the door this morning, I did."

Charlie suppressed a surge of frustration at missing their quarry again. "Do you know where Henry Ormsby might have gone?"

The nurse planted her knuckles on her hips. "I don't know and I don't care, as long as he's out of my sight and not harassing any nurses." She glanced behind him and waved. "Here's our Miss Penrose. She might know. We could do with a few more like her around. She's got more dedication to duty in her little finger than that Ormsby boy could summon in a lifetime."

Grace hurried towards them. "Gentlemen, Nurse Evans, good morning to you all. Have you been interviewing Gideon Alexander?"

Nurse Evans pointed to the sleeping figure, who hadn't moved an inch, despite the sudden arrival of a bawling child, with one arm twisted unnaturally to the side. The nurse rushed over to the distraught father and son and directed them onward into the hospital maze.

Declan Kelly turned into the corridor, his arm looped through Anne Macmillan's, supporting her as she struggled to keep up with Grace's rapid pace. "Charlie, Henry Ormsby might be here, in the hospital."

"He was, Declan, but the nurse shooed him out of the surgeon's bed this morning."

"Have you tried the old lying-in ward? Apparently, there is a place there where medical students will spend the night if they are too drunk to get to their own homes."

Charlie turned to Grace. "Do you know where it is?"

"No one tells me these secrets, Charlie. The maternity ward was closed a few years ago. We only get the occasional emergency delivery now."

"I know exactly where it is," Anne said. "And a sorrier excuse for a hospital ward I never wish to see again as long as I live. A cold, dank building, accessed by rickety stairs, not suitable for swine or even medical students. Deemed unfit for birthing women five years ago, and not before time. Come with me."

Anne led the way. Charlie had been in the hospital twice before, but he had been in no condition to take in his surroundings either

221

time. Once he had been seriously injured, the second time his sole focus was on getting Grace out of here. He had forgotten the evil smell of inadequate bathrooms and poor drainage, the overlying whiff of disease and boiled cabbage, and the pervasive air of decay. He felt sick just being here.

They took a short-cut through the women's ward, one end of which was sweat-inducingly close to the heating, while the other end was icy. Rows of metal-framed beds fought for space. In each bed, a pale, shrunken face peered at them above a tightly tucked sheet. Enterprising nurses had erected blankets to stop the chill coming in the loose window sashes. Most of the blankets were pulled aside this morning, as insipid sunlight streamed through the windows alongside the breeze.

Grace had told Charlie about conditions in the older wards of the hospital, but it was completely different to be here, in person, being assaulted by all five senses. When this case was over, Charlie was going to personally ensure that every hospital trustee, and every government health official he could get his hands on, visited this ward, preferably dressed in a thin nightgown. Even if he had to handcuff them and drag them in himself.

The livelier patients welcomed their presence as an amusing distraction from the boredom and discomfort of bed rest. Charlie and Declan returned the hellos and ignored the more ribald comments, which would have had him blushing back in the days when he was a raw recruit. Most of the women recognised Grace, who darted here and there, using Anne's slower pace to fit in a little extra bedside care.

A thin woman pushed herself upright, calling out in a stage whisper. "Don't let the tall one get away, Doctor Penrose. I reckon he's got an eye for you."

"Nice to see you've recovered both your health and your cheek, Mrs Jamieson. Must be time you were discharged. As for me, alas, I've no time for anything but work."

"Och, you know what they say about all work and no play, lassie."

Charlie detoured to the patient's side to whisper that Doctor Penrose was never dull and certainly not about to escape his clutches, earning himself a cackle from Mrs Jamieson and a raised eyebrow from Grace.

Eventually, Anne took them through an external door into the freezing bite of autumn. The wooden stairs, still slick from overnight rain, were no place for a pregnant woman. Grace turned and rolled her eyes, as she pushed through the door into the abandoned maternity ward.

"It's been years since I was here," Anne said. "The room that used to be reserved for the midwife might be our best bet."

The midwife's room gave the odd sensation of being both deserted and in occasional use, like an abandoned building used by squatters. The air was stale, but not without traces of human life. Discarded hospital cups and cracked enamel plates littered the bench. The narrow bunk still had a mattress, disreputable grey sheets, and a blanket. No nurse would have left it in such a rumpled state.

More to the point, if Henry Ormsby had been here, he was here no longer.

They retraced their steps to the surgeon's room. Wallace was still waiting there, but Gideon Alexander had departed. Wallace returned the reagent bottle Charlie had left with him, holding it by the top.

"I sent Doctor Alexander back to his lodgings," Wallace said. "He's been working non-stop at the hospital, doing his own work and Ormsby's, as well as filling in for the on-call duty surgeon, who is ill. Alexander hasn't been in touch with the Ormsby family since Sunday morning. He was only there for a short time, to pay his respects and see if there was anything he could do for his fiancée and her family. Cecilia received him, but she was in such a dire state that he gave her a sleeping tonic. Richard said the most helpful thing Alexander could do for them was to see to his father's patients until other arrangements could be made. And so he has, unstintingly. I've

223

rarely seen a man so close to being asleep on his feet. Had the devil's own job waking the poor man."

"Did Doctor Alexander talk to Henry last night?" Charlie asked.

"No, he left him to sleep. But he did wake Henry this morning and told him to go home and see to his family, like a man ought to do. However, he thought it was unlikely that Henry would follow his advice. Doctor Alexander is not very impressed by young Henry's character, or lack thereof. Reading between the lines, I think Alexander didn't want to force the issue, as he wishes to remain on good terms with Cecilia's family. That's when the nurse arrived and kicked Henry out."

"I don't suppose Alexander had a theory on where Henry Ormsby would hide next?" Kelly asked.

"I showed him your list of Henry's friends," Wallace said. "His finger went straight to one address on the hills above St Clair beach. Alexander was reluctant to tell me why until I informed him this was a homicide investigation. Seems young Henry is obsessed with fire. He was staying with his friend when Cargill's Castle burned down a couple of months ago. Went on and on about watching the house burn, leaving Alexander with the impression that Henry was mentally unstable. He was so worried about his future brother-in-law, he offered to come with us, despite being half dead with exhaustion. I'm not sure whether Alexander thinks Henry is a danger to himself or danger to others, but it's one or the other, for sure."

Charlie agreed with Alexander's doubts about Henry's mental state. No sane man would pay a man to abduct Grace, in order to convince her that his life was in danger. No wonder Cecilia was so obsessed with marrying a decent man like Gideon Alexander, before he had second or third thoughts about the family he was marrying into. However, Charlie couldn't shake the feeling that Henry was frightened, rather than frightening. Not that he would have been stupid enough to test that theory by turning his back on him, even for a second.

Wallace paced the corridor, deep in thought. On the return lap, the doubt had cleared from his brow. "We need at least two men to confront Henry Ormsby. He is either a killer or unstable. Either way, he is withholding vital evidence. Kelly, you and I will go back to the station. If Elliot and Weston are there, I'll send them to South Dunedin. Otherwise, we will have to go."

Charlie understood Wallace's dilemma, but he had a gut feeling that the answer lay within the Ormsby household.

Wallace pre-empted him. "Pyke, could I ask you to return to the Ormsby house? We cannot ignore the possibility that Henry followed Alexander's advice to go home. We'll follow as soon as we can."

Wallace and Kelly strode off down the corridor, before Charlie could voice his doubts.

Grace took Charlie aside, nodding at Anne, who was seated on a chair, looking her age. "I'd better take my great-aunt home, Charlie."

Charlie passed the two reagent bottles to Grace. "Can you give these two fingerprint samples to Lily, please? Once you're home, stay there. There's a killer on the loose, and I don't think it's Henry Ormsby."

"I agree. I didn't like to interrupt DI Wallace when he was in the mood for action, but I have information for you from our interview with Doctor Harvey. Declan knows, so he will tell Wallace. It may not be relevant, because it happened so long ago, but it confirms our suspicion that Doctor Ormsby had a dubious past."

"I'm all ears, Grace."

"Doctor Harvey loathed Edgar Ormsby because he let a fellow surgeon take the blame for Ormsby's fatal mistake when he lived in Edinburgh. The other surgeon, Iain Thayne, was struck off and ruined. He drowned soon after, either accidentally after drinking too much, or intentionally. Thayne's family vowed revenge. Thayne died exactly ten years ago – the same date as Ormsby's murder."

225

Charlie saw the sparkle in Grace's eyes and knew his own face was equally alight with excitement. "Did Harvey know anything about the Thayne family?"

"Iain Thayne left a wife and three children – two girls and a boy. The family left Edinburgh to stay with relatives, reverting to Mrs Thayne's maiden name. Harvey couldn't recall the widow's name, but Siobhan Mairi Thayne, known as Mairi, rang a vague bell. And Mrs Thayne was a pretty, delicate nurse, who was likely around the same age as Mrs Siobhan Ormsby. I'm going to see Doctor Harvey's wife as soon as I can, in case she remembers more about them."

Charlie touched her hand discreetly, all too aware that they were not alone in the hospital corridor. "What would I do without you, Grace? Send a message to the police station if you find out any more details from Mrs Harvey."

Grace gripped his hand. "I don't like the thought of you being at the Ormsby house on your own, Charlie. Please be careful. I can't afford to lose my favourite private protection agent."

A Hive Of Suspects

Revenge. Now there was a motive that rivalled greed in Charlie's book. To lose a loved one in tragic circumstances was bad enough, without the added stigma of a possible suicide and financial ruin. All caused by another man's mistake. The Thayne family had every reason to hate Doctor Ormsby.

Had Ormsby come to New Zealand to rid himself of his shameful past in Scotland? Had one or more of the Thayne family followed him, after the passage of years had chilled their grief into a bone-deep lust for vengeance? What better method to exact revenge than poison intended for a rat. An agonising death played out in front of colleagues at the rat's own soirée.

Charlie went through Doctor Harvey's evidence as he walked up the hill to the Ormsby house. Grace was right. Mrs Ormsby appeared to be a fair match for the widowed Mrs Thayne – a pretty, delicate nurse of about the right age. Wouldn't Ormsby have recognised the nurse on the ship as Mrs Thayne, from past social events in Edinburgh? Perhaps not if the men kept to themselves and left their wives to discuss non-medical matters. Besides, a clever woman would have no problem disguising herself, by changing her hair, clothes, accent, even her personality. The current Mrs Ormsby was a clever woman, without a doubt.

If the woman who had called herself Siobhan Conway was out for long-plotted, cold-blooded revenge, then killing Ormsby's first wife and taking her place was a masterful opening move. Why then would the new Mrs Siobhan Ormsby wait the best part of a decade to make the next move? To deflect suspicion? To gain more of Ormsby's wealth? Charlie had detected no hint of greed or vitriol within Mrs Ormsby. Quite the opposite. She seemed kind and caring – happy with her life, for the most part.

227

And what of Iain Thayne's children? Charlie couldn't afford to ignore the possibility that the Thayne children were so scarred by their father's death that they had set their sights on revenge. The children were probably of similar age to the Ormsby children. Thus, several members of the Ormsby household were about the right age. Miss Lawson, Finch, and Betsy Dean and her cousin, Duncan Grant, the gardener-stableman. Possibly even Pugh, if the Thaynes had married at a young age. Gideon Alexander too, and no doubt others within the Ormsby's wider social circle. One of Henry's unpleasant friends, perhaps. For that matter, Ivy Beechworth was the right age for Thayne's wife and disliked Ormsby intensely.

Most probably, it was none of them. After all, Charlie had plenty of suspects with motive enough in the present day, without dredging the past for more. He had not ruled out any of the Ormsby family, male or female.

Nor could he rule out a person from outside the household. Richard's lost keys niggled at the back of Charlie's mind. In all likelihood, Richard had merely dropped or mislaid them. But, Richard had assured the butler he had the keys on Saturday morning when he left for the hospital. How then did the keys end up on the mantlepiece after the soirée, to be found by one of the maids on Sunday morning?

If Richard had left the house with his keys, then the keys could have been taken at the hospital. Two men with hospital connections had visited Ormsby on Saturday morning. After the meeting, either might have taken the poison from the workroom and sneaked into the house to add it to Ormsby's heart tonic. Horncastle had been angry with Ormsby, but his motive was weak. Gideon Alexander, in contrast, had good reason to want Ormsby alive, in order to secure a coveted job and a rich wife.

Of all the maybes, there was one name Charlie kept circling back to more than any other. Nelly Lawson. A young woman with an unknown past, who sailed to this country on the same ship as the Ormsby family and captured the eye of both Richard Ormsby and Siobhan Conway, the future Mrs Ormsby. Lawson had ample opportunity to both steal and administer the poison. And motive aplenty. Charlie was fairly sure it was Lawson who had steamed open the will. With Doctor Ormsby out of the way, Lawson could land herself a rich husband and live a gilded life.

As Charlie walked up the path to the familiar front door, he wondered what the collective noun for a gathering of suspects was. A gang of suspects? Given the challenges of gathering this lot together without one or more buzzing off, perhaps it should be a hive of suspects. With or without Wallace, he was not about to let the opportunity to interrogate them pass.

Cecilia flung the door open before the bell had stopped ringing. "Gideon!" She turned her back and flounced off as soon as she realised it wasn't her fiancé, leaving Charlie stranded on the doorstep.

Mr Pugh, the butler, appeared from nowhere and showed him in. "Detective Inspector Wallace telephoned to advise us of your arrival, Mr Pyke. Tea will be served in the drawing room."

Charlie thanked him politely, happy to go along with the ludicrous pretence that this was a normal social gathering. With relief, he saw that many of the suspects were already assembled in the drawing room. Mrs Ormsby and Richard occupied the sofa. Cecilia was in the most comfortable armchair, sipping water. Nelly Lawson was in an inferior chair, seated a little behind and to the side of Mrs Ormsby.

Despite Pugh's discreet announcement of his name, Charlie entered the room into silence. Mrs Ormsby seemed not to notice his arrival, Cecilia glared at him for his abject failure to be Gideon, and Miss Lawson gave her usual impersonation of a waxwork figure, awaiting an order before springing to life.

Only Richard maintained the pretence of a polite morning tea. He stood and showed Charlie to a chair, signalling Lawson to pour the tea. Charlie accepted a cup and a slice of lemon cake. He bided his time, content to play the game, especially as the lemon cake showed every sign of being up to Mrs Brown's exacting standards.

"Doctor Alexander sends his apologies, Miss Cecilia," Charlie said, allowing the half-truth to pass for the sake of Cecilia's heavily bitten fingernails. "He had to operate through the night on account of a sick duty surgeon and a serious accident on the wharf."

"Oh, my poor darling. There now, Richard. Didn't I tell you Gideon had a good reason to be absent?"

Richard raised both eyebrows, which Charlie took to mean that it hadn't been Richard who had doubted Alexander's devotion.

Cecilia kept her eyes fixed on Charlie, as if trying to place a vaguely familiar face. The way she leaned forward and squinted at him suggested a mild short-sightedness she did not wish to correct with spectacles. "I hope you have come to cheer us up, Mr Sykes. The conversation has been quite dismal without Henry and Gideon, and Daddy, of course."

Charlie spluttered his tea. Lawson looked ready to take the birch to Cecilia's rear end.

"Cecilia, please have a care for what you say in a house of mourning," Richard snapped. "Your thoughtlessness towards your stepmother and myself is shameful. You will apologise immediately."

Cecilia put down her teacup and stood up. "Or what, Richard? As if any of you truly mourned Father's loss. You're all hypocrites, or worse. Come now, brother dear, don't pretend to be offended. Even you must think our dear stepmother's desolation is overdone, considering she is now a widow for the second time. To lose one husband is unfortunate, to lose two seems excessively careless. Especially when that 'carelessness' caused our real mother's death."

Lawson jumped up and shoved her chair aside, crashing it to the floor in her haste to get to Cecilia. Cecilia turned her head away, but Lawson jerked it back. "You ungrateful little sow. After all your stepmother has done for you and all the happiness she brought to your miserable father." Lawson whipped her hand up so fast, Cecilia had no chance to avoid the slap.

230

Shock paralysed Cecilia for a second, before spite regained control. "How dare you talk to me like that, you despicable gold-digger? Richard might take his pleasures wherever he can find them, but he will never marry an inconsequential busybody like you."

Cecilia took a step towards the door, but Lawson pulled her back. "At least Richard loves me for who I am. You couldn't get a husband without dangling a huge dowry in front of a poor man. Doctor Alexander will get cold feet long before he reaches the altar, you'll see." Lawson grabbed Cecilia's raised hand before the return slap connected. "Touch me and I'll tell Detective Pyke about you going into your father's bathroom on Saturday afternoon."

Cecilia jerked her hand away. "I was trying a dab of my stepmother's perfume, as you well know. You're on thin ice, slinging accusations at me, Lawson." She dashed for the door, letting out a shriek as she ran into a man standing outside. "Gideon, darling, I didn't see you arrive."

"I'm sure you didn't, Cecilia, given your appalling behaviour over the last few minutes." The young surgeon was as handsome as Grace had hinted and as bone tired as Charlie knew him to be. But, right now, anger mottled Doctor Alexander's good looks and overcame his exhaustion.

"I didn't mean it, honestly, my love," Cecilia pleaded. "I was only repeating what Henry told me."

"You would do well to think for yourself, Cecilia," Gideon snapped, "and show some respect for the family who nurtured you. After Henry came to me with his accusations about your birth mother's death, I requested the ship's surgeon's report from the coroner's archives. If you had bothered to do the same, you would know that there was never any hint of suspicion over your stepmother's role in your mother's death. Indeed, her actions were singled out for praise by the ship's surgeon, as her exemplary nursing saved many passengers from the same fate."

Alexander glared at the woman he had hoped to marry, as if seeing her true nature for the first time. "You will apologise to your stepmother, now."

"Gideon … darling …" Cecilia clutched at Gideon's arm, but she showed no sign of apologising.

Alexander pulled his arm free. "Enough, Cecilia. I have worked back-to-back shifts at the hospital for over two days. I am leaving now and not coming back until I have had a very long sleep and an even longer reflection on my future. If Mrs Ormsby has received an apology, and Inspector Wallace hasn't arrested you or Henry for murder, I will discuss this matter again then."

Alexander ignored Cecilia's outstretched arms and stalked away. His footsteps retreated down the corridor, then the front door closed with a bang. Cecilia was still staring at the empty space where her almost-fiancé had stood a moment ago.

Richard rushed towards her. "Cecilia–"

She vanished in a rustle of skirts. The ensuing silence was broken only by the sound of hysterical sobs, footsteps stomping up the stairs, and Richard's heavy breathing.

The Lady's Maid

Charlie did the only socially acceptable thing he could think of in the circumstances – he sipped his tea and pretended to ignore Cecilia's outburst. He wondered why Richard hadn't intervened earlier, before the situation careered out of control. If Charlie had been here as a gentleman visitor, he would have intervened himself. As a detective, he had learned more about the simmering undercurrents in the house in the past few minutes than he could have gathered in an hour of formal interviewing.

Charlie filed the "throw them all together and light a fuse" interview technique into his arsenal of useful methods and waited for the next round of recriminations to kick off. Meanwhile, he pondered on what he had learned. Not least the fact that both Lawson's neutral English accent and Alexander's upper-class drawl had slipped under duress and betrayed their Scottish origins.

But, most of all, Charlie's attention had been grabbed by Alexander's excessively angry response to Cecilia and especially his last words: "if you or Henry haven't been arrested for murder". To hint that one's own fiancée or her brother might be guilty of murder suggested that Alexander had strong cause to suspect them. Doctor Alexander had learned only this morning, at the hospital, that Ormsby's death was murder, not heart failure. Wallace had sent him back to his lodgings to get some much-needed sleep. What had Alexander recalled that brought him to the Ormsby house instead?

Richard closed the door and crept back to his seat. "I must apologise to you all for my sister's abhorrent outburst. Grief manifests itself in unexpected ways."

Miss Lawson went back to her seat and picked up her teacup, holding it in front of her lips to cover her glee at Cecilia's humiliation. Richard shot a daggered glance at her, which Lawson responded to with a sweet, mildly apologetic smile.

Mrs Ormsby patted Richard's hand, presumably to show she understood his weak excuse for his sister's rudeness. Charlie couldn't imagine that Mrs Ormsby would last long in this house after her husband's funeral, with two stepchildren who did not hide their contempt for her. He hoped, for her sake, she hadn't had to put up with such insolence when Edgar Ormsby was alive. The widow's only hope lay in her sensible future son-in-law pulling them all into line. That is, if Gideon Alexander wasn't lost to the family forever in the wake of Cecilia's outburst.

Richard picked up his teacup and slid a fragile façade of politeness over his embarrassment. He took the gentlemanly way out, by switching to a safer subject. "Mr Pyke, will you inform Miss Penrose and her ladies that I have written to the Hospital Trustees and pledged my support to the new women's ward, adding a donation sufficient to appease Mr Horncastle's ire?"

"That is very thoughtful of you, Mr Ormsby," Charlie replied, "given the many calls you must have upon your time at present. May I also wish you every success in your business venture? Miss Penrose swears by Mrs Ormsby's hand cream for healing rashes from regular handwashing." At this rate, he'd be commenting on the weather next.

Mrs Ormsby raised her head for the first time, revealing swollen red eyes. "Kind of you to say so, Mr Pyke. We will proceed with the venture, in due course." She cut off his reply with a wave of her hand. "Mr Pyke, you are not here to engage in pleasantries, although I admit it is nice to pretend otherwise for a brief moment. What is it you wish of us?"

"I would like to talk to Miss Lawson first, as we were unable to interview her yesterday."

Richard squirmed in his seat, not meeting either Charlie's eyes or Lawson's. "Miss Lawson felt an understandable need for a walk in the fresh air yesterday, Mr Pyke, after exposure to so much suspicion and anguish. Nelly is very sensitive."

Charlie kept his scepticism to himself. Lawson had definitely had her feathers ruffled by Cecilia, but you wouldn't think it to see her now. The Mona Lisa smile was back and all her feathers were in place, from down to primaries.

Charlie addressed Mrs Ormsby again. "Perhaps you would care to have a brief rest, Mrs Ormsby, while I talk to Miss Lawson? I will have to talk to you again after that. Mr Ormsby, would you escort Mrs Ormsby to her room?"

He held the door open for them, giving them no option but to leave. On his way back to his seat, he slipped the glass Cecilia had been sipping from into his napkin. Only four fingerprint samples left to get. He'd have to ask Richard to provide an item from Henry's room or make an excuse to search it.

Charlie resumed his seat, tucking the purloined glass into his bag. He watched Miss Lawson in silence, waiting for her to make the first move. She bore the scrutiny much longer than most suspects would manage, not even fidgeting. She simply sat, holding her cup in her lap, her Mona Lisa eyes never leaving the flames dancing in the fireplace.

Eventually, Lawson placed her teacup on a side table. "I shan't apologise for slapping Miss Ormsby. Somebody had to. However, in all honesty, I must confirm her statement that she was using Mrs Ormsby's perfume, when I found her in the Ormsby's private bathroom." Lawson paused for effect. "What Cecilia was doing before I entered, I cannot say."

"I will be sure to ask her, Miss Lawson," Charlie replied.

"If I were you, Mr Pyke, I would be asking her about Henry's whereabouts too. Cecilia is not as stupid as she pretends to be. She and Henry are as thick as thieves."

Charlie knew Lawson was trying to convey the impression of a dutiful servant, driven to an uncharacteristic act of anger against Cecilia. Her rapid return to her habitual submissive posture and lack of expression left him with the sense of a river flowing under winter ice. Time to break through the rigid surface with a pickaxe.

"Is Lawson the name you were born with?"

Lawson turned as pale as the chip of ice he'd just broken off. "I don't have to answer your questions. You are not a policeman."

"I am a private detective hired by the man you hope to marry, Miss Lawson. Do you want me to summon Richard Ormsby to clarify my right to ask questions?"

Lawson's terrified glance at the door gave her answer. "I am engaged to no man. I am merely a lady's maid in this household."

"Oh, I don't think that's true, Nelly Lawson. You are more a confidante than a lady's maid, and one of the few people trusted with unrestricted access to the workroom. Richard is in love with you and you will do anything to marry him, whether it is for his wealth or for romantic reasons."

She glanced at the door again, her icy composure cracked through to the fears running beneath. "I do love him. I would never, ever do anything to hurt Richard. Or Siobhan … Mrs Ormsby … after all she has done for me."

Charlie sat back and waited. Not long this time. Now the outer ice was fractured, the words came gushing through.

"If you must know, I took my mother's surname when I ran away from home. My father was a vicious drunkard. Innes, his surname was, and I was glad to leave that name behind. He would have killed all of us with his drunken rages eventually, so I saw a chance to make a better life and I took it. What better place to be than half a world away from the brute? Siobhan looked after me on that long, horrible voyage. She made me feel as if I was worth something – that I deserved a decent future. Whether or not Richard marries me, I will be honoured to work by Siobhan Ormsby's side. We will make her business a success for the betterment of those in need."

Charlie had heard the slightest creak of the door easing open during this heartfelt declaration and wondered if she had heard it too. He prayed Richard wouldn't barge in. "And if he does marry you?"

Lawson's voice softened. "I will continue my work, but I will also be the happiest woman in the world. I don't care whether Richard is a pauper or a lord. Not everyone craves riches, you know. Most of us are happy with a comfortable home and loving companions."

"Very commendable, Miss Lawson." Charlie caught the quick flick of her eyes towards the door, confirming his impression that Lawson was playing to an audience. "If you care so little for wealth, why did you take the trouble to listen at doors to hear what Doctor Ormsby was up to? And why did you steam open Ormsby's new will and search through his documents?"

The ice closed over again in an instant. "I most certainly did not."

Richard barged in, with Agnes trailing behind him, her eyes wide.

Richard moved across the room swiftly, taking Lawson's hand and pulling her from the chair to his side. "That is quite enough, Mr Pyke. Nelly has been exemplary in her behaviour from the first moment I met her, when she was mopping my sick mother's fevered brow on the ship. I can assure you, without reservation, that Nelly had nothing to do with my father's death. She would never stoop to eavesdropping. And steaming open Father's will? Absurd."

Agnes skipped around Charlie's chair, coming to a stop in centre stage. "Nelly told a fib. I'm not allowed to tell fibs."

"Agnes–" Richard began.

Charlie interrupted. "What was Nelly fibbing about Agnes?"

"Nelly does like to listen at doors," Agnes said. "And I've seen her in Daddy's study, searching through his papers. See, Mr Pyke, Nelly's gone all red."

"Nelly, it's not true, is it?" Richard's words trailed off at the sight of Lawson's defiant glare.

Agnes did a little twirl to recapture her audience's attention. "Nelly told Mummy that Daddy was going to take all the money

237

from her hand cream. My Mummy's very clever at making things. Everyone says so."

Richard gaped at his half-sister. Disbelief quickly turned to anger, as her words sank in. He swung around to Lawson, grabbing her arm. "Nelly? What's this about my father taking the money from the hand cream?"

Lawson wrenched free of his grip. "You're so hopelessly naïve, Richard. I had to stoop to deceit in order to protect your interests. Your father was playing you all like puppets, making you dance to his tune while he plotted behind your back. He could see from your business plan that the hand cream would make a fortune, and he wanted it for himself. I didn't kill him, but I'm not sorry he's gone."

Richard's expression wavered between fury and pain. As Charlie watched, Richard gathered his emotions behind rigid muscles. "And you told my stepmother all this, but didn't think to tell me? I can see you are right, Lawson. I have been a played for a fool."

"Richard, dearest, I was going to tell you. There was no time..." Lawson swiped away a tear and made a dash for the door before Richard could reply.

"Nelly, come back here, right now." Richard waited less than a second for her not to obey, before running after her.

Two pairs of feet ran up the stairs, followed by a door slamming. Seconds later, Richard hammered on Lawson's door and called her name. He stomped back down the stairs and through the house, leaving by the French doors, presumably to let off steam in the garden.

Agnes remained behind, observing Charlie with her head perked to one side and a small smile playing over her rosebud lips. "Can you make anything else besides paper angels?"

Charlie set aside a whirlwind of thoughts and tore a sheet of paper out of his notebook. "Do you like swans? Flowers? How about an elephant?"

The elephant received a vigorous nod. As Charlie folded, Agnes watched intently. "You're right about your mother, Agnes. My friend says her hand cream is marvellous."

"Is that your kissing friend, Miss Penrose? Mummy says she is going to be a doctor. Is that really true?"

"It is. Miss Penrose is very clever, like your mother. She is in your brother's class at medical school." The elephant was looking more like a lopsided teapot as Charlie waited for her response.

"Half-brother," Agnes corrected.

"Have you seen Henry recently, Agnes?" Charlie heard a door close upstairs. Light footsteps moved towards the stairs. He didn't have much time.

"Cecilia has," Agnes said. "I heard her say so. But you'll have to ask Betsy to find out where Henry is hiding."

"Betsy the maid? How would she know?" The memory of the pretty, flirtatious housemaid using Henry's first name so casually triggered an inappropriate thought. Was he going to waste an opportunity to question this inquisitive little girl for the sake of propriety? Not likely. "Are Betsy and Henry kissing friends?"

"Eww, no." Agnes screwed up her face and shook her head emphatically enough to make her curls swing. "Henry ignores Betsy now, but Betsy told me Henry used to play with her and the other children on the ship, even though he wasn't supposed to. Betsy only had a bunk, not even a proper cabin, or so she says." Agnes paused to observe his reaction. Not seeing a suitable level of shock and awe, she upped the ante. "Henry sneaks out of his room at night to go into town with Duncan Grant, the gardener. Betsy is jealous because she can't go and have fun with them, like she used to on the ship when they were children."

Charlie handed over the elephant-teapot, which Agnes promptly undid to see how it was made. There were so many urgent questions requiring answers. Should he track down Lawson to demand proof of her original surname, which she had probably discarded long ago? Question Mrs Ormsby about her origins? Go after Alexander to find out why he suspected Cecilia and Henry? Or find Betsy in the hope she would lead him to Henry Ormsby?

Fate intervened, in the form of Mrs Ormsby, who appeared at the door, straightening her rumpled hair. "What on earth is causing all the uproar in this house? Cecilia is locked in her room, Nelly didn't answer my knock, and Richard appears to have left the house." Her gaze went straight to Agnes, with a what-have-you done-now look.

"Mr Pyke made me an elephant, Mummy." Agnes inspected the refolded paper. "I think it is an African one, on account of the large ears, but it is rather hard to tell."

"Go find nanny, Agnes, and stay in the nursery." Mrs Ormsby accompanied her daughter to the door and waited for her to go upstairs, before taking a seat. "What has my little mischief-maker been up to now, Mr Pyke?"

Charlie saw no need to sugar-coat the truth. "Agnes saw Miss Lawson going through your husband's papers and steaming open his new will. She also overheard Miss Lawson tell you that Doctor Ormsby intended to take over your natural remedies business. Richard was upset at both her dishonesty and her decision to tell you what she found, rather than him."

Mrs Ormsby sank into the armchair and closed her eyes. "It was very wrong of Nelly to snoop like that. And wrong of Edgar to be so deceitful. For the record, I don't believe Edgar would have taken over the business. According to Nelly, he had jotted his thoughts on Richard's proposal – just thoughts, not necessarily a final decision. Naturally, if Edgar invested in the business, he would have some say, but he had no need of further wealth. I would have talked him around. I always do."

Charlie kept his views to himself. He doubted her naïve enough to believe a rich man was ever satisfied with what he had, when further wealth was attainable. Time to see what lay beneath the widow's superficial charms.

"Did you know Miss Lawson before the voyage, when she went by another name?"

Mrs Ormsby jerked her head up. "I met her on the ship. Nelly doesn't like to talk about her past, but I gather her father was violent, poor girl."

"What of your own past, Mrs Ormsby? Your previous husband's name was Conway, I believe, or am I wrong about that?"

"What a strange thing to ask, Mr Pyke. Why the sudden interest in my past?"

"The past makes us who we are, Mrs Ormsby."

She perked her head to one side, looking uncannily like an older version of her daughter. "Surely it is our character that makes us what we are, not our past."

"But our character is inevitably shaped by our past. I must ask you again, Mrs Ormsby, what was the surname of your first husband and why did you choose to leave Scotland for New Zealand?"

"I have a marriage certificate to prove my married name was Conway, née Anderson. My first husband was a good man who became swept up in the excitement of the new inventions of our era. He lost all our money investing in electrical therapeutic devices." She shook her head. "Don't ask. It was a fool's venture. My husband had a delicate constitution. He didn't last long in the debtor's prison. New Zealand was offering paid passage for qualified nurses. It seemed a better option than staying to watch the bailiff uplift the last of our belongings."

Mrs Ormsby made her tale sound plausible, just as Nelly Lawson had. Charlie prided himself on sniffing out lies and misdirection, but these two had him stumped. If their stories were true, they both had plenty of practice at surviving in a harsh world. "Does the name Iain Thayne mean anything to you?"

"No, I don't think so." Mrs Ormsby hesitated. "My husband may have mentioned him once. I seem to recall the name came up at his interview for the surgeon role in Dunedin. It's a long time ago, but I do remember Edgar being upset. An old rivalry, I assume."

Charlie tried a change of tack. "Did you see Mr Horncastle outside your workroom on Saturday morning?"

241

A faint blush painted Mrs Ormsby's cheeks pink. "I only went to see if the workroom door was properly locked. I admit I pretended not to see Horncastle, assuming he wanted to dissuade me from my support of the women's ward. That man is like a dog with an old bone, refusing to let go. As if I didn't have enough to do with the supper party that evening and the salon still to be decorated. Rather than talk to him, I exited via the stable."

Mrs Ormsby waited for the next question. When Charlie let the silence drag, she filled it.

"Mr Pyke, I didn't kill my husband. Edgar could be frustrating, but I did love him. When you meet someone you cannot live without, you will know what it is like, even if others do not see the attraction." She perked her head to one side again. "But perhaps you already know that feeling? Do people ask your beloved what she sees in you, never looking beyond the surface differences to the character at the heart of you both?"

She threw his tactic right back at him, letting the question hover in silence. When Charlie didn't answer, she smiled knowingly, as if he had poured out his heart. These darned women and their intuitions. The police force would be well served by recruiting a few to refine the interrogation techniques currently used.

Charlie had intended to ask about the first Mrs Ormsby's death, but now it seemed pointless, as well as offensive. "That will be all for now, Mrs Ormsby, unless you have anything further to add."

She rose and smiled again – a genuine smile that had him smiling back. "You have made a good choice, I believe, as I did. You need never doubt you are loved for who you are, Mr Pyke."

When she had left the room, Charlie realised he was still smiling. Mrs Ormsby was either one of the nicest and most perceptive women he had ever met, or a master manipulator. He was fairly sure that she was the former, but was that not merely proof of the latter? Charlie sat alone longer than he intended, but even another slice of the delicious lemon cake did not resolve the conundrum. Eventually, he brushed the crumbs off his waistcoat and went in search of Betsy Dean.

Memory Box

Grace ate her food without tasting it. Sharing a midday meal with her great-aunt was a rare treat and not one to be wasted with worries she could not control. Yet she couldn't dismiss the feeling that Charlie was in danger, alone at the Ormsby house. Grace couldn't send Sergeant Pyke or Alistair Stewart to Charlie's aid, as they were out. She couldn't go herself, as Mrs Harvey might send a message. Lily and Jasmine had eaten quickly, before heading next door to examine the new fingerprint samples.

The sound of her name cut through her distraction. "My apologies. What did you say, Auntie?"

"I said, I think you should give up medical school and learn how to cook," Anne replied. "I was merely testing whether you were listening to me."

Grace spluttered her mouthful of soup. "When I become a doctor, I will be able to afford to pay someone to cook for me, thereby giving two people a job they enjoy. If I can convince paying patients that a woman doctor can be as good as a man."

"There are more sick people than competent doctors," Anne pointed out. "Although, it is true that those who need help the most cannot afford a qualified doctor. Do stop fidgeting, Grace. Charlie can handle anything the Ormsby household throws at him."

"I cannot help but worry. The murderer will be anxious that we are close on his or her heels. A person ruthless enough to kill once will not hesitate to kill again."

The bell rang at the front door. Grace knocked over her cup in her eagerness to answer. She flung the door open with a crash, but it wasn't Charlie.

"Everything all right, Grace?" Anne's beau, Kenneth Drummond, held out a note to her. "The messenger was about to ring when I arrived."

Grace led the way to the scarred old wooden table, at which she and Anne had been eating. Anne had recently started receiving Drummond in the informal comfort and warmth of the kitchen, rather than the formality of the drawing room. A sure sign that Anne had accepted him as part of her inner circle, after a long period of pretending she was too old and cantankerous to have a gentleman suitor.

While Anne greeted Drummond with a discreet kiss on the cheek, Grace opened the note, which invited her to call on Mrs Harvey at her convenience.

"No need for sustenance, my dear." Drummond was saying. "I am on the way to my club to chase down a potential opportunity for young Charlie Pyke. A 'lead', I ought to call it, in the parlance of detectives. I am only here for a moment, to leave the official documentation for the establishment of the new business."

"Kenneth, I do believe this detecting business has given you a new lease on life. Did you settle on 'Stewart, Wu, Penrose, Pyke, Pyke, Pyke, Drummond, Macmillan and Brown' or Southern Investigations Agency?"

"The latter, I'm pleased to say, for the sake of the ink level in my inkpot."

Grace wanted to see the document – not quite believing that this crazy idea of a private detective agency was now official. However, she had other priorities right now. "Mr Drummond, do you know where Alistair Stewart and Sergeant Pyke might be found?"

"Visiting a police officer of their mutual acquaintance, I believe. The alternative being a visit to the manchester department of Dick & McKechnie's store. Lily and Jasmine have taken to home decorating with the fervour of a battalion under the Duke of Wellington."

"Do you know where the men are meeting? I need to find them, quite urgently, because Charlie may need assistance at the Ormsby house. I don't wish to overstate the level of danger, but he is there alone, potentially in the company of a cold-blooded murderer."

Drummond pushed his chair back with the energy of a much younger man. "Leave it to me, Grace. I believe they are at the same club I frequent, which does not allow ladies to enter." He flung an apologetic glance at Anne, but wisely left the argument over male-only clubs until a later time.

Grace made haste to follow Drummond. Sharing the buggy would get her to Mrs Harvey all the sooner. She waved a farewell to Anne, who was smiling to herself as she gathered up the dishes.

As Drummond took up the reins and urged the sleeping horse to life, Grace regretted her melodramatic words. Was Charlie really at risk in the presence of the Ormsby family? He would hate it if Alistair and his father turned up unannounced and interrupted a critical interview.

Grace jolted out of her musing as the buggy halted for traffic at the bottom of High Street. No matter what character they showed to the world, everyone in the family had a financial motive to kill Edgar Ormsby. The question remained, were there other, hidden motives, buried inside, which had driven someone within the household to take a life?

They pulled to a halt outside Drummond's club, where Grace took over the reins. Drummond trotted in at full septuagenarian speed. He returned less than two minutes later to report that Alistair and Thomas had already left.

"I don't know where they went, Grace," Drummond said. "I could come with you instead."

"No need, Mr Drummond. You have your meeting to attend. Charlie will be fine." Grace hoped she was right. After all, there wasn't much Charlie Pyke couldn't handle on his own. Except perhaps a firearm … or a bludgeon from behind … or poison in his tea.

"If you insist, Miss Penrose. But you ought to take the buggy."

Grace bade Drummond farewell and flicked the reins. She focussed on avoiding delivery carts, trams, meandering pedestrians and skittish horses, until she reach the Harvey's house. There, Grace tied the horse to a nearby rail and patted her glossy neck, promising not to be long. Grace expected no revelations from Mrs Harvey. A decade was a long time ago. The mare waved her tail agreeably, having discovered a patch of lush grass within foraging distance.

Mrs Harvey was charming, if rather puzzled at Grace's haste for answers. "My husband's note said you want to know the maiden name of Iain Thayne's wife. Siobhan or similar, he thinks, for her first name, but I only knew her as Mairi. I hope it's not important. It's so long ago and my memory isn't what it was. I only knew the lass after she married Iain."

"But you do recall Iain Thayne and his family, Mrs Harvey?" Grace asked.

"How could I forget? Terrible tragedy. I wish we could have done more for them, but Mairi's uncle was determined to take her away to a quiet place to recover. He had a croft on Skye, if I recall rightly. I'll never forget Iain's children at the funeral. The elder lass could barely stand upright, the younger lass crying a river of tears, and the son trying his best to hold his grief inside so he could support them all. Far too heavy a burden to bear for young folk."

Grace wasn't sure what else she could ask. "I know it is a long shot, but do you recall anything about the Thayne family? What his wife looked like? The names and ages of the children, perhaps?"

"Mairi was a pretty lass, as I recall." Mrs Harvey stared dreamily into space for a moment, before sitting up with a start. "Och, what a numpty I am. I'm forgetting it'll be in the 'hatch, match and dispatch' box. Why you want to know, I'll not ask, as I can see you're in a hurry." She went to a cabinet, rummaging within the overflowing contents and withdrawing a bulging box. "All the christenings, weddings, and funerals we ever attended are in this box."

It seemed to take forever, although Mrs Harvey's aged fingers flicked at speed through the pile.

"Here it is – the invitation to Iain and Mairi's wedding." Mrs Harvey held up a gold-embossed invitation. "It seems my husband was wrong about the name of Iain's wife. Not Siobhan, but Shelagh." She held the invitation to her heart, which was a touching expression of her feelings for her son's best friend, but added to the frustration for Grace, who could not see the writing.

"A terrible time she had, poor Mairi," Mrs Harvey continued. "I heard she went back to using her maiden name after the tragedy of her husband's death. Poor lass never left her uncle's house again, so they say. I believe the girls were forced to go into service. Such a shame, when they were so bright. But for the slip of a scalpel, they would surely have been wives in grand households."

The doctor's wife shook her head sadly. "Iain's children worshipped him. His death was a terrible blow." Mrs Harvey recollected her purpose and passed the wedding invitation to Grace.

Grace took one look at the elegant gold script and sprinted for the door, leaving Mrs Harvey slack-jawed in her wake. Grace tore the reins from the hitching post and vaulted onto the seat, urging the startled mare into a fast trot. She gave thanks for the manoeuvrable little buggy as she sped through the streets to the police station. Grace stopped only long enough to demand that the desk officer pass on the name of the killer to Wallace and Kelly with the utmost urgency.

Then she was back in the buggy, urging the horse up the hill, knowing deep in her bones that Charlie was in danger. She could only hope she wasn't too late. How she wished she had left a message for Thomas Pyke and Alistair Stewart to go to the Ormsby house immediately, but wishes would not magically bring them to his aid.

The Stables

Betsy was on her knees in one of the guest rooms, scrubbing the hearth. She put the brush down as Charlie entered, but only to take up the kindling to lay the fire. "I can't stop to talk to ye, Charlie Not-A-Copper. We've a funeral to prepare for."

"I've only one question for you, Betsy. Do you know where Henry Ormsby is?"

"Now, whyever would I know that?" Betsy fumbled the pieces of wood, collapsing the kindling pyramid.

"The police need to know, Betsy. Henry's life may be at risk."

She turned to face him. "You think Henry killed his father."

"No, I don't. And I mean it. I think Henry's life is at risk." Charlie didn't repeat Gideon Alexander's suspicion that Henry was mentally unstable and likely to be feeling desperate, knowing the police suspected him.

Betsy looked him in the eye and saw he was in earnest. "My cousin, Duncan Grant, has hidden him in the stable. Duncan's the gardener and stableman. He's the only person who ever goes into the stable, so we knew Henry would be safe there."

"I expect you have looked after your friend too, by taking him food and clothes, and telling him what is happening in the house." Her downcast eyes confirmed his suspicions. "Don't worry, Betsy, I won't get you into trouble."

Charlie took her downstairs with him, so she couldn't run to the stable to warn Henry. He made her wait, while he telephoned the police station. Wallace and Kelly were out, so he left an urgent message that Henry Ormsby was hiding in the Ormsby stables, not across the other side of the city near Cargill's fire-ravaged former mansion.

248

Charlie warned Betsy to stay in the house, while he went to find Henry. As he reached the French doors onto the terrace, Agnes rushed in from the garden, her little face pinched with fear.

"Henry is asleep on the floor of Mummy's workroom," Agnes squeaked. "I went around to open the door, but there are hay bales outside. Someone has lit a fire. It wasn't me, honest."

Charlie had heard enough. "Fire," he yelled at full volume, hoping the fire hadn't had time to take hold in the wooden structure of the stables. "Stay inside, Agnes. Tell Mr Pugh. Tell everyone."

Charlie pushed the French doors open, slamming them on their hinges. As he ran down the steps of the terrace, a tendril of smoke escaped from the entrance to the workroom lobby.

Duncan Grant was racing across the garden from the other direction. When Charlie reached the workroom entrance, the gardener had already stripped off his coat and was using it to beat out the flames, which had taken hold in bales of hay stacked in the lobby.

Charlie stripped off his own coat. Together, he and Grant beat the flames down. Inside the main house, a bell rang, creating an infernal din. He could hear shouts and running, dominated by Pugh's commanding voice at a full roar. "Stables on fire. Form a bucket brigade."

After a panicked few minutes, it seemed as if he and Grant had succeeded in quelling the flames. But, as soon as they stopped beating, Charlie could see that the fire still smouldered deep within the dry hay, beyond the reach of their coats. With a jolt of fear, Charlie remembered the store of flammable chemicals on the opposite side of the lobby from where the hay was stacked. They didn't have much time. If the flames took hold and spread across the lobby, it would soon be a bonfire worthy of Mr Fawkes and his gunpowder plot.

The fire was still concentrated in the front bales but spreading. Charlie leaped across to the rear bales, stacked up against the workroom door. The door was locked and the keyhole was blocked. He tried to kick the door open, but the angle was wrong and the door was far too solid. The heat from the resurgent flames seared through his trousers, forcing him to leap away.

"We could try to drag the bales outside," Charlie shouted, over the steadily growing crackle of the fire.

"It's too late," Grant shouted back. "I need to get the two horses out of the stable."

The gardener-stableman fled around the corner to the stable entrance. The fire was quickly taking hold in the dry hay, driving Charlie back. Behind him, Pugh yelled for him to stand aside. Charlie ducked as a bucketful of water sloshed past him. Behind Pugh, the terrified household staff passed buckets and basins and pots of water along a chain from a series of rainwater barrels around the side of the building.

Mrs Ormsby ran up, pushing past everyone, trying to enter the workroom. "Henry!" she yelled, but the heat beat her back. She stood in the doorway, mesmerised by the flames.

Pugh hauled her aside, pushing a baking bowl into her hand. "Help with the water," he commanded.

Mrs Ormsby grabbed the bowl and joined the bucket brigade. Cecilia watched, horrified, from the safety of the terrace, holding Agnes in her arms. Richard Ormsby and Nelly Lawson were nowhere to be seen.

The hay bales were all alight now, the flames licking at the thick door to the workroom. Worse still, the fire was spreading across the other side of the lobby towards the flammables store. The noise was ferocious.

"Pugh," Charlie yelled. "Get everyone clear if the fire reaches the flammables store." He had to repeat it before the butler got the gist. Pugh's eyes went wide, and he grabbed the incoming bucket with renewed vigour.

Charlie could see the bucket brigade was losing the battle with the fire. There had to be another way to get Henry out. He ran to the tree outside the workroom window and scrambled up into the branches. The flames had not yet penetrated the workroom, but the

250

room was slowly filling with deadly smoke, which streamed in around the edges of the door.

Inside, he could see Henry on the floor, motionless, despite the chaos unfolding on the other side of the workroom door. He couldn't tell if Henry was already dead, but he could see no signs of injury. Had he been wrong in thinking Henry innocent of his father's death? Was this the final suicidal act of a guilty man? Or a second murder by a ruthless killer? Either way, burning to death was a terrible was to go.

The bars on the window were embedded deep within the frame. Charlie would need help to get in that way. Out of the corner of his eye, he saw Duncan Grant leading two terrified horses out of the stable and down the side of the main house to safety. He waved to get Grant's attention, but the stableman was fully occupied keeping his charges from bolting.

Charlie yanked at the bars covering the window, cursing their rigid refusal to yield to his muscles, even when he planted his feet on the wall to gain maximum force. No matter how hard he heaved, the bars didn't budge. What he needed was an implement to provide more leverage. There must be a spade or some sort of pry bar in the stable.

Charlie dropped from the tree. As he ran along the path that led to the stable entrance, he remembered that the cupboard within the workroom had been formed from an old stall in the stable. Presumably the wall would be a standard interior wall, wooden framed and plastered. Much easier to break through than the window bars. And much safer, as the cupboard was on the other side of the workroom from the fire and the flammables store.

The inside of the stable was blissfully calm and cool, with only the faintest whiff of smoke. The horse stall that had been converted into the workroom cupboard was easy to spot. Charlie grabbed a mallet from a rack of tools and attacked the back end of the cupboard, smashing through the plaster with ease.

"Drop the mallet," a voice said behind him. "Walk back to the stable entrance and lie on the ground with your face down."

Charlie swung around, mallet at the ready. The black hole at the end of a revolver barrel pointed at him, unwavering.

"Put the mallet down. Now."

Charlie dropped the mallet. He looked into the face of a murderer, expecting to see evil or insanity. Instead, he saw compassion. And apologetic determination. A flicker of hope ignited. Charlie might still talk his way out of this situation, if he remained calm. Easier said than done, when standing a trigger-squeeze away from death. He walked backwards down the stable to the entrance, with his hands in the air.

Rapid footsteps crunched on the gravel drive behind him. He tensed, ready for an accomplice to attack. He heard the swish of fabric – a woman's skirt.

"You shouldn't be here," the killer said. "Best you walk away now. I'd rather you not see what happens next."

Grace stepped between Charlie and the gun. "Don't you dare tell me what to do, when you are holding a revolver on my sweetheart. You're not going to shoot me, Thayne, so why don't you put down the gun, and let us rescue whomever you are trying to kill in there. Your father was a medical man, who took an oath to save lives. He would not want this evil revenge."

"My father can no longer save lives, because Ormsby destroyed him with a lie. I can't let you interfere, although I would hate to have to shoot a woman of your undoubted skills. I intend to keep my vow to my family, that I will rid the world of every last drop of Ormsby blood. I was hoping to take over his fortune as well. God knows my family deserves it after what he did to them. But their deaths are my priority."

Grace stayed calm, even as the revolver barrel remained three feet from her nose. "Don't be a fool, Thayne. Edgar Ormsby did a terrible thing, letting your father take the blame for his mistake, but his family had no part in it."

"Grace, get out of the way," Charlie begged. "Let me handle this."

Grace ignored him and took a step towards the end of the revolver. "You won't shoot me. It's not in your nature."

The revolver didn't waver.

Charlie moved to go around her, desperate to get between her and the killer. Out of the corner of his eye, he spotted his father and Alistair sprinting towards them. He needed to distract the killer's attention, right now. Charlie grabbed Grace roughly. "Gracie Lee, don't you dare disobey me. You know what happened last time you did. Get out of the way." He shoved her aside, hoping she had taken the hint.

Grace stumbled backwards over a bale of hay, screaming as her left hand hit the ground. "You've broken my wrist, you brute," she cried, writhing on the floor, milking the drama. "Don't just stand there, help me."

The tip of the revolver wavered. Thomas Pyke jumped the killer from the rear, letting out a mighty roar as he jerked the revolver skyward. Charlie joined the attack at leg level. A shot rang out, showering them with sharp fragments of roof tiles and pigeon droppings. With the two angry Pykes squashing their captive, Alistair Stewart stepped forward and retrieved the gun.

Thomas pulled handcuffs from his coat and fixed one cuff to a wrist. "Threaten my son and his girl again and you'll regret it."

"You stay here, Pa," Charlie ordered. "I've got to get into the workroom. Henry Ormsby is about to die in there."

Thomas Pyke clipped the other cuff to Alistair. "You're not going in alone, son."

Charlie didn't have time to argue. Together, he and his father ran back into the stable and broke through the wall into the cupboard behind the workroom. It took them mere seconds, with powerful strokes of the mallet and a nearby axe. But seconds were precious, with the fire raging on the other side of the building.

Tendrils of smoke gushed out to meet them. Charlie thrust his head through the hole and saw a body lying in the cupboard. It

253

couldn't be Henry, who was in the main workroom. Through streaming eyes, he recognised Richard Ormsby's shoes.

Charlie and his father plunged in, grabbing a leg each and pulling Richard out. Both men were coughing. The victim was ominously still. The sickly-sweet smell of chloroform oozed from the rag tied around Richard's nose and mouth. Charlie ripped it off.

"Take him out to the fresh air, Pa," he ordered. "Grace will know what to do." Charlie grabbed an empty feed sack and wrapped it around his nose and mouth, before taking a deep breath and disappearing back into the rear of the cupboard.

He burst through the cupboard door into the thicker smoke of the workroom. His lungs demanded air, but he couldn't risk inhaling the smoke and whatever toxic chemicals lurked in the air. All he could do was crawl across the floor, feeling for a body in the middle of the room, trying not to breathe.

The only visible object was the main door to the workroom, glowing red around the edges as the fire ate away at it. Fortunately, its stout construction had survived so far, but it wouldn't hold off the wrath of the fire for much longer. Across the lobby, the flames must surely be close to the flammables store. And when that happened, the ether and alcohol stored inside would ignite and turn him into charcoal.

All Charlie could see was a dense swirl of black and grey. His fingers touched a leg. He pulled at the body, drawing it to himself to get a better grip. Desperate for oxygen now, he took a gasp of air from low to the floor. Smoke rushed into his lungs, sending him into an uncontrollable spasm of coughing. He hoisted up the body, hoping it was the only one left in this hellhole.

Now all he had to do was find his way out. Charlie took a step, before realising he couldn't see where the cupboard door was. Smoke swirled around in front of his eyes and filled his lungs, stealing his consciousness and turning the body in his arms to lead.

A muscular, Pyke-sized arm caught him around the waist and propelled him out the back route into the stables. Charlie ran blindly beside his father, knocking into the door frame and shelving, jostling bottles of herbs and potions.

As they emerged into the light, Charlie could hear screaming and an ominous roaring. Pugh shouting for everyone to run, in a parade-ground bellow that would have done a Sergeant-Major proud.

Footsteps crunched on the gravel at a run. Somebody grabbed Henry's body from his arms. Thomas Pyke lifted Charlie as if he weighed no more than a goose-down pillow, then dashed to safety at the far end of the drive. Powerful hands ripped off the feed sack and held him in a tight embrace, while Charlie sucked in blissful fresh air.

A giant whoosh cut off all other sounds. The fire had reached the flammables store. Flames shot up through the walls and roof, creating a fireball of scorching heat.

Charlie watched in dazed horror as the inferno raced through the roof-space and enveloped the stables. He would have died in there if his father hadn't rescued him. Grace had saved his life too, stepping in front of that revolver. Where was she?

The figures around him danced in front of his smoke-ravaged eyes. Alistair Stewart, still handcuffed to the instigator of this madness, stared at the blaze. Horror and despair battled for space on his face, turning to palpable relief when he swung around and saw Charlie.

Richard Ormsby was on the ground, moaning. Mrs Ormsby knelt beside her stepson, cooling his exposed skin with water. Agnes was next to her mother, using her own tiny handkerchief to wash away the soot from her half-brother's face. Pugh and Finch ran up with a stretcher for Richard. Nelly Lawson hurried behind them, calling Richard's name through sobs, but Richard kept his face turned away. Mrs Ormsby rose with the stretcher, accompanying her stepson into the house, with Agnes holding fast to her hand. Lawson let a moment pass, but none of them turned back. She ran after them.

Betsy Dean and Duncan Grant raced up with a second stretcher, passing Charlie by. He turned to see them roll Henry Ormsby's body onto it. Grace was beside Henry, on her knees, checking his vital signs and looking concerned, but not excessively so. Apparently, the Ormsby brothers would live.

As soon as Betsy and her cousin stretchered Henry away, Grace redirected her attention to Charlie. Instead of giving him the embrace he longer for, Grace ordered Thomas Pyke to hold his son still, while she plunged his singed fingers into cool water and prised open his eyes. "Charlie Pyke, what in heaven's name were you thinking, running into a burning building? And you too, Sergeant Pyke." Her voice cracked. She turned her face away and busied herself with checking him for injuries.

"Sorry, Grace," Thomas said. "I would have stopped him, but he was too intent on issuing orders to listen to his old man." Thomas glanced up at Alistair. "Didn't you teach Charlie to obey his seniors, Alistair?"

Alistair shrugged, but he wore the same proud smile as Charlie's father. "What can I do, Thomas? One case as a private detective and he forgets everything he knows. I suppose we'll have to forgive him, as he and Grace did solve the case and save two lives."

"Only with the help of everyone in the Southern Investigations team," Grace said as she gently washed the soot from Charlie's eyes.

"A grand start to our business venture," Alistair said. "Although, next time, it would be nice to solve the case without almost killing our client. I assume the man chained to me is our murderer?"

Charlie looked to Grace to reply. After all, she was the one who figured out the final piece of the puzzle.

"He is," Grace replied. "Let me introduce Gideon Alexander, previously known as Gideon Thayne. How did you know to come to our aid, Alistair?"

"Lily and Jasmine made a fingerprint match to the sample Charlie got this morning at the hospital," Alistair replied.

Doctor Gideon Alexander stood beside Alistair Stewart with such calm and dignity, it looked as if they were nothing more than old friends passing the time of day. "How did you work it out, Grace? I've been so careful."

"Unfortunately for you, Gideon, Doctor Beechworth recalled doubts had been raised over Ormsby's references when he started as a surgeon in Dunedin because of a scandal in his past. And Doctor Harvey knew all the details, because his son was best friends with your father in Edinburgh. Harvey even went to your father's wedding." Grace pulled a thick piece of card out of a hidden pocket in her skirt.

Charlie read out the elegantly penned words: "To celebrate the marriage of Shelagh Mairi Alexander to Iain Gideon Thayne."

"I'm deeply sorry for the tragedy your family suffered, Gideon," Grace continued. "Doctor Harvey told me how Ormsby lied to save his position, condemning your father to disgrace. You had every right to be angry. But murder?" She waved a hand to take in the burning building. "And this? Not even the unforgivable ordeal your family faced could justify such terrible revenge."

"You're wrong, Grace." Gideon Alexander Thayne spoke with the strength and certainty of a man fighting for a just cause. "Ormsby not only killed my father, he took everything from our family, including my father's good name. My mother never left the house again and died a broken woman, while my sisters were forced into a life of hardship and servitude. My uncle sacrificed his savings to put me through medical school, far away in London, so I wouldn't be tainted by my father's disgrace. Ironically, I could not repay my uncle, because I was unable to get a position without the right family connections."

Gideon looked at Grace, almost tenderly, begging her understanding. "All the while, Ormsby's family was living in luxury. His children had everything they could wish for. Not that they were the least bit grateful. Do you not think I was justified in taking back what ought to have been mine and my family's? To give my own sisters a chance for a decent life? To repay my uncle? To buy a headstone for my parents' graves? I would do it all again without hesitation. I may not have taken his fortune or wiped out his tainted bloodline, but I got my revenge on Ormsby."

Cecilia appeared around the side of the stables. She broke into a stumbling run on seeing them. "Gideon, my darling. Did you hear that Henry and Richard were hurt in the fire? Thank the Lord you have come back again…" Her words petered out as she saw the handcuffs.

Gideon looked down at his supposed love with disgust. "They will live, more's the pity. They will continue to be rich and pompous and ungrateful, when they deserve nothing but shame and penury."

Cecilia shrunk from the searing contempt of Gideon's words and burst into tears.

"Yes, that's right Cecilia, wallow in tears as you always do when you do not get your way. Did you really think I wanted to marry you for anything other than your money?" Gideon spun away from Cecilia. "For heaven's sake, take me away from these despicable people."

Thomas Pyke and Alistair Stewart led him away. Gideon held his head high and never looked back. Cecilia ran into the house, weeping, not realising how close she had come to marrying a man who would certainly have murdered her too, once her fortune had been secured.

Charlie and Grace were left standing alone on the drive in a haze of smoke. Grace stared after Gideon, her face tense with shock and pain. He put his arm around her and led her away from the chaos into the tranquil seclusion of the trees beyond, where he crushed her to his chest. He held her close until she stopped shaking. "My brilliant, courageous love. You were magnificent."

Grace ran a hand over his face. It came away black. "As I recall, you were the one who had the courage to run into a burning building to save two lives."

"I wouldn't have been alive to rescue them if you hadn't stepped in front of that revolver." Charlie lifted her chin, leaving a sooty smudge. "Promise me you will never try to sacrifice yourself for me again. I'd rather die than live without you."

"And how would I live without you, Charlie Pyke? Besides, Gideon would never have shot me. He's a doctor. His vocation is to preserve life, Ormsby excepted." Grace yelped as she attempted to put her arms around him. "I know you needed to deflect Gideon's attention, but did you have to push me quite so hard?"

Charlie stepped back. "Are you hurt? I thought your fall was a convincing piece of acting."

"It was mostly acting." Grace held out her swollen wrist. "Only a minor sprain. You may take a moment to finish singing my praises, before you bandage it."

Charlie sat her down on a tree stump and found a clean handkerchief to bind her wrist. "I hope to have a lifetime to sing your praises, Grace. I am a man of few words. I don't want to wear them out all at once."

"I don't mind if you repeat yourself, Charlie. Ouch, not quite so tight. You'll cut off my circulation."

"Darling Grace. The worst of it is that I would have killed Alexander before I let him hurt you. Am I any better than him?"

Grace's good arm slid around his torso. "Defending a loved one in the face of a deadly attack is one thing, Charlie. Planning and carrying out cold-blooded murder is quite another. Besides, you found a way to disable Gideon, rather than killing him, which proves your true character." She rested her head against his chest, above the beat of his heart. "Forget Gideon. Tell me again how you can't live without me."

Charlie buried his lips in her hair. "As if you didn't already know. Shall I take you home?"

"Home? That sounds wonderful. However, I suspect Detective Inspector Wallace will want us to make a statement. His eyebrows are going to dance a wild jig when he finds he's missed all the action. And we should see if Richard Ormsby is recovering. He is your client, after all."

"We should," Charlie agreed, but he didn't want to let her go just yet. "We don't want Richard to forget he owes us an enormous fee."

Grace didn't move either. "After that, I really must go home and have a fitting for my bridesmaid's gown. I need to finish my essay on the anatomy of the heart too. And we mustn't forget to practice our dancing for the wedding."

"Is it always going to be like this, Grace?"

She reached up to kiss him. "I certainly hope so, my love. Although I have to admit that I'd prefer fewer murders and more dancing. And kissing, definitely more kissing."

Charlie smiled down at her. "I can't do much about your uncanny knack for uncovering murders, Grace, but I can promise you as much dancing and kissing as we can fit into our busy schedules. Indeed, I do believe I can spare a few minutes right now."

Joy

On the afternoon of Lily and Alistair's wedding, Grace sat at her dressing table as one of Lily's friends worked with nimble fingers. Elaborate loops and curls appeared in her hair by magic, sculpted with an artistry Grace could never match. Alongside her, Lily and Jasmine chatted away, undaunted by the array of decorative combs, jewelled clips and flower circlets lined up in front of them.

Grace closed her eyes to the unaccustomed perfection in the mirror, savouring the moment of tranquillity after the tumultuous events leading up to the wedding. The horror of watching Charlie disappear into a burning building would stay with her forever.

But today was not the day for unpleasant thoughts. To distract herself, Grace ran through her bridesmaid's task list one last time. She was sure she had ticked off every item, but also terrified of letting Lily down. Her skill set had expanded dramatically of late. Frankly, it had been more exhausting than a twelve-hour shift at the hospital. Grace had more-or-less mastered the art of calligraphy for the place settings. She had crafted matching bouquets and buttonholes without too much bloodshed. She had folded linen napkins into swans under Charlie's tutelage, Lily having vetoed elephants and angels. And, the big one, she had learned how to walk.

Grace had been living under the misapprehension that she had already mastered walking, ever since taking her first steps as an infant. Not that her first steps had ended well. She had tottered to a nearby table, grabbing the edge and tipping a vase to its demise. Grace still favoured speed over elegance, but surely she could be trusted to walk down a church aisle on this one precious day.

Nevertheless, Jasmine Pyke had tutored her at length on the correct method of elegant locomotion. One had to glide like a swan, without appearing to move a muscle, whilst matching the precise

261

tempo of the music and avoiding tripping on the long train of Lily's wedding gown. Grace's grandmother, who had unwisely chosen the name Grace, would be having a fine old chuckle in her grave.

"Grace? Are you awake?" Jasmine touched Grace's arm. "Are you nervous, my dear?"

"Not nervous, Mrs Pyke, merely wool-gathering."

"Excellent. You look absolutely exquisite, dearest Grace. Charlie will swoon at the sight of you."

Grace smiled at the image of Charlie swooning. "That would certainly ruin his reputation as a tough detective."

"Lily and I were wondering if you had seen Mr Richard Ormsby lately," Jasmine said. "After such a tragedy, I fear the Ormsby family must be suffering most terribly."

"Nothing comes of revenge, except more pain," Lily observed. "Although there is always hope. A good man can rise above the sins of his father, just as a wronged man can choose a better path than revenge."

"I am sure Richard Ormsby is just such a man," Grace replied. "I saw him at the hospital last week. The grief caused by his father's death is still affecting him, of course, but I do believe Richard's self-assurance has grown too. He was off to sign a lease on new premises for his stepmother's natural remedies business. He felt it would do her good to have something to distract her from her sorrow. I believe Richard will forgive Miss Lawson too, in time. It is clear he still loves her."

Henry Ormsby had changed for the better too, in a small but important way. Henry and his friends had stopped tormenting Grace. Indeed, with them being polite to her and the absence of Clement, medical school was a much more pleasant place. Every cloud has a silver lining, she thought, as the hairdresser stuck another pin into her scalp.

"Love is all that matters." Lily held out her hand, for the twentieth time that day, to examine the beautiful ring Alistair had given her to pledge his love. "A shame Gideon Alexander was so obsessed with revenge. If only he had talked to Richard Ormsby, tragedy might have been averted."

"I believe you're right, Lily," Grace said. "Did Charlie tell you that Richard Ormsby visited Gideon in gaol? Richard has set up a trust fund to support Iain Thayne's two orphaned daughters – Gideon's sisters. Richard wanted his father's killer to meet his maker with peace in his heart."

Richard Ormsby had been very generous to the Southern Investigations Agency too. He had insisted on tripling the agreed fee for the investigation, as Charlie had saved the lives of himself and his brother, as well as solving his father's murder. Grace had asked Charlie what he planned to spend his share on, but she had received only an inscrutable smile in response.

Grace shared a knowing grin with the unfamiliar woman in the mirror. Detective or not, Charlie Pyke didn't have a hope of keeping secrets from her. The hairdresser threaded the last flowers through Grace's hair and stepped back to admire her creation.

Jasmine was giving Lily's hair a final inspection. "You look divine, dearest Lily." She touched her lips to Lily's cheek. "Almost time to go to the church. I do hope everything goes according to plan. I want it to be perfect for you, my dear sister."

"It will be, with you in charge," Lily said. "Anne is already at the church, attending to last-minute details, and I have my beloved family around me to ensure Alistair does not escape."

One of the helpers rushed into the room. "Your carriage is here."

Soon after, Grace stood behind Lily outside the church, trying to think like a swan. Jasmine Pyke adjusted Lily's gown until it sat flawlessly. Lily radiated serenity in pale ivory satin, richly embroidered with gold. With a gossamer veil and a restrained use of tulle, Lily looked both ethereal and elegant.

The string quartet struck the first notes of the wedding procession. Thomas Pyke stepped forward to take Lily up the church steps and down the aisle, with Jasmine and Grace gliding behind.

True to her word, Jasmine had crafted a simple, but gorgeous, gown for Grace. The dusky lavender silk was so subtle, it shimmered like quicksilver. Jasmine's measurements had been perfect, as long as Grace didn't indulge in the wedding feast or attempt an emergency resuscitation procedure.

Grace made it all the way up the aisle without tripping once or dropping her bouquet. Familiar faces gasped and shed tears as they passed by. Pew after pew filled with the people from Lavender House, policemen from near and far, members of the Chinese community, herbalists and doctors, suffragists and unionists, friends and family.

Alistair Stewart waited at the end of the aisle, his eyes never leaving the vision of beauty and poise approaching him. Grace took Lily's bouquet and stepped to the side.

As the minister spoke the binding words, Grace sneaked a glance at the best man, only to find his green eyes were fixed on her with an intensity that made her blush. She raised an eyebrow, before letting her gaze travel down the length of his body, from the white shirt trimmed with gold, to the Clan Stewart kilt that matched the groom's traditional Scottish attire, to the muscled legs that normally did not see the light of day. When she reached his face again, Charlie held her gaze for a long moment. His lips twitched. He turned to concentrate on the words of the ceremony.

Grace tried to focus on the words too, but her eyes kept coming back to him. Charlie Pyke looked every inch a man who had found his place in the world.

Not that the world knew it, as he had been careful to step out of the limelight during the frenzy of publicity following the Ormsby case. DI Wallace had brushed off the praise and remained tight-lipped about the involvement of the Southern Investigations Agency, as requested. The press had failed in their repeated attempts to track down the "family friends" who had risked their lives to save the Ormsby brothers. How long their anonymity would last was a moot point. Sooner or later, rumours of a detective agency in their city would reach the ears of newspaper reporters, eager for a novelty more diverting than a taciturn Detective Inspector Wallace doing his duty.

In front of Grace, Alistair and Lily shared their first kiss as man and wife. Mr and Mrs Stewart walked together down the aisle to cheers from the congregation. Thomas came forward to claim his wife's arm, leaving Grace to the best man.

"You look stunningly beautiful, Grace," Charlie whispered. "I hope you won't refuse to dance with me because I am wearing a skirt."

Grace's nervousness over the dance had nothing to do with what he was wearing and everything to do with her inability to keep her feelings under control when they moved as one to music. On the other hand, there was a lot to be said for relinquishing a little control, in favour of working together as a team.

Grace slotted her arm through his. "It's a full moon again tonight, Detective Pyke. Strange things are bound to happen."

Read On

In Book 5, *Murder So Rash*, Penrose & Pyke must stop a murderer, an epidemic and a scandalmonger.

When a shopkeeper dies during a robbery, Detective Charlie Pyke has a secret motive to track down the killer. If only it was that simple. A tell-all article in the local ladies' journal wrenches both his investigation and his private life off the rails. Grace Penrose can't come to his aid – she's too busy trying to prevent a deadly outbreak of measles.

Clues are thin on the ground until they combine their resources. The problem is, neither knows quite what is at stake.

Thank You

Thank you for reading this story. If you enjoyed it, I would be very grateful if you would leave a rating or review to help other readers discover it.

Find out about other books and sign up for notifications of new releases at https://RosePascoe.com.

Historical Notes

Although this story and the characters in it are fictional, the broader themes were inspired by the real social constraints under which women lived in 1892 and the health practices of the time.

Arguments over hospital facilities are nothing new. As I write, the scope of the new Dunedin hospital is the subject of heated debate, a hundred and thirty years after a new hospital was proposed to remedy substandard conditions towards the end of the nineteenth century. The hospital scenes in my story are partly based on actual descriptions of those perilous times.

After a commission of inquiry condemned the current situation, Dunedin hospital went through a period of upgrades throughout the 1890s. A new operating theatre was one of the first reforms. The much-needed specialist women's ward was not considered a priority. Instead, the Hospital Trustees wanted to shift the women's ward to an old area of the hospital, once the new Nurses' Home was completed in March 1892. In fact, the Trustees initially refused to accept the large sum of money raised by public donation for building the new women's ward. After a concerted effort by medical staff and women campaigners, the new women's ward finally opened within the new Campbell Pavilion in 1893.

Dr Ferdinand Batchelor, a specialist in midwifery and gynaecology, was a key figure behind the demands for reform. He really did have to operate once by the light of a bicycle lamp in the 1880s. The death of a woman patient in 1890 from a post-operative infection was the catalyst for his well-publicised campaign for reform. His wife was a notable fundraiser for the women's ward. The Batchelors provided inspiration for the Beechworth characters in my story, but their roles are fictionalised and in no way resemble the actions or characters of the real people. Needless to say, the murderous events in the story never actually happened.

I am grateful for historical accounts of the Otago Medical School and Dunedin Hospital, especially *Anatomy of a Medical School: a History of Medicine at the University of Otago, 1875-2000* (D. Page, 2008, University of Otago Press, Dunedin) and *A History of the Otago Hospital Board and Its Predecessors* (J. Angus, 1984, Otago Hospital Board, Dunedin).

Tutu (*Coriaria* species) was well known to the indigenous Māori population and soon became the bane of new settlers, who lost large numbers of stock to this poisonous native plant. Early newspaper accounts warned settlers of the lethal properties of the plant, especially the berries, which caused numerous deaths. One of the earliest research articles published by the Otago Medical School described the effects of tutu in detail.

The fingerprint analysis was based on Francis Galton's published papers. He was Charles Darwin's half cousin.

Acknowledgements

A huge thank you to my fabulous beta readers, Mary, Kathy and Ross, whose enthusiasm is very much appreciated. Thanks also to my friends and family for their encouragement.

This novel is dedicated to all the people who work tirelessly in the health services, during good times and bad.

About the author

Rose Pascoe writes historical mysteries with a dash of romance, when she isn't plotting real-life adventures.

She lives in beautiful New Zealand, land of beaches and mountains, where long walks provide the perfect conditions for dreaming up plots and fickle weather provides the incentive to sit down and actually write the darn things.

After a career in health, justice and social research, her passion is for stories set against a backdrop of social revolution. Her heroines are ordinary women, who meet the challenges thrown at them with determination, ingenuity, courage, and humour.

Visit her at: https://RosePascoe.com